THE INHERITOR

E F BENSON

New Introduction by
Peter Burton

Millivres Books
Brighton

Published 1992 by Millivres Books
33 Bristol Gardens, Brighton BN2 5JR, East Sussex, England

The Inheritor first published by Hutchinson, 1930

ISBN 1 873741 06 5

Typeset by Hailsham Typesetting Services, Hailsham,
East Sussex BN27 lAD
Printed by Billings & Sons, Worcester

Distributed in the British Isles and in Western Europe by
Turnaround Distribution Co-op Ltd, 27 Horsell Road,
London N5 1XL
Distributed in the United States of America by InBook,
140 Commerce Street, East Haven, Connecticut 06512, USA

Introduction

Although not yet twenty-one, Steven Gervase is a young man whose future seems assured: blond and surprisingly beautiful, he is heir to the immense fortune of his childless shipping magnate uncle. But his uncle has imposed conditions for making Steven his heir: he must join the shipping line as a junior clerk and he must marry and start a family as soon as possible.

Further, he is adored by fellow undergraduate Charles Merriman (although a strapping and sporting six foot four, he is always known as 'The Child') and adored by Maurice Crofts, a young don (himself barely older than his charges) who, appropriately, lectures on Classical Greece. The first lengthy section of E F Benson's 1930 novel *The Inheritor* returns the reader to the idyllic Cambridge of *David of Kings*, most specifically King's, Benson's own college.

However, Steven is heir to rather more than great good fortune and when Benson transposes the action to Steven's native Cornwall, the second of his inheritances becomes evident: a timeless family curse which may doom this child of nature to unhappiness and an untimely death.

The wild Cornish landscape Benson evokes is beautiful but mysterious and strangely threatening, a mythical kingdom in which England is but a distant memory. Readers should consult the Falmouth paintings of Henry Scott Tuke to gain an immediate impression of the locale and, coincidentally, the youths who feature in this narrative, most notably the Pan-like Tim, close but illegitimate kin to Steven, who, barely clothed, haunts the woods and pathways.

The Inheritor is suffused with paganism and it is

interesting to consider how much paganism and especially pantheism are a feature of the fiction written by late Victorian and Edwardian writers of clearly homosexual inclination. It now seems fairly obvious that allusions to things Greek or pagan were more than references to the seductivenes of Classical Greek and Roman cultures but were evident but encoded symbols for homosexuality and homosexual desires. Examples would include E M Forster's stories 'Albergo Empedocle', 'The Curate's Friend' and 'Other Kingdom' (and perhaps the characters Gino in *Where Angels Fear to Tread* and Alec Scudder in *Maurice*), stories by M R James and Saki and ' The Piper at the Gates of Dawn' chapter in that most wonderful evocation of male friendship, Kenneth Graham's *The Wind in the Willows*.

In fact, any reader in 1930 who didn't realise that *The Inheritor* was about decidedly 'queer' goings-on must have been utterly incomprehending. Besides all the allusions to paganism, the novel abounds with references to Walt Whitman and even includes a character called Dr Blaize, who must be a reference to David Blaize, hero of the eponymous novel (one of the most explicitly homoerotic of Benson's novels), *David of King's* and the curious tale for children, *David and the Blue Door*.

Although blindingly beautiful, Steven is 'without pity and love' and as events bring this core falling to the fore, those around him begin to suspect that something is seriously wrong. His relationships with his mother, wife, 'The Child' and Crofts come under pressure and it is only the symbiotic friendship between Steven and the Pan-like Tim which survives. And, although the novel follows the convention of what we eventually came to know as 'homosexual fiction' by having lovers die, it also most subtly defies that convention because the dying lovers have the assurance that they will be together when they 'awaken' in what they think of as 'home'

Steven Gervase is as much a wild thing as the untamable fox in *The Little Prince* or Evelyn Beaumont in Forster's 'Other Kingdom' and her cry "Oh, fence me out, if you like! Fence me out as much as you like! But never in . . . I must be on the outside, I must be where anyone can reach me is echoed by him throughout this book.

The Inheritor shows E F Benson writing at the peak of his powers: it is a compelling and disturbingly erotic novel in which an idyll slowly, chillingly and inevitably becomes a nightmare.

Peter Burton
Brighton, 1992

The Inheritor

Edward Frederic Benson was born in 1867, at Wellington College, where his father, later Archbishop of Canterbury, was Headmaster. Brother of the equally prolific Arthur Christopher and Robert Hugh Benson, Fred, as he was always known to family and friends, was author of more than one hundred books – autobiography, biography, social satires (notably the famous Mapp and Lucia novels), thrillers, tales of the macabre and the supernatural and short stories. Benson died in 1940 and his rediscovery commenced in the 1960s; there are now two Societies dedicated to his life and work. Millivres Books has also reissued Benson's *David of King's*.

Acknowledgements

Thanks are due to Allan Downend of The E F Benson Society who first suggested *The Inheritor* as a candidate for reissue; Cynthia Reavell of The Tilling Society whose notice in her society's newsletter turned up for me a copy of the book; Timothy d'Arch Smith of Fuller d'Arch Smith Ltd and James Burden of Red River Books who unsuccessfully but dedicatedly searched for the book and, most especially, to Johanna Hurwitz, herself a writer of books for children, who generously sent from America her own copy of the book so that reprint could again make it available to a wide readership – explaining her action by the memorable phrase that 'to be out-of-print is a kind of death for an author'.

PB

There are two societies devoted to the life and work of Benson and anyone wishing for further information should write (enclosing an sae) to:

The Secretary
The Tilling Society
Martello Bookshop
26 High Street
Rye
East Sussex
TN31 7JJ

and / or

The Secretary
The E F Benson Society
88 Tollington Park
London N4 3RA

PART I

CHAPTER I

The result of the May-week races at Cambridge had been considered satisfactory by the crew of King's College. Their boat had gone up a place on each of the four nights, and its emergence at the head of the river was certainly an event which demanded due recognition: something suitable had to be done. This evening, therefore, an extremely festive supper had taken place, and now, about ten o'clock, the front court of this studious establishment presented what may fairly be called "a very animated appearance." Gramophones and wireless sets were blaring from the windows that looked onto it; a little dancing accompanied by a little singing was in progress on the grass, and somebody had very properly put a top hat on the head of the statue of Henry VI, the founder of the college, which stood on a little island in the centre of the fountain. It all looked, in fact, as if a rag might possibly be developing, but the Dean of the College, Mr. Abel Stares, in whose department was discipline, and young Maurice Crofts, lately appointed classical lecturer, looking out of the window of Mr. Stares's rooms on the top floor of Fellows' Buildings, wisely decided that the time was not yet come for any official intervention.

"For after all," said Maurice, "the King has a right to be covered in any assembly."

Mr. Stares gave a slightly uneasy smile.

"Quite so," he said. "But I hope that the right to make a bonfire in any quadrangle will not enter into anyone's head. Prompt interference will then be necessary. The Provost spoke to me after Hall to-night, and was very decided about that. 'Safety valves, by all means,' he said, 'but no bonfires. Any symptom of a bonfire must at once be suppressed.' "

"I bet you he said, 'Boys will be boys,'" said Maurice.

"Of course. I thought you would take that for granted. How about a game of piquet?"

Maurice could not at once tear himself away from the window which overlooked the coronation of the Founder: there was not a coronation every day. He was quite young compared with Stares, who was thirty, and he felt himself no older than the very cheerful crowd which was diverting itself on the lawn outside, for at the age of twenty-five no tie that links a man to the late teens and earliest twenties has yet been severed, and the dancing and singing seemed to him perfectly suitable on such an evening. The moon was swung high over the roof of the chapel, and it was impossible not to sympathize with the actors in that joyful scene, rather noisy, perhaps, and some of them no doubt rather tipsy, but on the whole behaving in the way that the occasion demanded. Lawn-tennis balls were being lobbed at the top-hatted head of the Founder, which again was quite right; one had evidently hit, for the hat which a moment before had been staidly and decorously perched on his head was now at a rakish angle. And there without doubt was the officiating Archbishop, who for this aqueous ceremonial (since he had to wade through the fountain to get at the monarch) had prudently taken off his trousers. The prelate, he rather thought, was Steven Gervase, who during the week had been stroking the victorious crew, and fragments of gay conversation confirmed this.

"Hi, Steven, crown him again. Those nasty Bolshevists have been getting at him."

"Steven, there's a lydy coming. Put on your bags, dear, to be sure, and be a little gentleman. She'll be shocked at you!"

"Crown him with many crowns"—this was sung. "Aren't there some more hats? What about a tiara? What's wrong with a tiara?"

A voice very like the Provost's joined in with a falsetto croon.

"No Popery, I beg, gentlemen," it said. "Where's that bell? Far better go round college calling out, 'Bring out your dead.' "

The next voice was thoroughly tipsy.

"Lesh put every bally blooming thing into the river," it bawled. "Right place for Popery. See if it'll stink or swim."

There was a loud splash and a roar of laughter.

"Tommy's fallen in the fountain. Tried to walk upon the water like Peter. Dead failure. Pull him out, Steve. Noble fellow. Humane Society medal. He's shaking himself like a retriever."

Steven was now dancing with the Child, quite quietly and decorously though with no trousers, but, after all, he had drawers which were just as big as the shorts he publicly rowed in. The Child, who rowed five in the King's and the University boat, was so named partly because he was six foot four and partly because he had the face of a young and earnest choir boy. As long as those two were there, thought Maurice (and where Steven was there was always the Child) the rag would be kept within reasonable limits. Of course, if they were drunk it might be a different matter, but the Child never drank anything alcoholic, while Steven was like Socrates: the more he drank, the more lucid and tranquil he became. It was the oddest thing . . .

Maurice's figure was featurelessly outlined against the light in the room behind, and the silhouette attracted the attention of some of the young gentlemen on the grass who knew these windows to be those of Dean Stares and seemed anxious that he should not feel out in the cold when everything was so pleasant.

"Mr. Stares, I believe," said somebody with precisely the cold intonation affected by the Dean when he was addressing some delinquent. And then somebody else sang: "Pray what are you staring at, Mister Stares?" which went to the tune of "The Campbells are Coming." Maurice withdrew from his post of observation and pulled down the blind. Stares had his sympathy, but where was the use of trying to look dignified when people were singing about you like that? It was an impossible achievement: far better not to attempt it.

"Getting a little out of hand," said Stares with peculiar acidity. (Somebody had asked, "Who killed Cain?" and a moaning chorus intoned, "Abel.") "Steven Gervase seems to be a ringleader."

"Not quite," said Maurice. "Ringmaster would be nearer. There won't be any harm done while he's there."

Stares gave his famous ironical laugh, which withered the soul of mirth.

"The decorum of the College is in Gervase's hands to-night, is it?" he asked, as he threw out the low cards from the pack. "We are indeed privileged."

"It couldn't be in better hands," said Maurice. "I asked him and the Child to keep things within bounds."

Stares cut the cards.

"A very impertinent and insolent fellow," he remarked.

"Oh, but it wasn't he who sang just now," said Maurice.

"How do you know?"

"It didn't happen to be Steven's voice," he said. "Also that's not the sort of thing he does."

"Exceedingly rude, whoever it was," said Stares. "I shouldn't in the least wonder if it was that great oaf they call the Child. Merriman, I believe. He and your Steven have a thoroughly bad influence in the College. A good thing that Merriman is at the end of his time here."

That was like Stares, thought Maurice, as he dealt: he thoroughly disliked the types of which the Child and Steven were, in their respective ways, such excellent specimens—the one with his genial boisterousness, and enthusiasm for games and friendship, and the other (in spite of his dancing with no trousers on) rather aloof, rather contemptuous of the franker enjoyments of life, because he got what he wanted too easily. Certainly the fairy godmothers had bestowed on him all the contents of their spell-laden wallets, but he remained detached, slightly icy. . . . The sort of boy that Stares liked was the elderly earnest type which cared for cathedrals and architecture and Greek accents and academic jokes. He took such on bicycling tours in midland counties, and they stayed at inns and drank cider and improved their minds. . . .

"It's your turn to declare," said Stares, interrupting these fugitive reflections.

Maurice found it difficult to concentrate on piquet. Some current of time which should have carried his earlier youth away seemed only to have kept it circling in a backwater, and now it came flooding out into the main stream again, and he longed to be out on the lawn dancing with Steven and lobbing tennis balls at the Founder's hat. He always liked the society of undergraduates far more than that of his colleagues, and, after all, it was for them that Cambridge existed: he and the rest of the Dons were here to serve them, since Henry VI had provided funds to hire elderly and scholastic persons to minister to the intellectual advancement of the rising generation. And what a chilly and barren job they mostly made of it! He himself had been lecturing to a class this term on the Peloponnesian war, and he could almost hear his own dry voice saying: "In the following year, 424 B. C., was fought the battle of Delium, and Athens lost her newly acquired province of Bœotia. She would have done better to stick to her programme of naval Empire. . . ." As if you could learn Greek history like that, or, if you did, how could it cause the smallest seed of growth to sprout in any mind?

But that was the traditional manner for Dons, and when their lecturings and tuitions were over they pulled down the blinds and played piquet with each other.

"And I get the cards," said Stares avariciously. "You could have saved a trick if you had led clubs."

A loud and agitated tap came on the door, and the College porter entered.

"I beg your pardon, sir," he said, "but the young gentlemen are bringing out old basket chairs and faggots and putting them on the lawn. It looks like a bonfire."

Stares got up and began putting on his cap and gown.

"Thank you, Williams," he said. "I will come down at once. It must be stopped instantly. Have you taken any of their names?"

Maurice jumped up also; there was some excuse now for going out.

"You had much better not come, Stares," he said. "Do let me have a try first. And don't let us have any names yet."

"My duty as Dean——" began Stares.

"Oh, come if you like, then," said Maurice. "But it won't be my fault if they rag you. The point is that they shouldn't."

Stares, on his way to the door, had appeared opposite the other window, vividly silhouetted in cap and gown, and in a sort of Gregorian chant came the question, "Who killed Cain?" and the walls of the chapel reëchoed the reply.

"Do stop here just for five minutes more," pleaded Maurice, choking down a laugh. "I feel sure I can manage them better alone. Nothing's happened yet."

The shout of his own Christian name had slightly unsettled Stares: it was so voluminous, so whole-hearted, so welcoming, in case, as a preacher might say, "he cared to come amongst them," and leaving him struggling between a sense of duty and a strong disinclination Maurice slammed the door behind him and ran downstairs. Straight in front of him on the edge of the grass was seated Tommy, dripping wet from his immersion, under an umbrella, as if to keep any further moisture off. He was chanting quietly to himself.

"I'm a lonely mushroom," he warbled, "growing on the lawn. And I should like a nice li'l' mushroom girl to come and sit with me. Hullo, I believe it's Mister Crofts whom we gen'ally call Maurice."

Maurice plucked the umbrella out of his hand.

"You may call me what you like, Tommy," he said, "but go back to your rooms at once. Else I swear you'll be sent down to-morrow for getting beastly drunk."

"Am I drunk?" asked Tommy with great interest. "Sure I'm drunk?"

"Quite sure; also that you'll be sent down if you don't do what I tell you. Up you get. Where's Steven?"

"Dancing," said Tommy. "Horrid sight. Bare knees, like a boy scout. Made me blush. Lor! How everything goes round. World without end going round the sun."

Steven and the Child came fox-trotting round the fountain.

"Hi! Steven!" called Maurice.

"Hullo! Is that you, Maurice?"

"Yes. Come here, will you? I want you and the Child to help. The rag has gone far enough."

"Oh, do you think so?" said Steven. "It's rather fun; I'm enjoying it. Or are you here officially?"

"No, that's just what I'm not, and what I don't want to be. But they're collecting stuff for a bonfire, and it won't do."

"Not just a little one?" asked the Child.

"No. Otherwise there'll be a lot of Dons here officially in a minute, and people will be sent down. Rather a pity just when we've gone head of the river."

"Right-o," said Steven. "We'll do what we can. Perhaps they'd take me more seriously if I'd trousers on. Hi! Anyone seen my trousers? And do you want Henry's hat taken off?"

"No, never mind that. And get hold of some more fellows to be friendly bobbies."

Maurice, still quite unofficial, walked off to where a pile of highly inflammable material was being sumptuously built up. He saw with secret glee that one of Stares's young men, who was supposed to be the most serious and high-brow soul with a mania for cathedrals, was stuffing news-papers by way of kindling (and very good kindling, too) under the seat of a basket chair. Redcliffe hailed him with genial but marked intoxication.

"You're just in time," he said. "I'm going to light such a candle. Same as that Archbishop."

"Yes, I know I'm just in time," said Maurice, seating himself in the basket chair. "But I'm not so sure about the candle."

"I'll convince you, then. We've gone head of the river, you know. It's a celebration," said Redcliffe.

Maurice wanted to be unofficial as long as possible.

"It's so dark," he said cheerfully, "that I've really no idea whom I'm talking to. Much better for both of us to remain incog. if we can."

"Why? I'm not ashamed of my name. Redcliffe. George Herbert Redcliffe."

"I can't quite catch it," said Maurice. . . . It was all great fun, and it was quite right and proper to rag on this auspicious occasion, but he was determined to have no bonfire.

"Well, you'll catch light if you sit there," said George Herbert. "I warn you."

"Thanks. The same to you, and this is the last warning."

Steven and the Child had come up by this time, having collected a few friendly bobbies of large size. Redcliffe had just lit a match when both his elbows were clutched from behind, and he felt himself propelled forward by an invisible but irrestible force. He had to begin running, though reluctant.

"I say, leggo, whoever you are," he said. "I haven't hurt you."

"Not a bit, thanks," said the Child, trundling him along.

"But I shall be sick," wailed Redcliffe.

"Very likely indeed," said the Child, "and then you'll feel better." They disappeared under the strip of shadow below the chapel.

George Herbert Redcliffe seemed to be the chief champion of incendiarism, and presently the unkindled bonfire was shared up between those who had contributed to it, and chairs and waste-paper baskets were taken home again by their owners. The general idea seemed to be that a bonfire was not necessary, since so many large people disapproved of it, and that Maurice had behaved with high tact in not putting up any semblance of authority. He and Steven strolled off together with the dispersal of the rest.

Steven nudged Maurice's arm.

"Look!" he said. "There's our Abel still in his cap and gown standing at his window. I bet you he thinks that his presence there, just looking on, quelled everybody so that we all said, 'Ba-a-a,' and went home like lambs. Mayn't I ask who killed Cain once more to show him what an ass he is?"

"Much sooner you didn't," said Maurice. "I'm actually in the middle of a game of piquet with him."

"Not going back, are you?" asked Steven. "Come round to me instead. Have a drink; have anything you like."

"I'll come round presently. But I must go and report that all's quiet again. I'm a Don, you know."

"Damned odd one," said Steven. "I believe you'd have liked to rag to-night, too."

"Of course I should, bar the bonfire. Only a sense of my position restrained me. See you presently."

Maurice ran upstairs and found his colleague making a list of the obstreperous spirits he had seen from his window. Pathetic as it appeared, he really seemed to think that his epiphany at the window, prepared to make an official sortie, had produced this tranquillity.

"And Thomas was evidently quite tipsy," he said. "Under an umbrella, I think, until you took it away."

"Yes, and he told me he was a lonely mushroom," said Maurice.

"A disgusting fellow," said Stares.

"Well, he went back to his rooms quite quietly," said Maurice. "Very solemn, in fact."

"And Merriman dancing on the lawn and Gervase without his trousers," continued Stares.

"I know, but he put them on again," said Maurice. "What do you propose to do about him and the Child?"

"Gate them at nine for the rest of the week."

"It'll be a great mistake if you do," said Maurice. "It will also be extremely unfair."

"I don't quite see the unfairness of it," said Stares.

"Then I'll explain. Of course, I allow that Thomas was drunk, but he was sitting quietly there, as good as gold."

Stares gave his ironical laugh.

"Soberness is silver, intoxication is gold," he observed.

"Gold compared to your young friend George Herbert Redcliffe. He was the ringleader of the bonfire brigade."

"I didn't see him at all," said Stares, who was engaged to go over to Ely next day with George Herbert and study the decorations in the Lady Chapel.

"That's why I'm telling you about him," said Maurice. "I went and sat down in one of the basket chairs they had brought out for the bonfire, and G. H. told me I had better get up as he wanted to set light to it. It was touch and go whether there would have been a bonfire, if the Child hadn't taken him for a run. He was sick, I think. Steven and the Child saved the situation. Really, Stares, if you send for them at all, you ought to send for them in order to thank them."

"I shall deal with the matter according to my poor lights," said Stares. "Possibly I have had a little more experience than you. I shall act on what I saw."

"Yes, but I'm telling you what you didn't see," said Maurice. "I went down among them, you know, and I really know better than you what was going on. It was Steven and the Child who caused the rag to fizzle out: if it hadn't been for them there would have been a bonfire. And now you want to gate them for it. Do leave it all alone. There's been no harm done, but there'll be a lot of ill feeling if you gate Steven and the Child."

"Perhaps you'd like me to thank Thomas for getting extremely drunk," said Stares.

"Do, by all means," said Maurice, "but then you must thank George Herbert for doing the same. . . . Well, I'm off to bed now, for it's getting late."

Maurice went into his room, which was opposite Stares's, opened and shut the door rather loudly in order to give the impression of having gone to bed, and then tiptoed down the staircase and skirted along the gravel path that led to the block of buildings where Steven's rooms were. He rather laughed at himself for the instinct of secretiveness which caused him to decline further piquet on the plea that it was late, instead of saying that he had promised to look in on Steven; but Stares was a suspicious dog, and it might occur to him that his attitude towards rags and ringleaders might possibly form an agreeable topic of critical conversation. It was quite likely, Maurice feared, that Steven would have given him up and gone to bed, for he spent some time in trying to convince Stares that any retributive measure would be highly ill judged and that he couldn't choose more unsuitable victims than those on whom he had fixed. But Stares ought never to be allowed to deal with people. Gargoyles and lancet windows were the limit of his juster perceptions, inanimate objects of historical value . . .

Steven's windows were still alight, and Maurice went in to find that his sitting room was empty but that the door into the bedroom was open. A voice from within called out.

"Hullo, who's that?" it said. "Is it Maurice?"

"Yes. I'm late. Are you going to bed?"

"I was, but I won't. Do stop. I hate going to bed. Find some whisky; find anything you like. I'll be with you in a second. The Child said he was coming round, too."

Steven emerged from his bedroom in pajamas and slippers, a very suitable costume on so hot a night.

"Well, what's the bulletin from the Deanery?" he asked. "It's lucky our Abel didn't come out. There'd have been a riot if he had."

"Entirely my doing," said Maurice. "Alone I did it."

"Jolly wise of you. He rubs everybody up the wrong way, makes them see red. If he'd come out and told me to put on my trousers I should have taken off my shirt too: that's what he makes me feel like."

"He's thinking of gating you and the Child to-morrow," said Maurice.

"The dirty, ungrateful dog! Let's begin ragging again. Why, if it hadn't been for clear-headed, law-abiding highbrows like you and the Child and me, the flames of burning basket chairs would now be licking . . . go on, I can't finish that sentence."

"That's what I told him. Only I finished lots of sentences," said Maurice.

"I'm sure you spoke very properly. Besides, I only danced. And it's King's ball to-morrow. We're all going to dance; shall we all be gated? My girl's going to be there."

"Who's that?" asked Maurice.

"A bold bad Amazon from Newnham. Niece of the Provost's, but several sizes larger. About as big as the Child."

"I believe I've seen her," said Maurice.

"I don't see how you could help it. Emerald Mostyn: that's a spanking name! I sat next her at dinner at the Lodge the other night, and during the fish she told me we were affinities, and as there wasn't any soup I should think that's about the record. Rather red eyes, and she fixes me with them in chapel instead of thinking about her soul, and I wouldn't meet her on a dark night for anything, unless it was so dark she couldn't see me."

"I know her. . . . She looked at you all through the Creed when she turned round——"

"Yes, and asked me to come to tea bang in the middle of it. There's nerve!"

"Did you go?"

"Rather. I'd never seen a harem before. Five friends of hers all tightly squeezed together on a sofa, and two of them had moustaches. What their names were I don't know, as they all called each other darling. Oh, no, they called her Gem. I see why, too. . . . Emerald: very witty I thought it. And then she told them all to go away, and I've never felt such a confirmed celibate in my life. In fact——"

There was a sound of a step outside, and Stephen, lying full length on the sofa, kicked off a slipper, caught it dexterously in the air and hurled it at the opening door. It hit the Child on the chin, and he gave a loud squeal. Next moment he and Steven were wriggling on the floor.

"Oh, don't, Child," panted Steven. "It isn't dignified, and there's a Don present who hates ragging. Don't tickle me: if I'm tickled I die. It runs in the family."

The Child, for all the strength and size of him, was slow in movement compared to the cat-like, quicksilver quality of the other, and as often as Steven seemed laid out and pinned down he wriggled a hand free and pulled the Child's nose or planted a knee in his stomach. His other slipper flew off, and a breast-button from his pajamas catapulted across the room; finally, in the grip of the Child's encircling arms and apparently about to have the breath of life squeezed out of him, he struggled to his knees and, getting both hands free, snatched a siphon from the table and discharged it full in the Child's face.

"Not fair!" he gasped. "Man to man: no weapons!"

"Bosh. Apologize," shouted Steven.

The nozzle of the siphon was still within a foot of the Child's face.

"Right; but it's an awful swindle," he said.

"Say it, then. I apologize to Messrs. Crofts and Gervase for behaving like a blasted barbarian."

The Child obediently repeated this degrading confession and went into Steven's bedroom to find a towel, while Steven, in the sad tranquillity that succeeds a bear fight, collected his slippers and sat down, very much out of breath, on the sofa. The Child emerged again, mopping, and established himself on the floor, propping his back against Steven's legs.

"I hate ragging," he said. "Can't think why you began."

"Liar—I didn't," said Steven.

"Liar—you did. You threw a frowsy slipper at me. If that isn't beginning I don't know what is. What bony knees you've got."

"Well, I can't have them boned to-night," said Steven. "Anyhow, whoever began, we know what the end was. Grovelling apologies from a——"

"Shut up, or it will begin all over again," said the Child.

"No, it won't, because there's no more siphon. Oh, sorry, Maurice; there's nothing for you to drink. Perhaps I can find another one. Or whisky neat?"

Maurice got up with a sudden conviction that he wasn't wanted. This was accentuated, rather than the reverse, by Steven's lapse into these polite hospitalities.

"Nothing, thanks," he said. "And I'm off to bed."

"Not this minute," said Steven. "Tell the Child about our little Abel. Little Abel is thinking of gating us, Mr. Merriman, I believe."

"Well, I'm damned," said the Child. "After all we've done for this putrid College, putting it head of the river, and stopping a rag, and me seeing George Herbert safely to bed, sick as a cat——"

"No! Did you! Almost too noble——"

"I know that; and so they're going to gate me instead," said the Child. "You just wait till I take to drink, wait till I throw my moral influence on the side of tipsy womanizers."

"Oh, does he? George Herbert?" asked Steven.

"Lord, yes; always nosing round after giddy pieces. Oh, I forgot you were a Don, Maurice."

"He isn't; at least, not to matter," said Steven.

"Not an atom," said Maurice. "But don't throw your moral influence anywhere until you have been gated. I tried to wangle little Abel about you, and perhaps it will come off. I'm going. Good-night."

This time neither of the others made any attempt to detain him. But just as he was at the door, Steven asked him to come to breakfast next morning. He hesitated.

"I wish I could," he said, "but I've got somebody coming to me. Thanks, though."

The Child sighed deeply.

"Good chap, Maurice," he said, as the door closed behind him, "but I thought he was never going. Oh, by the way, I found my outer door was sported, and I can't get in. I'd better go across to the lodge and get the key."

"Won't they all have gone to bed?" said Steven.

"Probably. In which case I shall sleep on your sofa."

"You can have my bed, if you like. I'll sleep here: you're too long for the sofa," said Steven.

"Very hospitable. I say, Steven, it's rather ripping going head of the river. You've got to keep us there next year."

"We shan't stop there," said Steven. "I think I shall chuck rowing."

"And so of course . . . But why chuck it?"

"Because the fun of it was that we were doing it together, and now you're going down. I shan't bother to burst myself if you're not bursting yourself behind me."

The Child picked a lump or two from Steven's sugar basin and crunched them.

"Lord, what a lot of races we've rowed together," he said. "Two years at Eton, and then I left, and then two years here after you came up. You were sixteen when you rowed at Henley first, and three feet high. But don't chuck it; you've a good chance of your Blue."

"Of course I shan't chuck it."

"You said you would just now," remarked the Child.

"Well, I contradicted myself. It was only a formal expression of regret that you were going down."

"Compliments," said the Child. "But only formal."

"Oh, don't be an ass. It'll be rotten without you. A week more, and then it's the end."

"Why end?" asked the Child.

"Because it happens like that. Nothing goes on without changing. We've done the same things hitherto, but we're bound to develop differently. Things will come in between us and people. It can't be otherwise. Then you'll marry and I'll marry, and you'll grow fat and I'll grow bald, and we shall wonder how we could ever have been what they call wrapped up in each other. After all, we've had quite a decent time."

Steven leaned forward and picked the pipe out of the Child's mouth to light a cigarette.

"I don't suppose you've the smallest idea how devoted I am to you," said the Child.

The merest crease of a frown delved itself between Steven's eyebrows. That sort of protestation, even from the Child, always made him retreat into himself.

"Of course I have," he said, "so why tell me that? And if I hadn't, there's even less use in telling me. Thank the Lord, there's never been an ounce of sentimentality between us. Oh, those girls up at Newnham! They pawed each other, and were rather arch, and one didn't like the blouse another was wearing, and that was thought very unkind, and we pouted. Do you like my pajamas, darling?" he said in a high falsetto, putting a leg over the Child's shoulder.

"Too sweet; take it away," said the Child. "What's to be done next?"

Steven hitched himself back and lay full length on the sofa.

"I don't know," he said. "Sometimes I'm rather like a dog, delighted to do whatever anybody suggests, but unable to initiate anything myself, though mad keen if anybody else begins. But when I've done it I don't care about it any more. Yesterday, for instance, I wanted nothing in the world except to go head of the river, and now it's done I want something else, but I don't know what it is."

"Undervitalized," said the Child.

"Not an atom. I might as well say you were undersized. And then sometimes I'm rather like a cat that goes off prowling quite by itself, on the chase of something mysterious. You're exactly the opposite: you can always think of things to do, and you never by any chance want to prowl by yourself."

The Child considered this.

"To be quite frank, I don't know what you're talking about," he said.

"Nor do I," said Steven, "and the more I talk the less I know what I mean."

The Child had no answer to make to this, and Steven, having summed up the inefficacy of discussion, pulled a cushion under his head, and turning away from the light appeared to be making his bed on the sofa, as he had suggested. The Child shifted his position, and now, with his head against the seat of the armchair where Maurice had been sitting, wondered whether he should take the bed that had been offered him. But he did not feel sleepy, and he was quite comfortable where he was.

From where he now lay, stretched on the thick hearth-rug, he could see Steven's face with a plume of bright hair falling on his forehead, with his eyes shut down above his lean cheeks, and mouth drooping softly at the corners. Little as he was given to reflection on abstract matters, he wondered if, in spite of their profound intimacy, he really knew Steven at all. Often and often, and now more vividly than ever, he had felt that his friend kept some piece of himself in reserve. Or was it that there was something lacking in him, which gave him the sense of an unbridged gap between them? Either of those would have produced just the impression of which he was conscious. Nobody could have moods of more apparently complete self-abandonment, of riotous high spirits, of shining comprehension than Steven; but then he suddenly withdrew, and one had the feeling that he had spirited himself away, and that all that was left was some unsubstantial wraith of himself. He rowed, he ragged, he came close to one as if with all his heart, and then in a moment a tide ebbed, and one was left on an infinite sand, with the sea, that buoyant and candid comrade, which had laughed and sparkled and sustained your voyaging, quite out of sight. . . . Not an image, not a phrase of such pictured analysis actually came into the Child's mind, for the vocabulary of analysis was to him an unknown tongue, but this curious accession of loneliness, which he experienced with such vividness when he glanced at Steven lying there, perhaps asleep, perhaps much farther withdrawn, would have yielded, verbally, some such result. An odd emptiness, an odd aching as for something that never existed grew upon him.

It was a very hot night, dark now after moonset, and faint warm stirrings of air came in through the open window, and Steven, without opening his eyes, sniffed and stretched himself. Moths fluttered whitely across the black curtain of darkness outside, and now there came the harsh chime of the clock in the lodge, striking two, and the Child got quietly up and went towards the door. At the click of the door handle Steven stirred and opened his eyes, with a full yawn. The electric light shone straight into his mouth, and his teeth showed transparent against the brightness within.

"I wasn't asleep," he quoted. "I heard every word you fellows were saying. Or was I asleep? Is that you, Child? Going?"

"Yes. Good-night."

Steven rubbed his eyes.

"But how about your key?" he asked sleepily. "Didn't you say something once—oh, years ago—about your door having been banged to?"

"Yes, but I'll go round to the porter's lodge; there are all the keys there," said the Child. "I'll get it somehow."

"I don't see how. Everything will be shut up; they'll have gone to bed hours ago. And it struck two just now, didn't it? You can't rout Williams from his downy at two in the morning. It isn't done. And you said you would sleep here, didn't you?"

Steven swung his legs off the sofa and stood up, again stretching himself, and smiling.

"I believe I did go to sleep for a minute," he said. "Very rude, when you were conversing so agreeably. Lord! what a good smell of night there is! Usually I'm asleep and don't smell it, but when I do, it goes straight to my head. I suppose I slept for ten minutes; all the greatest people in the world, like Napoleon and Gladstone, could do that, and then wake again, bright as a button. You asked me just now what we should do. Anything you like. I'm on. God, what's happened? Electric light fused, I suppose."

The room was plunged in blackness: they were voices to each other.

"Serves this hellish College right," said the Child. "It's because they threatened to gate us."

Some current of night, some prowling instinct began seething in Steven. From sleep he had passed to waking, and from waking to some purring consciousness of life. He laughed.

"That's it," he said. "Total eclipse has come on this injudicious place. There used to be a moon: why doesn't it stop still instead of gadding about out of sight? But if anybody thinks I'm going to bed just because the lights go out they've made an awful mistake. Where's anything? I wonder if I'm drunk after all these years of futile endeavour. Yet I can't be, for if I was I should surely see two moons, and I can't see any. Nor can I see anything like a match box, which would be more to the point."

After some groping about Steven found a match box and, lighting one match after another, tried without success to discover some candles in his gyp-room. All the time this pleased purring of the spirit was going on: something was astir. He had felt the like before, but never so strongly.

"I'm much too wide awake to go to bed," he said, as he

came back, "and we can't sit here by the light of one match at a time, and only about five of them. Let's go out of doors, Child. It's night, it's wonderful. One can always go to bed, but not always for a walk at night, because one is in bed, and it's impossible to go for a real walk in bed. See? Sheets and blankets get in the way of free movement. I should think I was drunk if I was anybody else. And it's too hot to go to bed, and far too dull. Stroll down as far as the river, anyhow, and see if we find anything to do."

The two wandered out onto the immense lawn that stretched from Fellows' Buildings down to the river. Above, the sky had become overcast with skeins and veils of high-floating mist, through which a faint starlight filtered down. On the grass the dew lay thick, glimmering like frost; the print of their feet made black holes in it as they walked. In front dim shapes of trees, towering higher as they approached, made a blotted outline against the sky, and to right and left rose the more clear-cut edges of collegiate buildings. Some fresh mood, vivid and voluble, was on Steven now, expressing itself in a hopeless babble of nonsense, streaked with seriousness.

"Let's serenade the Provost," he said. "That's the window of his chaste bedroom, because I've seen him shaving himself there. Shall I sing 'Oh, That We Two Were Maying' in a fruity alto? At that he will stir in his sleep and remember foul nocturnal fancies of his when he was young. Did he ever run after girls? I wonder: we shall never know, because he won't tell us, and they're probably dead. I wish I was old, with a wig and a Bath chair and false teeth and somebody to blow my nose. So safe, you know, so serene, with nothing to be afraid of; all the awful things that happen to people would have happened. Only death ahead—and who minds that?"

"I do," said the Child.

"Then don't talk about it so much. A serenade for the

Provost, coming out of the darkness 'thick and hot,' might do wonders for him. He might learn to walk romantically about the lawn, arm in arm with Stares, just as you and I are doing. He might tell Stares that Stares didn't know how devoted he was to him, as you told me just now, and then you and I would come softly up behind them and push them both into the river. There was an old lady once who said you had no idea what passion could be until you were seventy. And when you've gone down, whom the devil shall I talk rot to?"

"Maurice, I expect," said the Child.

"I shouldn't wonder. There's something rather understanding about Maurice. He makes me feel as if we were both freemasons, though I'm sure I don't know what the secrets are. . . . How dead quiet everything is! I wonder if the end of the world has come and they've forgotten about us. I thought I heard something like a bugle just now, and as it hasn't come again it was probably the last trump. Are we the only people alive, do you think, and shall we go on creeping about a dead world in the darkness? Or are we all dead, even you and I, and are these our souls which will wander on together for all eternity? What shuddering possibilities; let's think of something else at once."

They had come to the edge of the river, which lay in front of them, smooth and faintly shining, like a wet causeway of asphalt. Not a fish moved, not an eddy nor a trail of waving weed wrinkled the surface. Suddenly Steven pointed into the shade of the willow by the bridge.

"Look!" he said. "That makes me feel better. Somebody's left a Canadian canoe there tied up to the bank. I expect it's the Provost, who means to steal out on amorous adventures. We ought to prevent that, Child; the credit of the College, as usual, is in our hands. In fact, we must prevent it, and the simplest plan is to take the canoe ourselves. We must thwart him; the College will go to the dogs if we allow the Provost to do that sort of thing. Come on!"

They pulled the canoe to the bank and got in, sitting opposite each other, then pushed off and paddled upstream till they came to the Mill. Then landing, they carried the boat across, and launched it again on the upper river. A barn owl, silent and white and ghostly, was hunting over the open ground to the right, and once or twice, far away, came a blink of lightning, but still no breath ruffled the surface of the river, and no sound ruffled the silence but the cluck of their paddles and the drip of the water off the blades. The Child, heavily weighting one end of the canoe, had stripped to shirt and trousers; his white starched front creaked as he plied his paddle. At the other end, facing him and above him, sat Steven, the red stripe of his pajamas black in the dim light, while the jacket with its missing button lay open at the neck, and slipping down his arm left one shoulder bare. The muscles of it, alternately taut and slack, rippled under the skin as he pressed on his paddle and withdrew it. Just the two of them slid up the river, with all the world asleep or dead, isolated in night and silence. The Child was utterly content with this companionship, absorbed in the sense of friendship; Steven, far more intensely alert, was conscious of the spell of the night itself; it held something for him, something secret and essential, of which the Child knew nothing.

It was not long before the flat monotone of the twilight began to brighten with the hinted dove-colour of dawn. A suggestion of greenness flickered and then grew fixed on the grasses of the riverside, the paddles dripped with globules of light, and in the bushes birds began to pipe drowsily. The first breeze of morning stirred; gray wisps of cloud in the east became tinged with pink, and the blurred shape of trees and distant roofs grew more defined in outline. For Steven that mysterious spell of the night which held something potent and vital and secret was quenched by the breaking of day, and as they slid up to the sheds of the town bathing place he broke the long silence.

"Why, of course we shall have to bathe," he said. "Look, it's all arranged for us; somebody has even left a couple of towels on that bench there. Good boy; he knew we were coming, and here we are on the tick of time with the dawn."

The Child reached out with his paddle and drew the canoe up to the bank; Steven climbed out with the painter in his hand and tied up. He threw his pajamas on to the bench, and running across the grass flung himself into the river. Next moment the Child followed, striking the water flat with the noise of musketry, and surged after him. The spell of the night for the one, for the other of that almost discarnate silence of their companionship, was broken, and with the spread of the light in the sky above, and the touch of the water's coolness, the dreamland of the darkness dispersed. The Child, churning through the water, heaved himself onto Steven, but before he could duck him Steven had dived sideways and, rising again on his flank, vaulted onto him as into the saddle of a horse, with his knees pressed close to his ribs. Down they went, locked together, and came up separate, gasping and spluttering and calling each other cads. Then, with peace restored, they floated and swam and dived again, and now the first ray of the sun caught the treetops.

"All over," said Steven, as he climbed ashore. "Good-morning, Mr. Merriman."

"Good-morning, Mr. Gervase. I hope you've had a pleasant night."

"Very. Slept beautifully. Do you take tea or coffee for breakfast? Personally, I'll have a cigarette, if you've got any. I have the four remaining matches which we spoke about earlier in the evening, and I'll give you a light."

"You score there," said the Child.

"Not at all. I save the situation because I've got matches. It's devastating to have cigarettes and no matches, because you think what a little would have made you happy, but if you have matches but no cigarettes, you don't think about smoking at all. Matches are worth boxes of cigarettes."

"Don't argue; give me a light," said the Child.

"Well, then, give me a cigarette and shut your mouth. Lord, you did look funny when I jumped onto your back just now."

"Horseplay in the water is very dangerous," said the Child. "If we hadn't been able to swim we should both have been drowned."

Steven inhaled a long breath of smoke.

"Do you know, I don't believe either of us spoke a single word for half an hour as we paddled up here," he said. "It was queer; the night was full of spells."

"I know nothing about spells," said the Child. "But I enjoyed it. Happy."

"So you are still."

"Yes, but it's day again, and other people will be butting in. We were alone."

They smoked on in silence again, and Steven realized how little the Child had entered into his consciousness at all. It was odd; he was very fond of him, but all the time there had been something calling to him out of the night, of which the Child was wholly unaware, and while it called the Child had not existed for him. Then they dressed according to the capacity of their clothes and prepared to return.

"But we must make a burnt sacrifice first," said Steven. "The gods of the night and the river have been kind. What's the most valuable thing we've got?"

The Child looked in his cigarette case.

"One cigarette and the rest of the matches," he said. "But it's frightful to think of. Isaac's not in it."

"We can't help it, and it will be a splendid burnt sacrifice. Collect some bits of stick and dry grass."

They made a beautiful altar of small stones and covered it with dry rubbish of twigs and withered herbage. The cigarette was shredded and put into the match box, and the three remaining matches used to kindle the priceless offering. The wisp of smoke fragrant with tobacco ascended into the still air, and Steven, reverently kneeling with his hands spread out like the pictures of Moses, recited prayer.

"Gods of wet places and of night," he intoned, "look favourably on two of the silliest of your servants and grant that their lives may be as fragrant with foolish deeds as is the breath of morning to-day with this offering of the most precious of our possessions which we have dedicated to the honour of Your Majesty. . . . Go on, Child."

The Child thought heavily.

"That's about all," he said. "Amen."

"*Selah*. Alleluia," said Steven. "What asses!"

The smoke of the oblation died away, and they dropped down the river again, from which, with the invasion of day, all enchantment had fled. Rather sleepy with reaction they tied up the canoe, now no longer a chariot of magic, and strolled back across the lawn, where still the black holes made by their walking in the thick dew were visible. Steven pointed at them.

"Look! There are our footprints on the outward journey," he said. "It seems years ago."

"Sort of Wonderland," said the Child. "I wish you were always like that."

"Why? What's the matter with me at other times?" demanded Steven.

"You withdraw yourself; you retire."

Clearly the Child had no idea what had filled the night for Steven, the spell, the mysterious beckoning. . . . He had had no part whatever in it.

"For goodness' sake don't let us talk about our natures," he said. "We're as we are."

"Well, I don't want to talk about them," said the Child. "You asked me."

"I know I did, but I didn't want to know. But it has been ripping. I wonder what time it is."

They came round the corner of Fellows' Buildings, in sight of the clock.

"Just six," said the Child. "I shall get my key from the lodge and go to bed."

"Breakfast with me?" asked Steven.

"Rather. About ten?"

CHAPTER II

MAURICE awoke early that morning, drowsily conscious that there was something rather pleasant ahead. He collected the threads of memory snapped off by sleep and began knotting them together again, and, still sleepily, reviewed the events of the evening before, in order to pick up the one that gave him the sense of something jolly at hand. The first thread was the rag in the court, snuffed out before it blazed into a bonfire; but that wasn't it, nor had Stares anything to do with it. After that he had gone to Steven's room, and the Child had come in, and he remembered that Steven had asked him to breakfast. That was what he was looking for, but immediately he remembered that he had declined on the excuse that he expected someone himself. So the pleasant anticipation expired.

He turned over in bed, wondering why he had said that he was engaged, for as a matter of fact nobody was coming to breakfast with him. Without difficulty he got hold of the reason, for it had struck him that Steven had asked him just by way of saying something polite to oil his departure. That was the reason why he had said, "No"; neither he nor the Child had wanted him either then or ever.

The clock in the lodge struck six. His blind was flapping sharply over the open window, and he got up to quiet this cracking noise. It was hot already; he would get more air with the blind up, and then he would go to sleep again. His windows looked out over the big lawn that ran down to the river, and there, halfway across the grass, the one in pajamas, the other in dress clothes, were strolling up the two whom he had left together, earlier in the night, to their evident content. And their content, it seemed, was not less now, as they drifted along absorbed in companionship, and quite unconscious of the anomaly of such attire at such an hour. Why was the Child still in dress clothes, or why, for that matter, was Steven in pajamas?

Maurice experienced a sudden pang of jealousy. It was born of a perception of his own loneliness, but perhaps it had been begotten last night when he had left those two together. Usually he felt very comfortably self-sufficient, but the sight of them gave him the sense that he was missing all that was really worth while. Then they turned the corner of Fellows' Buildings, and, rather ashamed of himself but unable to resist his curiosity, he went through to his sitting room, which looked out onto the front court, to see what they did next. There they were, standing at the entrance of the passage that led to Steven's rooms in the block of buildings at right angles to that from which he peered. Then Steven passed in, and the Child walked off to the porter's lodge on the far side of the court. He emerged again, carrying a key, and went into the entrance of his own staircase.

"I've been spying," thought Maurice to himself. "They thought they were alone, and I've been looking through the keyhole. A fat reward for my pains, too! But I wonder what they've been doing all night, and I also wonder what the devil it matters to me. It's no business of mine."

He felt no desire to go back to bed again, and he dressed and sat down at his table, where there were spread the notebooks from which he had been lecturing during this term, and from which he meant to extract material for a book of half a dozen essays on Athenian domestic life in the age of Pericles. Surely Athens had descended like the new Jerusalem from the very heaven of art and intellect, and yet, according to modern ideas of civilization, how barbarous was a city where women scarcely existed in the emotional life of men, but lived sequestered and periodically pregnant, and were in no way, with the immortal exception of Aspasia, either the companions of men or their inspirers. In the city of the Maiden Goddess there was no place for maid or matron; it was as celibate in purport and intention as a college at Cambridge. Fellows of college could be married, of course, just as were the philosophers of the Academe, but their wives lived in discreet villas in leafy suburbs, and the real life of the place, at Athens and Cambridge alike, was centred on the athletic and intellectual pursuits of men. A celibate community this: half a dozen of the Fellows were married; with the rest, as with the more numerous world of undergraduates, friendship and games and scholarship took the sting from the urge of sex. . . .

Just now he was conscious of a loneliness that was rare with him; generally he was quite content to be a young man of twenty-five without any close tie to any human being in the world, finding sufficient sauce for life in books and casual companionships, and evolving gradually, like most of his colleagues, a sort of horny protective integument which would soon sever him from all desire for intimate human intercourse. He felt he would soon begin to move sideways, like a crab; indeed, his refusal of Steven's invitation that morning had certainly an oblique motion about it. He was preparing for himself, by acquiescence in this environment, some hollow, scooped in the sand, where he, like Stares and the rest, would soon lie embedded, furtively peering out into the water where the brisk fish swam, ready with pincers and scratching legs to repel any intruder on his gritty privacy. In a few years more, if he did not take care, he would lose contact with the younger male life even that surged about him with its high ebullience and charm, and unless that kept him supple he would grow mailed and shelled much faster than those who lived, whether married or single, in the normal life of other cities, where a man and his friends grow old together. Here, except for the Dons, nobody grew old; a foam of young life continually poured in, and that made

Dons grow old faster than anyone, while still preserving some awful superficial sprightliness.

Steven and the Child: the Child and Steven; somehow the sight of those two coolly strolling over the grass an hour ago had stuck in his mind. What had they been doing all night that at six in the morning they were still habited as they were when he left them, the Child in his dress clothes, Steven in pajamas lacking a button? They had been together, of course, and none except a pair of boys under some bond of perfect comradeship could have come sauntering up, still together, in such intimate content. A boy and a girl couldn't have done it; man and a woman even less: sex would have intruded with its disasters and consummations and fatigues. An odd couple, too, finding perhaps in each other the complement of their qualities and defects: the Child with his boisterous waggings of the tail, like some splendid stupid dog, for all the obvious amusements and stick-throwings, and the other with some secret life of his own into which, sheathing his brightness, he so often withdrew.

How he envied them! How pinched and frost-bitten was his own life in comparison! Maurice had always avoided intimacy, keeping round himself some sort of thorny zareba where he entrenched himself. And yet always from boyhood he had longed and starved for close contacts, but he retreated from them, when they threatened to approach, in a panic of reserve and shyness. "I've always been a prig by nature," he thought to himself. "I've always suppressed any impulse of self-abandonment, and now here's the reward, that I'm already drying up." He had been through a few short and sordid experiences with women, but in no case had they been more than a physical guzzling to quench a physical thirst, and they had not either satisfied or caused any permanent desire for a woman as part of his nature. Lacking that, such episodes had remained as casual as any other gratification of the physical senses, like eating or sleeping; indeed, they were on a lower plane, for food and sleep were primary needs of life, and these others were wholly unnecessary, and he got on quite well without their satisfaction. They had been trumpery little excursions, like bank holidays to Margate, which produced nothing but a momentary pleasure, rather bracing perhaps, like a whiff of sea air, but they had left his imagination quite unkindled. He was well-off, he could have married comfortably if he had felt the smallest inclination for domestic life, or (what seemed to him) that curious passion of a man for perpetuating himself in offspring; but lacking that kindled imagination with regard to women, marriage seemed to him hardly more than legalized adultery with a lady housekeeper who would see after his home, and produce (*D.v.*) legitimate children. . . .

And then there was that strong reserve of his own to be reckoned with: he could not visualize himself as living under the yoke of even such daily trivial intimacies as marriage implied. He did not want any woman to take it for granted that he would like her to pat his hair or kiss his neck when she asked him what he would have for dinner, or to envelope him in that atmosphere of tenderness in the soft shadow of which there lurked for him the disquieting image of Delilah and her shears. Women, to his mind, sapped a man's virility rather than ministered to it. He knew he did not understand them in the least, and many of his friends, once apparently sworn to scholastic celibacy, pitied him, kindly and indulgently, for his want of comprehension. Women, in fact, except for the gratification of a recurrent but not very potent desire, were an enigma to him, of which he did not in the least care about guessing the answer.

And Cambridge, after all, with its intelligent monasticism, was rapidly becoming a habit, and it would require, so he knew, some very strong external stimulus to enable him to break free from it, or admit any intimacy, whether sexless or sexual. He could not imagine any mode of existence which would suit him so well, nor one that would keep him so wholesomely busy and entertained without effort or search for work or recreation. There were no household cares; his lectures and his pupils were sufficient mental occupation, and for diversion there was the society of his colleagues and of undergraduates. Something altogether new and surprising, some curiosity and lure of strange adventure would be needed to draw him out of this brisk little orbit in which he circled. A pang of jealousy certainly had jabbed him this morning when he saw Steven and the Child coming home, for he conjectured there some sexless engrossing intimacy which he knew he had envied. There was a freshness about it to his lonely eyes, an intensity . . . Of course that sort of thing was now utterly outside his scope; reserve had become a habit with him, an armour in which perhaps already there were no joints for the impact of a chance arrow. Besides, there was nobody who was in the least likely, man or woman, to pull a bow at a venture anywhere in his direction. . . . He settled down to the verification of some references in his essays and began to think them interesting.

Lectures were over for the term, and after breakfast Maurice strolled out without any fixed object in view, except the vague idea of picking up the news of the morning. The statue of Henry VI still wore its top hat at a rakish angle, but the porter, who had put a plank across from the coping of the fountain to the base of the stone pedestal in the centre on which the statue stood, was even now angling for it with a barbed pole used for the opening and shutting of high windows. It seemed to be difficult to insert the brass-hooked end of this between the monarch's orthodox crown and the rim of his adventitious tall hat, and at present the porter had only succeeded in adjusting the hat more firmly onto Henry's head. He wanted, so Maurice imagined, to pick the hat neatly off and use it for evidence. But he got impatient, and poked at it injudiciously, with the result that the hat fell into the fountain and floated up to where Maurice was observing these fishing operations with deep concern. An idea struck him, and kneeling down on the coping of the fountain he rescued the hat and looked inside it. There, as he suspected, were Steven's initials, S. G. in large adhesive gilt letters.

"I thought I had better see whose hat it was, sir," said the porter, "and tell Mr. Stares."

Maurice whisked the water off it.

"Quite right," said he cheerfully. "But I'll see to it. No damage done last night, was there?"

"No, sir. All melted away very quiet. Mr. Merriman came for the key of his rooms at six this morning. Dress clothes still, but that's none of my business. He and Mr. Gervase calmed things down wonderful last night. I thought we was in for a bonfire. You were out there, too, weren't you, sir?"

"Oh yes, but there was no bother."

Maurice went hat in hand to Steven's rooms. It was a good thing to have appropriated it, for if Stares had been informed whose hat had crowned the king, it would certainly have added weight to his ridiculous notion of gating him. He knocked, but there was no answer, and he entered to find Steven's sitting room empty and an untouched breakfast for two laid on the table. So he put the hat over the teapot, by way of an agreeable mystery, and withdrew. Coming out he ran into the Child, looking extremely fresh and cheerful.

"Hullo, Maurice," he said. "Steven up yet?"

"No sign of him; only breakfast."

"Let's begin, then. Aren't you coming to breakfast? Oh, no, you said you couldn't. And are we going to be gated? I've not had any gratifying invitation from little Stares yet."

"Can't say," said Maurice. "I did my best."

"Awfully good of you. I expect you did the trick."

Maurice did not care two straws whether the Child was gated or not, except on abstract principles of justice; the Child might be gated or sent down, for all that it personally mattered to him. It was not for the Child's sake that he had testified to Stares. This large elementary youth was certainly a splendid type, but it was strange that Steven, with his moods of withdrawal and secrecy, which gave one the sense of something rare and mysterious held in reserve, should find in him the perfect comrade.

"I should think you're all right," he said. "You'd have had a *billet doux* from Stares by this time, if he pined to see you. You're disgraceful sluggards, though, not having breakfasted yet."

"We were a bit late going to bed," said the Child. "We sat up after you left quite a long time."

Maurice knew that; he could have supplied some of the information the Child withheld.

"Just fooling about, you know," he added, and went on into Steven's rooms. Steven came out of his bedroom as he entered, and pointed to the unusual tea cosy.

"Hullo, what's that?" he said.

"It looks awfully like a top hot," said the Child. "In fact, I believe it is."

"But why and how?" said Steven, picking it off. "I say, it's mine, the one I lent to Henry."

"Well, then, Henry's finished with it and brought it back," said the Child. "Oh, I guess. I met Maurice coming out of your room a moment ago. I bet you he brought it."

Steven ran to the window; Maurice was strolling along the path back to his own staircase.

"Hi, Maurice!" he shouted. "Do come here a minute, unless you're busy."

"I am," said Maurice, coming back.

"I've found an awfully odd thing on my table," said Steven. "Have a guess."

"The Green Hat," said Maurice. "Still dampish."

"It was you, then. How did you get it?"

"I wangled it. Best to remove all evidence."

"Too angelic of you. Pleased to have met you. What can I do for you?"

Maurice smiled at that radiant face peering over the windox box.

"Go on being pleased to have met me," he said.

"I will. Come in and have breakfast; or call it lunch."

"Can't. I told you I was busy."

"Why this stand-offishness?" demanded Steven. "I asked you to breakfast last night, and you wouldn't, and even when I call it lunch you won't. What have I done?"

"I haven't the slightest idea," said Maurice. "Go and eat your breakfast. I expect you're hungry."

"I am, specially. Thanks ever so much for the hat. I shouldn't have known what to do without it. Not that I've worn it for a couple of years or so, but I always knew I could if I wanted."

The King's ball took place that night; dancing was in a big marquee with a swinging wooden floor on the back lawn, and a tented way led there from Hall and Combination Room which served for refreshments and the almost extinct genus of chaperon. The Child always felt he was too tall to dance without looking absurd, and Steven confirmed this impression by telling him that he resembled an enormous black and white spider tackling a small pink fly. After that, naturally, he had to dance once more to show his contempt of such comparisons, but conscious of the acid truth of it, he surrendered, and watched with a broad grin the Amazon tackling Steven. She was a stalwart young woman, like a guardsman or an athletic virile Diana with a bevy of attendant adoring nymphs, whom, in intervals of dancing with Steven, she twirled round in a desultory manner. Otherwise, even though there were more than enough men to go round, the nymphs seemed to prefer revolving in a virgin eddy of their own, till Gem gave them another turn. Maurice, who abhorred dancing and was acting as steward, was busy enough for the first hour, until affairs began to warm up, with introducing undergraduates to stranded damsels, but soon the rhythmical lure of band and natural law asserted themselves, and the instinct of dancing relieved him of his duties.

He strolled off alone towards the river for a cigarette and coolness. Rows of small lights in coloured glass globes outlined the paths, making luminous avenues for sauntering couples; above, the moonlight took charge of general illumination. But in that vivid foreground of bright specks of colour, and in the strong glow shining through the canvas of the lit marquee, the artificial seemed to be real, and the chapel and college buildings in that toneless brightness of the moon appeared theatrical, as if they were pieces of stage scenery. They were the illusion, run up there as a contrasted setting to the real thing, which was this mingling of the young sexes.

He leaned on the parapet of the bridge, and the idea began to spread in his brain. Certainly, in this starry decoration of coloured lights, all that was really solid and permanent here, with the moon thus shining on it, seemed like pasteboard; and with these mixed couples passing up and down the bright avenues, all that these solidities stood for, education, the celibate life of athletics and friendships and books, partook of the pasteboard quality. The rag last night, which had so wildly interested him, the achievement of the King's boat, and, more than all, his own work, appeared to him like trivial games for an idle hour, while the true business of life was now introduced into this academic playground by the fluttering figures which, with their black-garbed partners, strayed about or moved in pairs to the band. He and Stares and the Provost and all the rest of the tutorial body were charlatans and quacks with their bread pills of stale history, and their unmedicinal draughts of dates which they administered to the youth to swallow in faith. It was all a sham, like those moonstruck theatrical buildings where they worked and prayed and lectured; the marquee was genuine, and the gleam of the coloured lights, and the paired sexes.

"Shall I get hold of a girl," thought Maurice, "and prance round her, and tell her she is a dream of loveliness and an epitome of all the graces? Yet that would be a fake, too, for I know I shouldn't believe her to be anything of the sort. All the same, it would be a fake of something real. If I pretended it long enough I might get to believe it."

Maurice's attention was distracted from these sombre topics for a moment by the sight of Tommy, who had been a lovely mushroom at this time last night. Tipsy he had been then, but now, with his arm round a girl's waist, and his face extraordinarily close to hers, he looked to Maurice far tipsier than in his mushroom incarnation. He had been bemused (to put it prettily) with wine last night, but now he was dead drunk with a girl. They had stepped for privacy under the hanging festoons of the drooping willow, and Tommy in a hoarse whisper said: "Do give me a kiss . . . oh, that's ripping." Maurice thought it only kind to show them that their kissing-out place was clearly visible to anyone standing on the bridge, and he lit a match for his cigarette and appeared to be absorbed, with averted face, in lighting it. "Oh, Lor'!" said the girl, and they crept away.

That was real; Tommy was being a proper young man to-night, and doing what a proper young man should in kissing a pretty girl. That did not come into the scholastic curriculum; indeed, it was on the index expurgatorius, together with being a mushroom or anything freakish of that sort. But was it freakish to behave like Tommy? Was not such exuberance perfectly right?

Surely it was more freakish to take an interest in Ely Cathedral like George Herbert, or in domestic life in ancient Athens like himself. Of course you couldn't have tipsy mushrooms growing all over the court, or deliver a course of lectures on kissing, but who with any sort of humanity wanted young men to be always decorous? What a collection of bloodless prigs (like himself) Cambridge would turn out if the educational system perfectly fulfilled itself! Tommy was introducing a little judicious human nature into the sad, unreal cloister.

The strollers had gone back into the marquee, and Maurice went along the walk by the river. He sat down on a deserted bench, feeling again, as he had felt at six that morning, extraordinarily lonely. His whole life here, so he imagined it, was a very useless tissue of industry: it bore no relation to reality, it was busy with inhuman businesses and barren accumulations. When you were fifty or sixty or seventy years old, ages which to him from his altitude of twenty-five seemed to compose a flat uniform plain without any distinguishing features, it might be a suitable occupation to trace the details of Athenian life, or solve mathematical problems, but it was a vast mistake at his present age to treat such as the main business of life.

The proper study of mankind was what it always had been, and the proper time for the acquisition of first-hand knowledge on that subject was youth, when contacts were easily made and emotions were keen. Arts and sciences and the pursuit of knowledge were no doubt useful for the advancement of the race, but if they crowded out human relationships and made their students into men like Stares, knowledge simply became a disease and its unhappy devotees hypochrondriacs. . . . And then at the back of human relationships was the relation of each individual to the whole: out of that came all the religions of the world, Christian and pagan alike.

Somebody stepped off the grass behind him, close to where his seat stood.

"Hullo, Maurice," said Steven. "What are you doing here?"

"Precisely the same as yourself," said Maurice.

"In that case I'll go away, because I was seeking solitude."

"No, sit down. You don't count. How are things going?"

"Hectically," said Steven.

"The Amazon in full pursuit?"

Steven laughed.

"That's rather difficult to answer," he said. "If I say 'yes,' I seem rather a bounder, if I say 'no' rather a liar."

"Don't answer, then. I'll take it that you've come for a rest from pursuing her."

Steven sat down by him: he was all crackling, like something electricially charged, with vitality.

"Yes, a rest," he said. "The steady pursuit of enjoyment is frightfully fatiguing. You've got to enjoy yourself by accident if it's to be any good. Organized revelry is as tiring as organized work: I would as soon go to a lecture."

"And impromptu revelry stimulates: is that it?" asked Maurice.

"Of course: it's a rag."

Steven opened his cigarette case and found it empty.

"Damn that Amazon," he observed. "She has a true affinity with my cigarettes."

"I've got some," said Maurice.

"Hurrah. I've a true affinity with yours. Thanks. How long does the revelry go on?"

"Till everyone's thoroughly exhausted with pleasure. I daresay you'll get to bed about six."

"Same as last night," said Steven.

"Yes, it was just six," said Maurice.

"Now how on earth do you know that?" demanded Steven.

"Because I saw you and the Child coming up over the lawn at that hour. As he was in dress clothes, and you in pajamas, which was how I left you five hours or so before, I presumed you hadn't gone to bed."

"How frightfully secretive you are," said Steven. "If you knew all that why didn't you tell me?"

"I know I'm secretive," said Maurice. "It's the bane of my life. But, after all, you didn't tell me."

"It never occurred to me. Would you like to know what we had been doing?"

"Immensely. You looked so happy that I was jealous of you," said Maurice. "Go on."

"It'll sound awful rot, but really we had the most marvellous night, and I can't think why. Absolutely impromptu: perhaps that was it. We wandered down to the river, some time after you had gone, and found a canoe tied up under the willow. Naturally we untied it."

"I don't see what else you could have done with it, if it was tied up already," remarked Maurice.

"Glad you agree. And so we paddled up to the Mill, and hauled over to the upper river. And then we just sat there, without a word: drip, drip from the paddles. We got to the bathing sheds just at dawn."

"Obvious that you bathed," said Maurice. "I don't see what else you could do. I call it rather commonplace so far."

"Don't be so dry, or I shan't go on. It wasn't commonplace; there was something magnetic abroad."

"That sounds like a description from a novel by an elderly lady," said Maurice, continuing to be dry.

"If you had said from a poem by Walt Whitman you'd have been nearer the mark," said Steven. "The night was magnetic: it tingled, it pressed close."

Maurice felt a sudden thrill of comprehension. Something secret within him knew what Steven meant. . . . It was the relationship of the individual to the whole. . . .

"Ah, it wasn't commonplace, then, if something got hold of you like that," said he. This was interesting: perhaps it bore on that secret Steven who withdrew himself so often and so strangely. "Go on: did it get hold of the Child too?"

"Not an atom. He liked being with me, but he didn't know—how shall I express it?—that I had gone a long way off," said Steven. "Something had come for me out of the night, and there was a great force abroad, like a hammer which was welding me into—into the whole caboodle."

Steven was silent a moment. The moonlight falling on his face neutralized the hues of wholesome sunburn which stained it, and made it some exquisite ivory mask. It dehumanized it, and though it was still intensely alive, it was alive with the vitality that throbs in some sculptured faces. But the blanching of the moon could not decolourize the gold of his hair: sparks of the pure metal seemed to gleam in it; his head, like some temple statue of the Greeks, was of ivory and gold, burning with the life of an intense but unhuman spirit. His eyes looked out into the moonlit dusk, fixed and eager. But this impression, flashing through Maurice's perceptions, was but momentary, and Steven turned to him again.

"Good Lord, what an extraordinary thing that I should be talking to you like this," he said. "But somehow I felt you would understand, and if a fellow understands, you can say anything to him."

"I'll try to, anyhow," said Maurice. "Go on."

"Where had I got to? Oh, yes: we bathed just as the

sun came up. The usual rag, of course. The Child tried to duck me, so I vaulted onto him, and down we went together, into the green twilight ever so far away, and all the bubbles above us turned red as they broke on the surface. And though we were wrestling together down underneath the water, the Child wasn't there at all, or if he was he was only rather in the way. Then up we came, half drowned, and swore at each other. And what do you think we did next? You must promise not to laugh if I tell you."

"I swear I won't. I shan't even want to," said Maurice.

"We made an altar to the gods of wet places and of night," said Steven, "and burned on it the most valuable things we had got, which were some matches and a cigarette. And I said a prayer."

"I never heard of anything so suitable," said Maurice. "But when you say 'we' did that, you were wrong. I'm sure the Child hadn't really any part in it. That was you."

"I suppose it was; indeed, of course it was. The Child wasn't there really. And then it was all over, and we just paddled home again. All that had made the night marvellous had gone phut: there were just the Child and I in a canoe."

Steven laid his hand on Maurice's shoulder.

"I say, you do understand, don't you?" he asked. "Not what it was which made the night marvellous, but that there was something? I don't know what it was, but it was something primitive and wild and joyful. And to think of the Child not having any notion of its existence! It's an awful pity. Disappointing."

"Why; exactly?"

"Well, naturally," said Steven. "You see, we've been such friends, and now he's no use. It's odd, too, that just before we set off we had been talking about the Child going down, and I had said it was the end."

"And now the end's come another way?" asked Maurice. "Is that what you mean?"

"Yes, that's it. We've gone together as far as the road goes, and he can't see any farther or come with me any farther. Of course, I'm devoted to him and all that, but—but there's the end of him. It's a bore. But what a way of spending a night, and then the next night to come down to this."

Maurice laughed—rather a donnish laugh.

"To sit with me on a bench. Condolences," he said.

"No, I don't mean that. I mean the utter unreality of this evening. Fairy lights. Amazons. Hell! I said I would take her in to supper in ten minutes, and it's at least twenty. And yet all this wild raging mob thinks that it's having no end of a time. Come up as far as the tent. Have you been dancing?"

"No, I loathe it," said Maurice.

"That's no reason why you shouldn't do it. Discipline. I say, don't laugh at me for all the rot I've talked. I won't do it again. Indeed, I don't know why I told you at all, except that I suddenly thought you might understand. I expect you think that I'm dotty. Or was it that some bit of me came out and roamed? Some wild animal that's always lived deep in woods and thickets?"

"Let it come out again, Steven," he said. "And call me. I want to have another look at it."

It was little to be wondered at that next morning, to Maurice's well ordered and academic mind, that strange talk with Steven by the river appeared highly fantastic. But, though fantastic, it throbbed with reality: the truth, as everyone knew, could be fantastic. Above all, the image which Steven himself had suggested was vividly real; namely, that of something having come out of the woodland thickets of his mind, like some shy wild beast emerging to feed and prowl at night, or like some fabled creature that followed in the rout of Pan. It was that which had responded to the mysterious call of the night, which had given him a glimpse of something "primitive and wild and joyful." Shy it certainly was, diffident of having revealed itself at all. And was it, so Maurice asked himself, ruthless as well as shy, not with the deliberate cruelty of a reasonable being, but with the indifference of some gay and graceful animal which starts up from its pleased, purring mood and strikes with an unsheathed talon? Sudden and shadowy had been its appearance, and as fleeting as that strange glance he had caught of Steven's face all ivory and gold in the moonlight, and alive with the life of consummate sculpture. In that glimpse, he told himself, he had momentarily looked on the incarnation of this wild thing, which had usurped the use of Steven's eyes and his mouth and the gold of his hair, moulding the lineaments to its own projected image. Even as, so it was said, at spiritualistic séances, a spirit could inhabit and inspire the earthly tenement of an entranced medium. It had revealed itself to his eyes in outward form, just as, using Steven's tongue, it had told him something about itself.

But in the epiphany by the riverside there had been no possession from without; it was no external and discarnate soul, he felt very sure, that had used the features and speech of Steven, but Steven's own interior self, coming out of its withdrawn reserve and manifesting itself, neither male nor female, but some sexless entity, full of the joy of night and the woodland, and somehow, for all its infinite grace, terrible.

What it had said had been terrible too, if such was regarded as an utterance of a human spirit, but Maurice felt sure that it was no more cruel in intention than was the action of any wild animal. But humanly speaking, as coming from Steven's lips, there was something disconcertingly heartless about it. Those two, already knit close in the bond of their friendship, had spent the night up there on the river, not returning till after dawn, and surely that should have been to them both a jolly episode, at the least, in their intimacy, but to Steven it had been nothing of the kind. The Child had not understood; he had not been there at all, or, if he had, he had merely been in the way. Steven had no more use for him; his inadequacy, his want of comprehension had been to him the end of their friendship, and on that he wasted no regret at all: he shrugged his shoulders and dismissed him. He felt no regret and he feigned none; it was as if they had never been friends at all. And yet it was no deliberate heartlessness, any more than is the indifference of an animal to some amusement of which it has tired. Steven had discovered, or been on the verge of discovering some new emotional territory, and if his friend could not see that there was something there, his friend was no good to him. He might go or he might stop, but for the wild thing which had come out of its thickets he had no existence. . . . And what *was* that wild thing? Maurice asked himself. Some vibration of primeval consciousness, perhaps, some veiled recognition of the oneness of all that has life.

There had been a force, Steven said, like the stroke of a welding hammer. . . . Subconsciously, perhaps, he had felt that before, and it had expressed itself in his moods of withdrawal: now, like a bubble coming up from the depths of dark water, it had broken on the surface of his consciousness.

It must not be supposed that Maurice made any such ordered or consecutive dissertation on the subject: the substance of what has been said flashed across his mind like the glimpse caught of a street or a meadow during a blink of lightning. It came out of the dark, manifested itself in colour and in detail, and went back into the dark again. But in his mind, though there came at present no further illumination, the impression remained singularly vivid, and in the days that followed various points in it became more distinct. Little happenings recalled to him something which he had momentarily understood as he and Steven sat on that bench in the moonlight; they were like that fugitive conviction, so common and so inexplicable, of something identical, though trivial and unimportant, having happened before. It was as if signals winked distantly at him, and before he could focus them or guess at their significance they were gone again. But they came from Steven, not the Steven who was visible and audible to all, but from that which was far more essentially he, the wild thing shy and secret, which had come out of its woodland lair.

Several small incidents then, all of which would have been trivial or unnoticed by him had he not got that glimpse below the surface, occurred during those few days of the term that remained. The two friends, for instance, came up to his rooms after Hall, on the night succeeding the dance, for coffee and conversation and bridge if a fourth could be kidnapped. They had been together, it appeared, all day, as usual; no hint of a break had appeared.

"And thank God for a sensible evening again," said Steven, "without affinities and muck. Also for the prospect of eight or nine hours of sweet repose. Up till five this morning, and up till six the morning before . . . Yes, Child, Maurice knows about our excursion. I told him."

The Child's face expressed serene incredulity.

"Rot," he said, "you did nothing of the kind."

"It isn't rot, and I did," said Steven. "What are you looking like that for?"

"Oh, nothing," said the Child. "But I didn't think——"

Maurice got a glimpse then of the Steven who had no more use for his friend. It was evident that the Child had taken it for granted that their adventure was something utterly private, but Steven either perceived nothing of that or cared nothing for it. But the implied reproach clearly annoyed him, and he got up, interrupting the Child.

"That's right, don't think, never think," he said. "And why on earth shouldn't I tell Maurice?"

The Child shrugged his great shoulders.

"All right, then," he said. "It's done, anyhow. Yes, we paddled and bathed and played the fool and didn't get home till six in the morning. Hectic night."

Steven strolled to the window.

"There's Tommy," he said. "May I shout to him, Maurice, and ask him if he'll come and gamble?"

"Rather. Tell him he must."

A few *fortissimo* observations resulted in Tommy's saying that he would come at once. Maurice went through to his smaller sitting room to fetch cards and markers, and the Child got up and joined Steven in the window-seat.

"I say, don't be stuffy," he said. "But what made you tell Maurice about it?"

"Stuffy? It's you who were stuffy, it seems to me," said Steven. "Not that I mind. And as for telling him, where's the harm?"

"Harm? I'm not talking about harm. But I can't see how you could."

Steven laughed.

"Oh, don't let's behave like the Amazon and her friends. It doesn't suit us a bit. I told him because I knew he would understand. He'd seen us coming back across the lawn at six in the morning, and do you know what he said? He said we looked so happy that he felt jealous. Is that enough for you?"

Maurice came back again with cards and markers. He saw Steven bristling and impatient. Simultaneously Tommy entered, and Steven hailed him.

"Hullo, Tommy! I say, I'll back my girl against yours any day. The one in blue, I mean. Six rounds."

"Huh!" said Tommy. "Oh, good-evening, Maurice. You

did mean me to come, didn't you? Steven shouted from here. Match your girl against the Child, Steven: they're about the same weights. Heavyweight championship: man *versus* woman. Betting about even, if the Child's in good training."

"Good enough to pull off your little arms and legs, Tommy," said the Child, getting up.

"Well, I'm not contradicting you; don't be so personal," said Tommy. "You want to be like the lady spider when she's had enough of her gent. Pulls him to bits, she does, and eats him. Damned interesting piece of natural history, and that's what I thought was going to happen last night. I thought Steven was in for it. I thought we should find a big web made of corsets and garters hanging across the entrance to the marquee, and Steven's girl sitting in the middle of it, licking her fingers. Of Steven no trace."

Tommy, small, neat and ruddy, cackled with laughter at his own wit.

"Tommy, you're not drunk again, are you?" asked Maurice.

"Good Lord, no. Blind sober. What put that into your head? Oh, by the way, thanks awfully for making me go home when you found me sitting on the lawn two nights ago. You were a true friend, and I did just what you told me. I went back to my rooms, good as gold, and didn't know anything more till I woke with an awful head, wondering if I had really told you I was a mushroom."

"You did," said Maurice.

"Awful: I can't think how I came to do it. But I behaved beautiful last night."

"A chaste salute under the willow," said Maurice.

"What! Was it you on the bridge?" asked Tommy. "You seem to be everywhere."

"It was. You shocked me."

"Sorry, but it's another good mark to you. I saw somebody with a match on the bridge looking absolutely the other way. Tactful, delicate, Nature's gentleman, Maurice. And how did you wangle little Stares into not doing anything about me as a mushroom? I saw him looking out of the window when you were picking me. And you got Steven off too. Steven dancing without his bags. Horrible; worse than being a mushroom. I thought we should be sent down, but nothing. How was it done?"

"I wangled, of course," said Maurice. "I told him that George Herbert was the worst of you all. Incendiarist."

"Jolly clever of you. They wouldn't have gone to see the Angel Choir at Ely next day. How I hate cathedrals, and my father a bishop."

"I promise not to tell him," said Maurice. "But aren't we going to play bridge?"

"Yes, that's what I came for, on Steven's invitation. But there's lots to say, if you'd sooner talk. The idea of matching Steve's coal-heaveress with my little Sylph: Dempsey and Jimmy Wilde I call it. Oh, am I to cut? Queen of hearts: that's her."

Tommy, with his babble, had restored a normal atmosphere, which was a good thing, and Maurice felt he ought to be grateful for this readjusted balance. There was nothing the least mysterious about him: he was the true incarnation of the obvious and natural young man, and it was far better to be exactly like that, to walk and skip down the very middle of the road, than peer and sidle away into the shadowed margin. Most young men, if they had only enough natural exuberance to do what they thought most pleasant, and make no bones about it, were exactly like Tommy, and they, after all, were the race. He would sow a small field of respectable wild oats, and drink the strong wine of youth, and then, wiping his mouth from that normal but heady beverage, would probably take orders, and become his father's chaplain, and marry, and be presented to a country living, and rear a sturdy little family, ruddy and round, exactly like himself, who would do precisely as Tommy, in his time, had done, and thereafter carry on the admirable traditions of their class. . . .

But would all the Tommies of the race really further any conceivable sort of human progress? Wasn't it rather this host of perfectly normal people, who had not the slightest curiosity about the shadowy edges, who by their sheer weight kept back all chance of enlightenment? There they all marched along in the middle of the road, singing "Onward, Christian Soldiers" without any notion of what Christianity or fighting meant, except that you were kind and bluff and hearty and taught the village boys to resist the temptations to which you had yourself succumbed. But anyone who imagined that there were strange little-known districts in the hinterland of the human spirit, who ventured on the dubious and secluded places, was to them an object of slightly contemptuous pity. They were quite certain of themselves: they knew that there were no shy wild beasts which lived in the forests, just as they knew that there were no unicorns. . . .

And yet all new knowledge of every sort came from such unorthodox excursions, and though science laughed at what it called quackery and superstition, it generally, a generation or two later, netted in the results and roused the admiration of orthodox folk at what it had found. Two hundred years ago practitioners of X-ray or wireless telegraphy or hypnotism would have been burned as witches by an enlightened world, but the witchcraft of one century became the science of the next. And there were mysteries of the human spirit which could only be solved, if at all, by leaving the beaten track. It was in youth only, thought Maurice, that you had the power to leave it; later on such trespass became impossible, for there was not the vitality to strike into the unknown . . .

"My father thinks there's going to be the hell of a row

over the new prayer-book," said Tommy. "Two spades."

Tommy was partnered with the Child, and Maurice was on his left.

"Three clubs," said he. "But why?"

"Something about the Communion Service. Don't ask me. Three spades, did you say, Child? That'll make them think."

"No, it doesn't. I double," said Steven.

"Thank you kindly. Enough. I wonder if I might have a drink before we begin, Maurice. It's going to be thirsty and trying work. When I'm a parson——"

"Shut up," said Steven. "There won't be any church for you to be a parson in."

"I shan't argue," said Tommy. "At least not at present." He tasted his drink. "Did you happen to omit the whisky, Maurice?" he asked. "It's only an inquiry."

Maurice felt a sudden exasperation at this genial twaddle.

"Help yourself," he said. "It's by you."

. . . Yet all these fellows, three years or four younger than himself, had experienced, in their different ways, keennesses of emotion, human realities, which he had never known, had penetrated into regions where he had never been. Tommy, perhaps the simplest and most elementary, had found rapture in kissing the girl in blue under the willow; the Child, hardly less normally, had known devoted and passionate friendship; Steven, who had gone farther afield and into less trodden places, was on the scent of something rarer than they, of something that prowled, and was *perdu*, and Steven was certainly signalling to him out of that dark of things . . .

All of them, anyhow, were tasting in their different capacities the juice and the joy of life, the elixir of youth, which up to any age nourishes and alone makes it worth while to be alive. And the fruits of it, fed on that sap, were alone capable of supplying refreshment: even an obvious boy like Tommy was doing more for the human race than one who, like himself, drily reconstructed some detail in the ancient life of Athens. Industry, scholarship, research, study of fleas or of Greek prepositions, were all smaller and subsidiary influences compared with that which dealt with life direct: they were withered and dry unless they were stewed in the juice of humanity. All these boys were ahead of him here; never had he had a relation with boy or girl, with man or woman, that was vital. Somehow he must get rid of that reserve, that timidity which drove him into these bookish and barren ways. Even George Herbert Redcliffe, for all his lamentable interest in Angel Choirs, could get tipsy and want to light a bonfire. Maurice knew he could not make his approach to humanity on such lines, nor indeed on Tommy's, but something must be done, some surrender made. . . .

The first rubber was short, but the second lengthened itself out inordinately, with skyscrapers of penalties above the line and little foundation below, and it was getting on for midnight before it came to an end. The Child had long been in a swoon of drowsiness and yawning, a wild melancholy invaded Tommy, but there was something alert still in the other two: glance met glance, they were conscious of each other. Then addition was done, no suggestion was made of beginning again, and Maurice's three guests clattered away down the uncarpeted stairs. It was not till they had gone that he saw that Steven, who had amassed four shillings as the result of this interminable struggle, had left his winnings on the table. He went to the window to call out to him, but by now all three of them were at the far angle of the Court, where the Child's rooms and Tommy's lay, and it would be ridiculous to bawl after them. He would drop in to Steven's room to-morrow morning with these fabulous gains.

Maurice left the window, and in his neat, careful way began clearing up débris. He threw into the waste-paper basket the scribbled sheets of marking, and into the fireplace the contents of a couple of ash trays piled with cigarette ends, for these made a room smell like an unventilated smoking carriage if they remained there all night. He put Steven's four shillings into his pocket, poured out and drank the remains of the last siphon, and went into his bedroom, switching off the light in the sitting room. He had hardly got there when he heard his outer door open, and he went back.

"Hullo, who's that?" he asked. Stares, perhaps, he thought.

"Me," said Steven's voice. "Sorry; I didn't think that you'd have gone to bed. I left my year's income on the table."

Maurice switched on the light again.

"I know you did," he said. "I meant to bring it round to you in the morning."

Steven looked at the table where he had left it.

"Rather suspicious," he said. "You've pouched it already."

Maurice fished four shillings up from his trouser-pocket.

"I only removed temptation from my bed maker," he said. "There you are. Four. And stop and talk a bit."

"Shall I? Sure you don't want to go to bed?" asked Steven.

"Not a bit. I hope you intended to do so when you came back."

Steven laughed.

"Why, of course I did," he said. "You don't suppose I came up all those stairs for the sake of four bob. But I was quite prepared to be yawned at."

"I couldn't yawn at you if I tried," said Maurice. "Sit down. Drink? Smoke?"

"Neither, thanks. I came back because I'd got something to say. The Child didn't like my telling you about our night out."

"I guessed as much," said Maurice.

"I thought you did. We're beginning to understand each other a bit, you know."

Maurice hesitated; his shyness, his ingrained reserve tugged him away. But more potent was the charm of what beckoned him.

"I should like that," he said. "But I'm sorry the Child's vexed."

"I don't see that the Child matters if you and I are going to be friends," said Steven.

Some spell was at work that warmed and encouraged. Under it, Maurice felt that the frost of reserve which all his life had sheathed him in isolation and coldness was beginning to melt. But he still held back: loneliness was a habit with him, hard to break.

"I've never had a friend in my life," he said. "I don't know if I have the power of making friends with anyone."

"Try," said Steven. "Give me a chance. That's really what I came to say. So I'm off. Good-night."

He turned abruptly, and next moment his steps were clattering down the staircase. They died away, and Maurice saw that he still held in his hand the four shillings which Steven had won.

CHAPTER III

MAURICE could never trace any system or sequence of cause and effect in the momentous trivialities of these days. Little events, closely related to each other, touches, hints, stirrings and questionings and muttered answers, formed a network of meshes softly drifting in upon him, and it was with sudden and fleeting panics and thoughts of escape alternating with eager thrills of anticipation of being in the grip of a constraining force that he waited for the situation (and yet what *was* the situation?) to develop. . . .

That night he passed through an endless series of dozings and awakenings and of cool still sleep that seemed to come out of some well deep down in the heart of things. Sometimes in these dozings that ivory mask of Steven's face swung oscillating against a background of summer woodland thick with scents of the wild and loud with forest murmurs; slower and slower it swung till it melted into flickering gleams of light among the leaves, or solidified into Steven's real face, smiling and beckoning with that little backward toss of his neck. Vague and muddled the panorama of such visions seemed to him when he definitely woke next morning, but there still lingered in them some sense of reality, as if they had been born not of his own brain, but had come from outside altogether: he had passed through real experiences, now of childish happiness, now of vague horror. Processes of dressing and bath did not quite disperse them; rather it drove them inwards into those summer woods of which he had dreamed.

But his conscious reactions to life were normal enough: that threatened thawing of his own frosts of reserve seemed to have congealed again, and he could not imagine himself cultivating relations of unreserved friendship with Steven, or even of permitting such to establish themselves. Steven was a strange, fascinating fellow, but he almost wished that he had not come back last night with that gesture of welcome. He dreaded a renewed contact, he regretted that he had not repulsed the first and retreated, as he could so easily have done, into his own inviolable security, with faint but icy surprise. Yet when Steven had said, "Give me a chance," and bounded down the stairs, Maurice had known that it was his own chance that had come, and that his instinct had leaped to take and clutch it. A way into the perils and rewards of human relationship had been opened for him. Somebody wanted his comradeship, and it showed, he felt, how far his crustacean habit had grown on him, that, when the chance came of breaking through that shell, he was frightened at it.

The fact of Steven's four shillings being still in his possession gave rise to an oblique crablike design, one that should make a sideways movement in the direction he feared to approach directly. Steven was not an early riser, as Dean Stares had often had occasion to remind him, and Maurice went to his rooms, secure in finding him not yet up, with the intention of putting these coins in some silly place, so that when he discovered them later he would have to re-open matters himself. Under his tea-pot would be a good *cache*, or inside his box of cigarettes. He would find them there before long, and wonder what the devil a half-crown, a shilling, and a sixpence were doing there. He would perceive that they amounted in the aggregate to four shillings, and then he would remember his winnings of the night before. "I am exactly like a playful, frisky old maid," thought Maurice to himself, and grinned at the aptness of his comparison. Tall and dark and handsome, he made his dignified way across the Court and exchanged a few academic observations with the Provost.

He gave a perfunctory rap at the door of Steven's sitting room, feeling sure it would not be answered. Nor was it, for it was unheard, and he walked in to find him and the Child at breakfast in quite the usual manner. They were quarrelling over the remaining sausage.

"No. I'll go halves," said Steven, "but I'm damned if you have it all. Hullo, Maurice: if you'll take that sausage away from the Child you may eat it."

There seemed to be no place here for the dashing old maid. . . .

"No use to me," he said. "But you left your bullion on the card table last night. Four bob."

Steven just glanced up at him, an eyelid quivered, a smile hovered.

"Four bob it was," he said. "And do you mean you've brought them to me? I should never do that sort of thing. I should pocket them in complete ignorance of the owner, the more the bobs the completer the ignorance. I suppose I ought to tip you for your honesty. Have sixpence, won't you?"

"Rather," said Maurice, handing over the remainder.

"No, I didn't mean that," said Steven. "Threepence would be plenty. Too much, in fact, on the proportion offered by ladies who leave pearl necklaces worth a thousand pounds in taxis and proclaim a reward of five. Insanely generous, in fact. But I've offered you your chance, and I won't withdraw it."

Maurice caught that too: already he found himself in confidential communication with Steven in the presence of the Child, and the old maid popped out again. "We're like parents who talk French to each other so that the children shan't understand," he thought to himself. Steven was serious then about "the chance": he had not forgotten; he reminded him of it in the middle of this public drivel.

"It would be nice to be quite insane," he went on, "and live in a world of one's own. Once upon a time there was a Nonconformist who believed that one of his legs was a Roman Catholic. This naturally distressed him a great deal, and he wouldn't put his two legs in bed together for fear the Roman Catholic one would try to convert the other while he was asleep. So he left the Roman Catholic outside the blankets to prevent it talking to the Nonconformist. It got rheumatism, which served it quite right. And he wouldn't have it in the railway carriage with him on a journey, but stuck it out of the window, and a passing train cut it off at the knee. He was deeply thankful, and said, 'Praise God from whom all blessings flow,' and died from loss of blood that flowed. That's all. . . . Hurrah, the Child's cheering up. He was morose."

"Ass," said the Child.

"What's the use of telling me that? I might as well say 'Kill-joy' to you. But stale news never breaks no bones. Only I think you might try and get over the fact that you lost two shillings last night. Don't spoil the few days that remain before we leave our sheltered life here."

"If you go on like that," said the Child, "I shall be sick."

Maurice left them together, and for the rest of the day made no attempt to see Steven. He had had his signals confirming the proposition of last night; they had flashed to him in no mistakable manner, and he accepted them. There was a mutual understanding now, and it could be left like that, coding and decoding itself, till Steven was free of the Child. To him Maurice gave no thought at all, except of faint, contemptuous indulgence; he was at liberty to take what he could of Steven in the few hours that remained to him. He probably noticed no change in him, for he had never known him at all, since he had had no part in the true significance of the night on the river, when the "wild thing" sniffed the sorcery of the darkness and sought someone who, though he might not understand it any more than Steven himself did, could make some response.

The Child, Maurice felt sure, had ceased to matter, and though all day no doubt he would find Steven amiable and affectionate and foolish, as he had been at breakfast, the props had been knocked away from under their friendship: it was as brittle and empty as if through some minute puncture in an eggshell the contents had been sucked out of it though the shell still cohered. Maurice was rather sorry for him, but he didn't matter.

What mattered was Steven and himself, and he divined that they would start their friendship exactly at the point at which the Child had been discarded, the good blind muscular Child who had no idea that friendship comprised other ingredients than the attraction of high spirits, clean vigour of limb and the sympathy born from a community of healthy tastes. In these, sure enough, was a sufficient basis for devoted comradeship, but beyond that lay the untraversed country to which they gave no passport.

Here was the cause of Steven's having sought him: he wanted a companion to go with him farther. Perhaps that region was chimerical; perhaps Maurice himself would fail, even as the Child had failed. . . . Vague and dim was all this current of thought, and bewildering was it to one who had never cultivated human emotions, to be suddenly bidden to so intimate a partnership. Steven, as the world of his peers saw him, was surrounded by friends and laughter and popularity, but it was not to join that circle that Maurice had been bidden, nor yet to take the place of the Child, but to go with Steven where the Child had never been capable of going.

Reactions came in this fantastic dreaming, and often during the day he told himself that, blinking as he was brought out of the darkness of his own loneliness, his eyes dazzled, and he imagined things that were not; and such a reaction as this was strong in him as he went into Hall for dinner that night. As he passed the entrance of the building where Steven's rooms lay he came out. Neither of them smiled as their eyes met; they might have been strangers to each other, but though the Court, suffused with the late sunlight, was full of men going in the direction of Hall, Maurice felt himself more alone with Steven than he had ever been, and that reaction of sensibleness dropped from him at Steven's words.

"I've not seen you all day," he said, "but that's all right. Look in after Hall, if you feel inclined. There are some other fellows coming in. That won't matter: you'll be there."

"Right," said Maurice.

"The Child's going down to-morrow," said Steven, as they went up the steps to Hall. "I shall stop up another day. See you after Hall, then."

The dinner of the Dons at the High Table lasted longer than that of the undergraduates; the Provost was dining, and afterwards they adjourned for coffee and wine into the combination room. There was a gay brotherly spirit abroad, for term was over, the College had done very well in the Triposes as well as on the river, and friendly, slightly academic jokes flew about with great cordiality. Stares was starting for a tour of English cathedrals next day: Peterborough, Norwich, Lincoln, York, Ripon, with the abbeys of Fountains and Rivaulx, were his itinerary, and George Herbert Redcliffe his companion. Redcliffe's father was a Canon of York, and two days were to be spent in the domestic circle.

"Stares won't be satisfied till we have a Tripos of Ecclesiastical Architecture," said the Provost humorously as he sipped his port. "He will have to set examination papers for himself and, if he passes them, be sole Examiner in the Tripos."

"Or will he and Redcliffe examine each other?" asked Maurice.

"That would never do," avowed the Provost. "They might plough each other, and there would be no examiners."

Stares laughed.

"Upon my word," he said, "I think Redcliffe might be right in ploughing me, but I don't believe the British College of Architects would be able to plough him. I went with him to Ely yesterday, and though he had never seen it before, he knew far more about it than the verger who took us round. He proved quite clearly that the aumbry in the east wall was a later addition."

The Provost was not quite sure what an aumbry was, and led the conversation off this dangerous topic.

"Is he going to take up architecture as a profession?" he asked.

"He wants to. I am going to put in my word for him with his father. That aumbry has always been considered——"

"Redcliffe's father used to be a fine oar," said the Provost, raising his voice a little. "He rowed for Cambridge in 1890."

"Ninety-one, I think," said Torrington, who had been coaching the King's boat and had rowed for Cambridge himself in the year that they swamped.

The Provost shook his head.

"I should be shy of contradicting a Blue, a *cordon bleu*, I might say——" he began.

Stares's metallic laugh broke in again.

"Ha! ha! Capital," he said. "*Cordon bleu!* The soup was excellent to-night, Torrington. No doubt you saw to it yourself."

"But I think it was in ninety that Redcliffe rowed," continued the Provost, "ninety, I think. The year of that long frost. One began to think that a skating race might take the place of a boat race."

Torrington, who had learned the list of crews in the Boat Race from the year of its inception, by a *memoria technica*, and could reel them off without a hitch, was perfectly content to be right, and it was not etiquette to contradict the Provost.

"King's rowed a fine course on the last day of the races," he said. "Were you down on the river?"

"Indeed I was," said the Provost. "You must have been proud of your pupils, Torrington."

"A very good crew. But it was Merriman and Gervase who won for us. They were the inspiration of the crew."

Stares put his head on one side in a judicial attitude.

"I rather question the possibility of any individual inspiration making a crew more efficient," he said. "No doubt Gervase is a fine oar, but I doubt whether stroke can really do anything beyond rowing with judgment and vigour."

"You wouldn't doubt it if you had the training of a crew on your hands," said Torrington, for Stares was not officially exempt from contradiction. "Stroke undoubtedly has a psychical influence on his crew."

"I should call his influence entirely muscular," said Stares.

"No: psychical. Especially when he has behind him a great engine like Merriman, who is absolutely *en rapport* with him. A sort of wireless passes between those two."

("Lord! How much they know and how little," thought Maurice.)

"Damon and Pythias: Harmodius and Aristogiton," crooned the Provost. "Damon plus Pythias is more than Damon plus Robinson, though physically Robinson equals Pythias. Is that your notion, Torrington?"

"I consider it certain. The Child—Merriman, I should say—won't be up next year, and Gervase, even if he rows as well as he did this week, will be lacking something."

"There I differ," said Stares. "If Gervase's propelling power this year was x, and next year again it is mathematically the same, it will be x still."

"No; it will be x minus some indeterminable factor."

"An interesting contention," said the Provost, yawning slightly. "You must concoct a little manual of psychical athletics, Torrington. 'The coefficient of friendship in propulsive aquatics.' Where are you spending your vacation? Zermatt, as usual?"

Torrington was going to Zermatt, and the Provost was going to Aix-les-Bains. He therefore drank another glass of port, since Aix would soon frustrate all gouty tendencies.

"And you, Crofts?" asked the Provost, addressing Maurice.

Crofts expected to spend most of the Long Vacation term here, and to go to Devonshire in September, where his uncle was rector of a remote parish beyond Bideford. He would be working at the series of Essays in which he would embody the bulk of his lectures this term on the Peloponnesian War. But all he said in answer to the question which elicited this news seemed to him guesswork and meaningless gabble. Such had been his intentions, but what they were now he really had no idea.

"We shall many of us be up here in August, then," said the Provost; "and you, Vyse?"

Vyse would be here too; he had been examining in the Classical Tripos and retailed most amusing howlers made by candidates. This was always a popular topic, and Dons otherwise usually silent had contributions to make. The Provost reserved his for the end.

"One I heard the other day amused me a good deal," he said. "Rather profane, I am afraid, but I seem to be the only clergyman present. A boy in a board school was asked what was the character of the Pharisees; his answer was, 'The Pharisees were very stingy. They once brought

Jesus Christ only a penny, and He said, "Whose subscription is this?" ' "

The laugh was loud and general, for so comical a perversion of the text was felt well to excuse the profanity. Then, the session having been unusually prolonged, the Provost rose.

"A most amusing and agreeable evening," he said. "I look forward to our reunion when I get back from Aix. Would you feel inclined to come across to the Lodge, Crofts, for a game of chess?"

Maurice excused himself with unstuttering perjuries, in accordance with which he went up to his rooms and sat regarding the backs of his books for the London Library, which he had glibly said must be returned next day, and so must be finally consulted to-night. In a few minutes his colleagues would have dispersed. . . . But what a typical hour it had been: with what gaiety and sprightliness they had talked on suitable topics! As if it was worth the expenditure of a single breath to determine in what year Redcliffe senior had rowed for the University, or learn what cathedrals Redcliffe junior and Stares were about to visit. Who cared? And yet what else were they to talk about, seeing that none of them really cared about anything?

And then the academic humour so heartily aroused by the "howlers" in examination papers, and the interesting question arising therefrom as to what the derivation of the word "howler" was in that connection! Torrington had amusingly said that he did not see what else you were to call it; all mistakes were not "howlers," it was only a particular sort of mistake to be thus designated, and he reminded them of how a professional cricketer was asked why a particular type of ball was called a "yorker," and had so justly remarked that he did not know what else you were to call it. Maurice had left Stares and him trying to define a "howler" and planning to look up the word in the Oxford Dictionary in order to establish its derivation. Only once had they got near a living topic, when they discussed psychical communication between the Child and Steven: even then they contrived to desiccate it. Maurice fancied he could have supplied a little juicy information on that head which his colleagues would have found highly disconcerting.

The sound of Stares's piano in the room next his had begun: Stares was playing, as usual, Bach's first prelude which he performed with ever increasing accuracy, and after that he would play the slow movement out of Beethoven's Fifth symphony, arranged for the piano, and then he and Redcliffe would study guidebooks in view of their approaching tour. These were innocent, even laudable pursuits, if any pursuit was innocent that was not undertaken with a certain feverish enthusiasm, for surely the excitement with which one did anything was the sole justification for doing it. Or was this new view of life which was beginning to dawn on him a false idea; was the main purpose of living to find out something of scholastic interest, thus adding to the general stock of knowledge, and, in moments of social relaxation, just to pass the hour in this innocuous gambolling, like elderly lambs in well nibbled pastures? Subjects concerning religion or morals or life were always taboo in this hour of relaxation: even a discussion about Soviet Russia last night was soon abandoned because it showed signs of awakening a lively interest. Laying down the law quietly, as you sipped your port, over matters that did not matter was much safer. Then Maurice heard that Beethoven had begun, and went downstairs.

Steven had a small but excited gathering in his rooms. Tommy and the Child were there, and Isaacs, the cox of the King's boat, whose nose, irrespective of his name, would have given a correct clue to his race, and Dickenson, one of the crew. Steven was poring open-mouthed over *The*

Green Hat; the wireless, with an extremely loud speaker, was playing jazz music, and Tommy was arguing with Isaacs about a doctrinal point in the revised prayer book.

Steven only just looked up as he entered.

"Come in, Maurice," he said, "and sit on Tommy. He's got the revised prayer book on the brain. Who cares?"

"I do," said Tommy, "because I'm going to be a parson. And in any case, little Isaacs hasn't got a right to say a word, because he's a Jew. I might as well lay down the law about circumcision. We'll have another sacrifice of Isaac if he goes on."

"As it happens, I'm a Christian," said Isaacs. "Scored off. Besides, who brought Christianity to this heathen isle?"

"Augustine," said Tommy.

"Not at all. I thought you'd say Augustine. It was Joseph of Arimathea, if you've ever heard of him. He was a Jew first, like me, and then became a Christian."

"How do you know that?" asked Tommy.

"Because before I became a Christian I studied your religion, which is more than you ever did. I daresay you've never heard of Glastonbury."

"Theology barred," said Steven. "All Doctors of Divinity to leave the Court."

"Being the only Catholic present," said Dickenson from the window-seat, "I can tell you that you'll all be damned because you're heretics. It doesn't matter what any of you say. All your opinions are blasphemy."

"Do you really think that?" asked Tommy.

"I don't think anything about it. I know it."

Steven gave a loud whistle.

"I say, the Green Hats are a hot lot," he said. "All you've got to do when you meet a girl you fancy is to give her a cocktail and proceed."

"Make the most of your time, Tommy," said the Child.

"You'll be a parson soon, and then you'll have to take off your green hat."

"Oh, lots of parsons keep it on, if you look in the police reports," said Isaacs. "We had one at home: living vacant now. It'll just do for Tommy, if he'll hurry up and get consecrated. Fine tradition."

"'Tisn't consecrated," said Tommy, "it's ordained. You'd better study your religion a little more."

"Golly," said Steven, deep in *The Green Hat.*

"Spit it out," said the Child.

"I couldn't. I should blush like a red, red rose."

Tommy leaned over him.

"Where is it?" he said. "Let's look."

Steven shut up the book.

"Not good for you, Tommy. The girl in blue wouldn't approve. I like smut as well as anybody if it's funny, but I like it because it's funny, not because it's smut."

"That's swank," said Tommy. "Don't be so beastly pure in heart, but give me the book."

Steven threw it across to the Child who sat on it: it was therefore inaccessible.

"And you and the Child will gloat over it when we've gone," said the baffled Tommy.

"Oh, it's early yet," said Steven. "Don't think of going."

Maurice, during this conversational pea shooting, had sat down in the window seat, where Dickenson was gently fumigating with cigarette smoke a large speckled spider in the window box.

"What's that, Dickey?" he asked. Dickenson was a natural history student.

"Damned interesting," he said. "Female spider just eaten her young man. I thought if I fumigated her she might be sick and pieces of spider come out."

Maurice attended closely to the disgusting experiment. He had taken no notice of Steven, or Steven of him, but he was really aware of no one else. And as Steven had said, though other fellows were coming into the rooms, they didn't matter. . . . Suddenly the spider doubled up, and dropped on to the grass outside the window.

"You brute!" said Maurice.

"Oh, it won't hurt her. A little fresh air. I should like to keep a spider farm: you'd learn a lot that way."

The Child wheeled round in his chair, and *The Green Hat* slid from under him.

"Have you and the colleagues been talking right up till now, Maurice?" he asked.

"Yes. Animated and agreeable evening. The Provost in fine form. Subjects of high import instead of this piffle. He and Torrington disagreed about the year Redcliffe's father rowed for Cambridge."

"By gum! I should like to have heard that," said the Child. "Pretty keen debate, I expect. Any of Torrington's stories?"

"Rather. One about the man who didn't know what you were to call a 'yorker' except a 'yorker.' "

"I wonder where he gets all those new yarns from," said Isaacs.

"Invents them, I expect. He had a beauty yesterday. A curate was having breakfast with his bishop, and his egg was a stinker. But he said that part of it was excellent."

"Highbrow stuff," said the Child. "And little Stares?"

"Going for a Cathedral jolly to-morrow: Peterborough, Norwich, Calcutta, Rome, New York."

"A great traveller. Mr. Stares will be staring at lots of things."

Tommy had gently appropriated *The Green Hat* and retired into a sequestered corner to learn about life. Isaacs, in view of an early train to-morrow morning, went off to pack, Dickie found another spider, and the Child wandered off to Steven's gyp cupboard in the hopes of a cake. Maurice still sat in the window seat, and Steven on the sofa was shaking an indolent siphon. It suddenly responded to this treatment, and a fountain rose from his glass, drenching his sleeve.

"I'll say it for you: damn," said Maurice, which was the first word he had spoken to him, and their eyes met.

The Child came back with a cake, and, as Tommy would not leave *The Green Hat*, Dickenson was torn from his spider, and they played a couple of rubbers. Maurice and Steven argued rather acidly, so thought the Child, over the rule about penalties for undercalling; they got on each other's nerves a bit, perhaps, and this view was confirmed by their subsequent politeness to each other. At the end of the second rubber Maurice got up.

"I must go," he said. "I haven't done any of the work I told the Provost I was going to do when he asked me to play chess. Besides, it's close on twelve."

He looked at Steven a moment with a question in his raised eyebrows. Steven just perceptibly shook his head.

"So he's not coming round," thought Maurice, quite certain that his signal was read and answered. . . .

"He got a bit stuffy with you, Steven," said the Child, when he had gone.

"I thought he did, too," said Steven. "Funny of him."

The books from the London Library had still to wait, for instead of going studiously to his rooms Maurice turned down towards the river, with some inward thirst for the empty night and the open air and the furtherance of that expansion of himself in this thawing of the ice of his life-long reserve. He felt absolutely ignorant of himself: he had really no idea what sort of person he would find himself to be when he had cracked and peeled off the shell of isolation, but it was quite needless to attempt to scrutinize this. The only point was that he should be unsheathed and receptive. He even knew more of Steven than himself, for when Steven had told him of that night with the Child on the river he had understood something of what he had experienced, enough at any rate to make Steven seek his friendship and comprehension. They had that in common, the sense of some region of the spirit, intimate, yet infinitely remote, which Steven hailed as native to him. There was the bench on which they had sat on the evening of the ball, and from that moment, so he saw now, all that had followed was inevitable; it was then they had discovered their kinship.

He sat there again now, and let his mind wander over the events of the evening with a sort of greedy deliberation. There had been that long session over the port with his colleagues, and he licked his lips at the utter unreality of their prattle. Was that cathedral tour of Stares's the keenest interest in his life? Did the Provost really care about the date of a particular boat race? Did Torrington most revealingly express himself by the recital of his stale little stories, or had they all worn masks and talked through cardboard lips? He certainly had done so himself, therefore it was fairer to credit them with a similar disguisement. Then had come that hour in Steven's rooms, when Tommy babbled of high mysteries and Steven of Green Hats and Dickenson of spiders. That was better than the talk in the combination room, because those boys had been eager about their topics, they had found enjoyment and vivid interest, and yet all that had been unreal to himself and, so he was sure, to Steven. They had both worn masks; just once or twice a gleam had come through the rigid eyeholes or a word unmuffled by the edges of the set mouth, but except for that gleam they had kept themselves dark and withdrawn.

He had looked out in a volume of Walt Whitman the lines which Steven had quoted as indicating what had come to him on that night in the canoe and among addresses to wild ganders and contraltos in organ-lofts and other surprising invocations on which he turned a cold academic eye, he found with a thrill of recognition the lines:

Press close bare-bosom'd night—press close magnetic nourishing night!
Night of south winds—night of the few large stars!
Still nodding night—mad naked summer night.

And now he said them under his breath, as if they had been a spell of incantation. It was somehow into that region that Steven had looked, and, despite his intimacy with the Child, had found that he was alone there; the other had had no perception of it. Their comradeship had parted there, for this stood outside any relation they held to each other: it reached out into a more primitive love, it was instinct with that knowledge which in Greek fable peopled the woodland with shy presences, with Pan and his fauns, with Dionysus and his mænads. You could not go there alone, so Maurice figured it; you must have someone with you to keep step and aid perception. And that region lay outside sex altogether: a man who went on such an exploration with a woman by his side, thinking that through her he would attain that primitive craving of the soul, would find that the satisfaction of physical passion would only cloud his eyes and lure him away from his goal, so that he turned aside and pressed forward no more. Comrades who understood, and who were bound together by a sexless love, alone could advance there. . . . And then suddenly he tried to visualize Steven's face, and he could not imagine it, and he tried to visualize that ivory mask of him, seen here in the moonlight, but again it evaded him. It was odd: he could vividly picture Tommy's face, and Stares's face, and the face of the Provost, and all the ugly old familiar faces, but not Steven's.

The moon had risen over the trees, a clock clanged somewhere, and passing his hand over his sleeve he found it was soaked in dew. He sprang up, wondering if he had been asleep, and went across the shimmering grass to Fellows' Buildings. He saw that Steven's rooms were dark, but from his own a light shone out through the uncurtained windows, and his heart leaped at the thought that perhaps Steven had changed his mind and was waiting for him there. But his rooms were empty; he must have left on the light when he went out, after Hall. And what was Steven's face like?

The Child left Cambridge the next afternoon. All day again Maurice had not seen Steven, nor had he attempted to. He worked at his essays during the morning with close attention; they filled the foreground of his mind, and after lunch he played croquet with the Provost in the Fellows' Gardens, which was even more richly rewarding than usual. The Provost had cheated, as he always did sooner or later, moving his ball gently and surreptitiously into a more desirable position while Maurice seemed to be engaged on his stroke, and he, bubbling with inward laughter, found it far more subtly amusing to observe that and say nothing about it, than to request him to replace his ball where it had been. "That's part of my reserve," he thought to himself, and cannoning wildly off a wire, and hitting a ball he had not aimed at, upset the Provost's plan altogether.

"Rather a fluke?" questioned the Provost in his crooning voice.

"No, I played for that," said Maurice. . . . So there they were, a cheat and a liar, each known to the other.

It may have been in consequence of this annoying falsehood that the Provost did not ask him to have tea at the Lodge afterwards, and Maurice reached the front Court just in time to see the Child's luggage being wheeled across from his room by the porter, and him and Steven following: Steven was evidently going with him to the station. He would be back by five or thereabouts, and Maurice went up to his rooms and sat in the window seat to watch for his return. His tea had been laid out for him; the kettle was standing on the electric heater ready to be boiled, but he thought he would wait for Steven. Presently he heard the door opposite his room open, and Stares entered, followed by Redcliffe.

"Ha, Crofts," he said. "As the hymn tells us:

"Dark and cheerless is the morn,
Unaccompanied by tea,

—one of Torrington's best, and if you substitute 'afternoon' for 'morn,' you will realize my position. Redcliffe and I are off in half an hour, motoring to Peterborough, and my bed maker has omitted to put out my tea, having eaten, I suppose, the rest of my cake. We throw ourselves without reservation on your mercy."

Maurice got up with a smile of recognition at one of Torrington's best.

"Yes, of course, by all means," he said. "The kettle will be boiling in a minute. Come in, Redcliffe." He switched on the current and brought a couple more cups. There was Steven just coming in at the gate, and presently there was his step on the stairs, light and quick. Maurice felt his advent, as if it was the dawn. "The hounds of spring are on winter's traces," he thought to himself.

"Peterborough to-night," Stares was saying, "and we spend the most of the morning there. Then an early lunch in the motor by the wayside, and we shall get a good three hours at Norwich before dark. Then I think we had better flit again after dinner, and sleep at King's Lynn. . . . Come in! . . . I beg your pardon, Crofts, I forgot I was not in my own room."

Steven entered.

"Oh, sorry," he said, "I didn't know you had anyone——"

"Come in, Gervase," said Maurice. "You have come on the tick of tea. Mr. Stares and Redcliffe are off to Peterborough."

"You're not going down to-day, Gervase?" asked Stares.

"No, sir, not till to-morrow. I've just been seeing Merriman off, Mr. Crofts."

"Ah, yes, going down for good, isn't he?" said Stares. "You'll miss him. Oddly enough we were talking about him and you in combination room last night and Mr. Torrington propounded some idea, rather fanciful in my opinion, about your combined value in the propulsion of a boat."

"We both rowed as hard as we could," observed Steven.

"Just what I said. If Merriman is x and Gervase is y, the combined propulsive impulse of you both is $x + y$, and nothing more whatever."

"Oh, quite," said Steven, wondering what on earth he was talking about.

The kettle on that admirable heater was sizzling and lifting its lid, and Maurice busied himself with hospitable duties. The motorists would not reach Peterborough till late, and ate cake assiduously. It was China tea, and Steven, when pressed, said it was like faintly scented hay.

"When next Gervase honours me with his company, I must see that there is some Indian tea," said Maurice.

This was great fun, and then there was a good deal said about Norman architecture in the Eastern Counties and Roman brickwork. Remains had lately been found at York which were likely to throw fresh light on the Roman occupation of Britain, and on the presence there of the 10th legion, otherwise Valeria Victrix, but of these Stares would be able to speak with greater certainty when he had examined them. But it was half-past five now, and time to take the road, and the two travellers went clattering downstairs.

"So that's that," said Maurice.

"Just about. . . . And Crofts plus Gervase is *x* plus *y*. Is that right?"

"Perfectly. And I must remember about the Indian tea."

"I hope you will," said Steven. "By the way, it was rather funny last night after you had gone. The Child thought you were stuffy with me about the rule on underbidding."

"So I was. . . . Steven, when you shook your head you meant, didn't you, that you weren't coming round here after they had gone?"

"Yes, of course. That's what you asked me. You didn't wait up for me?"

"No; I strolled down to the river," said Maurice, "and sat on our bench. And I must have forgotten to turn out my light here, for it was burning when I got back. When I saw it I thought perhaps you had come after all."

"No. What time was that?"

Maurice considered.

"I've no idea," he said. "I don't know how long I sat there, but my coat was wet with dew when I'd finished."

"Finished? Finished what?" asked Steven.

"Finished thinking."

"Penny for your thoughts," said Steven.

"Don't be so spendthrift. You'll know in time."

There were crumbs on the sofa where Stares had sat devouring cake. Maurice whisked them off.

"A filthy feeder," he observed. "And . . . the Child's gone."

Steven sat down by him.

"Yes. He really went a couple of days ago," he said.

"Do you remember telling me you had never made a friend in your life?"

"Yes."

"I've been thinking that I'm in the same boat."

"But the Child?" said Maurice.

"It was a schoolboy affair, really. I see that now. Rowing and ragging and being full of beans. That's all there was to it. When it came to one's self, what one is, he didn't understand. But you do, or some of it. You know there's something there."

"I do, and I want to come with you and find out what it is," said Maurice.

"That's just what I want. The Child stuck: we couldn't go any farther together. In fact, we had never started. He didn't understand a single atom about it all. And then I suddenly saw that you did."

"I'm sorry for the Child," said Maurice.

"That's nice of you, but there's no reason to be sorry for him. He—I suppose this sounds fearfully conceited—he got as much of me as he could take."

"But you got all of him," said Maurice.

"I know. But in things that mattered there wasn't any. If there had been I shouldn't be here now," said Steven.

There was a moment's silence: then he spoke again.

"There's just one thing to be said before the Child ceases to concern us any more. It was neither his fault nor mine that we came to that blank wall. I've wished sometimes, ever since we met, that I could be as unimaginative as—as unpenetrating as he, for then I should have been perfectly content with his idea of friendship. And I've wished that I could be like Tommy, who can find a Wonderland in any pretty girl. But it's no use: what you and I are after is something outside all that kind of thing. . . ."

Steven turned towards him with his eyes aglow and his mouth tremulous with a smile.

"Come on, Maurice," he said. "We've got to go together."

Some flame soared and blazed and died down again and, still a little dazzled, they were sitting quietly there.

"We won't go in to Hall to-night," said Maurice. "You'll dine with me here. And you're not going down to-morrow, are you?"

"Good Lord, no," said Steven.

CHAPTER IV

THE two had known little or nothing hitherto about the circumstances and home life of each other, for such information does not emerge among young men till friendship draws it automatically out. Everyone, of course, was aware that Tommy's father was a bishop, since Tommy so often alluded to that fact with pride or pathos, but ordinarily the movement of the home circle revolved in an orbit far remote.

"Oh, I've lived with my uncle for the last ten years," said Maurice. "My mother I don't remember at all, and my father died when I was fifteen. Solicitor, rather well off, with side whiskers. I hated him: he was always down on me for offences and omissions. Hence my repressed nature. When I'm not travelling in vacations I always go to Uncle Henry now. Rather a dear: parish priest in North Devon. Family prayers. That's about all."

"Huh! I'm a proud and lofty aristocrat," said Steven, "because my uncle's a peer. He is indeed—though you might not think it to look at me. He made an enormous fortune in shipping, during the war, out of the government, and so they rewarded him for his magnificent patriotism. Otherwise he's a crashing bore. I also belong to the landed gentry, as I've a place of my own . . . Are you attending?"

Maurice rolled over on the grass; they had rowed up to Byron's pool this afternoon, and bathed, and now were lying on the bank, not yet dressed. Maurice had got as far as shirt and socks, Steven was content for the present in this caressing sunshine with a girded bath towel covering him from loins to knees.

"No, I'm not attending much," said Maurice, "I'm stewing in content."

"Well, listen as you stew. I listened to your sordid history, so you must listen to mine, which is far more romantic."

"Not much romance in what you have told me yet," said Maurice. "I don't consider a profiteer peer for an uncle romantic at all."

"The romance is coming. Lord Gervase, that's my uncle——"

"I guessed that," said Maurice.

"Lord Gervase was my father's younger brother, and my father is dead. So I'm the head of the family. Family place, I assure you."

"Well, my uncle's got a glebe," said Maurice. "I daresay it's as big as your estate. And several cows."

"My estate's too steep for a cow," said Steven. "It would have to have climbing-irons. A Cornish valley running down to the sea. Are you coming there?"

"Tell me about it first. I may not like it. Quantities of pleasant neighbours, I hope. I can't be expected to bury myself in a Cornish valley unless——"

"I wish you'd let me get on to the romance," said Steven. "The place, Trenair, has been in the family four hundred years, and there's always been a curse on it. It's supposed that it's over now because of me."

"I would back you against any curse," said Maurice. "Besides, you don't really believe that there can be such a thing, do you? I don't care a curse for a curse."

"I do believe in it; it's impossible not to. You might if you weren't a plebeian whose house was never cursed by anything worse than a busted waterpipe."

Maurice laughed.

"That's a nasty one," he said. "And all because my uncle has some cows and you haven't."

"Yes; jealousy," said Steven. "I want to get on with the curse."

"Fire away."

"It's very horrible: you must try to have some imagination and think what a frightful thing it was. Never until this fellow here did it, has the eldest son succeeded, not succeeded properly, that's to say."

"What's happened to them all?" asked Maurice. "Accidents?"

"Much worse. For generations back the eldest son has been hardly human. Monsters: hooved and hairy, or with goats' feet. Some of them lived a long time. My father was not the eldest son, and he never really succeeded till he was fifty, though his father had died twenty years before, because in a wing of the house was living his elder brother. He was almost a man, though he had no mind to speak of. And he had little horns, like a kid. I saw him once."

Maurice raised himself on his elbow. Steven's extremely matter-of-fact tone gave him a sudden thrill of horror.

"Good Lord! Are you pulling my leg?" he asked.

"I swear I'm not."

"Go on, then. Tell me about him," said Maurice.

"I was six or seven at the time, and one day I was out walking with my nurse. There's a wood of poplars and hazels just below the house, running down to the village and the harbour, and we were coming up through it. I lagged behind, and she got impatient with me and said she would go on and leave me, thinking I should be frightened at being left alone, and would hurry up. But really I was delighted, for the wood that morning seemed an enchanted place. It was spring, and the ground was a carpet of primroses and anemones, with the bluebells just beginning, and I remember suddenly realizing that I was I, and that here were trees and flowers, and that they were part of me. And then I heard shouting from the house above me, and somebody screamed, and then there came towards me through the wood the sound of someone running and leaping. The steps came nearer, and then a—a man burst through the thicket of hazel close in front of me. He had a pair of breeches on, shorts, and some sort of wreath on his head, but his chest was naked and covered with thick hair. His face was bearded with a short golden beard, same colour as my hair, and he had kind merry eyes, and on his forehead, just coming through his hair, two horns, and I don't suppose he was more than four feet tall. He smiled at me, and made some sort of babbling noise, but I couldn't understand him, and then there came the crash of people running through the wood: the coachman, the gardener, the butler, and my father. They caught him, and took him struggling away, and he tried to bite them and butt them."

"Go on," said Maurice breathlessly.

"I was furious with them, because I knew he was kind and jolly, and why shouldn't he have horns if he liked? And then my nurse came running back with my mother, and they all tried to persuade me that I had seen nothing. I never saw him again, and it must have been very soon after that that he died, for I remember a funeral starting from the house, though I wasn't allowed to go to it."

"But was he mad?" asked Maurice. "Why wasn't he in a home or an asylum?"

"There was no real reason why he should be: besides, they—those eldest sons—have always been kept in the house. Usually his keeper took him out at night for air and exercise, but that day he had escaped. He wasn't quite a man, of course, but a jolly little beggar. It wasn't till later that I was told about the curse: my father told me not long before he died. The curse was clearly over, you see, for I was sixteen then, and rowing for Eton, and there was no doubt that I was all right. I'm human, aren't I?"

Steven sat up as he spoke, slewing round a little towards Maurice, smooth-chested and smooth-chinned, with a torso like that of the young Hermes, and a face, if unhuman at all, unhuman from the sheer beauty of it.

"I had got to tell you, Maurice," he said. "A pretty foul family history, isn't it?—and as true as gospel. No record of why the curse existed, but it certainly did. So now you can say you'll have nothing more to do with me if you like. I shall understand."

Maurice lay back again.

"Do you know that you're talking gibberish?" he asked.

"About the family history?"

"No. It's ghastly rather, but not gibberish," said Maurice, "if you tell me it is true. The gibberish is the idea of my having nothing more to do with you."

"That's all right, then. I suppose I ought to have known," said Steven. "I beg pardon."

"Certainly you ought. Pardon? Granted. Isn't that correct?"

"Yes, in the highest circles, I believe."

Steven rolled over onto his stomach and plucked one of the tall grasses, pulling the stem out of its sheath and sucking the juicy end of it. The whole subject apparently was dismissed. Maurice had noticed before how abrupt and complete were these transitions.

"How good that tastes," said Steven. "Raw broth of the meadow in my mouth, and the smell of running water. I should like to be Joshua—why aren't I Joshua?—and make the sun stand still exactly where it is, warm on my shoulders. And then when we'd got tired of the sun, Joshua would just nod to the moon, and it would be night with the moon standing still."

"Press close bare-bosom'd night—press close magnetic nourishing night!"

quoted Maurice.

Steven drew in his breath with a long sipping intake of air till the muscles stood out on his expanded ribs.

"That tastes good, too," he said. "That man knew something about night, the solemnity and the wild glee of it. Think of spring nights, Maurice, when the sap hums in the trees; and summer nights—there'll be a beauty to-night—when everything is purring. But the spring nights are the best; I go crazy with joy. You'll have to come down to Trenair again then, when I come of age, and five tenants present me with a small electro-plate spoon. We'll walk all night in the poplar wood, and drink it in, letting outselves secretly out of the house. Oh, yes, at dinner we'll be rather icy to each other, same as we were over bridge the other night, so that my mother thinks we've had what they call a tiff. A tiff—what a word!"

"I haven't heard about your mother yet," said Maurice.

"No more you have; I've only been showing you the family skeleton. Best to introduce the skeleton first. My mother's a perfect dear, but weird. She's Cornish, of course: all my forebears have married Cornish women since the year one. She and I live there together: there's no one else. Distinguished family history, too, for her great-grandmother was burned as a witch in the market-place at Penzance. It was bad luck on her, for she only used her powers to heal and help; it was always white magic, though magic sure enough. She cured people when doctors could do nothing for them, and had the same healing touch for animals. But as she never would go to church and said that she got her power from Nature, not from God, they called it black magic and burned her. She must have been a fairy much more than a witch. And my mother's got strange powers, too, jolly ones, but for some reason she's frightened of them. When she was younger she used to get the great black-backed gulls, which are the shyest and savagest of all the sea birds and can crack a sheep's skull with their horny beaks, to come to her when she told them."

"Told them?" asked Maurice. "Called to them, do you mean?"

"No: I mean told them. But, as I say, she's frightened of her power and won't use it, though sometimes, when she walks in the woods, she can't help telling the squirrels to come to her, because she's fond of them. Of course, that's easy."

Steven's voice died away, and Maurice, looking at him, saw that he was lying now with his cheek laid on his arm and his eyes half closed, with a stem of feathery grass still in his mouth.

"Oh, wake up, Steven," he said. "You're talking in your sleep."

Steven raised his heavy eyelids and met his look with a glance gay and dreamy and remote. He spat the grass stem from his mouth.

"No, I'm not; I'm quite awake," he said. "It's as easy to me as it is to her. In fact, I was just setting about showing it you, as a surprise. But now I'll demonstrate instead, telling you that I'm doing it, for I saw a squirrel up in that tree just now. Come quite close to me; lean against my legs, and then he'll think you're part of me and won't be frightened of you. And keep quite still: he'll come skipping through the grass."

Steven raised himself and looked up into the tree.

"Yes, there he is," he said, "and he knows already that I want him. Lean back against me, Maurice, and learn a little natural history."

Maurice, still half wondering whether Steven was serious, did as he was told, and, leaning sideways on his legs, watched his face. His mouth smiled, his eyes half closed, as he lay back again, looked unfocussedly in front of him, and suddenly Maurice saw him just as he had seen him that night in the moonlight, a mask of ivory and gold. But now he saw that it was no mask made by the blanching of the moon, but that it was as if the spirit of the real Steven was shining through his features from within: the wild thing was stealing out of its thickets. . . . The impression, vivid and startling, lasted but a single moment and faded again.

Without moving his head, Maurice looked sideways towards the tree, and observed, still rather detachedly, rather sceptically, that the squirrel, which he had not seen before, was sitting on the lowest bough, perked-up and alert. Then it came scrambling down the trunk, which stood in the tall grass, and he lost sight of it. Presently the grass began to stir and rustle, and he got glimpses of the animal's chestnut back as it came leaping towards them. When it came close to them it paused for a moment, sitting up with plumed tail erect, and then with a little chattering sound it ran along Steven's bare and outstretched arm and nestled up to his chin with a gabble of squeaks and chatterings. There it remained pressed close for perhaps a minute, and then Steven's face, all alight with smiles, began to twitch.

"Furry little brother," he said, "you're tickling me something awful. That's all. Thank you for coming, and get home."

The squirrel hopped out of his nest and leaped away among the grasses. Steven sat up, scratching his chin.

"So that's that," he said. "I told you it was easy."

Maurice levered himself up, grasping Steven's shin for a rest. His heart was thumping: some mysterious excitement throbbed in him.

"I never saw anything so perfectly beautiful," he said. "I love you for showing me that, and I adore the power that did it, and that's you. I could cry, do you know, for the sheer beauty of it. . . . And to think that it was you who, only a few days ago, asked me to give you a chance of being friends with me! A fellow who can do that is holy. But I won't go on."

He sprang to his feet.

"I'm dotty," he said, "that's all about it. Let me be a

Don again. It wasn't a trick, was it? Promise me that. You didn't hypnotize me, or anything of that sort, to make me think I'd seen it?"

"Good Lord, no," said Steven. "Hypnotism's nasty, mucky work. You like it, then?"

"I've told you that I adored it. What's happening to me? Am I sloughing an old skin off like a snake, and is a cataract dropping from my eyes, so that they see a new heaven and a new earth? And how did you do it? Should I understand if you told me?"

Steven looked at him with his eyebrows knitted together, as if puzzling something out, not in answer to the question, but for himself.

"I couldn't tell you," he said, "simply because my brain doesn't understand it, and so my tongue couldn't say it. But something inside me understands, and it's so frightfully simple. I've got to *be* a squirrel: no, that's not quite it. But I know you'll learn; you've got the germ of understanding. Every now and then, if you come on with me, I shall say something that will be a clue—no, not quite that. I shall *be* something that will be a clue. Damn words; words are awkward and useless. Damn the sun, too; it's going behind the trees. Little Isaacs might stop it for us—oh, no, he's become a Christian."

"And can your mother——" began Maurice.

"Rather. I daresay I inherit it from her. And she's the only woman I ever heard of who could get anywhere near it. In the middle they'd begin powdering their noses and wondering if they looked fetching."

"Concentration is it?" asked Maurice.

Steven laughed.

"Oh, dear, oh, dear!" he said. "It's exactly the opposite. You've got to relax, to spread yourself out and bask. . . . Don't let's talk about it: you can't get at it except by feeling it."

Without pause Steven made one of those abrupt transitions, sudden as a changed mood of a child or an animal.

"By the way," he said, "don't be surprised to see some of the folk down at Trenair, one boy particularly, looking very like me. They've every right to, for certain of my wicked old family have been regular Green Hats, prize fornicators. Shocking! My grandfather had three families, two in the village and one at home, and the type, such as it is, has persisted. Oh, Mr. Crofts, I forgot you were a Don. I should never have said that to little Stares. Don't send me down."

Steven pulled on his shirt and threw the rest of his clothes into their boat.

"We must be going, Maurice," he said, "and the intrepid squirrel tamer is instantly going to become the famous, may I say, stroke of the King's boat. Quick-change artist, though I lay no stress on artist. No, please don't row: I really ask you not to, for if you do we shall never get anywhere except into the bank. Sit at that broad end of the boat, which is generally called the stern, and don't attempt to steer. By steering, I mean pulling those two bits of rope. Look at that bank of forget-me-not! What a terrible little flower; it's the one flower I really detest. It's like some maudlin little child in a book, who trusts everybody, and has blue eyes, and asks the burglar if he's the kind doctor who's come to see Mammy. What a name, too! Reeks of sentiment. Adam must have had a sentimental attack when he named the flowers. Love-in-a-mist; heart's-ease; love-lies-ableeding: all dreadful names. But there are a few good ones: stinking archangel isn't bad."

The river was low and full of shoals and snags, but Steven, left to himself, managed the boat with that ease and unconsciousness that only come from long dealings with the water and its ways. He glanced casually behind him, flicked a wrist or held it taut for a moment, and snags and shoals glided by the ungrating keel. Sometimes he shipped an oar and stood up, carelessly punting with the other, and fending off with it an encroaching riverside bush, without even seeming to attend to what he was doing, but pouring forth a stream of absurd babble.

"A man preached at Eton once," he said, "and recommended us to row the race of life with our eyes fixed steadily on the goal. Heads screwed on the wrong way, I suppose—a pretty picture. And Ouida wrote an account of the May races and told us that everyone rowed fast in Third Trinity boat that afternoon, but nobody rowed so fast as stroke. There again, a pretty picture: whack, whack, all the oars hitting each other. They must have gone the devil of a pace. Lucky we didn't have to meet a Ouida crew. I shall write a story about motor cars, and describe the carburettor skidding as it took a corner, and Maurice at the wheel calmly controlling the revolving sparking-plugs. . . .

"How can I amuse you? I'm afraid you're feeling dull. Shall I ask a nice fresh-run salmon to leap into the boat and lay its head on my shoulder? Quite easy. Shoals of salmon come flapping onto the beach at Trenair when my mother and I are building sand castles, and we grill some and boil others, just to teach them not to be so affectionate. Weasels too: they're supposed to be shy things, but I've found as many as half a dozen sitting on my pillow waiting for me to come to bed. Then I skin them and make them into tippets for my illegitimate cousins. Oh, we don't consider ourselves at all out of the world at Trenair: there's always something going on of that sort. We have penny readings for the rocks and concerts for the coneys."

"Oh, for goodness' sake, dry up," said Maurice.

"I'm not sure if I can. Oh, look, we're at the bathing sheds already. Do you see that scorched place on the grass? That was where the Child and I made burnt offerings at sunrise. 'Gods of wet places and of night,' said I, for Brother Steven had been asked to offer a prayer, or if he hadn't he volunteered, and he was fair inspired, so everyone said. Shall we land, Maurice?—and I'll take you over the hallowed spot. There's the altar: you can see it clearly, and I'm told it's quite a little Stonehenge already. Americans come here in parties. And it was here we bathed, and so they bring bottles to fill from the sacred stream, as they do from the Jordan, and they baptize the infant Yankees with it in the gilded saloons of New York. If you're very rich in New York you always baptize your children in the drawing room, which they call the saloon. Women are churched there, too, and they call it going to the drawing room——"

This flood of deplorable nonsense ceased as suddenly as it had begun, and Steven became quite grave.

"Oh, and I've never asked you if you believe in God," he said. "Don't be shocked, though the ordinary Englishman thinks it rather improper to talk about God. A shade coarse: not quite nice. Call him the First Cause, if you think it would be more genteel."

"Naturally I believe in something that never began," said Maurice. "You can't help granting that."

"You do it rather grudgingly," said Steven. "Rather as if you thought that you ought to have been the First Cause. Surely it's enough to be an effect of the First Cause. That brings you into touch."

"But there are such a lot of horrible effects," said Maurice. "Did the First Cause make mosquitoes and cancer and death?"

"Fancy coupling those together! I think death is one of the utterly lovely things."

"Lovely? It's terrible and wicked," said Maurice. "Why should keen, clear minds be blown out like candles in the wind?"

"Blown out?" said Steven. "Not in the least. Set free."

"And why should beautiful bodies decay and rot away?" demanded Maurice.

"Oh, don't talk about two things at once. You asked

why keen, clear minds should be extinguished. You can't really believe that such a thing happens to them at death. That would be shocking, but luckily it's inconceivable. Don't you feel, don't you know that at present your mind's tethered, like a goat browsing in a circle? Don't you want some kind man to untie it and let it browse where it wills? That's what death is to me."

"Don't tell me you want to die," said Maurice.

"I don't tell you anything of the sort. I adore my circle of grazing ground, but when the kind man comes along, how I shall skip, and butt him if he fumbles on the rope. As for the body decaying and rotting away, that's only a step towards its becoming something else. It's kneaded into new form. . . ."

Steven took two vigorous pulls on his sculls and let the boat work out that impulse.

"I want to become so many other things with my body," he said, "that I can't make up my mind where to be buried. I think it will have to be in the wood of poplars at Trenair, as it's the place in the world I love best, and I shall like to leave it something. Money, if I ever have any, is no good to poplars: all you can do for them is to give them some broth. Then the roots of the trees will fasten on me and suck up my liver and lights, and say, 'Thank God for that little snack,' and all their leaves will flutter with satisfaction. Other bits of me will become bluebells and primroses; I shall be a most popular restaurant. Or is it a pity we aren't cannibals, because then, if I died a nice clean violent death, you could eat some of me? My mother would send you a nice jar of potted Steven, and some of me would become you. I should like to be diffused too: I would leave a leg to the High Table at King's, and little Stares would have some, and I should nourish Torrington's brain, and he would tell hundreds more stories on the strength of me."

"Don't be so ghoulish," said Maurice.

"Ghoulish? It's anti-ghoulish. Also it's the only unsentimental way of looking at death, as well as the only true one. There can be no doubt that our bodies nourish other forms of life, and what more can you ask? It's the only possible way of continuing physically to live. Would you sooner be stuffed and put in a glass case in the hall? But your idea that the mind is destroyed by death is what really shocks me. It's inconceivable, too. If you blow out my brains you don't destroy my mind, you only break the organ through which it works. You might as well say that if you smash up my wireless you destroy the power that makes it function."

"Yes, but if I brain you I stop your individuality," said Maurice.

"Of course, if you know that for certain, there's no more to be said. But I should like to know who told you. When are you coming to Trenair? I believe it would help you tremendously: it's a sort of aperient to the mind, as you'll see. You've got the right sort of imagination, but you won't let yourself go. You can't be yourself till you cease to be yourself. There's a truly Christian sentiment for you! And you've always held yourself in and clung on tight to yourself even when you reach out after something else. You can't really learn anything about yourself and know what you *are,* till you take a header into the dark. . . . Good Lord! You're a Don, and I'm an undergraduate, and I keep forgetting that and lecturing you. We've got to teach each other: we've got to go forward together."

"I'll go to hell with you, Steven," said Maurice.

Steven laughed.

"I hope we shall neither of us do anything of the sort," he said.

"Where, then?"

"If we knew that, it would not be worth while going there. But we know the direction. It lies through woodlands, among the powers that hide there. We've got to see them and hear them. They're antique and lovely and always young. . . . Shall I write a book, Maurice, called 'Confessions of a Pagan Who Believed in God' and you correct the spelling and the grammar? And you don't mind the family curse: that's a good thing. About the squirrel trick: you mustn't think of it as a trick. You can't learn to do it by practice any more than you can learn to sneeze. But if you've got a cold in the head you can't help sneezing, and if you've got a certain touch with life you can't help doing the squirrel stunt. It just happens, if you want it to. Forget all about it for the present."

Steven was due at Henley the next week, when the King's boat was rowing in the Ladies' Plate, and after that he was to spend a few weeks in London with the aristocratic uncle. Lord Gervase was childless, and though he could scarcely believe that there could ever come a day to so rich a man when his house in Carlton Terrace and his mansion and park in Sussex would know him no more, it was only businesslike to provide for that incredible contingency and make arrangements for their ultimate disposal. Steven was his only near relation, and seemed the obvious person to become his heir, but at present his uncle knew little of him, though, since his father's death, he had made himself responsible for his school and university expenses, as the revenues of the Trenair estate barely sufficed for the upkeep of the house. But the time had come when he thought he had better get to know something personally of a nephew whose future, though remote, would probably be so fortunate.

As yet he regarded Steven with that faint instinctive dislike which many wealthy men have for their heir, especially when they have made their money themselves and the heir is not of their body: he was, in fact, prepared to disapprove of Steven. It seemed grossly unfair that, whereas he had worked hard for his wealth, a quite undeserving young fellow should come into the harvest of so much industry. His wife, though she had lamentably failed in her duty of giving him a son, would be amply provided for, for he scorned any such posthumous retribution, but on the whole, blood was thicker than water, and if Steven showed a proper appreciation of what appeared to Lord Gervase an almost quixotic generosity on his own part, he would some day be an extremely wealthy man. But that day, please God, was still invisible in the mists of the most distant future, for he himself was still only just fifty, and you could hardly look in the obituary columns nowadays without finding the death of some centenarian still in full possession of his faculties, and that made cheerful reading. For the rest, Lord Gervase hardly ever enjoyed himself, apart from his keen appreciation of his own importance, but that, after all, made life extremely well worth living.

The thought of Steven's arrival, however, which wore for his uncle the aspect of a rather distasteful duty, was to Aunt Florence the cause of many fluttering anticipations. She was a woman of remarkable fatuity of mind, but the lightness of her head was ballasted by a very solid warmth of heart, though of a quality revolting in its sentimentality. She lavished the affectionate yearnings of a middle-aged and childless woman on young folk and on animals; of the two, she got on better with the latter, because they seemed to understand her more, and, as long as she stuffed them with tit-bits, exhibited no divergence of taste from hers, whereas young folk occasionally regarded her effusiveness with a cold blank surprise which was disconcerting.

There was something foreign about them, their ways and their language: they did not quite conform to her private ideals of boys and girls, which had remained precisely the same since she was a girl herself. According to that ingenuous creed, all boys should be slightly roguish and hot blooded; all girls should be pure as lilies, but their purity should by some incomprehensible alchemy be transmuted into a passionate longing for the legitimate and therefore chaste embraces of one roguish boy. These embraces resulted, after marriage, in a large family, who all grew up rogues and lilies and did it all over again. That life so often ran counter to her ideals never made the least difference to Florence Gervase: she continued to believe that it followed her lines, and apparent exceptions, however numerous, only proved her rule.

To her, the coming of Steven was an event of the highest emotional importance. She had been down to Eton two years ago on the Fourth of June, when he was Captain of the Boats, she had visited him once or twice at Cambridge, and her own barrenness had stung her shrewdly at the sight of this incarnation of Gervase splendour. She knew, though under the seal of secrecy, the strange story of the curse, and in place of the traditional monster here was this miracle of manly beauty, while she, married securely into that line, healthy herself and with a great bull of a husband, so unlike, both of them, to that elfish Cornish woman and that dreamy moth of a man who had produced this joyful boy, was childless. But the sting of her barrenness, sharp though it was, had made in her no ache of jealousy, and with an unconquerable kindliness she had seen herself mothering Steven when now he was coming to them, and renewing her youth by virtue of his.

Tenderness was still alive in her to the point almost of soreness, but even if it was raw it was also luxuriously sensitive, and often at Easthays, with its park and its ornamental waters and its emptiness, she would steal down at milking time to the dairy to see the cows fragrantly yielding the juice of their motherhood. Completely out of touch as she was with the world round her, she clung secretly and rapturously to such elementary and cosmic processes, the fruitful ways of Nature and of nutriment.

Or when calving was on, and the nuzzling, slobbering, weak-kneed young were at the udder, she would waft silent, silly congratulations to the mild-eyed mothers: they were so infinitely tender and contented and had no money and no title and no longing for anything except what they had got.

And now the adorable Steven (was he duly roguish? she wondered) was coming to them for these three weeks in July before Robert put on his yachting cap and they went to the Solent for the Cowes week, because that was the proper thing to do, and Robert always liked doing the proper thing. Cowes was succeeded by Aix, and then there were parties for shooting at Easthays—she always had a difficulty in remembering whether partridges "came before" pheasants, but they were both called "birds"—and by that time perhaps Steven would already be taking the place of the child she had never had.

Would some such belated miracle befall her? In the few contacts she had made with him he had always been cordial and friendly, and the opportunity of making some real relationship with him was to be cultivated with tactful eagerness. She did not mean to embarrass him with attentions and appeals: she was merely going to do all she could to make his sojourn highly agreeable, and perhaps—romantic thought—he would take to her, and seek her with sympathy and affection. She would give quantities of little lunches and dinners, where he would meet agreeable young people. She would give a ball, perhaps, and soon, no doubt, he would be quite launched and asked here, there, and everywhere. But perhaps in the midst of all the gaiety and youth which was soon to envelop him, he would look now and then to the corner where the effaced and elderly fairy godmother sat, and tell her, because he felt she was a friend, something about himself.

She would specialize for him, too, and if she saw the bright signals beginning to wink between him and any one particular girl, she would do her part in subtle and imperceptible contrivances for their meeting. . . . These were golden visions, and the most golden of all, dazzling her, was this idea that it might be she who would be the procuress of his marriage. Her successes in this covetable line had not at present been very marked: it had happened before now that, when she thought she saw signs of mutual attraction between a boy and a girl, they had leaped apart with intuitive repulsion. But she was never discouraged: rogues and lilies were designed for each other in the main, though not in this particular instance. Something very special must be found for Steven.

She was alone when he arrived, with a tea table copiously furnished in front of her, for she made a point of being at home at this hour in case friends dropped in. Sometimes they did, but more often the tea kettle bubbled in vain, and it was so to-day. In he came, radiant, to her eyes, as Apollo, and rather untidily dressed in oldish gray flannels.

"How are you, Aunt Florence?" he said. "I couldn't tell for certain what time I should get here, or I should have let you know."

"That's all right, my dear, as long as you've got here. Tired with your journey?"

Steven laughed.

"Worn out," he said. "Forty minutes in the train." His eye fell on the cohort of teacups. "But have you got a party? I must go and make myself a little less of a scarecrow."

"No: have your cup of tea," said she. "I daresay no one will be coming, but I like to be ready in case a few friends drop in. Or would you rather have something else? Would you like a whisky and soda?"

"I should hate it," said he. "Yes, a lot of lumps, please. And Uncle Robert?"

"He seldom comes to tea. Usually at his club with a

rubber of bridge afterwards. And to-night he dines with some City company."

"But I'm not going, am I?" asked he.

"No; just a company dinner. There'll be dinner here, of course, but nobody except me. Perhaps you would like to dine at your club?"

Steven felt an impulse of liking towards this comfortable stout aunt. She was simple; she was also slightly pathetic with her pearls and her laden tea table with no one to eat of her bounty, and her prospect of a solitary evening. That it was worth while to make himself agreeable, merely because he was to be her guest for the next three weeks, never entered his head.

"But I would much sooner dine with you if I may," he said.

"Why, of course you may, and delighted," said Aunt Florence. "And perhaps you would like to dine early and go to a play, if I can get seats for something well spoken of."

Steven divined that Aunt Florence did not in the least want to go to a play. There was no lack of cordiality in her suggestion, but there was no body behind it.

"If you really ask me," he said, "I should like to stop at home and dine with you. That's for choice."

Her face brightened with a gleam of eager satisfaction. Steven evidently had good-will towards her, and she must cultivate that.

"Just a cosy evening at home, then," she said, "and I shall enjoy that; but after this, my dear, I'm not going to allow you to spend your time with me. I'm sure you must have got heaps of friends in London, and they'll be welcome here whenever they'll pop in to a bit of lunch or dinner."

"That's awfully kind of you, Aunt Florence," said he. "But what a responsibility for me! Perhaps you won't like my friends, and where shall I be then?"

"Just where you are now, Steven; and as for my not liking your friends, why do you imagine that could happen? And you must get to know your uncle's friends and mine. I can't have you going back to Cornwall saying you've had a wretched, dull time here."

Steven found himself feeling very much at home. He was as sensitive as a dog to atmosphere, and Aunt Florence's was a very agreeable one. She was genuine, she was kind, and though possibly there was nothing very interesting or comprehending behind that, kindness and affection were pleasant superficial qualities; they made for comfort.

"I know I shan't do that," he said, beginning faintly to wonder how long this interchange of little complimentary speeches was to go on. "I'm quite sure I shall have a delightful time. Probably I shall refuse to go back to Cornwall, and you'll have to turn me out."

"Well, that won't be done while I'm here," said she. "And you must tell me what you like doing. Dancing? Are you fond of dancing?"

"I'm not much of a hand at it," said he. "But really I like everything. Just now, another bun."

"And that's what I like to see," said this elementary lady. "Young men I notice often hardly touch their food, and have a cocktail and a cigarette instead. Girls the same. Dear me, how things have changed. But I love them both; I should be sorry to think the day would ever come when I shouldn't like to have young people about me."

Comfort was not so much to the fore in the communings with Uncle Robert, for face to face with Steven he was conscious of regarding him rather as the highwayman who, when death had robbed him of his life, would relieve him of his money. But the highwayman must be made acquainted, however sternly, with his opulent destiny, and it was Uncle Robert's intention to attach certain conditions to this remunerative rôle. He was a large, pompous, handsome man, all broadcloth and watch chain, who spoke to his nephew as if he were dictating a business letter of some peremptory kind.

"It's right that you should know what the provisions of my will are going to be, Steven," he said, when he had outlined them, "and those I have indicated to you. But you mustn't think that because at my death you'll be a rich man I intend you to live in idleness on your expectations. There'll be plenty of time for me to alter all that, if you don't come into line with me. You'll be of age in April next, and I shall make you a good allowance, sufficient to enable you to marry, subject to my approval."

Steven wondered for a moment whether the duty of raising a family was all the coming into line demanded of him, but it seemed unlikely, and he ventured on no such facetious suggestion.

"That's very generous of you, Uncle Robert," he said. "I'm a very fortunate fellow."

"You are indeed. I've worked hard for thirty years in order to hand over to you at my death a very big fortune. But, as I say, I have no intention of your living in idleness while you wait for it to drop into your pockets. You've got to work, too, and show me that you're capable of making money and of handling it. If my advice had been taken, you would have left Eton at seventeen and entered my business. But your poor father had always been very keen that you should go to Cambridge, though it was waste of time, in my opinion, and so I made it possible for his wishes to be carried out. Now you've been two years up there, I think, and that means one more in front of you, does it not?"

"That's the usual thing," said Steven.

"Well, I'll let that stand, but after a year from now I shall expect you to enter my business. It's a big concern: the Gervase Line is well known in most of the ports of the world. But you won't get any favouritism and soft jobs because you're my nephew, I can tell you. You'll have to learn about ships and trading and freights like any other young clerk entering the house. A shipping business isn't the same as having a yacht at Cowes and belonging to the squadron any more than it means rowing at Henley with a lot of ladies sitting in your lap."

This was not a very accurate description of Henley, as such a practice would certainly have impeded effective oarsmanship, but it seemed to Lord Gervase a remarkably apt expression of what he wished to convey. The fortunate young fellow must be made aware that his achievements hitherto, though so much admired by the idle world and productive of silver cups and portraits in the illustrated papers, were mere amusements of a highly frivolous nature. The picture of Steven in *The Times* this morning had filled him with commercial indignation, and he had said, "Pshaw!" with an intonation of infinite contempt, when fond Florence had announced her intention of cutting it out and framing it. That was the sort of thing to turn a boy's head and make him think himself an Adonis and a popular hero. It was clearly the duty of an uncle to turn his head firmly back again.

Lord Gervase paused so as to let his picture of Henley acidly etch itself into Adonis's mind.

"Then there's your marriage," he went on.

Steven interrupted.

"Oh, I haven't any idea of marrying at present," he said.

The pause this time was of astonishment, as if the secretary to whom Lord Gervase was dictating had criticized his subject matter. It expressed his feelings better than any words could have done.

"Then there's your marriage," he repeated. "I should wish you to marry early. You and I are the last of a very long line, the last, I should say, of the legitimate line, and I should like to see it firmly established again. So if, before my death, you should have a dozen children, I will guarantee that you shall feel no material anxiety about their education and support. You are not yet of age, but I think I am not making an unreasonable request of you if I ask that you should marry in the course of your twenty-second year. To allude to an unpleasant subject, it is also perfectly clear that that dreadful and mysterious curse which, though I believe tradition has vastly magnified it, cannot altogether be dismissed as being without foundation, is, in point of fact, over. You are yourself a sufficient proof of that."

"Oh, I haven't got horns or hooves," said Steven gravely. "But it might break out again, you know."

"We may dismiss that possibility: you are not defective in either physical or mental endowments. The curse (whatever truth there was in it) is therefore over. Now I have told you what you may expect from me, and I have also told you what I expect from you. There will be a place for you as a junior clerk in the office of the Gervase Line of Steamers when you have finished your Cambridge course, and you can make your home with me, as soon as you enter it, until your marriage, which I hope will take place as soon as possible. As long as you choose a wife suitable for the position which you will occupy as my heir, I shall not limit what I think we may call natural selection, ha, in any way at all."

Steven had a smile for this which he firmly adjusted.

"Then is it a sort of bargain, Uncle Robert?" he asked. "Do you mean that you will make me your heir if I fulfil these conditions and not otherwise?"

Lord Gervase was much astonished at anyone questioning his clearly expressed wishes, but he behaved with remarkable self-restraint.

"They are very reasonable conditions," he said. "They only lay down that you shall work and that you shall marry, which are two perfectly natural things for any young man to do, whether he gets anything by them or not. I would point out that you get a good deal."

"I know I do," said Steven, "and the conditions are most reasonable. I shall have to work, in any case, for my living, unless I choose to settle down without a penny to spend at Trenair; and you offer me an excellent opening. It's equally reasonable to suppose that in the natural course of events I shall marry. I should almost certainly fulfil your conditions in any case."

Lord Gervase permitted himself to be withering.

"Perhaps you dislike the feeling that the fulfilment of them will eventually bring you a very large fortune and in the interval will give you a most handsome allowance," he said.

Steven seemed not to wither.

"No, I don't mind being rich," he said.

Lord Gervase let the full blast of irony loose.

"That is a very unusual view to take of wealth," he said. "Perhaps you think I ought to beg you as a personal favour to be allowed to make you so."

Steven still seemed unaccountably unaffected. He took this furnace blast as if it had been a refreshing breeze.

"No, I don't think that at all," he said. "I told you I thought you were very generous; I told you that I considered myself a very fortunate fellow. But can't you understand that, being only twenty years old, my liberty seems of colossal importance to me? Or is that unreasonable of me?"

Steven saw at once that his contention conveyed nothing to Lord Gervase's mind. But he felt very distinctly, though he could not have found words to fit the thought, what he meant by it. What Maurice had called "the wild thing" saw the bars of a cage in front of it, and the fact that they would be there was not rendered more palatable by the fact that they would be made of gold. The wild thing did not care about gold, and it had the strongest objection to bars. It could not tell what they might shut off from it: nothing, perhaps, except the notion of liberty. Lord Gervase, on his side, was acutely aware that, if this most extraordinary young man refused to accept his very reasonable conditions, he would either be obliged to remit them or leave his huge fortune to various charitable institutions, in which case he would entertain a far more intense dislike against these fortunate establishments than he did for his nephew. To have worked hard for so many years, and at the end only to benefit the lame and the halt and the blind, was to make a far deadlier fiasco than to bequeath the fruit of his industry, lacking a son, to his nearest relation. His tone became rather less dictatorial.

"Certainly, if I was imposing distasteful conditions on you," he said, "I should only respect you for weighing them against wealth. But my conditions, as you pointed out yourself, are only those which, if left in entire liberty, you would naturally fulfil. There is therefore no question of weighing one against the other. I may remind you that, up till now, you have had provided for you all that you could reasonably want, and that I was the provider: you have felt neither the need of money nor the appreciation of what money can do. Before you despise wealth it would be wise to learn what it means."

Steven nodded.

"That's quite true," he said.

There was a dignity about Uncle Robert now. He was speaking of money, for which he had an immense respect, and his conviction of the truth of his words gave them weight.

"That's what I want you to learn, Steven," he said. "I want you to work and earn it. And that's not the only object of working: work brings you self-respect as well, and the habit of discipline. But money is a most desirable thing in itself too: it means power, and those who affect to despise power are the weak-kneed and the indolent. I want you to show you are not of that wretched breed before power comes into your hands."

That was all very sensible, and from the standpoint of sense Steven was in entire accord. But, even as his uncle spoke he knew that, however sincerely he agreed with him, there lay below that note of concordance another of discord. Money to his uncle was a hallowed image, a magician with powers of spells and miracles, and this magician Uncle Robert had already bottled like some Arabian genius and was prepared to hand over to his nephew, but required of him first to learn something of its potencies and of its control. But what his uncle called power was to Stephen only a synonym for convenience. Could the magic of money possibly procure for you anything worth having, like the magic that lived in the woodlands and the night?

There, for the present, with Steven's promise to enter the shipping business at the conclusion of his three years at Cambridge, the conference terminated, for he was taking his aunt to Lord's, and she was waiting for him. With her a far more genial relationship was establishing itself. The actual mode of her life, her groove, her succession of lunch parties and dinner parties, her bloated little lap dog with froglike protuberant eyes, on whom she lavished not only blankets, appalling little fur coats, and cream, but so much yearning affection, her manifest adoration of himself, as something infinitely superior even to her dog, and the entirely sentimental view she took of life generally were all ridiculous to the point of idiocy, but so much sheer amiability made a very pleasant atmosphere for the time. How long it would be tolerable was another question: the atmosphere was that of a room with every appurtenance of comfort, soft carpets, enveloping chairs, and a prosperous fire, but with all the windows shut and an excess of highly scented flowers. But at present the question did not arise; it was pleasant to chatter to Aunt Florence and suffer her unbounded and uncritical appreciation.

"I had to send in to tell you it was time to start, dear," she said, "or we should have been late, and then you would have scolded me. A good talk with your uncle?"

"Quite; most harmonious," said Steven. "Oh, Aunt Florence, you're not going to take your bull-frog dog, are you? Supposing he bites the umpire, the fierce thing? They'll stone us."

"My dinkie-dog would never dream of such a thing," said Lady Gervase. "Would you, Dinkie-pinkie?"

"But you really had better leave him behind," said Steven. "I know dogs aren't admitted to Lord's. Of course, they might not count him as a dog, darling Aunt Florence, if you assured them he was an insect, but——"

"Insect, indeed," said Aunt Florence in high indignation. "But if dogs aren't admitted, I must leave him. Dinkie won't think it very unkind of Mamma, will he?" she asked, kissing his fat little neck.

"You can order him a quail and a peach for his lunch, and a glass of Uncle Robert's best brandy," said Steven. "Then he'll get tipsy and sleep till you come home."

Aunt Florence, reluctantly giggling at this blasphemous picture, resigned her Dinkie-pinkie to two footmen and a major-domo and got into the motor with her Steven.

"And tell me about your talk, dear," said she as they rolled off.

"I expect you know," said Steven. "Uncle Robert is going to make me his heir. But he wants me to do two things: to go into his office as soon as I leave Cambridge, and to marry without loss of time. Of course, I should have to work, in any case, and his business is a splendid opening for me. Also I suppose I shall marry. But somehow the thought of them being made conditions gave me a feeling of being—being handcuffed. I don't think he saw my point of view in the least, and it is, I know, purely an imaginative one. . . . But do you see what I mean?"

"Why, of course I do," responded Aunt Florence. "Even if you want to do a thing, it becomes a task if you're told you're expected to. The feeling that you must do it makes it such a bore! Oh, I've got that sort of contrariness as much as you."

"And is it ridiculous of us?" asked Steven.

She liked him to say "us," to couple her up with him, and Steven had noticed that already. She beamed and glowed at this confidential touch.

"No, my dear," said she, "it's not ridiculous in you, because you're twenty, though it is in me, because I'm fifty. I ought to have got over my stiff-necked ways, while you oughtn't to. But I think you should go into your uncle's office: he's got a right to ask that of you, considering you'll inherit the business."

"So I must do what's expected of me. And how about the other condition, Aunt Florence? You must find me a wife."

"I'll find you twenty," said Aunt Florence with a glance at him.

"Do, and a nice big house with sufficient accommodation for my harem. Lord! What a sultan I shall be. And you shall come, heavily veiled, to drink tea with my wives."

"Oh, for shame!" said Aunt Florence. "I only meant I could find you half a dozen girls who'd make you a nice wife."

"Bring them along, then, one at a time, to be looked at. And I'll put little red labels on those who I think will do, like you put on pictures at an exhibition that have been sold. And then you can take them all away again, and find me a nice quiet corner in a cemetery, for it's just as likely that I should die within the next year as be married. But I haven't any real intention of dying, either."

"No, but, after all, at twenty marriage is more likely than burial," said Aunt Florence.

"But neither of them at all probable," said Steven. "And what plotters we are. But then we're extraordinarily good pals, aren't we?—and pals always plot."

Aunt Florence made no reply, and Steven, looking up at her, saw her kind vague eyes swimming. He had not dreamed that he would arouse this exhibition of emotion, and he felt at once that he had no use for it and no response to make. . . . She patted his lean brown hand for a moment with her fat little bediamonded fingers.

"You're a very dear boy," she said, "and I'm a childless old woman. A silly one, too, I'm afraid, for I've let myself think of you as if you were my son, and, oh, Steven, how wonderful that would have been. But you've got your own mamma, to be sure. . . . But it's lovely to me, my dear, to hear you saying that we're good pals. I hug that to my heart. And now I've said my say. . . . Dear me, we're in the queue of carriages already, and all going to Lord's! We shall find ever so many friends there. Nothing so pleasant as a day among friends! Look, there's Mrs. Nairn, who dined with us—if it wasn't Wednesday it would be Thursday; and her two boys from Eton—or is it Harrow?—and her daughter Betty whom you took in to dinner. I asked them to lunch with us to-day. How small the world is!"

The block seemed interminable, and the two got out, for the world was large enough to impede further progress. Lady Gervase pressed blue tickets and pink tickets into Steven's hand.

"Those are our seats," she said, "and the pink ticket is for our luncheon table. I ordered one for eight, the Nairns and you and me, that's six, and I thought you'd like to bid a couple of friends whom you came across."

Steven had written to Maurice to say that he would be at Lord's, and it was no surprise to find him waiting about just inside the gate. He, of course, would join them at lunch; and then there swept down on him, terrible as an army with banners, the Amazon, who wanted him to lunch with the Provost and her. Steven expressed his regrets and then, most imprudently thinking that he was quite safe, bewailed the fact that she could not lunch with them. But without a moment's hesitation she said she would be delighted, and so Steven had to be delighted too. He saw Lady Gervase to her seat and strolled off with Maurice for a few words before rejoining her.

"Maurice, I'm going to be a man of millions," he said. "My uncle's making me his heir, if I see eye to eye with him about entering his business when I come down from Cambridge; also he wants me to marry suitably and soon. Opulent bomb-shells, aren't they? Why aren't I more excited? Perhaps I shall be when I grasp all that it means. I only heard this morning."

For a moment Maurice felt as if some violent jar or jolt had shaken him.

"Lor'!" he said. There really seemed nothing better to say.

"Just about that," said Steven. "You phrase things well. But what next?"

"Who can tell? It depends on you—on how strong you are."

"What do you mean?"

"Exactly what I say. It won't change you if you're strong enough. I think I'll back you: I don't believe money has got much chance against you. Not so sure about the other."

"But the other would come in the ordinary course of events," said Steven.

Maurice hesitated.

"Yes, of course it would," he said. "It just hadn't

occurred to me. I haven't even congratulated you. But I do. How goes it otherwise? What plans?"

"My first is that you come and dine with us to-night. My aunt always wants to see any of my friends. And we'll talk plans then."

CHAPTER V

It was not till the short summer night was brightening into the hour before dawn that Maurice tiptoed up to his room at his club. Steven had quite forgotten that Lady Gervase was giving a dance on this first day of Lord's, and Maurice, arriving for dinner at half-past eight, found himself expected to remain for the ensuing festivity. "I should take it very unkind of you indeed," said that hospitable lady, "if you dreamed of running away after dinner: it really mustn't be, Mr. Crofts." . . . He did not dance himself, but the scene was brilliant and decorative, full of melody and movement. A big tented enclosure was built out overlooking St. James's Park, open in front to the hot summer night with couples flitting kaleidoscopically in and out of the ballroom for pause and coolness, and then plunging back into the flood of the rhythmically moving crowd within. Sometimes the reserved, stiff-lipped, donnish strain in him controlled his mood, and he wondered how much it all cost, and whether, apart from dissolving pearls in vinegar, a more lavish waste of money could be devised; and then again the spontaneous gaiety intoxicated him, and he laughed at himself for the recluse and scholastic habit of his mind, the length of his moral upper lip, the priggishness that reeked in the view that classical studies were a whit worthier than dancing. Lady Gervase, singling him out as Steven's friend, had introduced him right and left to early arrivals, and he had agreeable little chatterings with people whose names he had already forgotten; but underneath it all he felt his alienness. He no more belonged to this world than these others belonged to the society of the High Table at King's, but this was the world onto which Steven was being grafted. Would he ever really belong to it either? he wondered;

was he not rather a native of the moonless night outside, with the filmed starlight and the dim trees and the shadowed spaces? Or would the glitter suck him in and gild him?

There were bridge tables in one of the rooms. Maurice played a couple of rubbers with Lord Gervase and two others, but then he came back to this sitting-out place, and sometimes he was included into a little knot of recuperating dancers; sometimes he drank a glass of champagne which he did not want, but throughout he had an eye on Steven's exits and entrances. He seemed to have assumed an official status in the house to-night, for when soon after midnight his uncle vanished altogether, servants came to him with messages from Lady Gervase, and he took down to supper a cosy-looking woman with pearls and a slight German accent, before whom backs and knees were bowed, and sat at a small round table with men wearing orders. Occasionally he had a word with Maurice, hoping he would wait till this affair was over and they could talk, but he had little leisure for that. He was often dancing with Betty Nairn, who had been of the lunch party at Lord's, a tall slim boy, to all appearance, olive complexioned and black haired. Steven deposited her once with Maurice, telling him not to let her go till he came back, and he learned that she had only come out this year and had been to twenty-three balls since the first of June. Maurice felt himself entirely unable to cope with this very modern product, who felt about as much interest in him as in his shoe laces, and when, Steven still tarrying, some other young man took her away, he made no attempt to detain her. But evidently Steven found her again, for soon afterwards, through the open door into the ballroom, Maurice saw the black and the golden head weaving their way through the dancers. Then suddenly the Child appeared, and instantly some nameless antagonism began to show itself, like the quivering of hot air over shingle, not precisely visible in itself, but perceptible through its movement.

"Hullo, Maurice," he said. "Steven told me that you were about. I didn't know that balls were in your line."

"They're not. I dined here, and Steven forgot there was a dance afterwards. They're not in your line either, are they? You used to say you were too tall to dance."

Maurice was quite aware that some touch of hostility had come into his voice. He had not initiated it; it was rather reflected from the Child, but if that was the note of the tuning fork he was delighted to take it up.

"So I am," said the Child, "but I don't mind making a fool of myself occasionally any more than you mind sitting here and looking on. But I shall trot along in a minute."

Maurice tried to infuse some cordiality into this unpromising conversation. He wished the Child would go away and guessed that it was not pleasure that was detaining him.

"I'm feeling like a foreigner, Child," he said, "who has got plumped down here without a passport or any knowledge of the language. Somebody in a diamond hat or a skirt of pearls will ask to see it, and I shall be arrested. And the natives do this every night; that girl dancing with Steven told me she had been to twenty-three balls during June."

"Who is she?" asked the Child.

"Betty Nairn. She was lunching with us at Lord's to-day," said Maurice.

"Oh, are you staying here?"

Maurice felt that if catechisms were going on he might as well catechize too.

"No, but I lunched with Steven and Lady Gervase. Are you in London?"

"Yes, with my people. I'm going abroad the day after to-morrow to learn German."

"Where?"

"German family at Schaffhausen," said the Child.

"Sorry for you. Have you seen much of Steven?"

"Almost nothing."

"Busy, I suppose," said Maurice.

There seemed not much more to say, and presently the Child rose.

"I think I shall be off," he said, "I really came here to have a talk with Steven, but there doesn't seem much chance of it."

"Very little indeed," said Maurice.

The Child shifted from one foot to the other.

"Are you coming?" he asked. "Let's drop into my club and have a drink."

"Thanks, but I shall stay on for a bit," said Maurice.

The cordiality had been stillborn: it had died almost before it drew breath.

"I wonder you stop, if you feel so out of it," said the Child.

Maurice resented this. He did not want any criticisms on what he chose to do.

"Oh, it's rather interesting to study the ways of foreigners," he said. "You'll be doing the same three days hence in Germany. *Auf wiedersehen.* Have a good time."

It was clear enough, thought Maurice, what lay at the back of this: the Child had betrayed himself with raw candidness. He was a very elementary fellow, honest and affectionate, but a large stupid boy, with just perception enough to guess that his schoolboy friendship with Steven was outworn and to suspect that another friendship, just as absorbing but far more mature, had arisen. Maurice again felt sorry for him, but with the quality of sorrow that he would have extended to a stranger whom he passed in the street, whose face was swollen with toothache, for he could not, situated as he was, think of the Child with any sympathy. He knew and liked the Child, but it was clearly impossible that the three of them could form a trio of pals, in a communion of affection and "old chappiness," for friendships of this sort were by their very nature duets, not trios, and one of them had to go. The Child had been bowled, middle stump, just as his enormous young brother had been at Lord's to-day, and so he must go and sit in the pavilion.

The ball came to an end rather suddenly, as such gatherings are apt to do: everyone seemed to have had about enough of it simultaneously. The room was full for one dance, half empty for the next, and for the third there were but half a dozen couples. The tented enclosure had emptied too, and for a few minutes Maurice found himself sitting here quite alone. Then through the open door of the ballroom, from the dazzle within to the darkness outside came Steven.

"Maurice!" he called, "you here still? Ah, there you are; that's noble of you. Florence Nightingale sitting by a sick-bed isn't in it, and even she had a lamp. I wanted to have a talk with you, but I found I was by way of being host. Have you been awfully bored?"

"Not an atom! I rather enjoyed it," said Maurice. "Stars and garters and principalities and powers. I feel as if the devil had shown me all the Kingdom of the World in a moment of time."

"The devil's me, then, I suppose," said Steven. "Don't apologize. The devil enjoyed it, too: everyone was immensely friendly, and I fancy they've caught on here to my new position. Probably that was why they were friendly; they wanted me to tip them. And there is something to be said for dancing; there's something primitive about it, and you don't get rid of the primitiveness by bands and marble halls; the savagery of it wins. And there's something ancient and religious about it. It's a rite;

David danced before the Ark tc express a holy joy, and bishops ought to dance in full canonicals on the great feasts of the Church."

"Will you kindly explain what you're talking about?" asked Maurice.

"Certainly not: you have to guess, and besides, you understand. Just the fact of dancing both symbolizes the joy of life and quickens it. It doesn't matter whom you dance with as long as you dance; probably you could dance alone just as well as with a partner. It's primitive, it's primeval, it's just as primeval as night and burrowing into deep water. Something inside me answered to it. Oh, by the way, did you see the Child?"

"Yes, I had a little talk with him," said Maurice. "Rather iced. I tried once to put a little cordiality into it, but it wasn't any use. I told him I felt like a foreigner in this worldly scene, and he asked me why I didn't go away."

Steven laughed.

"That was a silly question," he said, "for I'm sure he knew. He was rather dignified with me, too; you might call it stuffy. As if it was my fault that I came to the end of him. I quite appreciate what there is of him, but there merely isn't any more. Friends have got to go forward together, they must always be new to each other. And they must never demand anything of each other except that they should be themselves."

"That's not a bad definition."

"Of course it isn't. The Child—— Yes, what is it?"

A footman had appeared at the door of the ballroom but was retreating again when he saw Steven.

"I thought everyone had gone, sir," he said.

"Yes, they have. I'll let Mr. Crofts out. Just leave a light here and there and put out the rest, and you needn't sit up."

With the quenching of the lights inside, the tented enclosure where they sat darkened into a deeper dusk. From outside the lights along the Mall shining upwards illuminated the striped roof, and across it moved angled shadows of the plane trees below, now gently stirring, now rigidly outlined. Big Ben from Westminster struck some hour, and the boom broke against the house wall like some soft ponderous wave, but Maurice had no idea what hour it announced.

"The Child's stuck," said Steven, "and we've got to leave him. There's nothing else to be done. He'll find somebody else to play with. How much better the dusk is than the glare; we can think. But there's got to be a glare for a second, as I want to light a cigarette."

He struck a match and held it in the cave of his hollowed hands. The flare shone through his fingers, making them red and luminous, and it vividly lit up his face as he bent over it; and once again, before he blew the match out, Maurice saw it as that mask, wild and exquisite, of which he had had a couple of glimpses before. It struck him now as strangely expressive of the things Steven had been saying: there was in it some primeval quality, like that which he had said was the spirit of dancing: there was in it too a certain joyous inhumanity which most aptly illustrated the indifference he had shown with regard to the Child. The Child had stuck, he had said, and, with a shrug, they must leave him. Maurice, it is true, quite shared that sentiment, but he had never been more than a casual friend, whereas Steven and the Child had till so lately been the most intimate of comrades. Yet no shadow of regret or of tenderness shadowed Steven's sunny indifference to him now: the Child was left behind, like a stretch of road that it had been pleasant to stroll along, but which was now traversed and finished with.

The psychological impression lasted only for the same space as did the physical impression of Steven's face shining above the lit match. That image, when Steven blew it out, lingered on Maurice's retina just a second more, and then broke up and faded into the surrounding darkness.

"You looked primeval yourself then," said he.

"I feel it: is it the effect of dancing?" asked Steven. "Enjoying one's self, too, always brings out what one is. Something pagan, something to do with woods and wet places. That got into the ballroom to-night; there was quite a whiff of it. Betty Nairn, whom I danced with a lot, has a touch. But we were to talk about plans. I'm here till the end of July, when my uncle and aunt go down in pomp to Cowes. What a way of being on the sea! Then I go to Cornwall—oh, and I thirst for it already, the blessed place, where I learn to be myself. When are you coming?"

"I've got to be at Cambridge till nearly the end of August," said Maurice, "as I'm coaching half a dozen fellows up there in the Long. But may I come to you as soon as that's over? And then you'll coach me."

Steven laughed.

"On what particular subjects?" he asked.

"On the Art—or is it the Science?—of being myself. Knowing one's self is a very unimportant matter: it is just the sort of semi-ethical advice which the Delphic oracle would give, and all that I know of myself doesn't encourage me to want to know more. But inside what I know is the thing that I really am. But it's like a kernel inside a nut: the shell that I know must be smashed up before I get to it."

"And how the deuce am I to teach you to do that?" demanded Steven.

"I learn by being with you. I can't explain; perhaps you will teach me that I'm only a Don after all, and then, when I'm convinced of that, I shall go back to my place at the High Table at King's, and the lectures, and the piquet, and the academic humour. But I'm going to adventure with you first."

Steven made no reply, and he sat very still. Maurice had

often noticed that about him; he was like a lizard on a stone, basking in some sunlight of his own. There was that quicksilver quality, too. . . .

"There's time for being a Don afterwards," said Maurice, "but I must go . . . go somewhere with you first. There *is* something primeval about you. Oh, it's all very well to prate about the progress of the human race, and its education, and its civilization, and its knowledge painfully picked up grain by grain, and for every grain the life of a man laid down, but I wonder whether we shouldn't progress more if we could only go back and recapture the spirit of man as it was before it learned its tricks and accomplishments. There are primeval instincts and perceptions which we have lost in this bloody thing we call civilization, just as a dog loses his dogship by being domesticated. He sits up and begs for a biscuit, but he isn't the better for what he has learned: he is the worse, because he has become less of a dog but more of a clown. Just in the same way man in the morning of the world was something finer and more sensitive than he is now. He has learned a lot of tricks: that is all, and he has lost touch correspondingly."

"Ha!" said Steven. He moved a little closer to Maurice so that their shoulders touched, and there they sat a moment in silence, vividly conscious of each other, but more vividly of some bond or spell that was weaving itself between them.

"Maurice, you're getting at it," said Steven at length. "You're telling me things which I have known all along, and ever so much better than you know them, but of which I wasn't conscious till you said them. Go on: we're together, you and I, in a way that I and the Child never were. Damn the Child: it's his fault we didn't get together sooner. Go on."

Maurice did not answer at once: he wanted to stop thinking altogether, to let himself lie open, without exercise of brain or imagination. But from habit he could not help thinking. . . .

"All that I've got at I've learned from you," he said at length. "It's vague and dim, it's like a misty night without stars, but I know the direction where we're going. Of course you knew it already; when your face becomes a mask you show all that and ever so much more. Be patient with me and go on being primeval."

"But what's happening?" asked Steven. "You tell me things I'm not conscious of till you say them, and yet you assert they come from me."

"I know they do," said Maurice.

"Then you're a sort of wizard. Perhaps you have the power of tapping my dreams. Somehow, that's what you've done. The dreamer forgets his dreams, but you remind him of them, and then . . . and then they're not dreams at all. Lord! What a rum world!"

Steven got up, and by one of those swift, rather disconcerting transitions, which were so characteristic of him, turned all the gravity of their talk, its yearning, its questing, into farce.

"Let's instantly found a society for the reëstablishment of primeval man," he said. "We'll burn all our books and wreck all the railways, and live in caves and take off all our clothes, and paint ourselves with woad, and dance beneath the trees, and eat raw flesh. Oh, Maurice, let's begin at once! I know there are some dodos or pelicans in the lake there; let's go and kill one, and sit under the trees with nothing on, and pluck and eat it. Then we'll dance under the trees and ravish people. I wonder if there's any woad in the house. What a bore that you're going back to Cambridge to-morrow; but you can begin preparing public opinion there for the new epoch, and we'll start in earnest when we go back in October. You'll know more about it then, as you'll have been through a course of instruction at Trenair. I know I've broken up all our talk, but I couldn't go on. My brain gives a click and runs down."

"Time it did," said Maurice. "I must go."

"Must you? It's quite early yet. Very early indeed, in fact, for I don't suppose it's much more than three in the morning."

They went together through the empty ballroom, still faintly odorous, to nostrils used to the night, of human presence, and down the carved marble staircase, where their steps echoed sharply through the silent house. One light only burned on the landing, leaving the hall below dim and shadowed.

Then with the same suddenness as he had inaugurated farce, Steven whisked back again, laying his arm round Maurice's neck.

"It's as if the house was waiting for something to happen," he said. "Maurice, how exciting and yet how utterly natural it would be if a great light like many full moons began to shine out, and if cracks opened in the walls, and moss grew on the steps, and wild woodland creatures peered at us through the banisters. Why not? Then we should see that we were looking on the ruins of some bygone race, and that the world had swung back into morning again. It might so easily happen; the present is not an atom more real than the past or the future. The present is flimsy; the stuff that dreams are made of is the only stuff that endures. We've just paused here, linked like this, until all the shams decayed and dwindled and vanished, and all the false gods crumbled."

They stood there silent, each looking into the eyes of the other. And then, somewhere from deep inside him, there came to Maurice some whisper of fear. What if Steven's words came true, now, on the instant, and all the shams forged by civilization to safeguard and protect the community vanished, and all the false gods, wealth and learning and morals, with all their fettering codes and futile quests, crumbled? Would he without fear and with only passionate welcome await the inconjecturable result? He had scarcely asked himself that before Steven seemed aware of his qualm. He laughed and withdrew his arm.

"Don't be frightened," he said. "It's not going to happen yet. You're not ready, and I'm not certain that I am either. Hat? Coat? There you are."

They stood on the doorstep a moment.

"I wish that I wasn't going to Cambridge to-morrow," said Maurice, "or that you would come there. I shan't see you again till the end of next month."

"Bear up. But don't be frightened again," he said. "That spoils everything." He looked down on Maurice, standing now on the pavement below the doorstep, and stifled a half yawn.

"But we've had a ripping evening," he said. "Good-night. Cornwall next."

The streets were empty both of traffic and passengers in this stillest hour between the businesses of evening and morning. There was no taxi in sight, but Maurice had no great traverse to make, and the untrodden pavements, shimmering with dew, slipped by beneath him as if he was steadfast and they moving with the circling earth. Carlton House Terrace, with Steven standing on the doorstep, half yawning, was sliding away eastwards. Somehow that intuition of Steven's with regard to his own tremor, followed by that stifled yawn and that abrupt farewell, had made him feel snubbed. Without intention he had said to himself: "That's one for me: Steven's had enough of me for the present." But now, more robustly, he saw that such a reflection, however lightly entertained, was quite inadmissible; besides, if nobody had the right to yawn after dancing and talking three quarters of the night, yawning must surely be taboo from the gamut of human gestures. . . . Yet still the image persisted of Steven sliding away eastwards with the revolving earth towards some mystical dawn and yawning. Maurice himself yawned from associative impulse.

The night porter, weary but polite, let him into his club, and he conveyed himself in the lift up to his bedroom floor. The evening to which he had been so hungrily looking forward, ever since Steven left Cambridge, was over, and reaction asserted itself in an immense fatigue: he promised himself, as he slipped off his clothes, a spell of dreamless sleep. But his brain, or some deeper consciousness than that, had business on hand, and no sooner had he got into bed than up sprang those internal illuminations by which the factory of thought is lit, when the looms clash at their weaving. Maurice figured himself as looking on at this crossing of warp and woof, and at the strange tapestry of thought that magically grew under its motions, as if he was the interested but detached spectator of his own mind.

Steven, Steven. . . . Who *was* Steven? Most people were, more or less, what they appeared to be: you could guess, anyhow, with some approach to accuracy, when you knew a man well, what sort of controller inhabited his corporal frame, and how, in all probability, he would act in and react to external circumstances and situations. But these days at Cambridge of unreserved intimacy with Steven, which had burst into a flower of friendship such as Maurice but a few weeks before would have thought inconceivable, had only convinced him that he was utterly ignorant of Steven's essential nature. Yet it must have been that essential nature and something answering to it in himself that had drawn them together, for Steven had been up at King's for two years, and though Maurice had frankly and wholesomely admired—who could help it?—his astonishing beauty and that exuberant charm which were like words set to the melody of it, never had there been any hint, till that night of the ball, that they were to be snapped together in this bond of the soul. Steven's charm and his physical splendour, to which Maurice was fully alive, had nothing whatever to do with it. There had come some flash of revelation, and this loverlike blood brotherhood was sealed. And all this, so Steven had said, was but the beginning of their friendship: they started where he and the Child had left off, and now together they were going up some unconjecturable path, and Maurice had no idea whether it led to heaven or hell, or with whom he was travelling in this rapture of white devotion.

He remembered trying once unsuccessfully to recall Steven's face; now with a livelier bewilderment he tried to outline the lineaments of Steven's soul. The attempt was no less vain, and yet, so he told himself, he must, below the defined and registered impressions of consciousness, know about him, for to-night, when he had said something concerning man in the morning of the world, Steven had claimed and hailed that as coming from dream-stuff of his own, while Maurice knew that he had learned it from him. Did there lurk somewhere within that, as the life lies hid in the seed, the secret of his own adoration of him?

His thoughts, as befitted the guidance of his neat scholarly mind, were expressing themselves to him with a strict verbal distinctness, and now at the word "adoration" he paused, wondering if he really meant that. But he had neither the power nor the wish to recall it. He adored Steven, not mentally or physically at all, but with the devotion of blind faith in the temple of an unknown god. Was it some fantastic psychical kinship which, without effort or design on the part of either of them, had forced itself in upon them? He did not know nor would he have it different. Was it (and at this check in the weaving of the loom he strained his ears for any whispered answer from his own consciousness) was it in very truth a relationship between the lower creature and the inspiring presence, between the worshipper and the adored? And now the image of Steven presented itself to him as of some young god, awaking in an early dawn of the golden years and stretching sun-stained limbs on his couch beneath the holy olive trees and murmuring to himself, as he smiled his way into the consciousness of a new day: "I have been dreaming, and I don't know what I dreamed. I want somebody to tell me what it was, somebody who understands dreams."

"And I came," thought Maurice, "and I bowed myself before him, and he said that it was I whom he wanted. He looked kindly on me, and saw that I was dulled with years of loneliness, and though I adored him and loved him, I feared him too. A squirrel was nestling under his chin, and he winced because it tickled him. And a great big boy with sad eyes looked at us out of the bushes, but the god told him to get away because he was stupid and did not understand. When he had gone I began telling the god about his dream. . . ."

Some impression of falling and of a wild crash and beating heart invaded him, and he started up in bed, but before he regained full consciousness he heard his own voice, faint and strangled, calling: "Steven! Steven!" The room was unfamiliar; for the moment he had no idea where he was, and wondered if he was in Cornwall, staying at Trenair. Then there filtered back the disconnected memories of the night, swiftly arranging themselves into coherent patterns. The square of his window showed bright in the very early dawn, he could see the details of washing stand and wardrobe, and localized himself. The secure world was all round him: there were no shrines nor recumbent god. He smiled to himself at his disordered visions.

"Something frightened me," he said to himself. "I was

dreaming so happily before that. Now Steven will have to tell me about my dream, not I about his. And that won't be till September. Damn!"

He lay down again, and almost before his head touched the pillow he fell asleep.

Cambridge presented its familiar countenance when he returned there that day, formal and academic and with its own peculiar spryness and self-sufficiency. That self-sufficiency was as solid as the flying buttresses of the chapel: it did not even trouble to proclaim that everything which could be learned was taught here, merely because nobody had ever imagined otherwise. It was sane, it was solid, it was stolid: Maurice had been accustomed to lean his weight on it, and as long as you trusted yourself completely to it, there seemed no chance of its giving way. Centuries ago pious Henry VI had founded the College, and since then, year by year, it had conscientiously petrified all those whose mental equipment enabled them to batten on his bounty. A capacity for learning to write Baboo Greek or digest the splintered bones of history equipped you for teaching others, and, as reward, rooms, food, and a modest but adequate income were given you. Comforting, too, in some odd motherly manner, was this assured stolidity, for his dream last night, emerging, surely, straight from the gates of ivory, had ended, for all its magic of love and worship, in a tumult of nightmare: it was as if some unsleeping sentinel within him had yelled out to him of a lurking and mortal danger and had plucked him from his sleep while yet he was unaware that he had even dozed. That sense of having escaped was with him all day, but the flood of common sense which he poured on it had not extinguished that smouldering sense of peril.

His mind acquiesced, in an attitude at once fervent and superior, when he told it that his dream had been mere rubbish, a haphazard dishing up of hours of his friendship with Steven; and the big sad-eyed boy in the bushes, the squirrel, the fact that he was called upon to interpret Steven's dream, all supplied their verifiable quotas to it. Even the image (though coloured and exaggerated by sleep) of Steven as some young god of the early world, awakening among the olives, was not absolutely a new thought, for Maurice had often harboured embryonic ideas from which this might naturally have developed. But though his mind acquiesced, when he thus talked sensibly to it and confessed to imaginings of fancy and folly, he had no sooner said to himself, "That's all finished with, then," and looked elsewhere for diversion or duty, than out of the corner of his eye, obliquely, he saw still ascending the little coil of smoke, which showed that his squirtings of common sense had not quite extinguished that persistent smoulder.

To his secret perception of fear and unrest, Cambridge with its bland self-sufficiency promised to be an effective sedative, and it was with a medicinal interest, like one taking waters at a spa, that he listened, as just three of them dined in Hall that night, to Stares's Gothic intoxications. He had spent nearly a week instead of two nights with Canon Redcliffe at York, and had catalogued all the scenes in the most famous of the windows. Indeed, he believed that he had made a new and correct identification of one of them, which hitherto had always been supposed to represent Samson asleep, with Delilah coming in on her barber's mission. But occurring as it did, as Stares acutely noticed, between two scenes in the life of Joseph, it more probably illustrated the nefarious advent of Potiphar's wife to the bedchamber of the austere young patriarch.

"Most interesting," said Maurice. "I should say that your identification was undoubtedly correct. But a curious subject surely for a stained-glass window."

Stares easily satisfied him that such unedifying scenes

were by no means rare in thirteenth-century glass; he instanced David and Bathsheba, tipsy Noah, Rahab the harlot, and several others.

"And then on to Ripon," continued Stares, "from which, of course, we saw Fountains Abbey."

Maurice noticed the "of course": it was in the authentic academic manner to say that. All Dons said "of course," when they were alluding to matters which they knew quite well, concerning which they were imparting information to their hearers. He knew that he often said it himself, and it struck him now that his bedmaker used the phrase with equal frequency. His glance strayed over the still sparsely populated tables where the undergraduates dined, unconsciously searching for a face that he knew was not there, and he remembered looking up like that on the evening when Stares was telling them about the projected tour, now so successfully accomplished, and catching Steven's eye. He intended to write to him after Hall.

"And I had the pleasure of convincing Canon Redcliffe that he had much better let his son become an architect," said Stares. "By the way, Torrington, you were quite right about the year in which he rowed for Cambridge. . . . He saw my point at once, namely, the advisability of deferring to a natural taste in the choice of a profession. That was how I put it."

"Very sensible," said Maurice. "I'm glad it worked. But most undergraduates haven't got a natural taste for any profession."

"Many, I allow, have not," said Stares. "That young Gervase of yours, for instance. I could never discover the smallest intellectual leanings in him to any direction whatever. Kicking up a row and looking beautiful is about the sum of his endowments."

Maurice fell into the academic manner almost with enthusiasm. He liked to feel its protective shell.

"Kicking up a row cannot strictly be called an endowment," he observed. "The endowment for it, of course, consists in robust lungs."

Stares was always fair.

"True," he said. "But you must admit it is a natural taste. And then, if that doesn't come to much, he will fall back on looking beautiful by way of a profession."

"I can't even admit that," said Maurice, "as I happen to know that he is to enter his uncle's shipping business when he leaves Cambridge."

"The Gervase Line?" asked Torrington.

"Yes. A good opening, I should think."

"His knowledge of racing craft, of course, will be of service to him," said Stares in his most withering manner. "Probably he thinks that products from the West Indies are conveyed across the Atlantic in outriggers. Ha! ha!"

Torrington laughed too, but intervened.

"I can't have you running Steven Gervase down," he said. "I don't, of course, maintain that he's a very intellectual fellow, but he's a thoroughly pleasant one and by no means a fool."

"And after all, he can't help looking beautiful, poor chap," said Maurice. "That is a burden which most of us are not called upon to bear."

This would all do nicely for his letter to Steven, thought Maurice. . . . "We were very sarcastic about you at the Dons' table to-night. We said you probably thought that you would personally row cargoes of bananas from Jamaica across the Atlantic in an outrigger. But Torrington stuck up for you: he said you were by no means a fool. . . ."

"I'm off to Zermatt to-morrow," said Torrington, "and hope to have three weeks' climbing. The Matterhorn from Breuil on the Italian side is my main objective."

"That, I believe, is where the Whymper accident occurred, is it not?" said Stares.

"No, that was on the Zermatt side," corrected Torrington.

"Possibly. The Matterhorn, I fancy, is the highest mountain in Switzerland after Mont Blanc."

"Mont Blanc," observed Torrington carefully, "is not in Switzerland at all, but in France. And the highest mountain in Switzerland is the Dom."

These were nasty jabs, and Stares thought it wiser to be pleasant.

"I am sure you are right," he said. "Personally I could never see the attraction of climbing, but, of course, there must be some fascination about it. *Chacun à son goût.*"

"I came across an amusing howler over that the other day," said Torrington, as they rose to go to the combination room. "A boy rendered it, 'Everyone has gout.' "

"Ha! ha! Very droll," said Stares. "I can't think where you get all your stories from."

"Uncle's Column in *Classy Cuttings*," thought Maurice, going on mentally with his letter to Steven: "And Torrington was in great form. He goes to Zermatt to-morrow, so picture me dining along with little Stares. No other Dons are up yet, and very few undergraduates, but a lot more of both varieties come up next week. I say, it will be dull here without you. Why aren't you here? I looked for you in Hall to-night, in a sort of absent manner, and if I had seen you there I should have thought it quite natural."

Torrington sipped his port with relish.

"I'm afraid I've got a fly-paper mind, as I saw it rather wittily described the other day," he said. "Small insignificant little things that buzz alight on it for a moment and stick there. But I must be careful about it: as we grow old I'm afraid we tend to tell stories too much. In fact, we don't fall into our dotage, as somebody rather aptly said, but our anecdotage."

"Rather neat," said Stares. "Go on, Torrington: tell us another."

Maurice felt that his eyes were beginning to wear a slightly glazed expression, and he roused himself.

"Really, on the spur of the moment," began Torrington. "Ah, that does remind me of a little *mot:* one of my own, if you'll excuse it."

"Not at all," said Maurice, meaning exactly the opposite.

"Well, down at the river the other day, the Child, Merriman, you know, tore his shorts, in fact, behind. I asked him if he had been sitting down on the spur of the moment. It amused him a good deal."

"That surprises me," said Stares. "Not, of course, Torrington, because your remark wasn't extremely witty, but because I shouldn't have expected Merriman to see the point of anything."

Torrington perked his head sideways, in his favourite judicial attitude.

"I can't quite let that pass," he said. "Merriman's got a certain sense of humour."

"Of a recondite order," said Stares. "I fancy it must have been he who balanced a hat on the statue of the Founder on the night of the boat supper. I imagine that seemed to him exceedingly amusing."

"But did he do it?" asked Maurice.

"Irrelevant, rather?" queried Stares. "I was merely using that as an illustration of what he would think humorous. But I should say that there was no doubt whatever that he did it."

This would do for the letter, and Maurice continued: "Stares said it was quite certain that the Child crowned Henry on the night of the little rag. . . ."

"I remember you made rather a witty observation that night, Crofts," continued Stares, "when we looked out of my window before going down to stop further proceedings. You said that the King had the right to be covered in any assembly."

"Very neat," chuckled Torrington, who was nearly as appreciative of the wit of others as of his own.

Stares rose.

"I'm afraid I can't ask you to have a game of piquet to-night," he said, "for George, George Redcliffe, is coming to my rooms at nine, and we are going over our catalogue of the York windows together and comparing the subjects with those in the chapel here. I have a theory about that which I must not divulge till I have been into the matter with greater minuteness. To-morrow night perhaps, Crofts. We shall be dining alone then, unless some other of our craft arrive. Good-bye Torrington: *au revoir* rather! For I trust the Matterhorn will spare you. I must look up what you told me about the height of the Dom in my Baedeker, for I still rather fancy the Matterhorn is the highest—I should say the higher. Everyone has gout! I must remember that."

Torrington gave a little gentle cackle as the Dean went out. "Good little Stares," he said, "he always knows best, in spite of innumerable proofs to the contrary. His saying '*au revoir*' just now reminded me of the amusing story of the young man who was making a tryst with his girl for the following night at the edge of a lake. So instead of saying, '*au revoir,*' he said, '*au reservoir.*' "

Maurice excused himself from the privilege of personally examining Torrington's ice axe and Alpine rope before he packed them, but noted that in view of his approaching foreign travel his luggage had become his "baggage." His rooms looked very dim and lifeless, as if the lamp which had lit them was not burning. But it was easy to rekindle that: a talk with Steven, even though Steven could not answer him, would make it luminous again, and he pushed some encumbering papers aside to clear a space for his writing. He could hear that Stares was busy next door with Bach's first prelude: he was a little rusty-fingered, presumably from want of practice on the Cathedral tour. The slow movement of Beethoven's Fifth symphony succeeded, but it broke off in the middle, and Maurice conjectured that George Herbert had arrived for the cataloguing of the windows. "High talk," thought Maurice, "about Potiphar's wife."

Though the mental composition of his letter had been so easy and material so abundant, Maurice's pen paused after half a dozen scribbled lines, for now these fragments that fell from the High Table seemed not worth picking up and displaying for Steven's perusal. They might have formed part of the chatter incidental to personal talk, but a letter must reflect the mind of the writer and his preoccupations, and those morsels reflected only the remotest and least focussed part of his mind. Half a dozen lines of them were enough: they would just serve for a humorous introduction to what he really had to say. He put a line of dots after the "*au reservoir*" anecdote in the fashion of novelists who have done with a topic, and started a fresh paragraph.

I'm going to have a dreary time up here without you [he wrote], for to me now Cambridge connotes (good word!) you, and you aren't here. Why did I ever say I would take pupils in the Long? I shouldn't have if we had really met before that. Indeed I've half a mind to chuck the whole thing, and come up to London while you're there, and go on with you to Cornwall. I expect you are more yourself in Cornwall than anywhere else; or did you tell me that? Anyhow, it seems very likely. Oh, I had an odd dream about you last night. You were yourself all right, but at the same time you were a sort of woodland god. . . .

Maurice got as far as this without check, and as he wrote he felt that strange quickening of his inner self which Steven, when personally present, always produced in him. But now as he began telling Steven about that dream he laid down his pen, for that which had ended in the crash of nightmare suddenly surged back in all its biting vividness. He saw, too, how secret it was, and he could hardly tell even Steven about it, for it represented, only too faithfully, perhaps, all that he tried to conceal from himself, and though, so evidently, if he looked at it in the light of academic reasoning, it was a mere fantastic hodge-podge concocted out of random memories by a drowsy brain, it contained something which, quite indefinably from any reasonable standpoint, he recognized to have a truth that scared him. What that was he had no definite idea: it was as if in his dream he had looked on a veiled image underneath the covering of which he divined some shape of terror, something that walked in darkness. Once before, when earlier in that night Steven, with his arm round his neck, had paused on the marble staircase of the house in Carlton House Terrace, and spoke of the end of shams and of false gods, Maurice had felt a touch of that same terror. It and the nightmare ending of his dream had an identical quality.

The ink dried on his paper, and once again, with the relish of relief, he found himself inhaling, in the quietness and emptiness of his room, that aseptic academical air of Cambridge, in which surely no germ of the fantastic could live. There was Stares next door talking about the windows of York Minster to the budding architect, and perhaps outlining the theory that must not yet be publicly announced; there was Torrington packing his rope and his ice axe, and he pictured himself going to one or the other of them and saying: "Have you ever noticed anything queer about Steven Gervase?" And if he explained, as far as explanation was possible, the qualm that had come to him, they would certainly (and how rightly!) be sure that there was something queer about Maurice Crofts. No doubt there was: nothing seemed more likely.

He tore up the letter he had begun; it was ridiculous to write to Steven merely about Dons and their chatterings, and it was impossible to write about real things, when those real things were so monstrously unreal. No doubt he would receive to-morrow morning some brief affectionate scribble from Steven, which would require an answer of similar tone, and in the saner light of morning he would find his own equilibrium again. He was disturbed at its having been upset in much the same way as a man who, feeling in all essential ways perfectly well, may be disturbed at finding that he has a feverish temperature. . . . But there was no such sanity of atmosphere anywhere as that which brooded over these scholastic courts, whether under the gray skies of winter, or, as the clearness of the night promised, under the warm wash of summer sunshine which would enfold them to-morrow. One way or another (and he left it at that) he had had an emotional shaking which clouded the clear liquor of perception. Where it came from and what it meant was quite mysterious, but it was uncomfortable to find that the fact that it was so fantastic confirmed rather than dispelled its reality.

He came into his room next morning, where breakfast was already waiting for him, to find that the post had arrived but that it had brought nothing for him from Steven. Oddly enough, that was rather a relief than otherwise. "Why should he write to me?" thought Maurice to himself. "And why should I write to him? We can neither of us get onto paper any touch of that which exists between us. It's the being together that is the whole of it. Damned fool I was last night. If he's got anything to tell me, he'll do so, and if I've got anything to tell him, ditto. All the same, he might have sent me a postcard, saying: 'I'm here, you're not.' But I might have done just the same to him."

This thoroughly British conclusion proved fortifying when every morning he found that Steven, like himself, had refrained from any communication. Sometimes, eager in spite of himself, he came in half dressed and experienced some odd sinking of the heart when he saw his letterless table, and the involuntary question would flash across his mind, red with danger, as to whether Steven had tired of him, whether he had finished with him, as he had finished, apparently without the smallest pang of regret or tender memory, with the Child. Yet he himself had not written to Steven, and Steven might be saying, with equal justice, just the same about him, and the absurdity of that made him view his own absurdity in the same light. Sometimes again, in the evening, when the session of Dons was over, and when he had played an acid game or two of piquet with Stares, he would feel that he could no longer endure to make no sign to Steven. But always next morning, when he saw his own barren breakfast table, an obstinacy bred of common sense made him put the impulse aside. If he had anything definite and concrete to say to Steven, then by all means he would write. Till then he would follow Steven's example (or was Steven following his?) and use his pen for other purposes.

Meantime the days started with a slow pace of passage, and then, as is the way of them when they are spent in repeated routine, they clicked by with accelerated motion. He had half a dozen pupils, whom he coached daily, two at a time, and their instruction took up three solid hours of the morning, while later in the day he was busy preparing for to-morrow's lecturing. The habit of exercise drove him out of doors in the afternoon; sometimes there would be tennis, sometimes, after the Provost's return from Aix, he would play croquet with that swindling clergyman, but more often he took a boat, and rowed himself up the river. This was directly Stevenish, for his efforts at oarsmanship had always provoked high mirth, and it was pleasing to think that when they went on the water again, whether in Cornwall or here, he would astonish his friend with a touch of his own unconscious ease. But so far from this budding accomplishment being a reason for letter writing, it was exactly the opposite, for it was designed to be a surprise, an amazement when they met. Thus it was frequently that he scooped his difficult way up to Byron's pool, sweating and cursing at the shoals, the presence of which Steven seemed to divine, but with a secret pride, silly and boyish and old-maidish, in his attainment of efficiency. And surely the river was lower in this August heat than it had been when they were here together: Steven himself would probably have been aground half a dozen times now, round these blasted corners. . . . Arrived at his destination he would strip and bathe, and then lie out in the sun just where they lay together on the day that the squirrel came bouncing through the tall grass in answer to that wordless invitation. Often he saw it or one of its kinsmen climbing among the trees, and he tried to relax, as Steven had said, and *be* a squirrel. Of course it was no use (there was the donnish "of course" again!) for Steven had told him that it was hopeless to practise the stunt like a conjuring trick. And then he would forget about the squirrel, and his mind lay still, soaking perhaps into the ground, until Steven's presence began to distil itself, drop by drop, from the air of the August afternoon. Most of all, then, he longed for him, most of all, then, he felt he must write to him, but even more he felt that, as wordlessly as the spell that brought the squirrel, they had made a pact with each other to be separate in body and soul, till September brought them together again. Sometimes, as in the nightmare ending of his dream, he said aloud: "Steven, Steven!" and he would hardly have been surprised if Steven's voice had answered him, or if he had seen him girt with a bathing towel, stretched by his side. The terror of the dream and of that moment's fear of him withered in these solitary haunted hours, dispersing like a puff of bitter dust, and he wondered in what aberration of the spirit he could ever have conceived it.

Day by day the date on which he would join him in Cornwall crept closer. Within three weeks, within a fortnight, and now within a week, the term would be over. He would be obliged to write before long, suggesting the actual day on which he would arrive at Trenair; and then again the notion that Steven had finished with him peered white-faced into his mind. Would Steven write back to say that as he had not heard from him, he had concluded that his promise to come was only vague and tentative, and that, with many regrets, his mother would not find it very convenient to receive him? They would meet at Cambridge in October, and he hoped that Maurice had been enjoying the term. . . . Again and again he chased the idea away, not letting it settle on him, but it remained hovering, impalpable, and shrilly trumpeting.

The last days of the term had come, and now, regretting his own long silence, and bitterly wondering what had caused Steven's, he knew he must do something. Yet still the impression that there was a silent understanding between them remained. Then, during his pupils' hours one morning, the porter appeared with a telegram for him. The moment he saw it there was no doubt in his mind from whom it came, but his fingers trembled as he opened it.

I expect you any day now [he read]. Will meet you at Penzance. Telegraph day and hour of your arrival. STEVEN.

"Excuse me a moment," he said, and he scribbled on the reply-paid form the date two days hence, and the train he had looked up weeks before in the A.B.C.

PART II

CHAPTER VI

STEVEN had slid away eastwards with the revolving earth as Maurice walked away from Carlton House Terrace on that taxiless night, and this morning as the great train swung along towards Cornwall a similar image presented itself of the earth spinning under its motionless wheels, and of Steven drawing nearer from the west. . . . Maurice made a festival of the journey, his mind invested it with the glowing colours of some adventure delightful in itself. He arrived at Paddington with a full twenty minutes to spare, and as soon as the long line of stately coaches had been hauled into the station by a bustling little engine that reminded him of a charwoman, he secured a corner seat facing the direction of travel in his corridor carriage, engaged a place in the luncheon car, bought a couple of illustrated papers, and then went to see the great monster of a locomotive strangely christened "Edward VI" backed onto the train. With such precision was it handled, and so exact its obedience, that the hind buffers of the coal-piled tender seemed just to kiss those of the first coach, and with this salutation it was coupled up, and the vacuum brake connected with a little fizz as of a syphon.

Edward had a mere stump of a funnel, three pairs of driving wheels, linked by coupling rods, and, slightly impatient to be gone, though behaving beautifully, he sent out a small hissing streamer from the safety valve as an intimation that he was quite ready. The driver came out of his cab, oil can in hand, and, holding onto the handrail along the boiler, fed a couple of oil cups near the cylinders. In front was a four-wheeled bogey, and Maurice longed to be allowed to sit on this, with his back against the smoke box, and see the riband of the line open out like torn linen as they raced westwards. Meantime the stoker was shovelling coal into the open mouth of the furnace and raked down more from the piled tender to be ready for the monster's meals.

The driver came back from his excursion, glanced at the pressure gauge and turned a handle, and the sizzling of escaping steam rose to a roar; then he leaned carelessly and at ease over the side of the cab, looking back down the platform. There were now but a few minutes more, and Maurice made his way through a grove of clanking milk cans and past three coaches and the restaurant car to his compartment. He settled himself in, and presently, without whistle or jerk or any sense of motion, the bookstall and the station clock and the refreshment room began to slide off eastwards on the revolving earth.

The enchantment of travelling continued to weave its spell. He knew really that it was due in the main to the anticipation of what and of whom awaited him when the earth should cease from its revolving and come to a stop when he reached Penzance, but it still had a magic of its own. The stations swam by, faster and faster, the great train squealed and roared through Slough, jerking aside over its shoulder the branch line to Windsor. The Thames at Maidenhead was like some narrow ditch, taken in a stride, a local train puffing industriously along in their direction was passed as if it had been stationary, and by the side of the line the lyre of telegraph-wires dipped and rose again between the posts.

After Reading they passed into a land of streams with cattle standing knee deep among ragged-robin and meadow-sweet, and soon cornfields were flying past, where the earth showed red through the bristles of the cut stubbles. Then came the summons to lunch, and the first stop at Exeter. Yet still the train did not seem to have moved: the earth had turned under it. Red cliffs and beaches fringed with the liquid rims of the sea moved past, and thereafter Plymouth, and they drew out again over the Saltash bridge into Cornwall, the land of ancient kings and sorceries. There were spider-webbed viaducts across gashed valleys with streams and treetops far below, and burrowings among steep hills.

The names of stations grew liquid and foreign, Menheniot and Lostwithiel and Double Bois, and then came Truro, with the estuary of the Fal beyond, and its houses lying dwarfed and huddled round the cathedral. Through the open window blew a soft languid air, laden with a breath of something more remote and antique than Christianity. Soon, opposite Marazion, St. Michael's Mount floated on a full sea, and the world slowed finally down as the train crawled into Penzance. . . . He was standing on the platform, hatless and golden and browned with sun, in a rough blue jersey and sea-stained flannels, looking up at the coaches sliding by, and Steven had come up from the west with the revolving earth.

Maurice's luggage was soon collected, and a porter, with whom Steven chattered, wheeled it out of the station to where an extremely ramshackle motor was waiting.

"Sometimes she moves fine, and sometimes she's rare and powerful at standing still, Dan'l," said Steven. "She went beau'ful, she did, coming from Trenair, aw, my dear, she ran like a hen when the farmer's wife goes to wring her neck for denner. Now, maybe, she'll sit and squeal like a rabbit when the weasel's after him."

Steven spoke, Maurice noticed, with an accent soft and mellow, as if it had been a breeze off the sea, and just so did Daniel answer him.

"A turrible machine, sure she is, Mas'r Steven dear," he said. "I wonder that you and your golden hair are not afeard to get aboard her."

"Afeard?" said Steven. "Why, dear soul, my belly's whambling to think of it. She's a spiteful bitch, too, ever on the growl and the snap. Thank ye, Dan'l. Good-bye, unless so be you'd like to take a ride along of we."

"Aw, my dear, indeed no," said Daniel. "I'd sooner walk every yard to Trenair and further too, than tempt the Lord so. My respects to your lady-mother, Mas'r Steven."

The car throbbed and shook as with some deadly ague, then suddenly sprang forward, rattling like a covey of skeletons.

"Here we go, and she's going to behave like a scared cat, bless her heart," said Steven, speaking again with the clipped English intonation. "Praise her, Maurice: say you've driven in a hundred Rolls-Royces, but never yet have you felt such smooth going."

"She's a beauty, a regular beauty," shouted Maurice, as the car scampered round a hairpin corner. "New, too, I see, without a speck of enamel off her. And eighty to a hundred horsepower, I daresay."

"That's good, she likes that," said Steven. "But that's enough. If you say much more she'll think you're pulling her leg, and that she cannot endure. Mad Maria is how we know her hereabouts, but call her Miss Maria till you know her better. And don't distract my attention till we get up this hill. Once on the top we're fairly safe till we get to the dip leading down into the combe. But very often the brakes act perfectly."

The hill was surmounted with brilliant success, but in silence, except for Maria.

"Ha," said Steven, as they topped the final ridge. "Well, Maurice?"

He turned to him radiant and smiling.

"Yes, I'm here," said Maurice.

"So am I. Very much here, in fact. I've not been entirely here without you. And why didn't you write to me?"

"Or you to me?" asked Maurice.

"I tried to once or twice, but it was no use. I knew you couldn't understand anything I had got to say from here, until you had come."

"Understand what?" asked Maurice.

"It; everything; you; me. What Trenair is and what we are. You'll have to let yourself go; you'll have to let it soak into you."

"That's what I came for—that and you," said Maurice. "And on my side, what was I to write to you about? I tried to the first night I was at Cambridge, and told you about little Stares. But then I tore it up: not a particle of good."

"I rather loved you for not writing," said Steven, "because I guessed the reason, which was exactly what you've told me. It showed your good sense. But now you've got to tip your good sense overboard. No use for it here and no demand."

The road lay for a mile or two over a bare and featureless upland, set in stone walls. Here and there was a copse of stunted wind-combed trees, and a more prosaic and duller stretch of country could not be imagined. The sea had slipped out of sight, and there was little sign of habitation: they passed only a small pinched farm or two, with dilapidated sheds and an air of decay. Then came a branch road dipping steeply down on the left between a disused shale quarry, and a small stream that trickled from a wayside spring.

"And now we'll know about the brakes," said Steven cheerfully. "Yes, I believe they're going to work."

With the swift dipping of the road the flanking hills on each side grew tall, rising in steep spaces of grass, and sown with clumps of gorse that spread an added sunshine on them. The combe into which they were descending broadened out from the narrow neck at its head, and soon the road lay through a strip of wood, while the runnel of water from the spring above, reinforced by streamlets from the hills on either side, expanded into gravelly pools the margins of which were fringed with cress, and the rocks round which it skirted with fronds of fern. The hills retreated farther yet with the widening valley, then came a sharp angle in the road, and as they turned it, suddenly the sea sprang up to meet them high against the steep contour of the hills.

Far below spread out a sandy bay with a small pier for the harbourage of the fishing boats, and a little above it clustered the gray roofs of the village, not more than a score, all told, with skeins of smoke adrift over them. The hills were far sundered now, and stretched to right and left in lines of tumbled cliff which bordered the shining expanses of the gorse and green, and a breeze fragrant with its blossoming, and spiced with the sea-scent, drove up through the valley, setting the treetops stirring. At this corner they turned out of the road that led down to the village and saw the house where they were bound, mellow-gray and creeper clad, set a little above them in this amphitheatre of the hills: a wood of poplar and hazel clothed the slope below between it and the village.

A short steep rise, between bushes that brushed the sides of the car, brought them onto the level where the house stood: a mossy lawn faced it, and up to its low gables climbed fuchsia trees and magnolia. Above it rose the rampart of gorse-golden hill, and the whole valley, secret and sequestered, closed in below by the sea, and surrounded on the landward from the haunts of men by those miles of empty and austere plateau, was like some fairy dell brought into being by the waving of a wand and a muttered incantation. Everything else in the world seemed to Maurice suddenly remote: here, visible, and invisible, was all that was real and that mattered.

Steven woke echoes from the hillside with a blast of his motor horn as they crackled over the gravel.

"Mother's sure to be out," he said, "so it's no use looking for her. Tea, don't you think, while they unpack for you, and then you can change into proper clothes, and we'll go out, too."

Maurice made himself, as Steven said, "more decent" and presently the two young men took a path through the wood of poplars down to the village. The path was narrow and much encroached on by thickets of hazel, and the roof of poplar leaves flickered and danced above them in the sea breeze. The ground for the most part declined steeply, but here and there were flat plots of a few yards in extent, as if at one time the hill had been terraced for vineyards. On one of these, considerably larger than the rest, and in the very heart of the wood, were some fragments of ruined walls, from the crevices in which sprouted the hair-like stems of spleen-wort and creeping tendrils of some minute mauve-coloured snapdragon.

"What a strange place to build a house," said Maurice, pointing at these walls, "with only just this path to it, and huddled among the trees."

"It's older by a long way than the trees," said Steven, "and perhaps it wasn't a house. It's thought to be the remains of a church. Not Christian, of course, but earlier even. A temple, they say."

"And all these little terraces?" asked Maurice.

"They must certainly have been made for cultivation, and the odd thing is that the wild vine, which you won't find anywhere else near here, grows everywhere over the hillside: tangles of it, mixed with ivy. Look, there's one in fruit, close to you. You can't call them grapes any longer, just berries. Grape-like, though, still to the taste; try them."

Maurice picked a cluster of these, five or six berries growing together, an embryo, or rather a degeneration, of a bunch, and crushed them into his mouth.

"They're like grapes an enormous distance off," he said.

Steven laughed.

"That's hit it," he said. "It's just what they are. At

least, botanists say that they are degenerated vintage grapes brought from goodness knows where."

Maurice spat out a blob of skin and stones.

"I know you told me something about this wood once," he said; "it's familiar to me. Ah! I remember: you were coming up through it with your nurse, and it was here you saw your horned uncle."

"Right again; you're making wonderfully good shots to-day, it was exactly here. He came plunging through that very thicket of hazels, looking just like an illustration out of the Dictionary of Mythology. A jolly little beggar. I wish he hadn't died, for I'm sure I should have been friends with him. I should have understood him all right."

September, as Maurice knew, was a silent month for birds, and it struck him now how vocal the place was with song. Blackbirds were richly fluting as in February, and thrushes as in nesting time. From somewhere among the treetops a green woodpecker laughed; a company of goldfinches were swinging on thistle heads in one of these open spaces of clearing, picking out the ripe seeds, and as the two approached they rose with dipping flight into the air and with soft whistlings. Presently they came to the lower edge of the trees, and now the smell of sea and wood smoke overscored the odour of its greenness. The village lay in shadow, so, too, the sea behind the western headland, though farther out it gleamed like a shield of roughly hammered gold, and high above them the gorse-clad cliff to the east flamed with blossom and sunlight. The tide was low, and half a dozen fishing boats lay stranded and slanting on the pebbles and sand of the harbour, sheltered by the little pier.

"It'll be high tide about midnight," said Steven, "and they'll go out fishing then. Some night we'll go with them and see the dawn on the water. That's the loveliest thing on earth, a moment when everything is rose coloured. That's what I should like to look on when I'm dying."

"Oh, put that off," said Maurice. "It would annoy me horribly."

There were but few folk about in the village, and those women. One or two were knitting at their doors, or mending the clothes of their men; two or three more, with the carriage of figures from some classical frieze, were bringing home from the spring big water pots which they bore nobly on their heads; another, young and active, was herding up the road a heavy-teated sow with a numerous farrow of piglets, which tugged at her for refreshment and scampered into the open doors of cottages, and ran between the legs of their inhabitants.

But all those who were sitting, Maurice noticed, rose to their feet as Steven passed, and the water carriers, with a hand to steady their burdens, curtsied to him, dimpling with smiles, and their eyes grew gay at his approach. He had a word for each of them in that broad soft tongue of his country, and he chased one of the piglets, which had turned into a backyard, and brought it, squealing, out, nursing it.

"Aw, Master Steven dear," said the girl who drove them, "thank you kindly indeed, but don't you muck yourself. Little devils, bain't they?"

"Iss, sure," said Steven, "and they'll be frizzling like little devils bymeby. How's Brother Tim, Janet?"

"He's fine. Been bathing and decking himself and piping his songs all day. 'Tis the full moon, and that's a rare time for him, poor lamb. But he ought to be coming home for his supper now, for he's eaten nought all day but berries in the wood, maybe, which wouldn't nourish a throstle, let alone such a big lad as he's growing. And liker to you, Master Steven, every day, though I shouldn't say that."

Steven laughed.

"And for why not, Janet?" he said. "We'll tell Tim to get home for his supper if we meet him."

At the end of the village the road came to an abrupt end against the hillside; from there only a sandy track, deep-rutted with the wheels of the hand carts that plied from the harbour to the village laden with fish, or round pebbles of the shingle for building, or seaweed for burning, led to the head of the beach.

"And here he's coming himself," said Steven. "It's Janet's brother, Tim. Don't be surprised at anything, Maurice. He's quite harmless."

Strolling along the shore towards them came a strange and beautiful figure, a boy of seventeen or eighteen, naked but for a pair of tattered breeches, with his skin tanned to iodine brown by the sun and the sea. A wreath of ivy and wild-vine was twined in his yellow hair, and to his mouth he held a reed-pipe on which he blew squealing sounds. There were but three notes to it, and sometimes he marched to his music, as if with processional solemnity, or quickening his time danced to it. So intent was he on his occupation that he did not see them till they were close to him. Then lifting his eyes from his pipe as he flung back his head in some corybantic gesture, he stood poised a moment, and then ran to Steven's feet and knelt there.

"Eh, Tim, but you mustn't do that," said Steven. "We settled to have none of that. Up you get."

Tim sprang to his feet and stood before him with eyes lowered. The likeness between the two was amazing, not alone in face and features and in crop of yellow hair, but in limb and build. Like Steven's, Tim's neck rose thick and round from low level shoulders, broad-chested was he, and slim-waisted, long-thighed and narrow of hip, and his feet, uncramped by usage of shoes, were not splayed and flat, but high-instepped, and delicately made even as were his hands.

Steven laid his hand on the boy's shoulder.

"Look up, Tim," he said. "Tell Mr. Crofts and me what you've been doing."

Tim looked up, grave and eager.

"I bathed in the morning," he said, "and when the sun grew hot I slept in the woods. I've made a pipe too, 'tis the best I've fashioned yet, Master Steven. Look! Rarely made it is!"

He held out his reed: he had cut it whistle-shaped at one end, and pierced two holes in it, smooth and well-rounded.

"Why, that's clever of you, Tim!" said Steven. "Give us a tune on it."

Tim put his pipe to his mouth and began playing, and with the sound of it his shyness vanished, and his eye, fixed on Steven, sparkled and smiled. There were but three notes in its compass, but they were clear and mellow, though shrill. Sometimes he made two of them, by rapid alternation, bubble like a musical shake, and he answered it with long repeated single notes. Tune there was none, but there underlay the performance some loose rhythm of joy, as when a bird sings and its mate answers it in that language of bird song which makes phrases of ecstatic import.

"Very good music, Tim," said Steven when the boy ceased. "I like it. Did you make it?"

"Aw, no. 'Twas what I heard when I woke from my sleep this day; 'twas in the bushes, just like that."

"Birds singing?" asked Steven.

"No, Master Steven: 'twasn't a bird. 'Twas music for dancing. I dance to it, too. Shall I show?"

"Yes, show us. Dance up the road to your house," said Steven, "for Janet's driven the pigs home, and she said it was time for you to get your supper. We'll watch you."

Tim began his tune again, and to its music he strutted up the road with slow steps, pausing and poising on each. Then quickening up his feet and his notes, he threw back his head, and broke into wilder measures and extravagant prancings, yet with some inborn inevitable grace of motion. At the door of one of the houses not fifty yards distant he stopped and leaped over the threshold.

"That's the happiest fellow I know," said Steven, "and he is as mad as a hatter. He's a cousin of sorts, as you may guess, all along of a girl in the village and my wicked old grandfather."

"But whom does he take you to be?" asked Maurice. "Why did he kneel to you?"

"Goodness knows. He spends half his day chanting and praying in the woods; he makes little shrines there, and as far as I can understand I've become part of his religion, whatever that may be. I wish he could tell us what it was. Something goes on in his brain, but he can't explain it. He's only just taken to that kneeling business; he told me he learned it. But I've told him he must unlearn it. I find it rather embarrassing to be knelt to."

They strolled on towards the little pier that ran out of the hillside at the entrance of the harbour; it was but thirty yards long, but it served to make a pool of quiet water when the surf was rolling in from seaward. The tide was beginning to flow again across the sandy beach, at the top of which, across a belt of shingle, lay smooth spaces of short grass, tufted with thyme and thrift, where the fishing nets were spread. Their owners were rolling them up again now for the night fishing, when the tide would be high; others were sitting smoking on the low parapet of the pier. Like the women in the village they all rose on Steven's approach, and all had for him the smile and the bright eye of welcome; clearly with their deference there was mixed an eager affection.

"Be ye gwine fishing along o' we to-night, Mas'r Steven?" asked one of them. "A rare catch we'll bring back, for 'tis the full moon of September, and the waters riot with fish then."

"Not to-night, Jan Pentreath," said Steven, "for my

friend Mr. Crofts has newly come from Cambridge in England, and I'll be biding at whoam."

He made a general gesture introducing Maurice to the company. He guessed what he should do, and shook hands with the whole half-dozen of them.

"Been in the train all day, sir?" asked Jan Pentreath. "Them mucky trains; thank the Lord, I never put foot in such since I was born."

Maurice felt quite cordial, but his manner somehow lacked the naturalness of habit.

"I'm sure I don't wonder," he said. "If you live at Trenair, why should you ever want to go away?"

Maurice looked at Jan Pentreath; he was a handsome straight-featured fellow, yellow haired and yellow bearded, and he saw that they were all of this type, fair men tanned by the sun, except one, a bent little man, black eyed and gray. He was conscious, too, that he was being quietly observed, in the pause that followed his polite speech.

"Eh, 'tis well said," piped up this old man. "Twoscore year it is since I came here from beyond Tamar, and I've not been in a train since. Messy, noisome things, not fit to carry aught but cattle and the catch of the sea. Nor ever shall I, and when I'm put in my coffin 'twill be only to make the journey to St. Buryan's yard."

Steven laughed.

"But who's to make your coffin for you, Tom Evans," he said, "when you're dead and gone?"

"Eh, I've made it already, and it's lain by my bedside more'n a year," said Tom Evans, "and when my rheumatics are bad I often think 'twill be easier lying there than in my bed."

"A rare good bit of sense in that," said Jan Pentreath. "Poor old Sally Morgan, she'll rest more comfortable in the coffin you're making for her, Tom Evans, than ever she did these weeks agone in her bed."

"Is Sally Morgan dead?" asked Steven. "Poor soul!"

"Eh, but she suffered cruel, Mas'r Steven, with that lump in her innards," said Jan Pentreath; " 'twas a rare release when she went out. He found her dead, did George Morgan, this morning at daybreak." He turned briskly to Maurice, as if hurrying away a gloomy subject. "And you're staying for long, sir?" he asked.

"A week or two, perhaps," said Maurice.

"Don't you believe him, Jan Pentreath," said Steven, "he's not come all this way for just to say good-night and good-morning."

"And you'll not be leaving us, never no more, we all do hope, Mas'r Steven," said Tom Evans, "when you come of age in the spring, but bide here."

"No such luck for me," said Steven. "I shall be biding at my work in London town. But I'll be back often, and some day, sure, I'll bring a wife with me."

"Eh, do," said Jan Pentreath, "and beget a dozen lusty sons. But choose her Cornish, and one who'll belong to us like your lady mother."

Steven laughed.

"Time for all that," he said. "But my mother will be expecting us at the house. Good-night, all, and may your net do all but break with your catch. I'll be out with you before the moon dwindles far."

Maurice went up to bed that night without a thought of getting to sleep, so full was his brain of strange bright images, which kept slipping aside as he tried to fix and focus them. They gleamed and beckoned, and when he set himself to study any of them, it dissolved into some other shape that allured and eluded. After Steven himself (and he somehow was harder to focus than ever) there came his mother: she had given him the kindliest of welcomes for her son's sake, and time and again during the evening Maurice had seemed to catch a hint that already she was liking him for his own. . . .

And then suddenly she would withdraw herself, and though her body was still in the chair next him on the lawn where they sat in the soft warm air under the blaze of the moonlight, and though she was still even speaking to him, she, her real self, had whisked away. It was not a mere absent-mindedness that played this disconcerting trick, it was a complete vanishing, as if, by a gift inherited from that great-grandmother of hers (who, as Steven had said, was a fairy rather than a witch) she had slid on to another plane of existence altogether and had vanished from human sense into the wood where the wild vines grew. In that she was like Steven, who had just that habit of suddenly withdrawing himself, and in that abrupt way he had of dismissing a subject even while you listened with eager attention to what he was saying.

But physically mother and son could hardly have been more dissimilar: she was small and dark in colouring, instead of his tall stature and fairness; she had little twinkling eyes, as black as sloes, small features that bunched themselves up together in the middle of her face, like the markings on a pansy, when she laughed. She laughed often, and her laughter was like that of a child of five, amused from top to toe; she made little staccato gestures when she spoke, she asked innumerable questions, and punctuated the replies with humorous little observations—and then, presto, she was not there any more. . . .

Maurice, lying with his face turned to the open window, tried again and again to fix her down, to form a coherent whole of her, but she was elusive, she flitted away, just as he thought he had got her, and next, in the manner of a student, he tried the place and the people, with a view to getting a comprehensive impression of them. Here, besides his own observation, he had learned something of them and their history, and the two sources together gave material for a fascinating picture.

This valley of Trenair with its handful of fisher folk

formed a little kingdom of its own, and undeniably Steven was the crown of it. They intermarried among themselves, seldom seeking a wife from outside, and though Cornish in blood, there was thought to be a stray strain of some other nationality altogether, which persisted in that big fair-haired type, as strongly as the type of Gervase, which doubtless sprang from the same, produced by the indiscretions of Steven's grandfather, persisted in that strange mad boy, who so marvellously resembled him. The Gervase blood had stamped Tim with that fineness of build and feature, because it had been impressed on a kindred clay. A strange legend it was that Steven had told him, how the Phœnicean traders who in antique days undoubtedly voyaged to Cornwall from the Mediterranean, had brought with them Greek women raped from the islands of the Ægean, and how some of these, with Greek slaves who manned the oars, had been rescued from a sinking vessel at the mouth of the harbour, and thus the ancient blood of Greece still flowed in the veins of these folk. Historically the thing was possible enough, and the type of these fishermen certainly supplied a confirmation of it, for the fairness and the beauty of them was not that of a Northern race: theirs was just the rich warm fairness of the Greeks, and theirs their straight-featured faces. Tim and Steven might have been models for the sculptor when he wrought the equestrian procession of youths on the Frieze of the Parthenon, and not less might Jan Pentreath have sat for one of the bearded gods of Olympus on the pediment, and those water-carrying women in the village have filled their pitchers at the Ilyssus.

Some fidget of disquiet and energy twitched at Maurice, and he got up and went to the window. The moon still rode high, the stars were dim in that superb wash of light, and on the sea twinkled another cluster of redder tone from the fishing fleet now far out from land. Close by an owl was richly hooting as it quested for its food, and even as Maurice leaned out, it swept whitely over the lawn, checked with a swift backwater of its wings, and then came the short squeak of a mouse, acid as the sound of a slate pencil. Straight before him, motionless in the tranquil air, stood the wood of poplars with its hazel thickets, dropping towards the village in a staircase of terraces which the wild vine wreathed and festooned. Steven had said that possibly it had once been a slope of southern-facing vineyards, and that some temple had stood on that clearing still toothed with ruined walls, and this again fitted in strangely well with the legend of rescued Greeks from a Phœnicean ship having settled here. It might thus be true that a temple had been built here by these exiles in honour of Dionysus, the god of the grape, and that round it they had levelled vineyards and planted them with grafts from Attic hills or Ægean islands.

Then his fancy, still lightly tethered, escaped from its bonds, and he pictured how, in dim dawns and flushed evenings, processions came winding up the hillside to the temple: the priest would stand at the door facing eastwards and wait for the rising of the sun to make sacrifice, and by him, piping the hymn to Dionysus and crowned with ivy, knelt the youthful acolytes. To their conception and belief Fauns and Dryads, spirits of the woodland, haunted the thickets and formed the rout of the joyous god, and sometimes these were visible to mortal eye, so that some minister of the temple or fervent worshipper passing by the precinct at night might see the screening thicket thrust aside, and one of those presences peering out, gay and kindly, from the dusk of the branches, horned and half human.

Distant as the lights of the fishing fleet, a notion, wild and fantastic, flickered at Maurice out of the dark places of his mind. He laughed at himself. "The place has bewitched me," he thought. "I'm silly and moonstruck and hypnotized. I shall go to sleep."

He got back into bed again, but the resolution to go to sleep had little weight behind it. He had extinguished with a summary douche of common sense that fantastic flicker, but his mind went back to the thought of the temple which might once have stood on the hillside. Collateral reflections suggested themselves: he had noticed, for instance (thinking of temples), that there was no church at Trenair, and, what was more remarkable in so strongly Wesleyan a county, no chapel. He had asked Mrs. Gervase about this, and she had replied with a guilty gesture of raised deprecatory hands, which had set Steven laughing.

"I know; most shocking, is it not?" she said. "Very pagan indeed. Of course, we are really in some other parish; that must be so, mustn't it? and I think it is St. Buryan's. But that's a long way off, and such a steep hill to climb, and after all, Sunday is a day of rest, and so the people don't go to St. Buryan's very much. Then there are the Wesleyans: earnest people, and they did begin to build a chapel for us, but somehow it never came to anything."

This set Steven off laughing again.

"Darling, what a hypocrite you are, pretending to be shocked," he said. "Tell Maurice about the chapel."

"Well, it was a very curious thing," she said, "and never entirely explained. The bricklayers used to come from St. Buryan in the morning and be busy all day laying their bricks and go back there in the evening. But when they came next day they would find that all the bricks they had laid the day before had disappeared. Not a trace of them. No one knew whc had been so mischievous and destructive. Most mysterious."

"Oh, you liar," said Steven. "Every man in the village had been mischievous and destructive. I daresay you had a hand in it yourself."

Her face bunched itself together as she gave that delicious little gust of laughter.

"Never, never," she said. "I thought it was a great shame, all that trouble and those pretty bricks and nothing to show for them! I suppose our people didn't feel they needed a chapel: that was how it was. They liked to be left free to go to St. Buryan's if they wished, or to that new chapel on the Penzance road."

"But did nothing happen?" Maurice had asked. "Didn't the contractors try to find out who had taken the bricks away? Surely they could have discovered that, if, as Steven says, every man in the village was concerned in it, and brought an action for damages?"

Mrs. Gervase laughed again. Maurice could not imagine what he had said that moved her mirth.

"Oh, no, that wouldn't have been any good in Trenair," she said. "No one would have told tales in Trenair. They did put someone to watch one night, but that was no use. He was found next day all trussed up like a hen and with his eyes bandaged, on the road to Penzance. And then they saw, the good Wesleyans, that nobody wanted a chapel, and that if they had finished it nobody would have come near it. A dreadful scene there was one day, before they quite gave up the idea, for the minister came over from Penzance, and called the wrath of God down on the village. Such a violent man and so un-Christian, was it not? But nothing happened: the fishing was wonderful that year, and never a touch of sickness nor a death. Perhaps we're a little old-fashioned in Trenair in matters of religion."

At last Maurice was beginning to get sleepy. This remark of Mrs. Gervase's had completely puzzled him at the time, but now, drowsily, he applied the piece, a queer bit from a jig-saw puzzle, to the rest, and it seemed likely to fit in: the temple, if such it was, in the poplar wood, for instance, had a complementary outline; Steven and Tim hovered near it. He was just awake enough to perceive that this brilliant idea was nonsense, and the nonsense and brilliance alike became of one texture.

The tide was flowing next morning when the two went down after breakfast to bathe, but as yet there was no depth of water round the pier, and a bathe from a boat or from one of the beaches outside seemed preferable. But before they had come down to the harbour, with their towels about their necks, their intention seemed to have been anticipated, and there was Jan Pentreath with a boat ready for them. The full moon last night had done what was expected of her, and there had been a monstrous haul of mackerel, and the whole village, men and women alike, were busy lading a trawler to sail round to Penzance; when that was full there was cargo for another, and the hand carts were being trundled up and down the sandy track to where on the road a trolley was being loaded for distribution inland. So Steven sent Jan Pentreath back to his work and said that he and Maurice would manage the boat for themselves. There was a crowd of workers round the place where the nets had been drawn up on shore, and now Tim, as soon as he saw Steven, came running out from among them. He wore his wreath of ivy, twined fresh that morning, and in his hand he held a mackerel which he was eating raw.

"May I row you, Mas'r Steven?" he asked. "Doo'ee let me come on the watter with you and row for you."

Maurice felt a qualm of shuddering disgust. In spite of his physical splendour, this daft boy with his gnawed fish, eaten as a man eats a biscuit, and with his lips and chin bloody and fish scaled, was more animal than human. But Steven had no shudderings for him: he smiled a welcome for him.

"Iss sure," he said, speaking in broad dialect, "sure you shall come along of we on the watter, my dear. But you'm all mucky, Tim, and stinking of your breakfast. Eat till your belly's content, and then, for shame, go and rinse yourself clean o' they messes."

Tim took one huge mouthful more of his fish, then threw the rest away and ran down to the sea and splashed in, breeches and ivy wreath and all. Waist high in the inflowing tide, he scrubbed and cleaned himself, and out he came again with the sea water dripping from him, none other indeed than the young Bacchus of Tintoret coming up from the waves with the wedding ring of Venice in his hand. Of Maurice he took no notice whatever and let him scramble into the boat, but for Steven he pulled it up farther, to steady it.

He rowed them out round the end of the pier; the sea was glassy still, hardly flecked by the runes of the flowing tide, and the reflection of the eastward cliffs on its surface scarcely wavered. Steven was gazing down on the water from the stern of the boat, and presently he called to Maurice.

"Look down below," he said, "if you want to know what happened to the bricks of the Wesleyan chapel which never got itself built."

Maurice looked: three or four fathoms down through the clear water lay a sandy bottom with ribs of rock, and among them, softly wavering in the water's movement, lay multitudes of bright new red bricks, scattered over the sea floor.

He burst out laughing; this too was Trenair.

"And everybody knew?" he asked.

"Naturally, since everybody did it. But never a soul outside Trenair knew. What do you take us for?"

Tim joined in.

"We worked hard, Mas'r Steven, we did," he said, "for they bricklayers were handy, and 'twas hard to keep pace. Night after night we carried the bricks down to the shore and laded the boats up wi' en, and tipped 'em over. 'Twas rare sport though to see the faces of them fellows from

St. Buryan's when they came back in the morning, and we all looking butter smooth and wondering."

Steven had kicked off his shoes and peeled off trousers and jersey.

"Hold her up, Tim," he said. "I'll drop in here."

"An' may I bathe too, Mas'r Steven?" he asked. "Lemme come into the water with ye."

"Why, of course, Tim."

The two popped overboard like water rats, with scarcely a splash, and Maurice followed. Creature of the woodland though he was, Tim seemed hardly less native to the sea. He did not seem to swim, if by swimming were meant those kickings and writhings and strugglings by which men have learned to be locomotive in the water. He ran, he strolled, he lay, he burrowed down to the sand below and brought up one of those admired bricks, dropped it, and caught it up before it had reached sea bottom again. Then vaulting straight from the water into the boat with only a hand on the stern, he rowed, towing the others, to a yellow beach of sand enclosed in a half circle of bush-clad cliff, where they lay sunning. His wreath had been lost in the water, and he wandered off along the thicketed slope and returned with a new crown of berried bryony. There was not one touch of self-consciousness about him: he wore his crown as a man puts on his hat, and dispensed with clothes as a man sheds an overcoat.

Steven lay with his arm across his eyes against the strong ray of the noon, and Tim sat at his feet. Maurice noticed that a fly settled on the boy's shoulder, and he dislodged it, as a horse does, with a twitch of his skin. Some spell of jubilant tranquillity seemed to be woven over the unclouded sky, the unwrinkled sea and this sandy bay over which the hot air quivered, and Maurice stretched out at length and, leaning on an elbow, felt all the familiar furniture of his mind crumbling into worm-eaten dust that could be dispersed with a breath. There was nothing real, except what was here (that seemed to express it best), the sun and the sand and the sea and his heart's comrade: while that which perceived them was not the reserved student, whose recluse ways had isolated him so long, but some being newly awakening, infinitely simpler and infinitely more in touch with life. Like Steven, on that afternoon at Byron's pool, he wished that the sun could stand still, not for the mere continuance only of the moment, but for its intensification, its burning of its way into him, its scrapping of all that worm-eaten rubbish. Perhaps the sun had stood still, and he planted a twig in the sand and for a long time watched its shadow. . . .

Steven rolled over onto his side.

"Damn, I'm hungry," he said. "What are we to do, Maurice? What a bore it is: why should one be shackled like that? Must we go home? We ought to have brought food with us. Tim, I'm ready for my dinner, and there isn't any."

Tim instantly jumped to his feet.

"But sure, I'll get 'ee your dinner, Mas'r Steven," he said, "and a savoury dinner."

Steven looked across the bay to where at the head the village stood diminished, and on the hillside his house was gray and small above the poplar wood.

"No, it's too far for you to row back and forth again," he said. "I should be squealing from hunger before you returned."

"Aw, there's no need of that," said Tim. "I'll cull your dinner from here." And he pointed along the rim of the sea and the bush-clad banks.

"But we don't like raw fish, Tim," said Steven, "and how are you to catch them if we did?"

"But ye have fire," said Tim, pointing to Maurice, who was lighting a cigarette, "an' there's plenty sticks for the burning, and I'll roast ye cockles in seaweed, and there's samphire and wild strawberries and mushrooms plenty.

Eh, Mas'r Steven, doo'ee let me get your dinner, such a good dinner."

"Aw, my dear, 'tis truly kind of ye," said Steven, talking broad again, "an' we'll come joyful and happy to your dinner."

Crowned with his wreath of bryony, and with a face of morning at this deed of service to his god, Tim raced off into the scrub and bushes, and they heard him laughing as he went. Presently he returned with precious parcels wrapped in big dock leaves, wild strawberries in one, crab-apples in another, and in another a wealth of mushrooms. Among these were some unfamiliar funguses, very questionable to the view, but he assured them that these were the best of all. He was off again on a second marketing, and now he returned with a bundle of sticks for his fire. He dug in the wet sand on the sea's rim with a baling-tin from the boat, and brought back two handfuls of cockles. Again he quested along the shore and returned with a bunch of sea-samphire, with greenish stems, semi-transparent like immature asparagus. He built an oven of shingle stones and laid his fire of sticks within its enclosing compass; he wrapped up the cockles in pads of seaweed, laying them in the centre, and they heard the shells crackling like gorse pods in the heat. Intent and eager he plied his tasks, looking up now and then into Steven's face with a lift of his eyebrows to ask if he approved, and a chuckle of laughter when Steven said: "Aw, 'tis a beau'ful dinner, Tim." Maurice did not exist for him: it was not for him that he made burnt offering and oblation.

"Eat, Mas'r Steven," he said, when all was ready. " 'Tis fine food and good."

"But bain't ye gwine to eat with us, Tim?" he asked.

"Eh, no," said Tim, very decidedly, and, leaving them, he squatted down in the shade of the bushes that edged the beach.

They ate the baked cockles and the mushrooms fried

in the baling tin, and the roasted crabapples, the samphile, and the strawberries. It was a strange meal, savoury and sweet, but there was a more potent savour and sweetness which underlay it and fed the soul. Maurice felt himself dwindling into the personal nonexistence in which Tim held both himself and him, and as the spell of this trivial picnic began to weave itself over his mind he felt himself becoming part of the setting of it. The sun was warm on his naked shoulders, and they ceased to be his, and were pieces of the whole. The hot air over the beach quivered and trembled, no breeze stirred in the bushes, and only a little ripple occasionally sighed along the liquid edges of the sea. Above all, the time was not *now* on this day of early September and in this year 1929, but it was the noon of some remote immortal morning of the golden days when the blithe spirits of sea and woodland still made themselves manifest to eyes that were enlightened with understanding. His own were dim still, but not quite closed, as they had been so long.

Some little peevish eddy of his own identity stirred in him again: he knew he was Maurice, and that Steven was lying by him on the sand, and that a little way off the idiot of the village, beautiful and wild as a young Greek god, and crowned with bryony, was squatting with his hands clasped round his knees, watching them (or rather watching Steven) eat the savoury sacrifice he had prepared. But to him there was something mystic about it; his brain, that of a child who lives in a fairy story, was all alert and alive with vivid adoration; he was in the presence of a god whose eyes were full of affection for his servitor. And it was no image of wood or stone or legendary relic that Tim adored, but a living and beautiful presence, one whom Maurice also regarded with some inexplicable feeling of worship, dim and troubling as compared with Tim's, but existent. Such worship was quite distinct from any human passion of friendship, it was outside sex altogether, and altogether void of that desire for possession which makes the urge and the ache of mortal relationships. And once again, "What *was* Steven?" made its question.

There had been silence after their meal was done, whether long or short Maurice had no idea, and now Steven sat up, brushing the sand from his chest and his girdling of bath towel. He spoke drowsily, as if he had been half asleep.

"Ah, it's slipped away again," he said, "but something came close just now. What scared it off, I wonder? You, too, didn't you feel that knowledge was in the air? Did Tim give us mystic food to eat, and was there magic in the mushrooms, or is it only that I've been half asleep, stewing in air and sea? But I seemed to be nearly slipping out of this silly sheath of limbs and flesh."

He rubbed his eyes, yawning.

"Oh, I praise God for simple things," he said, with one of those abrupt transitions. "Think what a botheration there is on most days when one has lunch. A cook sweats away in the kitchen, and a scullery maid peels potatoes, and a butler lays a table with four-pronged spears and knives for us to eat with and napkins to wipe our greasy mouths, and then he rings a bell to tell us that all is ready. And we muck up plates and glasses, and somebody has to wash them. Let's start a cult of simplicity at Cambridge next term. You and the Provost and Stares and Torrington will all take off your clothes and sit on the lawn and eat slugs. Umbrellas allowed in case it rains, and an occasional dip in the fountain in case it doesn't. By degrees all the learning will be washed out of you, and you'll get nice blank minds, like new notebooks, on which you can put down real impressions. Lord, I wish I knew what Tim knows, mad stuff though it be. It's always close to him; he's in it."

Maurice tried to summon up the Cambridge sense, but Cambridge seemed infinitely remote.

"Something has been getting close to me too," he said. "I was spreading into the sun and the sea, and to-day began to be not to-day, but something timeless, and infinitely distant, and yet here all the while. . . . Then this person, myself, got hold of me again."

"Ah, that's it, that's it," said Steven. "And it comes in sudden waves and tides, and they ebb again. Can't be helped, I suppose. . . . Oh, the quiet of noonday; can't you feel how much stiller it is than any hour of night? Everything's throbbing at night, the dynamos are at work, charging you, but now always there comes a pause. The people of the woodland, satyrs and dryads, always used to have their fling at night and sleep when the sun was high. Look at Tim there."

Tim's head had sunk onto his knees, his forehead resting against them, and his arms hung limp by his side. The shadow of the bush by which he sat was spread over him; his shoulders and back were dappled with specks of sunlight yellow against the warm brown of his body, and with dark patches where the shade lay deeper. It was just as if he was clad in a leopard's skin.

Steven got up, and with his stirring Tim awoke. The two wandered a little way up the hillside where the wild strawberries grew thick, and Steven was just picking some that grew under a shrubby-looking plant with ugly mottled flowers and sticky leaves when Tim screamed at him.

"Eh, don't touch those, Mas'r Steven," he said. "They're growing under the death plant, and it drips poison on them."

"Is that the death plant?" asked Steven.

"Ay, sure, and powerful. Henbane, that's what they name it. If you make a broth of them leaves or the seeds of it, and drink it, you'll go swift asleep and not wake again. A rare thing for those as are gripped with pain and wait for death."

"And have you ever made broth of it, Tim?" asked Steven idly.

"Iss sure. Why, 'twas only two days gone."

He stopped.

"Go on, Tim," said Steven. "You needn't be feared of telling me."

Tim came close to him and whispered.

"Eh, if you bid me to tell you, Mas'r Steven, tell you I will," he said, "though George Morgan bade me never speak of it. 'Twas he who sent me two days agone to gather it, and we made the death brew of it, and he gave it to old Sally. A merciful thing, sure, for she cried nor moaned no more, but went off quiet to sleep."

"Good Lord!" said Steven.

"But I did no wrong?" asked Tim, "nor George Morgan either? We wished his old Sally not to suffer no more."

Steven did not hesitate for a moment. He was quite sure that for himself, had he been writhing in the atrocious agonies of mortal disease, he would have been swift to send Tim to gather henbane for his relief.

"Not a bit of wrong," he said; "but never open your lips about that again, Tim, save I speak to you of it. 'Tis secret between us. And now we'll be getting home."

A week of crystalline weather was succeeded by the earliest of the autumn storms. The evening had been warm and windless, but Maurice, waking at some timeless hour, found his blind blowing out horizontally in the room and cracking like a whip. Before morning the wind had risen to a gale, and sheets of rain were being flung against his panes. A big fire of logs was lit in the open hearth of the panelled hall, and the raindrops coming down the hooting chimney hissed on the embers. The poplar wood below the house writhed and struggled in the blasts, and soon the yelling of the wind began to be punctuated by the thump of breakers. The waves drove straight into the bay from the open sea and mounted in towers of solid water, fringed with spray as they struck the wall of the pier. But the fishing boats had all got home safe before the fury of the gale had burst, and now, drawn up high and dry on the beach, they were like great sea beasts leaning on their sides.

The riot pleased and excited Mrs. Gervase; she sat in a window of the hall watching the fury of sea and sky, with childlike applause at its achievements.

"Right over the pier again," she cried. "What a beauty that was; it leapt the pier and poured over it. Oh, it's a lovely storm! Shan't we go out, Steven? It will blow us about like withered leaves."

Steven was sitting in a chair close to the fire, with bellows in his hand. The strong wind and tempest had got on his nerves; he had been snappy with the servants, he was like a cat in a thunderstorm.

"Who wants to be a withered leaf?" he said. "I can tell you, I don't."

The fire was roaring now; it sent out little aromatic puffs of smoke into the room. Steven plied the bellows again and curled himself up in his chair.

"Mother's got a passion for the wind," he said to Maurice. "She'll ring the bell presently and order her broomstick, and then she'll go flying across to Penzance. She often does that when there's a storm. A dash of witch's blood."

"Well, darling, you've got it, too, then," observed Mrs. Gervase.

"I suppose I have. But the other strain's the strongest. I want to huddle up in shelter and go to sleep till the storm has passed. All the woodlanders do that."

Her face, puckered with glee, suddenly relaxed.

"You're talking nonsense, darling," she said. "What have you got to do with the woodlanders?"

"Oh, God knows," said Steven. "Anyhow, we're both talking nonsense."

Maurice had followed this but lazily. He was conscious, however, in an interval of reading his paper, that there was tension about, and that Mrs. Gervase wanted to go out of doors, and that Steven didn't. . . . Also Steven was jumpy; they had argued over some nothing-at-all at breakfast, and Steven had been rude. Not that it mattered; nothing really mattered where Steven was concerned except Steven.

"I'll come out with you, Mrs. Gervase, if you'll let me," he said.

She jumped up; Steven just as obviously settled himself down. He wanted to be rid of both of them.

"Ah, do let us go out, then," she said. "We'll go to the top of the hill. The gale will be terrific up there; just what I like."

"Put my mother on a leash, Maurice," said Steven, "or she'll certainly fly away, and you will be arrested as the last person seen with her."

The rain for the present had ceased, but the wind was solid as a cataract of water pouring uphill from the sea. Steep though the slope was above the house, it carried them up it, like flotsam on a rising tide. Now and then a high clump of gorse, thick as a fortress wall, and impervious to any gale, took them behind its sheltering bastion, but then, leaving it, they were pressed forward again by the invading force. They stopped behind one of these ramparts, hearing the wind whistle through its battlements, bearing with it a peck of flying blossoms. Mrs. Gervase seemed to expand in this elemental riot.

"Not a word have I had with you alone," she said, "though you've been here a week, Maurice. Dear me;

I called you Maurice—so forward, and yet that's how I feel, and it's done now. I've wanted to talk to you about Steven, but really I've had no opportunity, and I was delighted you offered to come out with me. This offer of his uncle's, you know, to make him his heir and take him into his office: what do you think about it? Steven in an office? I can't imagine that. And Steven rich? That's almost as difficult. What will he do with money? Buy some more beer?"

"But if he marries?" asked Maurice.

"And he's not twenty-one yet! Think of something more reasonable."

"But he'll have to do something," he said, with the Don slightly in the ascendant. "You want him to have a career of some sort, don't you? And a family?"

"Yes, but for the moment he's so complete as he is," she said. "And yet he can't go on being twenty, I suppose."

She plucked a gorse blossom and gave it him.

"Just suck that, my dear," she said, "and then see what you think about a career for Steven, when you taste the honey of it. And then say Steven Gervase, Member of Parliament, or Director of the Gervase Line of Steamers, and see if you don't have a nasty taste in your mouth."

This was Trenair, thought Maurice, and with becoming gravity he sipped the honey heart of the gorse and said: "Steven Gervase, Member of Parliament."

"Well?" said Mrs. Gervase.

"I don't say they go very harmoniously," he said. "But what do you propose? That he should suck gorse flowers all his life?"

She grew pansy faced with laughter: she bobbed him a curtsey.

"Oh, reverend Don," she said, "I make my obeisance to you. But now you must be Maurice again, and I won't be a mad witch any more, but just Steven's mother. Let's sit down, may we? The wind goes over our heads like a curling breaker, and we're in the hollow of the wave, that lovely green cave, between the foaming crest of it and the shingle. I really want to talk to you, because Steven says you understand, and I take it he is right, and I want you to understand a little more. Perhaps when I've done you'll think I'm crazy, but where's the harm of that? I shan't care. So listen to an old woman who's younger than you will ever be, unless you crack the shell that's growing round you. You've got to be young to understand Trenair and its ways and remember that Steven *is* Trenair. Perhaps you've got to be a little mad, too, for who understands Steven best? Why, that wonderful lunatic boy. So try to be like Tim for ten minutes."

As she had said, the wind poured over them: they were in a cave with the wall of gorse behind them. It was like the hollow of a wave before it breaks, dead calm with a hiss and stir of shattering force encompassing them.

"Of course, Tim's an idiot in mind," she said, "and the wise gentlemen at Cambridge think that mind is everything. At least, most of them do, so Steven tells me, and it was just because you had some perception beyond that, that he was drawn to you. I don't say that intellect is a bad thing, and sometimes I wish I had some myself, but it's a blinding thing. Intellectual people are always surrounded by a mist of brain and never see what lies beyond, and the poor dears think all the time that it is only they who have the light and the clearness. Fiddlesticks, my dear! Real vision begins just about where intellect ends."

"Are you speaking of faith?" asked Maurice, a little puzzled by this iconoclastic philosophy.

"Faith comes into it, of course," said she, "if by faith you mean the perception of what lies beyond the things we see. All religions are based on it, not Christianity only, nor Buddhism, but all beliefs that scientists and intellectuals scoff at, which transcend the intellect. Trenair hasn't any use for a Methodist chapel, but if you think Trenair hasn't any religion, you make a sad error. Try to be like Tim for a moment."

"In that case I should worship Steven," said Maurice.

Mrs. Gervase turned briskly to him.

"And are you sure you don't?" she asked.

It suddenly came over Maurice what a preposterous scene this was. Here was he, an austere student of Greek culture and a classical lecturer in the most intellectual college in the University, sitting under a gorse bush in a southwesterly gale, and being expected to tell his hostess whether he worshipped her undergraduate son. And then an even more preposterous thing happened, for quite gravely he said:

"I'm sure I do."

She laughed. She clapped her hands, and in the riot of the gale these jubilant noises sounded far away, as if some elf or sprite hidden in the bushes had been moved to applaud him.

"Well done, my dear," she said. "Now you've doffed your donship altogether and we can talk sensibly. You've always had your academical cap close by, you know, ready to pop on; now you've chucked it away. I almost saw it flying down the wind away inland to England."

He had made his confession, and now he faced her squarely.

"I'll tell you all about it," he said. "A few months ago I was a very lonely and reserved old man, though I longed not to be. And then Steven made me come to him, as he made a squirrel come to him the other day. I was tremendously attracted by him already, and when he singled me out and told me he wanted my friendship, it was the most beautiful thing that had ever happened to me. And then I found that behind his charm of body and mind there was something else, and I adored it. Now what is it that Tim and I adore in him? You're his mother; you ought to be able to tell me."

"I know I ought," she said, "but I can't. I can make guesses, but they're no more than that, and if I'm to speak of them at all you must put right away from you all the standards of what is sensible, for if you judge them by that they are delirious nonsense. But anyone who understands at all, who has the slightest touch of real vision, would know that there was something true about them."

"Go on," said Maurice, as she paused.

"I know Steven told you about the curse," she said. "Probably you didn't believe it; probably you thought it was some ridiculous old family legend which wouldn't bear looking into. But I assure you that it's literally true: the record is quite trustworthy, and it is a literal fact that for many generations, as far indeed as we can go back, up till twenty years ago, when Steven was born, the eldest son of the direct Gervase line at Trenair has always been a monster, too human for doctors to destroy or let die at birth as being an abortion, but not a man. For some years after my marriage there was such a one living in the house, who was my husband's elder brother. But with the birth of Steven the curse seemed to have been broken."

She paused again, and her elfin face grew soft and womanly, but over it too came that withdrawn look which she shared with Steven.

"Ah, can you imagine what my heart was like when the time came near for Steven's birth?" she said. "I knew the legend: my husband told me before he married me, so that I might choose with my eyes open, but I truly loved him, and I chose. But how I had been dreading Steven's birth, how I had been imagining, in those sick dreams that women have before their child is born, what sort of monster he would be. I gave the curse every chance (I couldn't help it) of imprinting itself on my first-born.

And then the pains came on me, but when I had been delivered I saw that I had brought forth a man child the most beautiful and wonderful that had ever been seen. Thick yellow hair had he when he came out from me, and from head to foot there was no blemish on him. Never an ache or a pain or an illness has vexed him from that day to this; it was as if in his person God had made up to the race for all those ghastly abortions. . . . And I adore something in Steven too, and I'm akin to it, though not in the ways of motherhood. It's the wild thing in him, that's without pity or love, but gay and sunny as the old gods of the woodland. . . . And then sometimes I'm terrified, for that makes me wonder whether the curse is over yet."

She stopped; she put her hands over her eyes with the gesture of someone suddenly waking and brushing a troubled sleep from them. Her shoulders shook and the shudder passed down her arms to her fingertips. She sprang to her feet.

"Dear me, what have I said?" she asked. "I must have been dreaming to say that. Forget about it at once, Maurice; I was babbling nonsense. . . . What were we talking of just now? Ah, yes, I was saying that I couldn't imagine the darling sitting on a stool in an office and getting rich. But I suppose it must be. And then, of course, he will marry; it would be unthinkable for him not to marry, and then once again it will be proved that the power of the curse is spent. It is now, I know that. . . . Let us walk on and get into the river of wind again. We will go to the top of the hill, shall we, and I will show you something very curious there which you have not seen yet, for you've spent every day and all day on the sea or in it."

They threaded their way between the scattered gorse bushes up the final steep rise of the hill, with the wind still pushing them on, so that the steepness of it made their progress no more effort than level walking. There, straight in front of them on the flat hilltop, was a great circle of stones, monoliths, some six to eight feet high, a couple of dozen in number, tracing the circumference. They stood at regular intervals from each other, except that between the two most easterly there was a double spacing, as if some gate of entrance had been there. The enclosed area was of virgin land, old turf of the downs, never yet ploughed (though up to the edge of the circle came corn-land), and covered with tall grasses, ox-eye daisy, scabious and trefoil, swept flat by the storm. Across its diameter, stretching nearly from side to side, stood a line of small gravelike mounds.

"Ah, interesting," said Maurice, rather donnishly. "One of those Druidical temples, unless archæologists have settled they are something else."

Mrs. Gervase pointed to the line of mounds.

"Where the eldest sons are buried," she said. "Look, twelve of them; that's twelve generations. There's room for one more, but that will never be. The tale is finished."

CHAPTER VII

MRS. GERVASE, three days after this walk in the gale, had to leave Trenair to pay a short visit to a sister of hers, who, with her consumptive husband, had taken a house for a month at Falmouth. Her intention had been to ask them here: her change of intention was due to a discussion between her and Steven on the subject.

"But he's so horrible," said Steven. "He has a little blue glass bottle and spits into it."

"You wouldn't want him to spit on the floor," said Mrs. Gervase.

"He can spit where he likes at Falmouth," said Steven. "Of course, I'm extremely sorry for him, but I'm sorry for him best when he's out of sight. Besides, Aunt Kate is the most awful kill-joy. How she came to be your sister I can't understand. Perhaps you've got a family curse, too, darling, and the eldest daughter is always a crashing bore. Fifthly, we're so happy as we are. Do you want a kill-joy or a consumptive to join the circle, Maurice? No, I don't, says he. You've got to consider your guests, mother."

Mrs. Gervase's face was a web of perplexity. She looked like a fairy suddenly confronted with a moral problem which completely puzzled her.

"But really I think I must ask them for a couple of nights, Steven," she said. "It would be very unkind not to. You and Maurice will be out all day; you'll see very little of them."

"But we don't want to see anything of them," said Steven radiantly.

"But just for two nights, dear," she said.

Steven meditated a moment, the picture of good-humour, and when he spoke his voice had not a trace of annoyance.

"Very well," he said. "Do just as you like, and I shall do just as I like too. If they come here I shall go and stay in the village: Jan Pentreath's got a spare room, and I shall be perfectly happy. And when they've gone I shall come back."

The fairy's perplexity increased.

"But you can't do that, darling," she said. "It isn't done."

Steven laughed.

"You wait: it's going to be done this time," he said.

Maurice glanced from one to the other over the top of his newspaper; minute though the subject of their contention was, it profoundly interested him. Steven had never spoken more pleasantly; his voice expressed the utmost of agreeable unconcern. One would have thought that he would actually prefer spending a couple of nights in Jan Pentreath's cottage. His mother's point of view, his mother's wish evidently did not even present themselves to his mind as worth consideration, nor did his admonition to her to think of her guest appear to apply to him.

"You're very naughty, dear," she said.

The significance of this trifle began to loom larger to Maurice. Steven acknowledged no claims: his mother's sense of sisterly duty had no existence for him: it could not be weighed against the objectionable spectacle of a man spitting into a discreet bottle. Never before, as far as Maurice had seen, had her wishes come into opposition to him, but that was because she had never expressed a wish that did not jump with his inclinations. And now, quite serenely and pleasantly, he went on his own way. He dismissed the whole affair as settled, and picked up an outside sheet of the daily paper, which Maurice had dropped, and with a shout of laughter read out to them a surprising desire on the part of a lady at Twickenham to exchange her set of croquet, nearly new, for sets of false teeth. Then the list of births, marriages, and deaths claimed his attention—it was nice to know that the wife of Elijah Pobgee had given birth to twins.

"Elijah and Elisha must certainly be their names," he said. "I shall write anonymously to tell Mrs. Pobgee. Oh, I say——"

Whatever he was about to say was cut short by his mother.

"I suppose I could go to Falmouth and stay with them there for two nights," she said.

Steven dropped his paper to applaud.

"Hurrah!" he said. "I knew you would think of some perfect plan. That meets everything, and it will be a little change for you, and none for me. Mind you give Aunt Kate my love. It was clever of you to have thought of that. But I don't in the least mind staying with Jan for a couple of nights, if you want them here."

He picked up the paper again.

"An awfully sad thing, Maurice," he said. "It must be the Child: Charles Merriman drowned at Schaffhauser, bathing in the Rhine."

"Good Lord!" said Maurice.

"I know. Horrible. Poor chap."

He threw the leaf of the paper across to Maurice and strolled away to the window.

"The sea's gone down a bit," he said. "Shall we have a sail after lunch? We might go round to Land's End. There'll be some grand waterworks against the cliffs there. Would you like that?"

Mrs. Gervase had gone to telephone to her sister about this visit, and the two were alone. Maurice joined Steven at the window, and put his arm in his.

"It's too dreadful about the Child," he said. "And I am so sorry for you, Steven. You were such friends."

"I know; it's dreadful," he said. "I've said so already.

But then my friendship with the Child was over. So I'm not sorry for myself, though it's nice of you to be so. But it would be silly of me to pretend to be cut up. If it had been you, now, or Tim, people I want——"

Something in his words, or in the light intonation of them, seemed to stab Maurice. He felt it was Steven himself who spoke them, that adorable wild thing, which suddenly popped out and in again behind the charm of his more superficial personality.

"But your affection for him, and his for you: years of it," he said.

Steven looked at him slightly puzzled, slightly impatient.

"But it was over," he said, as if repeating some explanation to a rather stupid child. "He was dead already, as far as I was concerned. I shouldn't have seen him again in any case, so it can't make any difference to me. By the way, I heard from him this morning: I just glanced at it, and forgot about it; he must have written it just before. He asked if he could come down here when he got back. I needn't answer it now."

"What would you have said?" asked Maurice.

"Oh, some amiable excuse," said Steven, "though I don't know why it concerns you. I didn't want to see him again. . . . What's the matter?"

"You're rather horrible about it," said Maurice.

"And you're rather hypocritical about it and want me to be the same. While the Child was alive you were delighted that he had quite gone out of my life, but now he's dead you want us both to be sorry for it. It can't be done, Maurice. Do be logical."

There was just enough truth in this to make a direct reply difficult. But there was missing from it something of far vaster import, the absence of which struck at the roots of humanity. And to speak of that was not difficult only but impossible.

"Of course I'm sorry," Steven went on with that childlike clarity and charm, "but I'm not sorry for myself. If the Child was happy and enjoying himself and wanted to live, I'm sorry that he hasn't got his wish. . . ."

He was withdrawing himself, Maurice felt. He wasn't here any more, he had gone into the poplar wood.

"Death!" he said. "What the devil does death matter? Very likely something else has begun for the Child which he likes much better. Oh, how you're beginning to lag behind, Maurice! Do come on! Besides, where would be the good if I pulled a long face and squealed?"

His shoulder twitched.

"About sailing round to Land's End," he said. "Don't come if you'd rather not, for the sea is a bit rough still. I'll take Tim; he'd love it."

The telephone conveyed an immediate welcome from sad Aunt Kate, and after Steven had returned from conveying his mother in the crazy car to Penzance, where she would get into the "mucky train," he and Maurice went down to inspect the sea at nearer range. A big ground swell, the sequel to the storm, was here more evident, and Maurice found the proposed expedition to be entirely unattractive. But his refusal, in which Steven fully acquiesced, brought rapture to Tim, and he saw the two set out. It was quite uncertain when they would get back, for all depended on the conduct of the sea and the wind, and Maurice was enjoined to sit down to his dinner punctually without waiting for their return. They might find, however, that the conditions outside made it impossible to carry out any sort of programme, and then they would come back at once.

Maurice strolled up the cliffs to the west of the harbour when they had put out, and watched them for a while, inwardly congratulating himself that he was on shore. The wind was very light, and they made small headway westwards, first taking a long tack out to sea, then turning landwards but with little gain in their direction, and out to sea once more. On the outward tack they met the big swell directly, climbing the long slopes of steep water on an even keel, poising on the crest and then gliding down again, like a swooping bird, into the valley of their troughs. But when they put about and came landwards it was a dizzier business, for their boat seemed to slither and slip sideways, heavily tilted, now to one side, now to the other, now poised and hovering, now helplessly slewing into those gray ravines.

But they held on their course, and Maurice, turning inland for a walk, mounted the gorse-golden hills which encompassed the village. It soon lay below him, fringed with sea and woods and utterly remote and apart. How sundered it was: the great humps and bulges of the hills isolated it from all external intercourse of any neighbourly sort, the traffic on the road to Penzance passed it at two miles of distance. Even the postman never came down the dipping track that led to it, but left his budgets of letters and newspapers in a wayside box at the head of the combe, and someone from the village went up there once a day and gleaned its contents, carrying with him to deposit therein the rare letters for the outside world that came from Trenair. Next day the postman would clear this out and deal with them. All this was typical of its remoteness. There was the telephone, it is true, at Steven's house, but since he came here it had not once been used, until Mrs. Gervase had occasion this morning to speak to sad Sister Kate.

Yet Trenair had, as it was impressed on him more day by day, a life of its own, intense and primeval and vivid. Its own spiritual atmosphere, pagan and alive, englobed it as if in some tough transparent bubble, which isolated it more hermetically from the current beliefs and conceptions of the modern world than did its enfolding hills from commerce and communication with neighbouring town and hamlets. Just as England was foreign to Cornwall, so Cornwall was foreign to Trenair. There was a knowledge possessed by these fisher folk, and in especial by Tim, of which, even after his fortnight's sojourn here, Maurice had formed no definite idea. And yet this secret lore was not so much a knowledge as an awareness. Probably, so he felt, not one of them, not Jan Pentreath, nor Tom Evans, nor Tim could, if tackled in cross-examination, give account of it any more than the layman in medical matters could give an account of the pulsings of his blood through artery and returning vein. But just as in the latter case the layman's life depended on the adequate functioning of the blood, so the interior life of these remote folk sprang from this mysterious source.

It concerned them all, it was a freemasonry, never spoken of, but vitally there, and he himself was completely outside it. It was a belief, a religion, a matter of faith, and Steven, as Maurice was becoming aware, figured in its primeval hierarchy. He had thought at first, when he saw the affectionate reverence with which he was regarded, that here in this sequestered place, owned from generation to generation by Gervases, it was the effect of a strong feudal instinct, but now he was sure there was something more than that. Tim, that daft creature of the woodland, with his uncontrolled impulses, expressed it when he knelt to Steven; the others were more controlled. Then suddenly and disconcertingly there came to him the question: Was he himself an unwitting co-religionist?—for he knew that he shared with Tim, surely though inexplicably, the same instinct of adoration. And then there was the curse. Somehow Mrs. Gervase connected that spell which Steven cast on them all with the curse. She had withdrawn that strange signal of terror at once, and begged him to forget about it, but it was in genuine terror that she had waved it.

"But that is midsummer madness," thought Maurice,

and he put himself to a brisker pace with the truly British idea of walking off his lunatic notions. But they kept pace with him, hovering round him like a company of gnats, one settling here, one there, with innumerable stinging contacts. And it was out of the dark that they assailed him with their shrill trumpetings and touches; he could not see his assailants, those creatures of the night.

He walked fast, and now the great empty serenity of the open hills high above the glen of Trenair and the "awareness" which brimmed it, like some cup, with that insidious liquor, began to drive from his brain those dangerous fumes, and common sense, like cold water dashed on his head, restored a saner and soberer outlook. Half an hour's steady tramp brought him to that "cirque of Druid stones" to which Mrs. Gervase had taken him on the morning of the gale, and he sat down leaning his back against one of the eastern monoliths, to think coolly and academically over the mad stuff which had been disquieting him. Far below now, small as the furnishings of a box of toys, glimmered the village, and he felt out of the range of its influence: across the circle, nearly from side to side, lay the row of little mounds which marked the resting places of those generations of eldest sons in whose bodies and minds had been incarnated the curse which now surely was broken in the person of his friend. Steven was far off on that blue shield of the sea, and, free from the spell of his presence, Maurice called up all his latent donnishness to help him to get a cool, correct image of him, built not out of fancies but of facts.

"An athletic boy," he said to himself, "who rowed for Eton and will probably row for Cambridge, popular and of silly, skyscraping spirits, possessed of an extraordinary personal charm, and in no way different in kind from hundreds of others. A curious power over animals, for did I not see the squirrel come to him at his unspoken bidding? But others have that power, too, and among them his own mother. A great gift of attaching others passionately to himself—for was not the Child as devoted to him as I?—but a singular indifference to those who care for him. The Child's death did not affect him in the least, and perhaps, essentially, he cares as little for me; yet I've no right to think that, for I've not a shred of evidence to support it, and all the evidence possible to disprove it. . . . A strange family history on his father's side, which I suppose can't be doubted, but that has come to an end. He intends to enter his uncle's shipping business and will probably marry before long. And that's all I *know* about him. I must be more sensible: I have been shy and reserved all my life, and like a man coming out of a cold, dark room into a blaze of sunshine, I'm dazzled. I've never known what friendship was before, and I can't view it rightly yet; it has gone to my head. And as for the feelings of the fisher folk here about him, I have merely been investing them with my own. There's room for one more grave here, and herewith I dig it, and bury my absurd fancies in it. I've regained my common sense, thank God, and having recaptured it I'll hold on to it."

He jerked himself to his feet, satisfied that his reflections had been eminently sensible, and that being a man of sense again he was now armed with a stout bludgeon of security to use as a weapon when next assailed. So absorbed had he been in its fashioning that he had not noticed the change that had come over the face of the day. The breeze on which Steven had intended to sail to the Land's End had fallen to dead calm, and in the west a huge bank of cloud had risen over the sea, dulling its blue brightness to lead colour and expunging the sun that had so warmed the stone against which he had been propped. It must, too, be much later in the afternoon than he had guessed, for a little rift, opening low down in that bank of cloud, showed a hint of sunset red, but in spite of the waning of the day and the shrouded sun, the atmosphere, fresh but warm, as he had climbed the hills had grown oppressively hotter. The outlines of cliffs and headlands were carved with a curious distinctness against the sea; they were etched and hard instead of being veiled by the intervention of the soft humid air; the edges of that advancing cloud were made not of vapour but of steel, and it was evident that some storm, not like that of three days ago, with its gale of riotous wind and rain, but one of thunder and explosion was gathering fast. The leagues of gorse were of golden brightness no more, but darkly smouldering, and a few drops of rain, large as a crown piece and swiftly evaporating, splashed on the stones of the circle and hissed in the short down grass. If he was to escape a drenching he must lose no time in getting home.

Just as he reached the corner of the house, the rain began in earnest, not in drops any more, but in solid rods of water. He ran at top speed to the front door, past the windows of the hall, and saw that the room was brightly lit within. Steven then must have come home, and that was good.

The front door, as usual, was open, and from inside came a smell of aromatic smoke, sweeter and stronger than that of a log fire, and the sound of a pipe, clear and mellow, though shrill. Surely that barbarous music with its repeated notes and artless staves could be none other than Tim's. Then he stepped inside.

Tim was squatting on the floor, crowned with his ivy wreath, and on the hearth there went up a thin streamer of blue smoke from a little fire of twigs and leaves that glowed and crackled there. In a chair just in front of him sat Steven, and he, too, was crowned with a garland of wild vine. On the table beside him was a silver two-handled cup that stood on the dinner table at night, and into it he was pouring a bottle of Burgundy; another bottle, empty, rolled on its side by his feet. Just as Maurice entered, Steven handed the cup to Tim.

"Drink," he said, "and then dance again."

Tim leaped up, and taking the cup from Steven's hands, drank long and deep from it, swaying tipsily as he stood there. Then he peeled his jersey off and tossed it on the floor. His face was flushed, his eyes sparkled.

"Ah, 'tis better like that," he said. "Now I'll dance as I dance in the woods by night."

Surely Tim had stepped straight off some Bacchic vase of Athens. . . . He moved in a small circle, slowly at first, his bare feet soundless on the carpet, to the music of his pipe. Then his pace quickened, he leaped in the air, and came down poised on one foot; he whirled round with short steps, naked to the waist and clad only in short sea-stained breeches. Then, with knees lifted high and galloping movement, each foot coming down where he had sprung from it, he bent this way and that, now with arched back, and now bowing forward. In one hand he held his pipe to his mouth, the other arm beckoned and gesticulated. . . . Maurice, in the shadow of the doorway, watched for a few minutes, his eyes fascinated by the wild grace and beauty of the boy, and in his mind some strange excitement seething and bubbling. That dance expressed something, the inspiration that prompted it was drawn from the secret lore of this strange place: there was in it, too, if he could but seize it, the key to what puzzled and entranced him in Steven. . . . Neither of the two, he could see, had the slightest recognition of his presence: they might perhaps be aware that he, Maurice Crofts, stood there by the door, but he was no more to them than the door mat on which his feet were placed. Meantime Steven had got up from his chair; his face was alight even as Tim's, his shoulders twitched, his fingers beat the measure of the boy's dancing. If he was lord here, he was also learning.

Then suddenly, with some qualm of disgust, Maurice saw the other aspect of this strange scene, and his sense of decency revolted. Steven had brought up here this splendid crazed creature, in whose deranged mind he was something godlike, and was amusing himself with making a drunken dancing faun of him. He stepped out into the middle of the room between him and Steven.

"I say, Steven, this won't do," he said. "You've made him tipsy. It's not right, it's not decent."

At the intrusion of his presence and his voice Tim stopped. He staggered and swayed, then fell at full length on the floor. Steven's face, radiant and alight with excitement, hardened to a mask of fury.

"You damned ignorant fool," he shouted. "What do you mean by interfering like this? You come here with your sanctimonious donnish airs, and tell me—me—what's right to do! You blind, stupid brute; learn something of some sort before you begin to teach!"

That gust of uncontrollable anger spent itself; his face cleared, but not into sunshine again.

"Sorry, Maurice," he said. "I lost my temper, I'm afraid, but you startled me coming in like that. Let's see to Tim first: we'll talk afterwards. Why, the boy's absolutely blotto, and it never struck me. God, how it's raining—I wonder if a shower bath would pull him round. Help me to lift him up; he can't lie there. Why, he's as limp as a sleeping kitten. Chuck me his jersey . . . more decent, as you say."

He propped Tim against his knee, and with Maurice to assist him, pulled his jersey over his head and steered his slack arms through the sleeves. Though a couple of minutes ago, inspired by that huge excitement that filled him, he had been dancing like some faun in the presence of his god, Maurice's intrusion had broken to fragments the spell that moved him, and now he lay against Steven, nerveless and relaxed in a coma of tipsiness. He was no more than a jointed doll, neck, knees, and shoulders fell this way and that, as uncontrolled by living sinews and muscles as the limbs of the dead before the eternal rigor has stiffened them.

Steven finished his valeting and picked Tim up in his arms to carry him to the sofa. The boy's head lay on his shoulder, and their two faces, and crowned heads now close together, were so alike in line and colouring that they might have been twins. A spasm of wonder shook Maurice as to whether two creatures so beautiful should ever be interfered with. The miracle of them surely justified all they did.

"He must lie there for the present," said Steven, "and sleep it off. I can't get drunk, you know, and I never thought about Tim. Sit down, Maurice, and I'll tell you what's been happening. Lord, how you startled me just now; I believed I saw someone standing in the doorway, but I heeded him no more than the umbrellas in the stand, and I had no idea it was you. And then, suddenly, there you were standing between us and jawing me like little Stares. What on earth made you do it? I would cheerfully have killed you that moment, because you interrupted everything—not Tim's dancing alone, though that was bad enough, but all the power that was playing on us. Why, it was realizing what you said yourself on that night at Carlton House Terrace; we were going fast back into the morning of the world. Tim was dancing himself and me back into it. Did you ever dream that dancing could be like that? It was bursting with the joy of life."

Steven put back his head and sniffed the air, which was aromatic with the combustion of the leafy fuel Tim had kindled on the hearth. Strangely heavy and scented was the smoke of it, and with it mingled the sweet odour of wet earth which came in through the open door. Outside the ramrods of rain still pushed home their fertile charge.

"Dancing helped it," Steven went on, "and that fire

which Tim lit there. Once, I remember, the Child and I lit a fire by the river at dawn, just for fun, as I then supposed, but there was more in it than that. It was a rite that I was feeling after. And Tim lit that as a rite, and he knew what he was doing. He was going back, going back to what he had known: he wasn't inventing anything, he was just remembering. He may make obeisance to me, but he knows more than I, his memory of it all is infinitely clearer. Good God, what devil from the High Table at King's made you come butting in then? Tim was laying a higher table than that."

Again through the resentment smouldering in Steven's eyes, the flame of anger flared high. It died down again.

"But you couldn't have told what he was getting at," he said, "for you were outside it altogether. And I made a stupid mistake in making Tim drunk. I had no intention of doing so; I simply forgot that he had probably never tasted wine in this life, and it seemed so suitable to take great draughts of that strong Southern stuff. Lord! the place reeks of the rapture of it: storm and sweat and dance and incense and worship and wine. They were bringing out the secret things; the clues were floating like gossamer in the air, and my fingers were on them."

While he spoke, Maurice seemed to himself to be following him, trying to catch up with him, but with the cessation of Steven's voice, as he leaned back in his chair, mopping his forehead, the half-grasped comprehension of what he said vanished, like a dream that fades utterly on the awakening. He was surrounded by material aspects again: a mindless boy from the village was breathing heavily in drunken sleep on the sofa; Steven had been hurling abominable abuse at him, and he himself was donnish again, quite interested in what had happened, slightly disgusted and detached, and lighting a cigarette.

"You were going to tell me what—what has actually

been happening since I left you putting out to sea," he said drily.

"Yes, I will. For goodness' sake, try to understand, to see what it means. . . . Let's think: yes, you saw us start off. It was fearfully rough, and if I had been managing the boat I should have had it half full of water in no time. But Tim was at the tiller, and though he scarcely seemed to be attending at all, he coaxed her, this way and that, as if by magic, and we never shipped a drop. Half a dozen times I, who thought I was in charge, told him to do something, but he only laughed and by degrees my eyes were opened just a little. But soon the wind dropped altogether, and we couldn't get on. I lay at the bottom of the boat watching him and trusting him now, and now he was swung high above me, and now far away below me, and the huge swells came up chuckling and lifted us, and then poured away from under us, and all the time we were like a bird swimming on the sea, though the boat was heavy and clumsy to manage. At last I said, 'We can't get on, Tim; we must try to get back, but I don't know how to do it.' And he said, 'You'll do it all right, Mas'r Steven. You can take us where you please' . . . and I sitting at the bottom of the boat all the time. 'Then I'll go back home,' said I, and he answered, 'Sure you will, then. There's a breath of wind coming out of the west.' "

Tim stirred on his sofa and gave a little moaning sigh.

"I hope he's not going to be sick," said Maurice, rather primly.

Again in Steven's eyes flickered the flame through the smoky resentment.

"What the hell does it matter if he is?" he said. "Don't be so idiotic. . . . Tim was right: a breath of wind made the sails shiver, and then it grew stronger, and we put about and slipped away homewards. The waves toppled astern of us, but none pooped us, and the biggest of all—

never have I seen such a mountain of water—caught us, just as we were rounding the pier, so close that you could have spat onto the edge of it. Then, with a sudden turn of the rudder, as if it had been a fish's tail, Tim shot in round the corner of it. You don't know anything about sailing, but you may take it from me that it was so masterly as to be miraculous. The whole village was down there on the beach watching us, and half a dozen men ran into the water to pull us in, for the seas were breaking over the pier, and Tim cursed them for interfering. When we had got ashore, I said to him, because I had to say it, 'Are you coming up to the house, Tim?' and he smiled, and said, 'Iss, sure,' as if I had already asked him. As we came up through the wood he left me and strayed off among the bushes, and I went on alone, but I knew he was coming. And presently he pattered in, with his hands piled with leaves and little branches, and without saying anything to me he built them up on the hearth and lit them. . . . And then I knew—don't you understand?—that he and I were not *here*, and we were not *now*, or, if you like it better, some hour from remote years had come up like a bubble through the sea of time, and inside it were Tim and I."

Steven had begun his story with manner and voice eagerly alert, but now he was lolling back in his chair, all relaxed, with heavy eyelids half closed. He paused, then roused himself.

"I don't know what leaves Tim had gathered," he said, "but the air grew heavy with an odour which something in me recognized: once it had been familiar, and behind it was the smell of early morning. What morning was that, I wonder? . . . And the smell suggested to me what I must do, so I fetched a couple of bottles of Burgundy, and the silver cup from the dining-room table, and I filled it with wine, drank myself, and then gave it to Tim, as—we used to do. He drank and danced, and I opened another and again we drank, and then he danced again, and while he was dancing you interrupted. I knew there was someone by the door, but that was all. How long had you been here before you spoke to me?"

Was it the strange odour of the burnt leaves, Maurice wondered, or this stranger narrative that surely was infecting him, too? He felt that the bubble coming up through the sea of Time, of which Steven had spoken, was beginning to enclose him also, and while some secret instinct quickened and grew jubilant, the conscious, controllable part of him protested and refused to be enmeshed. With a strong effort he braced himself to support it.

"I had been here a minute or two, I suppose," he said. "I looked at Tim dancing, I confess, with marvel and admiration, and then I was overpowered with disgust that you had made him drunk. It revolted me: so I told you."

Steven looked at him quietly; his angry resentment had quite vanished, and in his eyes there was regret.

"It was the stupidest thing you ever did," he said. "Instead of coming along with me in friendship you spoiled everything. You were afraid, I suppose; you were afraid of me once before. I don't think I have ever been so disappointed in anyone. Instead of helping, you hindered."

All that for the last few months had made Maurice's life, that had built for him this temple of friendship, shook and tottered. But such a catastrophe was incredible, and he gave to his answer the tone of the most flippant and impossible suggestion.

"So I suppose you'll chuck me," he said, "just as you chucked the Child."

Steven shook his head.

"Oh, I never chucked the Child," he said. "The Child chucked himself. I thought you understood that. He couldn't come on with me: he didn't know what it meant. You're not like that, are you?"

He swung sideways in his chair, as if this was the most

trivial of questions, and looked at Tim: his face grew radiant and tender.

"Oh, and he knows so much more than me!" he said. "Happy, blessed fellow!"

"And yet he thinks you're his lord," said Maurice.

Steven got up and stretched himself: some spiritual density and tenseness seemed to ease and clear, and Maurice remembered how he had said that there were tides that flowed and ebbed again.

"One of his cracked notions, I suppose," he said. "Oh, I feel as if I had been wonderfully dreaming, and that I had awakened again to that stale little bedroom of mine at King's. And I've been rude and quarrelsome, Maurice. I'm sorry, but then you were damned irritating. The rain's over: it's going to be a clear evening. Now what are we to do with Tim? As you so justly hinted, it isn't very dignified—shall we call it?—to be sitting here with a mad, tipsy boy snoring on the sofa, even though he is a relation of mine. It puts you in a false position; you can't pretend not to see him. Let's consider what the voice of respectability would counsel us to do. . . . Hullo, he's coming round, and I don't believe he's going to be sick at all."

Tim stirred and sat up; he rubbed his hands over his eyes like an awakening child, and looked round.

"Hullo, Mas'r Steven," he said. "I've been asleep, have I? Turrible rude of me."

"Iss, sure, you've been asleep, Tim dear," said Steven. "But 'tis late, and presently, if you feel rested, you'll be thinking of getting whoam."

Tim struggled to his feet.

"Eh, a bit dizzy-like," he said. " 'Tis that wine you gave me. Beau'ful it was, like our sail together. I'll be off, then; I've been dreaming of the woods and the gay things dancing. Thank ye, Mas'r Steven, and we'll go there again; doo'ee let us."

As he moved across to the door he stumbled into Maurice, as if he had not seen him. They watched him cross the lawn, still heavy footed, and plunge into the wood. Then came the sound of his pipe, clear and mellow like bird song, growing fainter till it died away.

The relations between the two young men continued apparently unaltered; that scene of the drunken dancing had been allowed to obliterate itself from the surface of intercourse. They boated and bathed together, they rattled about the roads in the crazy car, and their intimacy seemed externally unbroken. But below the easy conduct of life Maurice was aware that something was brewing. If he attempted to get back into that closer touch of comprehension which had originally drawn them together, Steven withdrew. If, with such ease as he could command, he spoke of Tim, Steven had nothing to say about him, and this was not due, Maurice unerringly felt, to the fact that Tim had been dismissed, as the Child had been, but that he was too intensely there to be talked about with one who had shown himself so void of understanding. Discussion was useless: why argue about algebra to a child who could not yet grasp the simple rule of arithmetic? Tim never joined their expeditions now, and Steven, lying out after their bathe on the sunny beaches, and full of pleasant chatter, would suddenly absent himself. Once Maurice attempted a direct assault, and asked him if there was anything on his mind, and he reached out an affectionate hand and said, "Nothing, except that you're going away so soon now." And then he talked with unconvincing enthusiasm over the delightful term that they would presently be beginning together at Cambridge. But this was a gabble that quickly ran dry, a tissue of reassuring politeness, as to an acquaintance, which scarcely interrupted, so superficial was it, the current of all that remained unspoken, and from that region, cloud beset and thundery, there sometimes zigzagged out like a streak of remote lightning that glance of ugly anger, which Maurice had seen first in Steven's face when he interrupted Tim's drunken dancing. Never before that had Steven looked at him with hostile eyes, but since then scarcely an hour passed, when they were alone together, in which he did not catch a glimpse of it. It was not a glance of deliberate hostility, nor of any reasoned animosity, but rather the sideways look of an animal which betrayed an instinctive, involuntary repugnance. Steven might be talking all the while with the friendliest geniality, and then this flash of natural dislike popped out, quick as a lizard from a dark cranny, into the sunlight, and back again.

Hitherto they had always spent practically the whole day together, but now, during this last week of Maurice's long visit, Steven always absented himself for an hour or so during the afternoon or evening. On these mellow September nights the three of them would often sit on the lawn in front of the house after dinner, and Steven just sauntered away, whistling and leisurely, leaving his mother and Maurice to keep each other company. Or they would be lingering in the hall after tea, and again he would get up in the most casual manner, as if going on some insignificant errand, and not be seen again till dinner-time. No word on the subject passed between Maurice and Mrs. Gervase; neither she nor he ever alluded to these absences, though each wondered if the other had any private conjectures or conclusions about them. Still less did Maurice question Steven in their regard, for he rightly held that complete freedom was essential to intimacy: you might, if you chose, be inquisitive with an acquaintance, and risk a snub, but you must never ask a friend for information about his movements if he did not choose to offer it.

One afternoon, the last day but one before his departure,

it idly occurred to Maurice, during one of these absences, to stroll down to the village. He took, as usual, the short cut through the poplar wood, and when now in the middle of it he caught sight of Steven standing some way off the path, among the trees. The glimpse was only momentary, for without a sign Steven, as if he had just caught sight of him and wished not to be seen, stepped behind a screen of hazels. So be it: if Steven had a fancy to wander alone in his own wood and say nothing to his friend nor wish for his company, it was certainly not that friend's business to peer into his privacy, and Maurice, stifling his sense of puzzled curiosity as best he might, went on his way without calling to him. He spent a half hour wandering about the beach and lounging on the pier, where, as usual, a few of the fisher folk were gathered, and more markedly than ever to-night he felt his remoteness from them. They talked to him about the fishing, they inquired into the length of his stay, they answered his casual questions civilly, but never a sparkle of warmth or welcome came into the eyes which regarded him with the level, far-focussed gaze of men accustomed to look out over the flat plain of the waters for hours together. They neither liked him nor disliked him; he was a neutral object which simply had no more existence for them than it had for Tim, and when he wished them good-night and turned homewards again, he was sure that no winks or shrugs would pass between them behind his back, nor would his departure occasion any sense of relief: nobody had been there, and nobody had gone away.

Dusk was beginning to fall as he passed through the village again, clear dusk with a greenish wash of sky spreading up from the west, and entering the wood was like stepping into some cave of deep water. His step was noiseless on the mossy pathways, and suddenly turning a corner in the windings of the track he saw Tim leaping and bounding down towards him. At the same moment the boy caught sight of him, and instantly his exuberant antics ceased, and he dropped to a walk. As hc drew near he raised his eyes with a glance of something too neutral to call contempt.

"Hullo, Tim," said Maurice. "What have you been up to?"

Tim stepped wide of him, and without word or smile in reply passed on down the path. At that Maurice guessed what he had been doing: without doubt, so it sprang into his mind, he had been with Steven. A further angle in the path brought him in sight of the central clearing in the wood, the plateau where stood the ancient ruined walks, and there, sitting on one of them, was Steven himself. This time he must pass close to him, and it was ridiculous to pretend not to see him.

"I've just been for a stroll," he said.

Steven got up. In his hand were half a dozen of those degenerate grapes, and he ate these, one by one, before he answered.

"I saw you pass an hour ago," he said, and in his voice as well as in his eyes there was a hostility clear and unveiled. "And you met Tim, I suppose, just now. Are you spying on me?"

Again the question was too neutral to be even contemptuous, but it struck Maurice like a blow in the face.

"You are perfectly at liberty to think so, if you like," he answered.

Steven hesitated.

"I—I beg your pardon," he said. "That was a monstrous question of mine. I know you haven't been spying on me. I suppose I asked you because I've been secretive with you myself. Look here: for the last few days I've had a habit, haven't I, of vanishing without saying a word to you? Every time I've been with Tim."

Maurice could see that there was some struggle going on in Steven's mind: the words came out with difficulty, something held them back. He put the utmost geniality into his reply.

"But why not?" he asked. "It did rather puzzle me to know what you were doing, but it wasn't my business, and it's not my business now."

Steven had no smile to meet his; this answer seemed to irritate him.

"You're too civilized," he said. "You're too well-bred and genteel. Why can't you be natural?"

"Perhaps it's natural to me to be genteel, as you call it," he said rather drily. The rebuff had brought a little donnishness into his voice.

"I'm afraid it is," said Steven, "and that's why there's a gulf spreading fast between us."

Maurice knew it too, but the statement of it made him sick at heart.

"Rot," he said. "There's no gulf. There can't be, between you and me."

"But there is, and you know it. I'm sorry too: it's a damned bore. But I can't help it any more than you can. And all the people here are on my side of it, and that's why you can't get near them."

"I won't accept the fact of there being a gulf between us," said Maurice. "It's a mistake, it's a misunderstanding. I'm just as devoted to you as ever. Leave it at that."

"I can't leave it at that," said Steven. "That only represents half the situation. You and I came together because I thought I saw you had some inner understanding. You get glimpses of it, perhaps, but then you get frightened, you get genteel. The other day, for instance, you only saw a tipsy boy dancing. . . . Well, it's no use going back to that. But to me he brings something that gives the wider air. I breathe. I'm myself, or learning to be."

"And with me you stifle," said Maurice. "Is that it?"

Steven looked at him without pity.

"That's about it," he said. "I want what you can't give me: you know it as well as I do. You seemed to understand when I told you about that night on the river; you saw there was something in me which you called the wild thing; you appeared to know what I meant when I talked about the magnetic night, the night that pressed close. It was all new to me then: I wanted us to go forward together. But you've gone such a little way; you're lagging behind."

"As the Child did," said Maurice.

"Yes, as the Child did. But——"

Steven's face, hitherto cold and blank, began to glow with animation.

"But when I'm with Tim," he said, "it's I who lag behind. He dances on in front, and I pant after him, but, oh, I breathe the real air. He remembers vividly in some subconscious way an existence of which I only have the faintest glimpses. It's more than memory with him: that world is much more real to him than this. I don't mean reincarnation or anything like it; I don't believe that he and I were ever mortal men before. But there are other intelligences besides men, presences and powers that used to haunt the woods. They haunt them still, they exist now just as much as they did when the Greeks built temples to Dionysus and carved friezes on which the fauns and dryads followed him. Christianity thought to destroy them, but they aren't dead. You might as well set out to destroy seas and springs; only ridiculous Puritans like Milton and people whose spirits are blinded with civilization think they've perished. They're here, and I know it, and their life is quickening in me day by day. I just sit by Tim as he dances or plays his pipe, and my heart sings because it's the hot hour of noon and I'm aware of the spirits of the woodland lying couched in the bushes, or because evening is coming on and they stir again. And they're not only around me, but in me."

The mask, soulless and exquisite, and burning with some life of its own, was on Steven's face again, and over his eyes, blue as a clear noonday, there passed shadows as of swift-moving clouds blown on the spring breeze, and brightnesses as of the sun. Strange was that speech on the lips of one living here and now, for it breathed with the ardour and the freshness of the antique woods. The dusk had deepened; above the clearing where the two stood was a pool of pale green sky in which shone one star like a jewel sunk in translucent water, and round it, motionless in the still air, grows the encircling belt of trees, enclosing arched aisles of darkness. And indeed some spell, felt even by Maurice, was at work, which for the moment drowned the bitterness that filled his heart at Steven's repudiation of him. Almost he adored the callousness which now, as once before, tossed away like a broken toy mere human affection, with its stupidities and unperceptiveness. The young god of the woodland—was it thus that Tim looked on him?—might permit the worship of such, taste their burnt offerings and sniff their incense, but why should he care for them? His delight was in his fauns and dryads who understood his nature and like him were unfettered by the sad codes and compassions of humanity. And suddenly, coming from nowhere, there sprang into Maurice's mind the question which Mrs. Gervase had asked and withdrawn, "Is the curse over yet?"

That thought broke in upon the spell, shattering it. A breeze set all the poplar leaves a-tremble, and Steven passed his hand over his eyes like one awaking.

"Hullo, Maurice!" he said. "Let's get home, or we shall be keeping Mother waiting for dinner."

The path was narrow and they walked in silent single file up to the house.

"We must have a talk to-night," said Steven as they

crossed the lawn. "There are one or two things I've got to tell you."

"I expect I can guess them," said Maurice.

Steven laughed.

"Bet you a bob you can't," he said. "Done?"

"Rather."

CHAPTER VIII

THE train began to move out of Penzance station, and Steven took his elbows off the sill of the carriage window.

"Good luck, good journey," he said, still walking alongside.

Maurice jumped up and fished in his pocket for a shilling.

"I quite forgot," he said, "I lost that bet."

For half a second Steven looked puzzled: then he remembered. "Honest fellow," he said, "I'd forgotten, too."

Maurice pulled up the window: the breeze off the sea was rather chilly. It lay gray and lead coloured on this cloudy morning, with a streak of sun near the horizon. There was St. Michael's Mount looking like the drop scene in a musical comedy; there ought to have been the deck of a man-of-war for foreground instead of a train. He wondered how Steven's crazy motor car would behave on his drive back to Trenair; he wondered whether that streak of sun would vanquish the clouds and let Steven bask and bathe. . . . The train had started on the tick of time, and he might catch his connection at Exeter, otherwise he must telegraph to his uncle to say that he would arrive by the later of the two trains he had mentioned. A week's golf at Westward Ho! would be pleasant, and in eight days from now he would be back at Cambridge again, and Torrington would be telling them about the Matterhorn. The general prospect seemed rather interesting and agreeable. . . . And then he began thinking about that shilling he had lost to Steven. He had lost it fair and square, for among all the things which he had anticipated that Steven might have to say, the announcement that he would not come back to Cambridge had been wholly unexpected, and Maurice had not quite realized it, or adjusted himself to it even yet. At present the fact seemed a mere black and white outline: his mind had not got hold of it in the round.

He began to recall again that talk, brief and quiet, as it had taken place two evenings ago. Steven's mother had left them at the end of dinner telling them not to be too long before joining her, for she wanted a game of piquet with Maurice. There was something on her mind, he thought, for she had been silent and withdrawn, unlike Steven, who had chattered away in the highest spirits, and, as his custom was, had drunk a good deal of wine. Now, as she left them, he poured himself out a big glass of port, and drank it at a draught.

"I'm afraid I shall never realize my ambition to get drunk," he said. "It must be delightful to feel a rosy cloud softly enveloping your mind. Tim's a lucky young devil—oh, I forgot that you didn't approve of my hospitality to him. . . . Yes, I've got something to tell you which I think will be a surprise to you; perhaps you won't like it. I shan't come back to Cambridge in October. There goes your bob, I think."

Maurice felt, the moment that this was said, that it had happened before. It was surely ages ago that they had sat here, and Steven had told him that.

"Rather a sudden decision, isn't it?" he asked.

"Yes; all decisions are sudden," said Steven. "I came to this one as we walked back before dinner from the wood, and I've told my mother. But of course things have been leading up to it."

"Among which, I suppose," said Maurice, "is the fact that I didn't approve of what you call your hospitality to Tim."

Steven looked up at him with a gay nod of assent.

"Quite right," he said. "I'm awfully sorry about it, for I thought we should go far together. But when two fellows have been to each other what you and I have been for these last few months, they can't relapse into casual acquaintanceship. I couldn't drop into your room every now and then and you into mine and talk about Stares. It's far better to cut the whole affair. I should hate seeing you about and meeting you in the Court, and I've no doubt you would really feel the same."

"In fact, it's because I shall be at Cambridge that you've settled not to come up," said Maurice. "That's what it comes to."

"That's only partly the reason. As I say, we should keep on meeting, and that would be very tiresome. . . . I hate saying these things, you know, but there's a good deal of sense in them."

"And what's the rest of the reason?" asked Maurice.

"Because I can't dream of leaving Trenair," said Steven. "I'm getting at something here: the place is aware. I'm beginning to catch glimpses of what lies below the world that we see."

Maurice was silent a moment.

"Steven, I've been doing the same since I knew you," he said at last and very simply, "and what I find beneath it is love."

Some small frown of impatience showed itself on Steven's face. Maurice was not looking at him and did not see it.

"Rough luck, Maurice," he said. "I'm sorry."

Maurice shook his head.

"I don't want your pity," he said. "Besides, you haven't got any. You can't know what it means, unless you care."

"Yes, perhaps that's true," said Steven.

Again there was silence; he refilled and emptied his glass.

"If you want to know my plans," he said, "I shall stop here for the present, because this is where the secret lies. I may not be able to get on beyond a certain point; there may be something terrible which will scare me away. If so I suppose I shall enter the shipping business and marry and settle down to being just one among the blind millions. . . . Shall we go? I rather think my mother wants to talk to you: that's what she meant by saying she'd like a game of piquet. She disapproves most strongly of my plan. She's frightened at something, and she won't tell me what it is. In fact, she's deserting me too."

Maurice could hardly believe he had heard this said.

"She's deserting you, *too,*" he repeated. "You mean, I suppose, that I'm deserting you. That's rather a singular thing! You've just told me that you've no more use for me, and then you say I have deserted you."

"So you have. You've refused or been unable to come farther with me. That's deserting, to my mind."

Maurice got up.

"There's no need to say any more," he said.

For a few minutes, as the train stopped at Truro, this sharp-edged unwinking picture of that scene faded from the screen of his mind. Somebody got into the carriage and sat in the far corner seat. Then, as the train slid out of the station, the film of memory began to move again, so well lit, so firm. . . .

Mrs. Gervase had been sitting in the hall with the card table ready when they came out of the dining room, and she and Maurice began to play. Steven fidgeted about the room, went to the door and stood there, as if listening, came back, took up a book, dropped it again, and finally strolled out, whistling, onto the lawn, closing the door behind him. Mrs. Gervase was in the middle of dealing the cards, but she laid them down.

"What is happening, Maurice?" she said. "Steven tells me that you've dropped him. Is that true?"

"No. He's dropped me," said Maurice. "It's he who has

given me up; he's no more use for me. He told me so in so many words. But he says I've deserted him."

"He says the same to me, just because I begged him to go back to Cambridge," said Mrs. Gervase. "He tells me I want to get rid of him, that I want to drive him away from his home. And there's truth in that, too. I do want him to go. There's something happening here, there's something at work, and it's getting hold of him. . . . Maurice, I'm terrified. Again and again I ask myself—I can't help it—if the curse is finished yet."

Maurice knew well that of all maladies there is none so infectious as fear, and none so paralyzing. Neither of them could do any good if they were frightened; that was the first thing to get rid of, and with a violent effort he jerked himself out of the grasp of some terror, vague and dim and deadly, that was closing with him.

"Look at Steven," he said, "and tell me if you ever saw a fellow more superbly human," he said.

"And observe Steven," said she, "and tell me if you ever saw one less human. That poor boy who was drowned: for years he was Steven's greatest friend, and Steven didn't care. Then there's yourself: does he value your love for him, or mine either? Love and friendship mean nothing to him, he doesn't know what they are. And he's without pity."

Maurice heard these last two words set themselves to the rhythm of the wheels of the train. "Without pity, without pity, without pity," they beat out in some brisk tripping measure. He saw that he was alone now in the carriage; the train must have stopped somewhere, and the passenger who had got in at Truro disembarked again, but all that had happened without his seeing it. . . . He had had no answer to this, for ten minutes before he had told Steven just exactly that himself. Yet the fact that anyone else, especially his mother, should accuse Steven of that ultimate baseness which takes humanity from man and merges him in the brute roused his stricken loyalty.

"Don't let us admit that of him for a moment, Mrs. Gervase," he said. "He's so set on one aim that he can't regard anything else. He brushes aside, carelessly, not wantonly, anything that seems to get in the way."

"And what's that aim?" she asked.

Maurice chose his words carefully, as if he was giving some important definition to a class of students.

"Realization of himself," he said at length. "He wants to get down to the bed rock of himself. And he believes that he will arrive at that here. There's something in this place, some old inherited instinct or knowledge, some spell that will reveal it. It comes out of the woodland: Tim knows about it; it's he who knows most."

"But what is it?" she cried. "What is the aim which you attain by being without pity or love? What do you become if you throw these over? Don't you see?"

Their eyes met over this, and there grew in them some horror that became intolerable. "If we look at each other like this," thought Maurice, "we shall get panic." He broke off this dumb staring contact.

"You're thinking of the curse," he said. "Put it out of your mind. Refuse to believe it."

The handle of the door through which Steven had gone out clicked and turned, and he sauntered in again. Dew had condensed in minute drops on his hair, and the strong light from the electric lamp just above him turned it into a halo, an aureole. His eyes were alight, his mouth smiling and gay.

He sat down on the arm of his mother's chair.

"Darling, you and Maurice have had a clear ten minutes to pick me to bits," he said. "That's sufficient, isn't it? Don't bother to tell me what awful conclusions you've come to, or what a devil you think me, because I shan't care. And don't try to argue with me: if you do I shall simply go to bed. Chuck me a cigarette, Maurice, and try to be friendly; I'm friendly enough."

Friendliness and charm had been the keynote of his behaviour next day. Maurice and he had strolled and sailed and bathed; they were together, as in earlier days, from morning till night, and he had made no quiet disappearance to seek communion with Tim. When they went to bed that night Steven had wandered in and out of Maurice's room which adjoined his, chattering in the old way as he undressed, and finally, ready for bed, he had put two intimate hands on Maurice's shoulders.

"Really I'm awfully sorry about it all," he said. "It's a pity, but neither of us can help it."

As Maurice watched this final scene of his memory film, the rattle of the train boomed hollow as it rolled over the viaduct at Saltash, then sounded solid again on the earth of Devon. Cornwall, and all that was mysteriously brewing there, was left behind.

Some sort of numbness settled on him. These things were written, and nothing could erase them. They seemed to finish a page in the book of his days, and the next leaf was not turned yet. He spent a week with his uncle, a week of normal pleasantly occupied days, but below them lay some vast emptiness. These ordinary employments seemed all that existed in life: there was nothing in them or in the energies that enacted them which came from within. During these last few months every thought and deed of his had been tinged with the colour of the emotional affection which possessed him; the most trivial of them had been a festival because he had a friend. Now Steven had finished with him, and life, such as it was before Steven had come into it, must be pursued along its normal course, not with stoicism, for there was nothing painful about it, but with a sense of its profound meaninglessness.

Soon he was back at Cambridge, with the business of the term to tackle, and he, a Don like all the rest of his colleagues with plenty of work to give body to the day, and with the usual relaxations to fill his leisure.

Steven had already written to the Provost to say that he was not intending to spend his third year at Cambridge, and the announcement had roused a mild interest in the session in the combination room that night. Torrington much regretted it, for the King's boat would be sadly weakened by his loss, and it was quite inexplicable to him that a man who had so good a chance of stroking the University crew should abandon one of the most dazzling prospects that life offered. It was sad, too, that poor young Merriman had been drowned at Schaffhausen: there were strong and dangerous currents in the Rhine, and if he had known that Merriman was going there to study German he would have warned him. He wondered whether Merriman's death had contributed to Gervase's curious decision: they had been such great friends that perhaps he felt a distaste for Cambridge. He suggested this to Maurice, but they agreed that Gervase had too much vitality and rebound to let himself be knocked down by his loss. . . . As for Torrington himself, he had had a glorious month's climbing at Zermatt: the Matterhorn (from Breuil), the Zienal Rothorn, the Weisshorn, and the Dent Blanche had all, for brief moments, lain beneath his feet. But he reverted to Steven again and said he would certainly write to him and urge him to reconsider his singular determination, if the Provost thought he might be given a few days' law before his letter was taken as final.

The Provost was quite willing: he hoped that Maurice would add his weight.

"We should all be glad to see Gervase back," he crooned. "A round robin, in fact, almost might be sent to him, though I am afraid the precedent of all the staff requesting an undergraduate not to desert them would be scarcely judicious. He would have the whip hand of us, would he not? He would say he had only resumed residence as a favour to us."

Torrington wrote to Steven that night, though Maurice did not. But he received no answer, and in a few days packers appeared, who by order of Mr. Steven Gervase despatched his books and other properties to Trenair. George Herbert Redcliffe took over at a valuation the rest of the furniture that he had left there, and moved into his room, and pinned up on the walls many architectural drawings.

Maurice, as recorded, had added up the items in the history of these last months, up to the date when the train took him out of Penzance on that gray September morning, and this removal of Steven's books and bric-à-brac seemed to draw a double line below the total and formally close it. He put the statement away in his mind, finished and done with as far as he was concerned. But whoever opened that drawer again, he resolved it should not be he: Steven, or perhaps Steven's mother, might possibly, one of these days, fumble at it, and finding it was not locked examine his account. If so, he had nothing to add or subtract from it, for it seemed unquestionably correct.

He had no comment to make on it, and though he did not attempt in any real sense to forgive Steven for his treatment of himself, he believed that if Steven had any remarks to make on it he was willing to consider it fairly. But he felt that nothing could ever induce him to enter into relations with Steven again; he had given him all that his nature contained of affection and love, and Steven had fingered and examined the gift, such as it was, and had tossed it away, not only as some flower now withered, but as one that had never been worth the plucking. Yet Maurice had no animosity towards him, for though a more wanton betrayal could scarcely be imagined, and though his determination never to attempt to renew the intimacy showed how far he was from forgiveness, his deliberate refusal to pore bitterly over the account was in itself an acknowledgment that there was something about Steven which he could not judge. His own confessed adoration of him confirmed the existence of that, for that which he adored in him was exactly that of which he could not judge. But that which he had adored he now believed was none other than that which from the beginning he had found terrible and which Mrs. Gervase feared.

Yet how fantastic, and increasingly so, as the staid academical days began to tick smoothly by, with the regular striking of their ordered hours, became the notion that Steven was anything other than an extraordinarily attractive and heartless fellow. For weeks, it was true, in that withdrawn and magical combe of Trenair, some spell had been working on Maurice: that enchanted wood with the clearing that was once perhaps the site of some Greek temple, the wild vines that so strangely wreathed it, the "awareness" of the fisher folk. Tim and his mad fancies about Steven, and that strange family history of the Gervases which hovered there, all these had combined to form in his mind some wild, vague surmise of what lay at the root of it all.

That history was authentic enough; there in that circle of stones on the hilltop were the graves of those generations of eldest sons who had not been wholly human, and the curse had persisted up to the last generation, for Steven had himself seen and his mother had testified to the merry, horned little monster who had been his own uncle. Linked up with this was her terrified apprehension that the curse was not over yet, and Maurice saw what she meant by that: Steven's pitilessness, his utter lack of human feeling, in spite of his perfect physical manhood, had caused that deadly doubt to assail her.

But now in this quiet progression of Cambridge days there grew in Maurice an incredulous wonder at himself for ever having suffered such a notion to present itself. He was surrounded by sane and educated colleagues, and about him seethed the young gay life in which Steven till a few months ago had been taking a conspicuous but entirely normal part, and there was not one of those colleagues nor a single undergraduate of the entire University who would not, if he even hinted at what he had allowed himself to imagine, cheerfully regard him as a lunatic. Or if by some preposterous plebiscite this entire body of sane persons was asked to vote upon the question as to whether Steven Gervase, late of this college, was by virtue of a family curse not human at all, there could be no doubt as to what the unanimous verdict would be. The conviction that this was so acted like some warm sun ray on these perilous mists; he told himself, with the admitted force of such reasoning to back him, that under the spell of a most fascinating personality, which had showed itself so ruthless and inhuman, he had woven a tissue the most fantastic and incredible.

But there were other moments as well, when his reason was not on its guard. He would wake, for instance, in the darkness before the late autumn dawn and find his brain swarming with ideas that had broken prison. The end was not yet, he told himself: there was something brewing in that Cornish combe, some ferment maturing. The spell was still weaving there, forces were astir which were developing in Steven that which he really was. But with the repetition of his normal days, that assault on his incredulity grew fainter, or the power of his resistance greater, and by the time the term was half through they troubled him but little. Steven had rather taken the taste out of life, but then, after all, life had had no very great savour before. Emotionally Maurice had always been withdrawn and shy of contacts, and this excursion, fiery in quality, had scorched him. He would attempt no further adventure but get back into his cool, safe shell again.

It was not so difficult to do this as he had imagined it would be. The imitative instinct is universal, and to be surrounded by intelligent people who went about their work with placid industry enforced by the conviction that life could not be spent better than they were spending it, had on him an effect similar to that of a course of medicinal treatment for some bodily ailment. It was cumulative in action, and though sometimes still, as he walked back to his rooms after Hall and saw a long chink of light shining out between the drawn curtains in the windows that had once been Steven's, some flash of involuntary association made him say to himself, "Hurrah! I'll look in on him," he could now extinguish it before it blazed high, and there would follow it a trickle of relief that Steven was not here. Steven had sought his friendship, and when he had tired of it had dropped it and passed on. *Requiescat in Trenair.*

It was a tepid December night during the last week of the term, and as he passed these rooms on his way to his own for a game of piquet with Stares and an hour's work before going to bed, the reaction after seeing the light within them came instantaneously and strongly, and he was thankful that he had done with Steven forever. Life had become peaceful and rather pleasant again, and for the first time he found himself unreservedly glad to be rid of him. No longer did he feel any ache of emptiness, but a sort of exultation, such as a man may feel when he realizes that he has got rid of a bad habit, at having broken the craving for a drug. He had not searched for the image: it had leaped into his mind; but once there he acknowledged its aptness. Strange was it that what had been so ardent an affection should suddenly represent itself as a craving for some ruinous poison of the spirit, strange that he should mentally applaud for its appositeness so ruthless a labelling.

But there, so it struck him now, was the key to Steven: the fascination of his personality was evil, as is the longing for a drug; but his personality itself was not evil any more than there is something inherently immoral in cocaine or morphia. They are agents for undoing, but in their essence they are as innocent as bread or wholesome fruit. In just the same way Steven was without evil purpose. His indifference to the code of affection and compassion and the moral responsibilities which redeem human existence from the callousness and the cruelty of animals was not deliberate. He was not a fiend: his attitude towards such a code was neutral rather than hostile; not satanic, or loving evil for its own sake, but purely pagan. He was pitiless, not because he desired to hurt, but because he did not care.

Maurice went slowly up the uncarpeted staircase to his room with this new light on Steven illuminating his mind. At once he saw how it fitted in with the terror at which Mrs. Gervase had hinted, that the curse was not over yet, and that more grimly and more tragically than ever before it was working out the inscrutable decrees. It had allowed her son the perfect human form, but within its contours of unique grace and beauty there was wrapped this spirit of bland indifference to all that gave grace and beauty to human life. . . . And was there within himself, thought Maurice, some secret craving for the moral liberty of the animal, the "wild thing" which, coupled with Steven's physical charm, had produced in him this inexplicable adoration? Though just now he had figured himself as one who had escaped from Steven as from some deleterious habit, he felt a wave of compassion flooding his mind for the innocent, terrible fellow. He would have scorned himself for shrinking from some exquisitely minded man who laboured beneath a birthright of abominable physical deformity, and yet he had been shrinking, with a misbegotten sense of righteousness, from one who from brith had been deformed in mind and whose soul was soaked in some inherited sorcery.

All these were disordered thoughts, vague, fitful searchlights which vainly tried to pierce the mists which hung so closely round the little creatures which danced or crawled about their urgent businesses till death crushed them between a careless thumb and forefinger. It was wiser, no doubt, to take example by his colleagues, to turn off the searchlight, and to stop his ears to the menace of these questionings which assailed him, now from this quarter and now from that, so that his mind veered and shifted like a weathercock before a storm. Far better was it to accept the overwhelming vote of the majority, to dismiss all thoughts of Trenair and the crazy conjectures which it inspired, and devote his faculties to historical deductions which could be checked and verified by inscriptions and chronicles. Yet even as he turned on the electric switch close to the door of his room, he wondered what he would do, what he would say, if by some magical trick he found Steven waiting for him in the dark. But "of course" (in academical parlance) there was no one there, and on his table, spread out, as he had left them, his notebooks and classical volumes. Stares's piano was tinkling next door: Stares was waiting for him to play a game or two of piquet. After that he would have an hour's work, for he was lecturing to-morrow on the return of Alcibiades to Athens after his campaign in the Euxine. There could be no better antidote to fantastic dreamings than the study of the career of that remarkably clear-headed scamp.

He worked later than he had intended, slept dreamlessly, and came next morning into his sitting room to find breakfast already laid and a telegram placed conspicuously on the table. It was from Steven, and it ran:

> I must see you and shall arrive at Cambridge this afternoon. Please put me up for the night.

It had been sent off from Penzance an hour before.

Maurice's mind was instantly made up: whatever the reason was for which Steven wanted to see him (and as to that it was impossible to frame the smallest conjecture), he was determined not to let himself enter into any relation of friendship or of friendliness with him again. It was impossible now to stop his arrival, or he would have done so, but Steven had evidently sent this telegram from Penzance just before catching the train. But if Steven was coming to him with any appeal that would reassociate them, that appeal would fall on deaf ears, whatever its nature. Though last night he had felt compassion for him as for one deformed, or at least had blamed himself for feeling none, he now repudiated any such impulses. Certainly he would arrange to get one of the guest rooms for him, certainly he would hear what he had made this long journey to say (and curiosity perhaps more than anything else prompted that), but nothing would induce him to do more than perform a cold office. He crumpled up the telegram, ate his breakfast, and went out to the performance of his scholastic businesses.

In these short days of December it grew early dark, and Maurice had just lit the light and drawn the curtains when he heard a step on the stairs. If he had not even known that Steven was coming, if he had believed him to be buried in the remoteness of Cornwall, he thought he would have recognized that step, and from mere untutored habit his heart leaped. There was a knock on his door (imagine Steven knocking!), then the handle clicked and turned and he entered. For a moment he stood there, as if waiting for the word of welcome which was absent, and then he advanced into the fuller illumination by the table. Some change had come on his face since last Maurice had seen him standing on the platform at Penzance, and he instantly perceived the quality of it. Darkly he rejoiced at that, for from Steven's eyes, now fixed on him, there looked out fear.

Maurice spoke first; his voice, cold and indifferent, expressed him perfectly.

"I got your telegram," he said. "I noticed that you sent it off just before you left yourself, so that I could not stop your coming."

Steven shook his head.

"I did not do that on purpose," he said. "Do you mean that if you could have stopped me you would have done so?"

"Yes, I think I should," said Maurice. "I am not sure, because I own to a certain curiosity. But you told me you had finished with me and had made up your mind that the break should be complete. I have grown to be of the same mind. I never want to see you again."

With the sight and proximity of him, with the charm of his bodily presence, the whole of the past, his own devotion and Steven's callous betrayal of him, surged back into Maurice's soul, bitter as bile. He had not known, till he saw him again, how strong the poison had been, and Steven's presence set it working in him again. He had thought he had no animosity against him, but now he hated him.

"You chose to come here," he said, "and you made it impossible for me to stop you. Presently I will hear what has brought you here and why you wanted to see me. But first I'll tell you the truth about yourself. Don't interrupt me, just sit down and listen."

He pointed to the sofa, and without taking his eyes off him Steven sat down. Maurice noted that when he said,

"I'll tell you the truth about yourself," the fear in his face was kindled into a burning terror, and that filled him with some sort of sadistic delight.

"It won't take long," he said, "because I shall be very direct, and a few sentences will tell you everything I think of you. You've got a black heart. You don't know what love is or what pity is. You took all I had to give you, and then you shrugged your shoulders and said you had no more use for me. I gave you love, and since you couldn't understand it, it bored you, as if you had been bidden to read a book in some unknown tongue. Since then, and in spite of that, I have given you pity, because I saw you as some monstrous deformity, with a soul crippled and twisted and dwarfed. But, now I see you again that pity is extinguished, and you are absolutely horrible to me. And you've changed, too: did you know that? You're frightened, and fear is a horrid feeling. Perhaps you've come to tell me about it. I'm glad you know what it is like."

This stream of cold deliberate hate had burst from Maurice under some impulse that he did not try to control; it was as if Steven's presence had smitten the rock, and the entombed liquor had sprung from it. But now the flow was spent: he had no wish to squeeze out any last drops, and already he wondered what had been the good of it. Steven, being what he was, would not care.

"That's the gist of what I have to say to you," he said. "It doesn't do the smallest good, for neither love nor hate exists for you. And I find it's no satisfaction to me, so I shan't enlarge on it. I only want you to pass out of my life altogether. But as you're here you may say what you came to say, and then I think you had better go. I've ordered one of the guest rooms for you, as you wished to stop the night, and I've told them in the kitchen to send dinner in for you if you want it."

During this Steven had sat without making the smallest gesture or movement. He listened closely, a chill fear, as in the eyes of a hunted animal, couched smouldering in his. He let a pause follow Maurice's words, as if of courtesy, to be sure that he would not interrupt him, and then he leaned forward.

"I acknowledge the truth of every word you have spoken," he said. "I must have seemed to you, as you say, deformed in soul. But you don't understand anything about me."

Maurice gave a short crack of laughter; this was surely egoism *in excelsis*.

"That is very likely the case," he said. "The only thing I ask for is that you should continue to be a complete mystery to me. I know something of you, and if I don't understand you I am content to abide the loss."

Again Steven paused.

"Maurice, if you found me lying on your staircase," he said, "with a string knotted round my neck, which was strangling me, would you walk by, or would you cut the string?"

Maurice shook his head.

"It's no use saying that sort of thing," he said, "if it is meant to be an appeal. I suppose I should try to save your life, because I happen to be human, and that is a human instinct. But you must remember that you wouldn't do the same for me, if you were in a hurry, and wanted to make Tim drunk, or something of that sort."

"I daresay that is quite true," said Steven quietly. "And what terrifies me is that it is true."

"I'm very glad to hear it. I hope you'll go on being terrified. Terror may teach you, perhaps, what pity means and what love means. But that's your affair, not mine."

"But I want you to make it yours," said Steven. "Terrible things have happened, and there's no one to whom I can tell them, except you. I can't bear them alone. I must have your advice, and your view of it all. I am being strangled."

"Well, go on," said Maurice. "I told you I would hear what you had to say."

Steven got up and stood leaning over the table towards him.

"It's the curse that is on me," he said, "and it is beginning to tighten its hold. I thought that because I was like other men physically it was over, and all this time, since first I began to pry into things that I thought mysterious and lovely, it has been gaining on me. I wanted, as you know, to learn about the powers and inheritance that are somewhere dormant in us. You understood something of this, so I believed, as that was why I was drawn to you. You agreed: you felt something of that call, and you too saw how friends who were devoted to each other could go farther than one alone. And then you hung back, and, as you say, I chucked you. I didn't see that all the time I was becoming something not human. I was brutal to the Child and to you and to my mother, not deliberately because I liked cruelty, but because I didn't care."

"Oh, have you treated your mother in the same sort of way as you treated me?" asked Maurice.

The horror deepened in Steven's eyes, and he covered his face for a moment as he sat back on the sofa again.

"It's hideous," he said. "You liked her, I know. . . . . And she's been drowned. Her body was washed up three days ago on the beach where we used to bathe. Maurice . . . I am sure she drowned herself."

For the first time Maurice's hostility wavered. He sat down by Steven with hand held out.

"Oh, Steven, how tragic!" he said. "Tell me about it."

"It's grim, it's ghastly," he said, "and the worst part of it is that I'm not sorry. I don't grieve for her: I'm only hideously frightened for myself. But I'll tell you. After you left she kept urging me to go back to Cambridge, but that I was determined not to do, and, as you know, I wrote to say I was not coming up again. Then she kept begging me not to remain at Trenair but to enter my uncle's office at once. I treated it all quite lightly at first: I chaffed her, I said she wanted to get rid of me. But she was serious about it; she kept on like some endless litany, beseeching me to go. And when she wasn't nagging at me she was watching me, all day and at night even, for I woke up and found her by my bedside. I was angry at that, for several times I thought somebody had come into my room, and she said she did look in occasionally, to see if I was safe. What did she mean by safe? I asked her, and she said she didn't know: just safe."

Steven stopped; he looked round the room.

"We had jolly times here in the summer, Maurice," he said. . . . "Well, it went on like that for weeks, and she never would tell me why she wanted me to go away. She would only say that it wasn't a natural life for a young man to lead, with no work to do, and no one in the house but his mother. I still tried to laugh her out of it; I told her that she would be the most adorable companion if she would only cease nagging and watching me. I reminded her that we had often spent delightful holiday weeks together under just these conditions. Besides, now I had Tim, whom I saw every day. But when I mentioned him she begged me not to be with him so much: she said it was dangerous, that I was encouraging what she was afraid of, whereas I ought to be fighting it. But still she wouldn't say what she was afraid of or what I ought to be fighting. At last it all got so bad that I told her that if she wouldn't cease worrying me, either she would have to leave Trenair or I should go and live down in the village. There was an empty cottage there, and I should get Tim to look after me."

Maurice knew very well—for had not she told him?—what was the secret fear under which she sickened, namely, that the evil sap of the curse was not yet dry. And easily he understood why she would not tell Steven of her dread, for the mind is like some fruitful plot in which the seed of any suggestion, when once idly dropped there, may terribly flourish, and to have put it into his head that the doom of the eldest sons of his race was continuing its further incarnations would have been of all things the most dangerous. His knowledge of her fear would have nurtured the peril she dreaded. Steven guessed it now, but not from her: she had wanted, without hinting at anything of the sort, to get him away, to surround him with human influence and normal pursuits. Clearly, also, his intimacy with Tim disturbed her: the woodland animal with his pipe and ivy wreath made an atmosphere congenial to the working of the curse.

"She got worse and worse," Steven went on; "she tried to get Tim away, she tried to let the house, she was full of transparent, silly devices, all so futile. But it was her fear—that fear—and her nagging and her watching that were the worst, and I couldn't go on living with her. So one day, when she had gone over to Penzance, I did as I had threatened. I sent a cartload of furniture down from the house to the empty cottage in the village, and when she came back she found I had gone. She came down after me and wept and wailed and promised she would control herself more and not worry me, but I told her it was too late. Besides, the relief of getting away from her was so immense: I had got to hate her, and I didn't want to hate her; simply I could not help it.

"I don't think that ever in my life I have been so happy as I was that evening. I had broken with all the ties that could hamper me: the Child first, then you, then my mother. Tim cooked some food for me, and we ate together, and then we went out. It was one of those warm winter nights that we have there, when already, though it was only December, the woods were listening for the footfall of spring, and there was a full moon, which always made Tim wild with some primeval passion. We wandered to his piping, and I felt, in a way I had never experienced before, the whole stifling burden of self-consciousness slip from me. I, and Tim far more than me, were becoming part of the earth and the trees, and the owls that quested, and the moon that poured down on us. . . . And we were more than part of them: we were the very spirit that animated them, not the mere material part of them, but the life of them. We ran, we danced, we lay on the ground panting for the ecstasy of it; we were the children of the woodland, but also its lords. . . . No, I wasn't mad, and I'm not mad now, but my God, I was happy. Or is it madness to be happy? Never for a moment did a thought of my mother enter my head, nor even the thought of myself. I wasn't young any more, I wasn't old, or, if you like, I was eternally young and eternally old, poised there. And all the time I knew that it was the merest glimpse that I had yet got of the reality that underlies the mask of life. We did not want to run any more or dance; it was bliss just to exist and to be aware."

This was wild raving stuff, but never did it enter Maurice's head that Steven was mad. Indeed, as he listened, Steven seemed to be telling him what in some secret cell of his mind he knew to be soberly true. That secret cell had knowledge of these things; Steven was only reminding it of them, and it thrilled with the recollection, faint to him as some remote echo, of an ancient and catholic inheritance. Steven's excitement had lifted him on his feet, and now he stood there, alert and tall, and from his eyes, as he spoke, all trace and semblance of fear had vanished: they shone with the glory of a flushed sky, and his face glowed as with dawn.

Then slowly that light faded, as when a lamp burns low and lower yet, and the shadows creep out from their lairs.

"We got home just as the east began to brighten," said Steven. "It had been a night of sacrament; it had fed and nourished me. But I suppose my body was tired, though I had no sense of it myself, for my body had been to me no more than my jersey was to it, something that conveniently clothed it for a time: and I just lay down on my bed and was instantly asleep. It was still early when I awoke. I yawned and stretched, knowing, as one does sometimes when one awakes, that there was some huge happiness all round one; I was swimming in it. I was very drowsy; at least, my body was still full of sleep, and I lay very quiet, not wanting to awake further, but just go on floating in that happiness. Slowly I began to remember the night I had spent in the wood, and I knew it was that, and what had been soaking into me there, which made my happiness. Then I awoke more, and there began creeping over me, coming from nowhere, some horror of the spirit, blacker than pitch."

Steven's throat was twitching: he commanded his voice with difficulty.

"All that had filled me with that wild happiness," he said, "filled me now with terror. I knew what had caused my mother's fear for me, and her fear was mine. What I had thought to be enlightenment was a gulf of darkness into which I had dived deep. The curse was working in me, for I was ceasing to be human. I had been welcoming and aiding it: it was that she meant when she said I ought to have been fighting it."

Some ghostly enemy was invading Maurice's mind, breaking through the flimsy defences of Cambridge, where he thought to be secure from such phantasmal attacks.

He tried to rally himself against them, to tell himself that he was allowing himself to harbour ludicrous imaginings, but he could not make himself mock them.

"I slipped off my bed," said Steven, "leaving Tim there, and went up through the woods to the house. The grass in the clearing, where last night we had lain and danced in the moonshine, was shimmering with dew, and I saw, as I had seen on that morning when I returned with the Child from our night on the river, on the lawn here, the marks of our footprints. And though one part of me was still flying panic-stricken from the horror of what I was becoming, there was another part, which hungered and thirsted, as the saints of God yearn for the sacrament, after the bliss and the freedom that were its paradise. It tugged at me, bidding me go no further, but wait here for Tim to join me again. I only had to let him know, as I let the squirrel know, that I wanted him. But the horror tugged at me, too: I must see my mother and find out whether it was this she had feared for me. Perhaps it was only some damnable reaction after last night that had blackened my awaking, and she would laugh at me for my trepidations. So I went on up to the house. It was early, and there was no one about but a housemaid sweeping in the hall, who looked at me in a frightened way. I ran upstairs to my mother's room and knocked, and as I got no reply I went in. She was not there, and her bed was unslept in. I rang the bell, and her old maid Lisbeth came, and I asked her where my mother was. She had been my mother's nurse and mine, and she worshipped her: that gray-haired old thing, do you remember? who always looked in about eleven in the evening and told her it was time for little girls to get to bed. When she saw my mother's smooth bed, just turned back with her night things lying on it, she burst out at me. 'What have you done with her, Master Steven?' she cried. 'It's you to tell me where she is. Her heart broke last night, when she went down to fetch you home and came back without you.'

"I got her quiet presently, and she told me all she knew. My mother had come home from seeing me the evening before and had locked herself into her bedroom. Lisbeth had come to the door once or twice, but she would not let her in, but finally she opened to her and told her to go to bed, for she would want nothing. Then she kissed her and turned her out of the room. . . . We searched through the house, but there was no trace of her, and I went back to the village to see if there was any news of her there, or if she had come again to the cottage. I think I knew then that I should never be bothered with her any more, and I wasn't sorry, I wasn't troubled, and I kept thinking to myself how tiresome she had been all these weeks and how I had quite done with her already, as I had done with the Child and you. But all the time the terror was there, too, and for that reason I wanted to find her and learn whether her terror for me was the same as mine. . . . Give me a drink, Maurice, and then I'll finish."

Steven poured himself out a half tumbler of neat whisky, the decanter clinking against the rim of the glass in his unsteady hand, and drank it off.

"The fishermen had gone out late the night before," he said, "on the top of the flood, and one or two of them, as their boats passed the pierhead, had seen a woman sitting there, and in the brightness of the moon they knew it was she. But that was no very rare thing; she often used to come out after dinner and stroll about, and though the lateness of the hour was queer, that was her business. Besides, they knew I had left the house and come down to the village, and she might have been seeing me. The boats were all back now when I got down that morning, and the catch was being landed, and the nets being put out to dry, and I went from one to the other to find out what they could tell me. Then I saw Jan Pentreath on the pierhead shading his eyes against the sparkle of the sun on the sea and looking across to the beach where we used to bathe. There was something lying there on the sand, and the beach was covered with a company of those great black-backed gulls. We rowed out to it, and as we approached all the birds rose wheeling in the air with that hoarse barking of theirs. And what we had seen lying on the beach was she, and her eyes were open, and there was fear in them as they looked at me. I still wanted terribly to know what her fear was, but I was pleased that she would not pester me any more. That was just what I thought when I first knelt by her, but then quickly my terror began to gain on me again, obliterating everything else, and I felt that the fear which had caused her to drown herself was the same fear that was clutching at me. I had to find out, and possibly you could tell me. She talked to you, I know, about me, and she may have told you what her fear was. That was my only chance of finding out, so I came to Cambridge to ask you that. You may share it yourself, though I know you care nothing for what happens to me. So tell me: did she fear that I was under the curse? Out with it."

Maurice did not hesitate for a moment. There was no longer anything to hide from Steven: he had guessed what his mother's terror for him was, and in his own soul it was now appallingly echoed. He saw that not once nor twice only, and that to those who loved him, he had shown himself soulless or brutish of soul, and in that his mother as well as himself had beheld the workings of that grim legend. Possibly this might be a turning point for him, this dread of his ghostly inheritance. But Maurice felt the need of presenting his own case to him with wisdom. Fear never helped a man to struggle successfully against stubborn facts or superstitious fancies.

"Yes, that is exactly what she feared," he said, "and that I learned from her own lips. And it is that you have to fight. Listen to me, then! You've got to tell yourself that the curse is a wild tale akin to incredible witchcraft or sorceries. It doesn't exist: you can't inherit a mere bogey, but what you can do is to bring a curse on yourself, and you've been working for that, God knows, industriously enough, by being without pity or human instincts.

No wand waved hundreds of years ago can turn you into a brute, but you've been doing it for yourself. All your life people have loved you, and when you got tired of their love you dropped them like a burden that chafed you. I know that, for I was among them, and I'm telling you the truth. All your life you've been doing your utmost to realize the curse in yourself, by being heartless and cruel, and I don't wonder that you sit there and shudder because of what you've made of yourself."

"Maurice, am I as awful as that?" asked Steven.

"Oh, don't interrupt: you came up here to get help, and I'm giving it you. If it hurts, so much the better. I've no doubt, too, that all your hocus-pocus with Tim has brutalized you. You thought it would be wonderful to get back in your own person to things antique and spacious: in other words, to the age when man was scarcely removed from the brute. You spoke just now of being the child and the lord of the woodland, but don't deceive yourself with thinking that there is anything fine or marvellous in that. It's a brutish retrogression: it's a deliberate attempt, though not intentional, to invoke the curse you're afraid of. When you go dancing in the woods and making Tim drunk, you're doing the best you can to lose your manhood and become like the beasts that perish. You're cultivating and forcing the curse which you believe in, and which your efforts may make real."

"My word, how you hate me," said Steven suddenly.

"Yes, I suppose I do, and I think that if ever you become a decent average human being yourself, you'll understand why. All the same, I should like to see you recover your manhood, and I suppose that's because I was once devoted to you. Otherwise you might rot in hell. And there's another thing——"

Maurice paused.

"It's this," he said. "I know something also of that lure of the wild. You made me see it, and I thought of yourself and me linked in a marvellous friendship and finding our way back to a morning of the golden age. I see now how hopelessly I misunderstood your aim, which was to free yourself from all that makes human life tolerable. You enchanted me, you made life seem something undreamed of in loveliness, and then you turned away with a shrug. I've learned my lesson, and it was a sore one, but now I welcome and embrace the thought of the old humdrum life which, under your spell, became a creeping thing, deaf and blind. It's sane, anyhow, and it's human."

Steven looked at him in silence, puzzling.

"You hate me, and yet you'd like to save me," he said. "I can't understand that."

"You'd better take it on trust then," said Maurice.

"But you decline to have anything more to do with me."

"Until you show some signs of seeing the horror of your nature, yes," he said. "It's hopeless to talk to you; you don't know the language I speak in. Pity and love are words which have no meaning for you: they're gibberish."

Steven sprang up.

"But, by God, don't you see that it's just that which terrifies me?" he said. "I know I don't understand them, and that's why damnation stares close at me. There must be a human soul in me, mustn't there? or I shouldn't want to understand them. It horrified me to find that I felt no atom of grief when I saw my mother lying there on the beach. I shuddered at the fear in her dead eyes, but I shudder also at myself. And I acknowledge that I treated the Child and you abominably, but I've got to feel it."

He flung out his arm in some helpless gesture.

"Where am I to begin?" he said. "I fled from Trenair as one flies in a nightmare from some throttling horror, and yet already I long to be back there, under the spell of the moonlight in the wet woods with Tim. Besides——"

Into his eyes there came an expression Maurice had never seen there yet: something cunning, something foxlike peered out.

"Besides, what would happen to Tim without me?" he asked. "I'm knit into him, and I'm his God. Am I just to shrug my shoulders once more and leave him? Wouldn't that be damning my soul as much as anything I've done yet?"

"Ah, that's not your reason for wanting to go back," said Maurice. "It's your excuse. You're making him a pretext. It isn't tenderness for Tim that moves you, it's the indulgence of the craving that you say you're fleeing from."

Steven considered this.

"That's quite true," he said at length. "Maurice . . . what am I to do?"

"Turn your back on it all. Root the idea of the curse out of your mind, and root out the idea of being a Lord of the woodland. Go ahead with ordinary human life; don't think you're a victim of the curse or the Messiah to a blind world. If I were you I should go to live with your uncle, and enter his office at once. The curse doesn't exist: you've just been an absolutely selfish young devil, and you're going to do better."

PART III

CHAPTER IX

STEVEN was sitting on a balcony overlooking the Park outside the windows of his uncle's house in Carlton House Terrace. It was a Saturday afternoon in mid-October, and thus he had a day of leisure from his work in the shipping office in which he had been a clerk since before Christmas. He had shown the most exemplary industry at his work, and so much quickness in getting a general comprehension of what business was "about" that Lord Gervase had almost begun to feel that a classical education need not necessarily unfit a young man for the more serious pursuits of life. Nor was his docility confined to his meeting his uncle's wishes in the matter of his business career: he had done all that was expected of him in other matters as well, and had now been married for some months to Betty Nairn, who was also satisfactorily engaged on the first duties of a wife. The marriage had taken place last March, on the day that Steven had come of age, and thus instead of that event being celebrated at Trenair, St. Margaret's, Westminster, had been the scene of the more important ceremony. Betty had wanted to spend the honeymoon at the house in Cornwall, but Steven had been unyieldingly firm on that point. His reason was a very natural one, namely that, so few months before, the place had been tragically associated with his mother's death. But he arranged that any of the tenants who cared to attend his marriage should be provided for, and a conspicuous company they made at the church, that score of tall, fair-haired fishermen. "Steven's Vikings" was the phrase instantly coined for them, and there was considerable curiosity about one amazing boy who was the very image of the bridegroom. As the procession passed down the church he had darted out of his place and kissed Steven's hand, and this was supposed to be a pretty but awkward attempt to kiss the bride's. The Provost of King's College, Cambridge, also was present; he had been surprised that Maurice did not come.

After the honeymoon a fortnight's holiday in September was all the remission he had yet had from his work, and once more Betty had fruitlessly begged to be allowed to spend it with him at Trenair. But again he had ingenious evasions: many of the staff at the office were on holiday, and it was thus far better, in case any emergency of work arose, to be within closer range. Moreover, his uncle had expressed the hope that they would spend it at his house at Easthays, where the parties for partridge shooting and week-ends would be taking place, and help in the hospitalities of the home that would sometime be theirs. Also, so said Steven, Trenair was often very sultry and airless in September: Betty must not get an impression of its languor for her first experience of it. In fact, Steven perhaps had too many reasons for not acceding to her; but she consoled herself with his definite promise that they would go down there for Christmas, and that her first-born should come into the world at the house of his heritage. Of course it would be a boy: she knew it would.

The afternoon sun was warm where Steven sat, and inclined him to a drowsy rambling of mind rather than to a perusal of the illustrated papers which he had brought out of the house. As yet there had hardly been a touch of night frost, and the trees in the Park were towers of full foliage. But through them he could see a gleam of the sun on the lake, just as, sitting on the lawn at Trenair, glimpses of the shine of the sea twinkled through the poplars of the wood below the house. For months now he had banished from his mind, as often as it intruded there, all thought of Trenair and of the panic that had been brewed there for him. It had been a task of the sternest difficulty to do so, for the whole of his consciousness had been blackened by that terror, but unremitting effort to detach it from the harbourage of his mind, and let it drift out to the dim sea from which it came, had met its due reward, and now, as the glint of the lake recalled those glimpses through the poplar wood, he found he could let his mind dwell on Trenair without any responding involuntary tremor. But it had been a stern struggle, for he knew that when he had gone up to Cambridge to see Maurice, after his mother's death, he had been undermined and tottering from fear, and then gradually, gradually consolidation had come. There had been times when that fear had gripped him with a force that seemed undiminished; there had been times, too, when a sick longing for Trenair and the magic of it had almost overwhelmed him, but at such times his terror had befriended him, and he shrank from it again with shuddering repulsion. Of his mother he never thought at all: she was too intimately knit up with that nightmare.

But this afternoon the emotional tension of his craving for the place on the one side, and of his fierce reaction from it on the other, were both relaxed, and he let himself picture it, enchanting rather than enchanted, as it would be basking now in this mellowness of its Southern October. He did not populate it either with the presences that lived there to-day, or with the wraiths of those who had gone from it: he imagined it empty of all inhabitants. The houses were unlived in, the roads unpassengered; the fishing boats lay tilted on the sand of the harbour waiting for the flood to float them, their nets were spread out on the shingle, and the woods lay dozing. No bird call even sounded there, and the great gulls had flapped seaward for their fishing. Pictured like that, and liberated from the fret and rapture of all animal life, the place was harmless to hurt. . . . Then, suddenly, how it pulled at his heartstrings!

It was as if he were there: it was as if he were descending from the high road that lay above the combe, cautiously looking round and pausing on his step to make sure that no perilous footfall pattered in the woodways, nor any dire presence watched his approach. The gorse flared on the encompassing hillsides, the stream grew louder with its affluents. Now he was come within sight of the smokeless roofs of the village and turned up the short rising road that led to his house, which stood empty and swept and garnished. He passed across the lawn to the hall door that stood open for his return, looking up at the windows to see that nothing evilly furtive waited for him. Inside was the faint odour of wood smoke, dear and familiar and constant there, and on the table a bowl of magnolia flowers, but no presence, human or diabolical, was within, and it was home, beloved and welcoming. No curse nor any haunting of ancient malediction dwelt there; it was only his imagination, surely, disordered by grim or ecstatic experience, that had invested it with terror, and he had but to strip off from himself the festering rags of superstition to restore its sweetness. And that, so he told himself, was already done, for by banishing the curse from his mind, as the sage Maurice had counselled him, he had robbed it of its vitality, and now it lay, harmless as a dead rabbit, rotting in the woods.

And for Betty surely as well as himself the place was safe now. She knew nothing whatever about the curse or its history, for in his person was sufficient proof that it was over, and to-day, healthy, happy, exuberant, she was within two months of her deliverance, and that would set the seal of its extinction on the second immune generation. Then, perhaps, over the cradle of her first-born, he might tell her of the worn-out legend, for husband and son alike would testify to its obsolescence. But till then no hint of it must reach her, for fear of those strange prenatal influences which mould a child while yet it lay in its mother's womb.

But he had been right, he felt, not to have taken Betty yet to Trenair, for it was only now that he could look on the face of his dead terror. It had been vital enough to him when first he fled from the place, but now it seemed no more than some vanquished phobia which had never had any existence save such as his own mind had given it. At the time of his marriage, at the time of his holiday, it had still lain coiled there lithe and stale eyed like a snake and ready to rear itself and strike, but now it was there no more, and Betty's desire that her child should be born there might safely be given her. She had always longed to go there, and his refusal at present to take her had puzzled her, in spite of his most admirable excuses. Sometimes he had wondered whether she had suspected any hidden reason for it. But she need puzzle over that no more, for her wish was soon to be granted, and he himself, as well as she, now longed for the sight and scene of its sequestered tranquillity. And yet . . . did he long for it because of that alone, or because of the secret springs that lurked and boiled up in its woodlands?

He had fled from them just as he had fled from the curse, believing that in some strange fashion they were its allies and auxiliaries, but when once the curse had proved doubly effete they would surely be but empty masks that had no face within. There had been wonderful moments in those woods, when his pulses seemed to beat with the very blood of the wild, but not yet did he allow himself to think of them freely, nor hold them in focus: they were out of the field of the direct vision of his intentions, obliquely seen. He did not contemplate the resumption of them, but would let everything develop naturally, when he and Betty got down there. She would not be capable of much activity, she would walk and drive a little, and rest a good deal, and afterwards she would be quite laid up for a while.

He would be a good deal alone, he thought, and would have to make employments for himself, and he wondered whether he had better get a friend to come down there while Betty was laid by. Perhaps (the idea presented itself suddenly) Maurice would join him for a bit of the Christmas vacation. Then he remembered that Maurice had indicated in the clearest manner possible that he wished to have nothing more to do with him. But that did not seem an inexorable decree; conditions had changed since it was issued. . . . And at once he felt how much he wanted to show Maurice how dead the terror was and how normal he had become. A married man in a shipping office: there was a nice and respectable change!

This change was further illustrated on the moment by the sound of his name called from within the house by Betty. It was repeated, but still he did not answer. She had been out to lunch, and if he was at home when she returned there was a vague plan of driving down to Easthays to dine with his uncle, who was there with Aunt Florence, and to return some time to-morrow. Lord Gervase had been unwell lately and had settled in the country for a time, only coming up to London for a day or two when business imperatively demanded him, and leaving Steven and Betty in possession of the house in town. He had suffered a good deal of unexplained pain, and Aunt Florence was anxious about him. When she was anxious she was a very worrying and fidgeting companion, fluttering this way and that like a flustered hen, and Uncle Robert, when in pain, lost all his geniality and a large part even of his pompousness. It therefore occurred to Steven, now that Betty was calling him, not to answer, for he had been out since lunch, and no one had seen him return. Probably Betty would inquire of the servants and find he had gone out, and then the afternoon would slip away, and very soon it would be too late to think of going down to Easthays. Instead, they would go to the theatre to-night, and there was a good concert to-morrow: that would be far pleasanter than spending a dreary evening at Easthays, with family bridge, during which Aunt Florence would cast sad and watchful glances at her husband and forget whether the ace of trumps and other trifling cards of the sort had been played, and Uncle Robert would grow more and more morose. . . .

Since he had been ill he had developed an unpleasant habit of being easily and causelessly irritated by Steven, whose intelligence in the office and obedience in marrying had previously caused him to stand in high favour. Steven interpreted this snappishness as the jealousy of a sick man towards his heir when he thinks that the day of his inheritance may be rather rapidly approaching, and always remained most creditably undisturbed by these growlings, and never failed in being patient and unprovoked. But no one could enjoy them, and though he would have been the first frankly to congratulate Uncle Robert on getting well again, he felt that if that happier alternative was not to be, it would be a relief to all concerned if he was spared a lingering and painful illness. Besides, it was impossible to like people who were ill: were not the lame and the blind hated of David's soul? Physical infirmities were a *gêne* to others beside the invalid. Let him have all encouragement and aid to get well and be pleasanter again, but if he couldn't manage that . . .

Steven wondered if these were rather inhuman reflections: he had quite got into the habit of pulling himself up over thoughts as well as actions which could be considered lacking in compassion. If he could not make himself feel pity, he could, and often did, avoid deliberate indulgence in its opposite. But he decided this question in his own favour: he would be quite pleased if Uncle Robert got better, and surely it was not a failure in pity to hope that, if he was only going to get worse, his sufferings and the inconvenience they caused to other people should not be unduly prolonged. He was in no hurry to step into his inheritance, so long as Uncle Robert found a reasonable enjoyment in life, but if he was only to find it increasingly uncomfortable, the most compassionate would surely be right in wishing him out of it. Steven did not covet wealth in itself: an immense balance at the bank and a careful reinvestment of money for which he had no real use had even less attraction for him than has the hoarding of bones for dogs, or the making of a magazine of food for birds. His uncle's death would not bring him, in spite of the great wealth that would be his, anything that he really wanted or valued: he was singularly indifferent to the aroma of money, and the smell of the woods after a shower was worth more, for the actual joy it brought him, than a check of many figures. The very handsome allowance which he already enjoyed was more than sufficient; he was no hand at either spending or hoarding. It might be pleasant not to be so tightly tied down to work in which he felt no particular interest, but he had no intention, when he became master of a great fortune, of living in idleness. His brain (such was the lesson the last months had taught him) had to be busy, and its business must be concerned in material pursuits which gave it a tethering occupation. There were seductive pastures he knew where it longed to graze at will, and fascinating regions, dim and perilous, where it longed to wander, but these were secret cravings neither to be indulged nor dwelt upon. Man was not free as the trees and the furry, bright-eyed beasts of the forests were free: he had hedged himself round with codes, and palisaded himself with commandments, and it was through obedience to them that he had differentiated himself from the brutes. He must not desire reinless irresponsibility, or, if he desired it, he must obey the curb. Steven hoped that with him this would become a habit, and that surrounded by human cares and calls he would cease to desire anything else. Above all, he must continue to direct his life by the laws of consideration and kindliness, so that out of obedience to them might spring the instincts which would make the curse impotent to harm him. In time he might even get to love people.

A step coming across the big drawing room inside towards the balcony where he sat interrupted these edifying meditations. He knew it was Betty's; there was a deliberation about it, as if she was walking a little stiffly, which now took the place of her usually light and brisk tread. Her face had changed too, it had become fuller, and her figure had lost its boyish slimness. It was a pity . . . Out she came.

"Darling, there you are!" she said. "I've been calling you."

Steven yawned.

"Have you, Betty?" he said with admirably feigned drowsiness. "When? Just now, do you mean?"

"Yes, a few moments ago."

"Then it may be just possible, though not likely," said he, "that I've been to sleep. Nor forty winks, nor anywhere near. About ten, I should say."

She moved close to him and stroked his bright hair where it grew short on his neck. He wished she did not like doing that, and it was always an effort for him not to move his head casually away from her hand, but he always succeeded in remaining still; indeed, now he pressed his head against it, with an answering caress.

"When a man says that he may possibly have been asleep," she observed, "you may take it for granted that he certainly has. It's supposed to be slightly unmanly to go to sleep."

"And what did you call me for?" he asked.

She sat down on the arm of his chair, leaning against his shoulder.

"There was something," she said, "besides just generally wanting you. Something at the back of my mind."

"Let it stop there, then," said Steven, knowing very well what it was. "There's nothing at the back of mine except generally wanting you. You've been out to lunch, haven't you? Pleasant?"

"Yes, darling, quite. There was a man there who knew you."

"I call that very remarkable," said Steven, still gently distracting her. "Was he a detective, do you think? Am I wanted by him as well?"

"I expect so, because he asked several questions about you. He remembered me, though I didn't remember him."

"Always rather a superior position," remarked Steven.

"Yes, but an inferior memory. He said he hadn't seen you for ages."

"That's true detective cunning," said Steven. "He wanted to disarm any suspicions you might have. We shall see a man in plain clothes this evening watching the house."

"No, darling, you won't," said she, "because he's leaving London again this afternoon."

"That's just the sort of thing he'd say. Fancy being taken in by that! I shouldn't wonder if there were two of them this evening. Are you by any chance going to tell me his name?"

"No; I shall will you to guess it."

"You're a mesmerist," said Steven. "I've guessed. It was Ananias Methuselah Higginbotham."

"Quite right. Now I'm going to will you to guess something more. Where is he going back to this afternoon?"

"Cambridge," said Steven, quite at random.

"Right again. What college?"

"You ask absurdly easy questions. King's, of course."

"Right again, and Mr. Higginbotham has got an alias or an alibi—I never know which is which, because they both mean something else. I mean, what is the name he's usually known by?"

"Maurice Crofts," said Steven.

"Darling, you really are clever!" said she.

"I know that. And I'll tell you a question he asked you. He asked if we had been to Trenair."

"Black magic!" said Betty, rather impressed.

"Black magic it is," said Steven. "Now I'm going to ask questions. What was his—his tone? Friendly?"

"Perfectly. Rather prim, perhaps: rather donnish, but quite friendly. Why not?"

"Because though I was very great friends with him at one time, we had a row. He thought I had behaved badly to him. He was perfectly right, too."

"His manner had no trace of that," said Betty, "though naturally he wouldn't say, 'Beware of your husband.' What did you behave badly about?"

Steven was silent a moment.

"The fact is that I got rather tired of him," he said. "But I think I should like to see him again."

"Ask him to Trenair when we get down there in December," she said. "He told me he had been there. You'll want a companion when I'm laid by."

It was odd, he thought, that she should say just that, for the very same idea had occurred to himself just now. If Maurice would come his presence would be a sort of safeguard: it would remind him of the days of terror, it would keep him from trespassing on perilous areas. And yet, did he want a safeguard? Did he really believe any longer that there was danger in wait for him in the enchanted woods? And did he not in some secret cell of his brain hunger and thirst for that from which he had fled in panic? He must think it all out.

"That's not a bad idea," said Steven, "but I should think it's quite likely that he'll say, 'no.' Perhaps if I let him know I have mended my ways . . ."

Betty's interest in Maurice was apparently of the faintest. She picked up Steven's hand, and drew her fingertips across the palm of it. He disliked being pawed, but no intimation of that escaped him.

"Steven, how I long for that time to come," she said. "I'm Early Victorian about it. I think I would almost cut the next two months out of my life to bring it close, and yet I can't spare one minute out of the hours I pass with you."

Steven judged that the sketchily designed visit to Easthays had now been obliterated from Betty's mind by other topics and chanced it.

"I won't spare a minute of them," he said, "so where's the use of your doing so? And what are we to do about the minutes this evening? I got tickets for the new play, which I'm told is wildly funny, so be prepared to be bored stiff if you would like to go."

"Would you?" she asked.

"Oh, answer me, woman!" he cried, imprisoning her fingers. "I asked that question first."

"If it pleases my Lord, the King——" she began.

"Oh, you're hopeless. You've no initiative; I've got to settle everything. We'll go, then. Dinner at seven and a half. Now I must trot round to the club and sit in a row of bald-headed old gents with my back to the window, and read the evening paper and puff and blow. Everyone should practise being old and bald, and then it's no shock when—when you're it."

"Practise hard, darling," she said, "you haven't got too much time, you know."

Steven got safely away to his practice before the idea of the projected expedition had recurred to Betty, and she slid into the chair he had occupied, content to laze away this last half hour of afternoon sunshine without further occupation than random thought for her mind which, like her body, basked in the mellow warmth. Marriage and love and motherhood seemed to spread a golden haze over life, through which it was impossible to see details. It absorbed and enveloped; it made everything else so simple because nothing else mattered. Dim shapes, lovely in outline, moved through the radiance of it.

She smiled at herself: indeed she was being what Steven called Victorian, a term which covered all such indulgences of sentiment. They argued about it sometimes, she maintaining that Victorianism lay at the root of love, but such argument never lasted long, for prolonged discussion on any subject bored him: a few clipped sentences expressed his own view, and having stated it there was nothing more to be said, for he never modified his own conclusions, and had not the slightest wish that she should modify hers. She smiled again at the thought of that, for she knew that on the subject of his fatherhood he was just as Victorian as she. He did not muse and dream over it as she did, but it was abundantly clear that if ever there was a Victorianly expectant papa, that papa was Steven. The thought of the child that was fast ripening to birth was as precious to him as it was to her. A dropped word, a glance, a silence constantly betrayed him; she know (and hugged the knowledge) that her approaching motherhood infinitely enhanced her to him.

Aunt Florence had noticed that, too, and often the two women, secretly conspiring, would wink to each other like augurs at some indication that Steven, even while he was chaffing her about her Victorianism, was with sublime unconsciousness exhibiting his own. And he was just as Victorianly minded about Trenair, although he had twice refused to go there on suitable opportunities, and often a chance word showed how he loved and longed for it. He would allude to the poplar-wood below the house, to the harbour with the fishing-fleet coming in at dawn, to the hot sandy beach, to the steep Atlantic seas that broke over the pier, as one who by the waters of Babylon absently whistled a phrase out of the songs of Zion.

She knew she was right about that: the valley broadening out between the gorse-clad hills was holy and beloved, the home of his heart. Strange it certainly was that neither for his honeymoon nor for his holiday would he go there: against the former there was his mother's tragic death still recent, but for the latter, his excuse that Trenair was a stuffy hole in the summer was laughable, for again and again had he spoken to her of the bathings and baskings of August as the most utterly delectable way of passing a morning. It was rather mysterious, but then Betty knew that there were many things she did not understand about Steven, all of which somehow contributed to the endless charm of his personality: sudden little savageries, sudden little withdrawals of himself, even at the zenith of intimacy, sudden little heartlessnesses, flicking out like a whip lash, and instantly vanishing again. His treatment, according to his own avowal, of this Mr. Crofts, seemed to her to be possibly one of these: he had just got tired of him.

Queer little inexplicable traits they were, and, whenever they occurred they struck Betty not as being superficial impatiences and *ennuis*, but as coming from the very heart of him, from some layer of soul stuff closely knit into his nature, and somehow antique, as if they were a throwback to an ancestral instinct. She could make nothing of them; they seemed altogether antipodal to his sunny geniality, as if an iceberg had floated into a warm Southern sea. She hardly knew whether she wanted to understand them, for she had no sympathy with the proverbial error, *Aimer c'est tout comprendre*. That was exactly what love, so she figured it, was not. *Aimer c'est ne pas tout comprendre* was much nearer her instinctive definition, for these little mysteriousnesses about him were wholly adorable.

But now, when Steven had left her, to practise the necessary art of senility at his club, she sought with a keener curiosity than ever some solution which should explain his attitude towards the home which he loved and had hitherto shunned. She had thought sometimes that he feared going there, as if it contained for him something sinister, but against so unfounded a supposition there was to be set his devotion to it, and his indwelling memories of it, which surely came from his heart.

A few days ago, for instance, there had been a white autumnal mist over the Park, and Steven, as if involuntarily, had said, "Oh, Betty, the sea mists at Trenair, with the hooting of the foghorns coming through them! And if a fog has come on after a gale you hear the boom of the breakers on the coast. Scrumptious!" One night again, at Easthays, the owls were hooting round the house, and he said, as if thinking aloud, "They come closer than that at Trenair: they scout over the lawn just outside my window." Certainly there was some intimate bond between him and Trenair of which he never spoke directly, and also, so his refusal to go there testified, something that he shunned. Or was it (the thought was new) was it for her that he shunned the place? Did he want, for some unknown reason, to keep her away from it while her child was crescent?

All this was fluid and vague in her mind, drifting in and out of it, and perhaps it was no more than one of these fantastic imaginations which were common in pregnancy, one of those defensive instincts of the mother for her unborn child. But still it seemed to have some sort of anchorage, even as a strand of seaweed, swinging this way and that in subaqueous currents, may be attached to and rooted on rock. If a natural occasion arose she determined to put some definite question to Steven about it and press for an answer. She knew he adored his little gray ancestral home in its withdrawn valley, and yet he had been unwilling to go there. He knew also that she longed to see it, but he had put her off with really untenable excuses. For some reason her curiosity was thoroughly aroused.

It was not long before Steven was back and came up to

her sitting room. He had a couple of letters in his hand, one of which gave her just such an opportunity, or the makings of one, that she wanted, for it was a report with regard to the establishment of power and plant for electric light at Trenair: this was a gift from Uncle Robert.

"Of course it's awfully good of him," said Steven, "though at the same time I rather wish he hadn't thought of it. But I couldn't tell him I didn't want it, could I? So it will all be installed and ready by the time we get down there. But somehow, you see, lamps and candles are much more like the house. They may be less convenient, but they are more suitable."

Betty laid down her book.

"Do you know, I don't think I've ever seen a house without electric light," she said. "I can't quite imagine it. What happens if you go into a room which is dark and there's no switch by the door?"

"Matches," said Steven. "And after a few have gone out you light a candle. Usually we hadn't got any matches. Dear me, now you mention it I don't know what does happen. . . . Oh, yes, you ring a bell, and nobody answers it. So there you are."

Betty laughed.

"It sounds lovely," she said.

"It's right, anyhow. When you go to Trenair you'll feel what I mean. At least I suppose you won't, because the electric light will be in by that time. Or perhaps you wouldn't feel it: you might think that the absence of it was a damned nuisance."

He stood by the fireplace, not seeming to notice that she had drawn up her feet on the sofa with a wordless invitation for him to sit there.

"I want to feel it," she said. "I want to get the sense of Trenair before I go. But you're a bit mysterious always, darling, about it."

He looked at her sharply.

"I mysterious?" he asked. "What do you mean?"

"I mean you never tell me anything about it," said Betty.

"I never heard such nonsense! I've told you about it again and again."

"Yes, in guide-book fashion," said she. "Perhaps I don't mean that you're mysterious about it, but that it's mysterious. No, I think it's both. You've let me walk about it, so to speak, but you've never let me understand what it is to you. You wouldn't take me there in September, and really, darling, your reason that it was hot and stuffy there was ludicrous, wasn't it?"

"But it's true," he said.

"It may be, but that wasn't the real reason why you wouldn't come there."

He made a clicked tongue of impatience: one of his little savageries was coming.

"You're always going back to that," he said. "Do leave it alone. You've got an obsession of curiosity as to why I didn't want to go there then. I've told you why. And you're going there in December. That's enough."

"You're being a little dictatorial," remarked Betty.

"If it comes to that, you're being a little inquisitorial. Why on earth should there be any reason except the one I've given you?"

Betty had no answer to this, and she picked up her book again. Steven's peremptoriness on the subject had only the effect of convincing her that there was some reason, beyond those he had given her, for his refusal to take her to Trenair, and her silence, to his thinking, certainly partook of that quality. But she asked no further question, and he was content to leave her in ignorance. Luckily, by no manner of means could she guess at anything so fantastic as that he had still then been fearing the spell of the place, and the curse that menaced not himself alone but the unborn child. Never had she heard a syllable about the curse. . . . Meantime he might prevent her mind from nosing round what she had declared to be mysterious, by telling her something that she would take to be frank and reassuring.

He came and sat down at the end of her sofa, leaning sideways against her knees. That looked intimate and confidential.

"Betty, darling," he said, "I'm sorry for snapping at you, and I'll confess that there was a reason, beyond what I've told you, for not taking you there at present. You guessed quite right: you're too clever for me, and I strongly suspect you of being a witch like that poor old great-grandmamma of mine. But I'm not going to tell you what the reason was, for I've come to believe that it was a pure fancy on my part, a sinister and ugly fancy, and I don't want to suggest ugly things to you, even for the pleasure of hearing you laugh at them. Frankly, then, I long to go to Trenair just as much as you, because there's no place in the world like it, but I haven't done so until I was sure in my mind, as I am now, that that ugly fancy of mine was dead. But if all goes well, you blessed darling, I'll tell you before we leave Trenair this winter, and then you'll know what a pack of nonsense I allowed myself to imagine. Do trust me."

Betty could not fail to respond to this frankness, even if she had had the slightest desire to do otherwise: neither could she press to know more of a matter about which he felt thus. It was one of his secrecies, one of the privacies into which she must not attempt to force her way. She was content to leave it like that, for, if she construed him rightly, it was his tender care for her that did not admit her there at present: he wanted to keep far from her all ugly fancies, which might conceivably work ill for her child; nothing must enter her head and pass into her blood which was not lovely. She felt sure that such was his design, and so poked her curiosity back into its cupboard, and slammed the door on it. . . . But it seemed to herself, even while she heard it bang, that she had shut in with it a doubt, a misgiving as to whether Steven truly believed that this mysterious notion of his was wholly fantastic.

He had been sharp and peremptory with her when she challenged him, angrily warning her off from any attempt at trespass on his secret. Surely if he was convinced that it was rubbish he would have told her so at once, instead of admitting it afterwards. But he did not really laugh at it yet, so she concluded, nor would he do so till the birth of her child demonstrated its absurdity. Possibly there was no logical connection; it might have been, as he had said, that he only wanted her not to know about it. But she could not believe that he himself was entirely at ease, for he could not have minded her asking any question about a matter that gave him no concern. It was just that doubt which had got shut in with her curiosity: it was perched there in that dark cupboard which she did not intend to open again.

"Of course I trust you," she said. "Oh, Steven, get up: I must go to dress if we dine early."

There came disquieting news from Easthays next morning. Aunt Florence requested Steven's personal attendance at the telephone, and told him that she and Lord Gervase were coming up to London that day. He had been having severe attacks all night of internal pain, and the country doctor had recommended an immediate examination by X-rays. Steven was warmly sympathetic in response, pouring out encouragement and cheerfulness, but his mind registered annoyance more acutely than any other emotion. It was a bore, it was upsetting, and though he was quite sorry for his uncle and for Aunt Florence's anxiety, an invalid intrusion into this house which he and Betty occupied so pleasantly could not be welcome. But all should be ready for them, he assured Aunt Florence, and no doubt it was wise to bring Uncle Robert up at once, for the X-rays would certainly show that he needn't have come. So Aunt Florence said he was a dear boy, and he went to Betty with these tidings.

She proposed what had never occurred to him.

"My dear, we must go down there at once," she said. "It's quite early still; we shall get there before they start. Poor Aunt Florence is all alone with him, and she'll be so fussy and inefficient."

Steven thought this a very wild idea; there seemed no sense in it.

"But that would be quite ridiculous," he said. "They've only got to get into the motor at that end and get out at this. We can't do anything for them."

"It's being there which matters," said she.

"But we probably shan't get there in time," he said. "As likely as not we shall pass them on the road without seeing them, and they'll find nobody here when they arrive."

"Ring them up again, then, at once," said she, "and tell them we're starting immediately. Ask them what time they are leaving and see if we can catch them."

"But there's no point in it if we can," said he. "It's a perfectly useless thing to do."

"Very likely, but it's one of the things that has got to be done," she said.

Steven suddenly realized that just for the moment he hated her. She was sentimental, she was utterly irrational in wanting to post down to Easthays on this pellucid morning, just to be with fluttering Aunt Florence for two minutes and possibly give a hand to Uncle Robert to help him into the motor. Thereafter he and she would get back into their car and drive up to London again: nothing could be sillier. And yet he knew for that moment when he hated her that he did so not because she was sentimental and silly but because she was human and pitiful. Of that he felt nothing at all, and he was jealous of it, as a sightless man might be who hears beauty spoken of not as something marvellous, but as something ordinary and obvious. He could not see it himself, while to her it was a thing taken for granted. . . .

And then from somewhere far off, in the dimmer confines of his consciousness, there came to him the sense of fear. It was just this, this entire unsensitiveness on his part to what was so ordinary to others, from which he had fled in panic from Trenair, nearly a year ago, seeing in it the menace of the curse fulfilled in himself. He had realized then that he was without pity and love, and now this incident, tiny in itself, yielded the same analysis. Betty was proposing, insisting, indeed, as a matter of course, on sacrificing this morning of sun and splendour to this fetish of humanity, and he had hated her for the instinct of which his heart was barren.

The spasm passed, but it had frightened him. His safety lay in acting as if he cared. . . .

"You're quite right, darling," he said. "I'll just telephone and tell them we're coming, and then we'll start at once."

Her face had been set and determined as she argued with him, but in her eyes there had been trouble. Now at his answer all that cleared, and her devotion to him beamed out again unclouded.

"Ah, I knew you would see with me," she said. "But you frightened me for a minute, Steven. You looked fierce, you looked hostile."

"Fiddlesticks," he said, kissing her. "Ready in ten minutes, Betty."

But the memory of that infinitesimal moment when Steven had glared at her wickedly and hatefully still haunted Betty as they drove through the Sunday streets with all the motor traffic setting countrywards on this golden morning. She tried not to think about it, but the stab of it kept coming back to her, as pain creeps back and thrums on the nerves of one who is trying to distract himself by firm occupation. For that black look of his did not come, so it seemed to her, from without, under a sudden provocation, as a startled look comes into a man's eyes at a crash of unexpected noise: the provocation of her insistence drew back some curtain in Steven's soul and showed her what dwelt within. Quickly indeed had it been veiled, for his acquiescence had been swift and complete, but what she had seen was not gone, it was only covered up again.

And yet was she being wholly fantastic and imaginative? For here was Steven, sitting beside her now, sweet and gentle and genial, and full of solicitude for those to whom they were journeying, and of care for her. Yet even while she sunned herself in his tenderness, which surely should obliterate that one short evil moment, a doubt obtruded itself again. Did his gentleness now come from his heart? Was it an instinctive unthought-out expression of what he was, or was it careful and studied?

Their passage was swift, and it was little more than an hour from the time when they set out that they turned in at the big gilded iron gates of Easthays, with their posts emblazoned with the recent coronet, and hummed up the mile-long drive to where the front of the red-brick house glowed in its setting of yellowing beech woods.

"Here we are," said Steven. "Pray God we get better news of poor Uncle Robert."

But his voice rang false as a cracked bell.

CHAPTER X

STEVEN had been doing things thoroughly for nearly a couple of months, and now at Victoria Station he was keeping it up till the very last moment. He had even said he would come to Folkestone with Aunt Florence and see her safely onto her boat, and it had required solid firmness on her part to dissuade him. With a sister and a maid to look after her, and a cabin engaged and a guard heavily tipped, she insisted that there was nothing he could possibly do: he would be wanting to escort her across the Channel next, and see her into the Blue Train southwards for Cannes, where she had taken a villa for the winter. . . . So in ten minutes more he would have brought these really awful weeks to a conclusion.

He had engaged a compartment for her and sat in the seat beside her. She was dressed, of course, in the deepest mourning that money could buy, and he noticed that she had her black pearls on, and wondered why she had not blacked her face as well. The bull-frog dog, odious asthmatic creature, whose orange coat was the only note of colour, sat in her lap, and Aunt Florence looked like a great black hen. In the opposite corner sat her sister, also in black, but she, being lean, looked like a jackdaw. It was a raw, foggy afternoon of December, and Betty had a cold, and so, very reluctantly, she had not come to the station to see the travellers off.

Steven had learned early in these woeful weeks how vastly appreciative Aunt Florence was of little material attentions, of being companioned and read to and gently chaffed and cosseted. She took all these ministries as being symbols of affection, and he had been assiduous with them. He stroked the disgusting bull-frog.

"Bull-frog will come back barking in French," he said, "and he'll want his *déjeuner* at half-past twelve instead of his lunch at half-past one. And your maid's got his coat for the crossing."

"My dear, you think of everything," she said.

"I thought of getting him a small tin basin, in case it should be rough," said Steven, "but I looked at the bulletin, and the Channel's smooth. So you'll have an excellent crossing, and all you've got to do is to step into your bright Blue Train and get out at Cannes. The servants will have arrived there this evening, so they'll have everything ready for you. And mind you send Betty or me a telegram the moment you get there: I've put a form in your bag. A proper one, never mind the expense, not just 'Arrived love bull-frog safely.' Really, I've half a mind to come with you and see you installed. If I can't get a ticket for the Blue Train I'll run behind through the pleasant land of France. . . . Now what else is there? Illustrated papers: there they are. Why does one always get illustrated papers to devour in the train, though one never looks at them on any other occasion? And then on Saturday Betty and I go off to Cornwall. How I wish you were coming with us, but I'm sure it's the wise thing for you to get right away. A real change, and you can't get a real change without crossing the sea. Abroad everything's different."

"And you'll write to me," said she, "and say how Betty is. And then one day I shall expect a telegram."

"You shall have it, and I'll write constantly. Lord, how sick you'll get of my screeds. Oh, I heard from Trenair this morning: the electric light is installed and working. That was a nice present of Uncle Robert's."

Steven glanced at the illuminated face of the station clock. There were only a couple of minutes left, and it was time to say final words.

"Aunt Florence, you've been too wonderful all these

terrible weeks," he said. "I can't tell you how Betty and I have admired and loved you for your bravery and your—your naturalness, and how helpless we've both felt to help you. All we could do was just to go on loving you. You are such a darling!"

Lady Gervase's hand closed on his, and he saw her mouth working. That little speech of his had gone home, she had felt it and loved it, and now it was time for a taste of cheerful idiocy as a stirrup cup. He jumped up and kissed Bull-frog on the top of his horrid dome-like orange head.

"Good-bye, Bull-frog," he said. "Keep the French dogs in their places, but don't bite them hard for fear of endangering the *entente cordiale*. And don't allow him to lose too much money at Monte Carlo, Aunt Florence. Why, of course there's a dogs' table: didn't you know? They gamble like anything. There's the guard's whistle; that always means that nothing happens for a while. Good gracious, the train's moving; it's started punctually. Some poor devil will get in a row for this with the directors of the Southern Railway."

Steven jumped out onto the platform and stood there waving to the black hen at the window till the fog engulfed her. . . . Never had he felt so swift and joyful a reaction: it was as if his spirits had floated up like a bubble through the murky air, till it rose iridescent into the winter sunlight above. For nigh on a couple of months now he had been keeping a hand on himself, checking hourly exasperations, drilling himself into sympathy and tact and tenderness, and not once, so he verily believed, had he betrayed himself, or let his impatiences, boiling below, disturb the surface of his cheerful solicitude. He had been a tower of strength, so Aunt Florence had assured him with tremulous mouth and weak swimming eyes: she could never have got through this terrible time without him. He had been like a son to her, she said; she had held to him, leaning on his devotion and judgment, and it was in obedience to his counsel that she had taken this house at Cannes with her sister for the next months. She had wanted to come down to Trenair with him and Betty, and it had been a long job to persuade her to abandon that appalling notion. She must have a complete change of scene and companionship.

She had gone, and he walked on air: even this throat-catching fog was delightful, for it gave him the sense of being alone. Shapes and shadows came into his ken for a moment and passed out again, much as they did in domestic life. Once a large black woman loomed close to him, frighteningly like Aunt Florence: she had perhaps lost her husband too; and he whistled as he went for sheer light-heartedness at the thought that Aunt Florence had gone. She would not be waiting for him at the great house which was now his, he would not have to sit with her, reading her scraps from the evening papers and hearing her gently rambling on about Uncle Robert. She had not really cared very much for him in his lifetime, but now it seemed to her the correct thing to find in him an epitome of every grace and virtue and accomplishment. His patriotism during the war (out of which he had got a fortune and a peerage), his amazing skill at bridge, his admirable prowess among the pheasants (or was it partridges?), his devotion as a lover, his delightful companionship as a husband; even sometimes, on her more cheerful days, his funny little ways and precisions, and his playful tantrums!

And then his thoughtfulness in leaving her Easthays for her life, and the gratifying remarks he had made about her in his will. Every day Steven had been the recipient of these interminable memories: she seemed to think that he enjoyed talking about Uncle Robert as much as she did. But, after all, that was a compliment, though an onerous one, for it showed how convincingly he had played his tedious part.

Ever since the middle of October, when he and Betty on a Sunday morning had driven down to Easthays, had this tragedy of horror and boredom been going on. Lord Gervase had been brought up to London that day, and during the week the sentence of incurable disease had been passed on him. The growth, being on a vital area, could not be removed, but the surgeon had been able to give him relief from acute pain by an operation. That had been a dreadful morning: Steven had hoped that they would insist on his going to a nursing home, but he had preferred to have it done in his own house, and two nurses had come in overnight, and early in the morning surgeon and doctor and anæsthetist arrived. Already Aunt Florence clung to Steven, and he had absented himself from the office that day in order to be with her.

They had sat and talked and seen the surgeon afterwards, and for hours the faint sickly smell of ether hung about the passages upstairs. For a plethoric man, Lord Gervase had borne the operation well, and good reports came from the sick-room. Steven saw him every day: he brought home bits of news from the office of a satisfactory kind, for Uncle Robert liked to know the business of the Gervase Line, whatever happened to Gervase, and Steven exerted himself with all that quick wit of his to interest the invalid. He listened to accounts of the disabilities the operation had entailed, of the ingeniousnesses which rendered them more tolerable, and he hated and loathed it all.

His uncle had a sort of Job-pride in his sufferings; he bore them with admirable patience, and recounted them, like Job, with gusto, and never once did Steven fail in displaying a suitable and wincing reception of the recital of them. It was abominable that anyone should have to go through such physical degradation as Uncle Robert, but it was almost equally abominable that he himself should have to take an interest in these gruesome narratives; and every day, as he came home from the office, he hoped that the nurse would meet him with grave tidings and tell him that he could not see his uncle that day. After all, was it not a compassionate desire to wish that such a parody of life would soon cease, for who could want it to be prolonged? That day was not long in coming: the disease suddenly flared into raging activity, and the end was swift.

Steven, groping his way in the tawny gloom, made rapid pictures of all this, and of the days of his devotion to Aunt Florence which followed, with a sense of luxurious content that it was all over. Scrutinize those days how he would, he could not convict himself of a single omission of kindness and consideration to the dead or to the widowed: he had conformed with ungrudged self-sacrifice to the codes of humanity. He had smothered distaste and disgust; he had brought gleams of brightness to a sick-room; he had concealed his boredom and impatience and had made himself a tower of strength for Aunt Florence.

Throughout he had had one object in view, namely, to prove to himself, to demonstrate to his own conviction, that his fear that the curse was fulfilling itself in him was a mere phantom of the night. The very apostle of love could not have done more than he: how then could such carry the doom of having the soul of a brute? Never since the first shadow of his terror had fallen on him had he felt so bathed in the sunlight of confidence: surely he had shown himself to be as magnificently human in spirit as he was in body. No doubt heretofore he had behaved infamously to the Child, to Maurice, and to his mother, and the result had been that he had experienced a hideous fright; but in these last weeks he had atoned for that.

The fog had cleared a little, and now the sun, already westering and low, hung like some red copper plate above the trees of the Green Park. There was but a thin layer of this muddy vesture of smoke and stagnant vapour; a little way up there was a serene and windless radiance of winter day. How it would be sparkling on the dim blue sea at Trenair: how it would spread its golden mantle on the hillside and filter down in spangles and flecks of soft brilliance through the aisles of poplar wood below the house! Often much of the leaf clung to the trees up to Christmas, and the woodways were but thinly carpeted with the fallen foliage which gave forth that damp, delicious odour that hung about there till spring replaced it with the fragrance of young growth. That gentle autumnal decay was the food of the imperishable life of the woodland, of the eternal spirit which made it green. The thought of Trenair, its noons, its midnights, and the magic of it, caused his blood to tingle. He had been afraid, surely, where no fear was; he had evoked phantoms for his own terror, like a child who deliberately conjures up hauntings and evil presences in its secure nursery. . . . And on Saturday, two days from now, he would be back at Trenair again, protected and armoured by his own compassionate achievements. Perhaps, till Betty's child was born, which would put the seal on the annulment of the curse, he would go warily, but after that he would let that thirst of his for the wild and the secrets of it take its fill. He meant to stop down there for a couple of months at the least, and had already arranged for the promotion of one of the junior clerks in the office to take over his work, and now, in the full confidence that the curse was clean gone from him, he began to consider whether he would ever go back to that desolating desk again. If Betty did not care to spend so long a time at Trenair, she could join Aunt Florence at Cannes for a few weeks. That would be nice for both of them: Aunt Florence was very fond of her, and perhaps Betty would not suit Trenair.

She welcomed his return; the house had been curtained and shuttered for the night, for there would be no more daylight now, and the fog, which had penetrated a little into the cosy room where they sat, gave a sort of substantiality to the glow of the fire and of the electric light, making it solid and palpable.

"You look absolutely the last word in comfort," he said, standing opposite the big chair she had pulled up towards the hearth. "How wise to shut out the flickering light of the day. It's warm and rich and sheltered in here, and no one can possibly come in to disturb us. I was so right not to let you come to the station: it was odiously raw and bleak."

"And Aunt Florence went off all right?" asked Betty.

"Beautifully; nothing forgotten," said Steven. "She had a reserved compartment, and Aunt Matilda sat in one corner like a dumb jackdaw, and she in another with thirty-seven packages in the racks, and Bull-frog slobbering on her knee. I like dogs, but Bull-frog's not a dog but an insect. And I sat by her, and with one eye on the clock timed my conversation to a T. I said exactly all the right things, grave and gay. And she said again that I was a tower of strength, bless her. I really think she was quite comfortable."

Betty was silent a moment.

"Tired, darling?" asked Steven. "How's the cold?"

"Not a bit tired," she said, "and the cold's going to be nothing at all. Will you ring for tea?"

Steven looked at her narrowly, with that scrutinizing glance that seemed to be looking for something not visible on the surface.

"What's the matter, Betty?" he said crisply.

"Nothing whatever."

Steven moved a little closer to her.

"Oh, nonsense!" he said. "You've got something on your mind; you're criticizing something I've said. What is it?"

She raised her face towards him, half in appeal, and a little troubled.

"Steven, you do puzzle me so sometimes," she said. "I've not the least doubt that you were charming to Aunt Florence and did it all perfectly. But you didn't feel charming to her. What you say and how you say it show that. Your tone mocks her, and it's touched with ridicule."

He laughed.

"Why, of course it is," he said, "because she's a ridiculous old thing. We both know that, and you feel it just as much as I do. And you're glad she's gone, and so am I. Where's the difference between us? Why should you be criticizing me in your mind?"

She got up, putting her hands on his shoulders.

"I daresay I've got no right to," she said, "for I think—I genuinely do—that you've been quite marvellous during all these weeks which have been horrible to you."

He gave no response to the caress of her pressed hands: he stood there as indifferent as a sculptured figure, or as a very polite animal submitting patiently to endearments.

"An unsolicited testimonial," he said, "and so all the more gratifying. I'm glad to know you think so. These haven't been very jolly weeks, have they? Not the sort of days one would ask for on a wishing ring. I hate illness, it's a filthy degradation, and day after day I had to listen to accounts of its most disgusting details. And then, when that was over, there was the interminable recital of Uncle Robert's graces and virtues."

Betty felt that she was clinging to something slippery which was gradually sliding away from her. Steven had behaved splendidly, and she tried to cling to that, but what lay below his unwearied patience, what had it sprung from? That was a disturbing thought, and every word he said gave solidity to it.

"I know, I know," she said. "You never failed her; she leaned on you as on no one else. And you were the same with Uncle Robert, and he looked forward every day to your coming and sitting with him."

"What more do you want, then?" he asked. "How is it that I puzzle you so?"

She couldn't tell him: perhaps, when all was said and done, it was one of the strange suspicions of pregnancy that she should be doubting whether a single impulse of pity or love had ever prompted his ministrations. But that doubt was loud in her ears, and it roused echoes from a dozen little rocky incidents which had puzzled her about him, situations in which he had acted with kindliness that had no touch of warmth in it, with indulgence contemptuously granted. Sometimes it had assailed even her own personal relations with him, and she had wondered whether he truly cared for her. And in his eyes now there seemed to be the look of one who guessed or even knew what she was thinking, and still he stood there wholly unresponsive.

"I am waiting to hear how it is that I puzzle you," he said. "Not, I hope, because I've behaved decently."

There was a certain tenseness about him, as of one waiting in suspense for some critical verdict: that and the hardness of his face, his irresponsiveness, the irony, bitter and accusing, of his words frightened her. She could not bring herself to tell him.

"Steven, it's nothing," she said. "Please don't ask me any more, and I won't be puzzled. Women in my condition have sick fancies. This is one of them; it's nothing more than that."

It was as if, waiting for evil news, he had been told

that none such was in store for him. With a sudden movement he folded her in his arms.

"Betty, you mustn't indulge sick fancies, darling," he said. "You must put them away from you. I've had sick fancies too, I think. Put yours right away. I won't ask you about them, and you don't want to tell me: I take it from you that they're vain and idle. Will that do?"

To her own immense surprise she burst into tears. Her heart, which utterly loved him, accused her of base disloyalty to him in ever imagining that all his marvellous kindness and patience during these weeks had no real root in his nature. She, too, she knew, was glad, though she had made this an accusation against him, that Aunt Florence had gone . . . that she was left alone with Steven . . . that she would soon be the mother of his child . . . that his love, as now his arms, enfolded her. These thoughts came in sobs.

"Oh, Betty, don't cry," he said. "*We're* here, you and I, and nothing else matters."

It was already dark when, on Saturday evening, they arrived at Penzance. Steven had sent down a motor from London, which met them there, one that purred softly and swiftly up the hill where Mad Maria used to have her stationary ague-fits, and that slid gently, rocking a little, down the steep incline of the combe. They slowed down and turned up the short rise to the house, where the lights of the car illuminated thick banks of rhododendron, and trees trailed slender fingers on its roof. The house front was only dimly visible in the dark, but Betty saw that a broad-leafed creeper climbed to its eaves, and that great cream-coloured flowers were in blossom upon it. The scent of them hung thick on the night air.

"But it's magnolia," she exclaimed. "Magnolia in December!"

Steven pushed her into the house.

"Not a step, not a look outside, Betty," he said. "I want it all to burst on you to-morrow."

She went in, and there was the panelled hall, and the faint incense of wood smoke, and the sense to her of a door having been opened into some deep antique tranquillity, the tranquillity of trees and pools of tree-shaded water, a forest lair where no hunter comes, of the children of the woodland.

They stood for a moment, while their luggage was being carried in, beside the jewels of the burning logs, and she leaned close on him.

"Oh, Steven, Trenair at last!" she said. "I've come home. But can I ever forgive you for not letting me come before? I wonder why you did that. No, darling, I'm not going to ask you that: I'm there now . . . and . . . and it's you."

She slept late into the morning, for her journey had tired her, but when she woke it was to the tide of warm fresh air, sea spiced, that came in through her open window. The room looked east and south, and to the east climbed the gorse-clad hills, sparsely golden, and to the south the treetops in the poplar wood were like a hurdle over which leaped the line of the sea. In a trance of content she leaned out and looked on the exquisite cradle of the race, and the child stirred in her, as if it, too, knew that it had come home to be born. But it was Steven who still presided at this banquet of her heart.

He came out of the house as thus she drank in the light and the freshness and the sense of home-coming. He was coatless and bareheaded; a fisherman's jersey came down over his hips. He looked up at her window.

"Awake at last?" he said.

"Very much; I feel as if I was never awake before."

"It'll do, then? Trenair, I mean?" he asked.

"It's awful, Steven. How could you bring me here? So sunless, so dreary, so noisy! Let's go back to London at once."

He laughed.

"Come down quickly, then," he said. "We shall just catch the morning train at Penzance."

"Right, and we'll have time for a stroll first. Wait for me, I shan't be long."

He was basking in the sun when she came out, and now she saw that though it was mid-December it was indeed the fragrance of magnolia that had greeted her the night before. The flower bed along the house front was bright with polyanthus and squill and crocus and aconite; spring had already come to this vale of Avilion, tender and promiscuously blossoming, and now, as they took the wood-path through the poplars down to the village, she saw that the hazel buds were already swelling, and the clumps of primroses in full flower.

"But is there no winter here?" she cried. "Is it always spring except when it's summer? No frost and snow?"

"I remember snow once here," said he.

She took his arm, pressing against him.

"And will it always be spring in my heart?" she said. "I feel as if nothing existed except this valley shut off by sea and hills from all the world. Was it we, you and I, who lived in a dark hole called London?"

He laughed: he was pleased, but a little tired of her raptures.

"I believe you've caught the disease," he said.

"What disease, darling?"

"Trenair. But you've only seen a corner of it yet."

They were crossing the clearing where the ruined walls stood, and Betty stopped.

"And what was this?" she asked. "An odd place to build a house, right in the middle of the wood, with trees growing close up to the walls on every side."

"Perhaps there weren't any trees when it was built," said he.

"As old as that? Oh, Steven, how thrilling! And look at those creepers on the walls. Are they vines? They look just like vines."

Certainly Betty had caught the infection of the charm and outward tranquillity of Trenair, but he, as she asked these silly questions about vines, was beginning to tingle with that mad, silent energy that underlay it. The tide of the joyous irresponsible life was swirling round him again, and on its bubbling waters there seemed to float, like stale and barren fragments of some wreck, all that suppression of himself which had manifested itself in weeks of patience and forbearance and kindliness. His sittings by the bedside of his uncle, his sympathetic audience to the horrors of his condition, his contributions to the panegyrics of Aunt Florence, all these appeared to him now as senseless sacrifices. But quick on the heels of this there came again the memory of his own panic, and with that the thought of Betty, from whom all hint of the hidden life must be guarded. Not till her child was born must she dream that under this fair peace and sunshine there had lain for him any secret and perilous stuff.

"Oh, come on, Betty," he said. "Yes, they do look like vines. Perhaps they are; I'm sure I don't know. But we must get on. I want you to see the village and the harbour."

She followed him down the narrow wood path, where two could not walk abreast, winding in and out of the little terraces on the hillside, and presently they came out of the trees onto the clustered houses above the harbour. Smoke curled up from chimneys where Sunday dinner was cooking, quickly losing itself in the sparkling air above the house roofs, and at the cottage doors sat women knitting. They rose as the two approached, with beaming eyes and hands of welcome for Steven, and he had a word with each in the soft Cornish tongue, introducing Betty to them. There was Janet among them, Tim's sister.

"Why, Janet, 'tis a year since I've set eyes on you, and you're a year younger, sure. Aw, my dear, you'll be 'mazing us all with your beauty. And Tim? How's Tim?"

"Tim's fine, Mas'r Steven," said she. "Eh, and it's good to look on you again. And when Tim heard you were come back yesternight, he danced and he piped; there was no stopping him. I could scarce keep him from going up to the house this morning to greet you: a pretty thing for him to be wanting to visit you and your lady wife, to be sure!"

They passed on with a word here and a word there.

"But they all love you, Steven," said Betty. "How could you keep away from them so long? And Tim? Who's Tim?"

These complimentary remarks seemed very stupid to Steven. What did Betty, this stranger, know about them of Trenair? And she had nothing to do with Tim: there must be no question about that.

"I think you saw Tim," he said. "The boy who came up with the fishermen for our wedding. I know you noticed him, in fact: the very image of me, and for an excellent reason. I told you, didn't I?"

"Oh yes, of course," said Betty hurriedly (that rather unpleasant story). "But do let him come up and see us, Steven. That's not his fault. And he danced and sang when he heard you were coming. That was dear of him: he must adore you. Tell me more about him."

Once again Steven had to stifle his irritation. Betty and Tim belonged to different worlds.

"Poor chap! He's the village idiot," he said. "Absolutely dotty. But if you want to see him, here he comes, top speed."

They had walked to the top of the steep decline down to the beach: the tide was low, and a broad belt of wet sand, blue as the reflected sky above it, stretched along to the landward end of the pier. Across this Tim was running towards them with dollops of wet sand flung behind him from the stroke of his flying feet. Up the soft deep-rutted incline he sped, and half knelt at Steven's feet, clutching at his hand. Shirt and shorts were all his attire, and the ivy wreath which he had twined in his hair. Of Betty he took no notice whatever; he seemed not even to see her.

"Eh, Mas'r Steven, you've come, you've come," he said. "'Tis long I've yearned for you. But you've come and the woodlands are kindly with spring already. There'll be no winter this year. And you're gwine to bide with us now, Mas'r Steven dear?"

Once again, and now with a more intimate thrill, Steven's blood tingled, for here was he who understood more than any of them of the hidden life, and it was Betty who understood nothing: she was the idiot. But Betty must not understand anything: the rôle of idiot was cast for her.

"Come, Tim," he said, "we settled to have none of that. And where are your manners? Don't you know this lady whom you came up to London to see married to me?"

Tim looked at her, and his eyes, just now wide and alight, narrowed and grew dull. He stood up, his mouth sullen.

"Iss, sure. Your servant, ma'am," he said.

Betty held out her hand to him.

"And I'm so glad to see you again, Tim," she said. "Master Steven's not going away for a long time, now he's come back."

Steven could have laughed or cursed at her for this kind condescension. Tim's family history was not his fault. How broad-minded!

Tim took her hand, no more than just touching it.

"And I'm going to stay here, too, Tim," she said. "This is my home now."

Tim stood with his eyes on the ground, still sullen, and kicking the soft sand with his toes. He had grown during this last year: he was as tall as Steven now, and not in face only, but in grace of limb and movement he was his peer. She noticed how extraordinary was the likeness, and Tim was just as finely bred in hand and foot (those awful indexes of "class") as he: he was straight-flanked and broad in chest, with his neck rising round and full from level shoulders. And how eager with devotion had been his approach and his kneeling to Steven; he must often have done that before, and she wondered at it. She was sorry that Steven had spoken roughly to him, and apparently Steven was sorry, too, for now he laid his hand affectionately on the boy's shoulder.

"And how has all been with you, Tim, this long while?" he asked. "You danced and sang yesterday, Janet told me, when you heard I was coming. I like being welcomed."

Tim's face brightened.

"That did I," he said, "for 'twas good news. And it was a beau'ful summer, Mas'r Steven; you should have been here. I slept in the woods, weeks together, and the vine berries were fine: many a dinner have I made of them. I thought sometimes to send a passel of them to you in London, but Janet said nay."

So Steven knew all about the wild vines, thought Betty, though he had professed ignorance. Perhaps he had forgotten.

"And you've been playing your pipe, Tim?" asked he.

Betty seemed to have vanished for Tim altogether. He used to disregard Maurice like that, not deliberately, but because he didn't exist.

"Iss, Mas'r Steven," he said. "And I've been making new tunes for the springtime. May I come one night at the full of the moon and play to you?"

"And to me too, please, Tim," said Betty.

At her voice Tim's face grew dark again, but again

through Steven shot a thrill of some secret joy at the thought of Tim's spring tunes. But here was Betty looking puzzled again at Tim's ungracious reception of her kindly intentions, and she must not be allowed to be puzzled.

"Sure you shall, Tim," he said. "And now we'll be going on, Betty. I want to take you onto the pier and make you known to the fishermen, and after that we'll stroll up the headland and get a view of the whole valley. Take my arm: the sand's heavy here."

They went down to the beach, where the sand was firmer with the moisture of the retreated tide, and Steven, glancing back, saw that Tim was standing where they had left him, still looking after them.

"Such a strange fellow," he said. "There's something awfully pathetic about him, isn't there? He lives in a world we've got no notion of. I should like to know what it is. Somehow I'm part of it: I'm somebody great to him in his poor mad world."

"He hates me," said Betty.

"Nonsense, darling," said Steven. "All these folk are suspicious of a stranger at first, even if he comes here under my noble protection. They were just the same with Maurice. Oh, by the way, I never told you: I heard from him last night, and he'll come down here next week. But Tim mustn't bother you. I'll see that he doesn't come up to the house. . . . Now, put your weight on me again as we go up the steps. They're slippery with weed. . . . Here we are on the pier. Eh, there's Jan Pentreath, and Tom Evans, and all the rest of you. And I've brought my wife here at last, Jan, as I told you I would. She's gwineter bide here now, and we'll make a Cornish woman of her, no fear."

Tim's rather discouraging reception of Betty was certainly not repeated by the fisher folk, for whom the fact of her being Steven's wife was an ample passport to their favour, and her heart warmed to these fine, smooth-spoken men. This was the real Trenair, to which she had awakened that morning with the sense of a tranquillity, far away from the world in a little kingdom of Steven's, and Tim's queer ways and sullen looks, no less than some vague feeling that he and Steven had a secret understanding between them, began to melt and lose its outline. It was all nonsense, of course. . . . Then on they went again over the down that mounted up to the headland outside the harbour. That was the view he wanted her to get, and this was enough of a walk for her, said Steven, and they sat themselves down on the dry, short grass, with the coast trailing away right and left into a dim haze. Landwards was the circle of hills that lay about the village.

They were at the edge of the cliff, and straight below them was the sandy bay, where Steven was wont to while away half the summer day, basking and bathing and basking again. There, too, it was that his mother's body had been washed ashore, and now to him, as he lay here looking down, that morning seemed faded and remote, and far more vivid was the memory of summer days passed there. His mother's death had been a horrible episode, but surely he had only read of it in some creepy, poisonous book. Even if it was real, it was decayed and done with, like the leaves that fell in the autumn and became mould for the fruitfulness of the earth at springtime. But he had still a grudge against her, for she had believed he was under the curse, and he had guessed that, and Maurice on that rather frightful night at Cambridge had confirmed it. She had been the author of the panic that had driven him away from Trenair, and kept him exiled from it till he had fought it down. Occasionally it still rose up again, but it was the merest wraith of what it had been; and a wraith, too, light as the wisps of cloud that formed and disappeared again in the heavenly sunshine of this winter noon, was the thought of her, and of her tragic and futile end. She had drowned herself for a fear of her own invention: deadly indeed it was, for he had had experience of it, too, and it had driven him half crazy with terror. But he had got the better of it, and Maurice had helped him there, good donnish Maurice, and he had defied it and fought it. He had married, he had spent months of patient ministry to a pair of very tiresome people (God rest the soul of one, and God send a sunny winter at Cannes to the other), and now his wife was beside him, shortly to reindorse the extinction of the curse and of his own unfounded panic. There was the futility of his mother's death: it was a pity, for, until she became so obsessed by this fear of hers, she had been a gay, pleasant companion. But now she was dim, she was dead, the victim of her own terrors, and for him the panic was gone and the horror that had come over him at the finding of her body on the beach. Far more vivid were those basking and bathing days there, and, winter though it was, he might perhaps go out there with Tim this afternoon for a dip while Betty, as he would insist on her doing, was resting. The memories of pleasant days, one above all when Tim had prepared a strange meal for him and Maurice there, alone haunted those sands.

The slope down to this beach at the top of which they were sitting now was dotted with clumps of low-growing bush, blackthorn and gorse, under shelter of which the growth of the spring was early maturing. There were dozens and dozens of young foxgloves there: in early summer it was a congregation of their belled spires. Other young green was already bursting out, and Betty, leaning across him, picked from a stem newly pushing out of the soil two or three half-folded leaves. They had steep-angled edges and were gummy to the touch.

"Look how things are sprouting already," she said. "These pretty young leaves: sticky, though! What are they, Steven?"

Instantly that disclosure of Tim's, made on the day of their picnic, shot into his mind.

"Good Lord! chuck it away, Betty," he said, "and rub your hands on the grass. It's henbane; there's lots of it here. Deadly poisonous stuff: they make hyoscine of it."

She threw the shoots away, laughing.

"And when they've made hyoscine, what next?" she said.

"As a matter of fact, people kill their wives with it," said Steven. "Didn't you ever hear of Crippen? Famous fellow: classical murderer."

She rubbed her hands on the grass.

"Horrid stuff," she said. "The serpent in Paradise. Steven, what a darling little bay down there."

"That's where I'll teach you to swim in the summer," said he. "What a queer thing that you shouldn't be able to: I cannot remember a time when I couldn't. What would have happened to you all these years, darling, if you had been wrecked?"

"Why, I should have drowned," she said. "Probably I should have in any case, whether I could swim or not. Is that the beach you told me about where you bathe so often?"

It came into Steven's mind what a bore Betty would be if she came down with him every morning, kicking about clumsily in shallow water and wanting him to hold her up. It would spoil all the spirit and charm of the place, with its long silent baskings, if she were here, learning to swim and proud of how quickly she was getting on. How absolutely idiotic of her not to be able to swim! It would spoil it for Tim, too: there would be no more wandering naked along the shore, looking for cockles and glasswort, with

Betty there in a pretty bathing dress and sandals. The whole of it would evaporate, and he wished he hadn't said he would teach her to swim.

"Yes, I have bathed there," he said. "A good little beach. But very often I bathe from a boat in deep water, which won't suit you yet awhile. But we must be getting home, Betty."

She leaned on his shoulder as she rose.

"Steven, tell me another thing," she said, "and then we won't ever talk of it again. When you found your mother's body, you know—where was that?"

Steven had not the least intention of telling her.

"Oh, right away on the other side," he said. "I couldn't point it out to you exactly. But over there. I can't think why you ask: it's one of the things to be forgotten."

They strolled down again across the thyme-sown slopes, past the pier, now empty of loiterers, and the deserted village street, for all were within at Sunday dinner; then they took the path leading up through the poplar wood to the house. Steven was walking in front of her, and suddenly he saw the glint of something white among the tree trunks ahead. The glimpse was only momentary, for that flicker vanished at once, but he felt sure it was Tim's white shirt he had seen. Soon they came to the corner where it had appeared, but there was no sign of him. But Steven knew that Tim was looking out for him when he should be alone.

Betty paused, a little out of breath. The roofs of the village were visible here through the trees.

"Enchanting place!" she said. "But where's the church, Steven? I didn't notice it."

He pointed to the head of the valley.

"About four miles away, somewhere over there," he said. "Five, perhaps."

"The people are Wesleyans then, Methodists?" she asked. "They've got a chapel, I suppose?"

He laughed: enchanting though she found Trenair, Betty had not apparently got hold of it much as yet.

"Well, not very fervent," he said. "In fact, when the Wesleyans tried to build a chapel here they took away every night the bricks that had been laid during the day. They didn't seem to want a chapel."

"Oh, Steven, how heathenish," she said.

Steven was rather pleased that Betty was so far, so very far, from understanding anything about Trenair.

"I know; shocking," he said. "But what's one to do? Perhaps you'd like to go to church this evening at St. Buryan's?"

That was turning the tables on her, and she laughed.

"No, not very much," she said.

She went up to her room after lunch with orders to have a real siesta and not dare to come down again for a couple of hours at least, and Steven let her understand that he would laze and stroll. But as soon as she had gone he fetched a towel, and stole off down the wood path, sure that before he had walked far Tim would see that he was alone and step out from some thicket where he watched. Even so was it: before he had come to the clearing he saw the flicker of white again among the trees, and he paused and whistled. He heard a laugh from close at hand, and there Tim was. He saw the towel round Steven's neck.

" 'Tis lovely in the watter to-day," he said. "May I row you out to the beach, Mas'r Steven?"

"Of course you may. Were you waiting for me, Tim?"

"Sure I was. I heard someone coming, and I hid myself, so's I could see when you got to the clearing if you were alone. I shouldn't have come out if not. Mayn't I wait for you like that?"

"Yes, but be careful," said Steven. "I don't want you to be seen by—by anybody."

"No, she shan't see me," said Tim, understanding perfectly what Steven meant, and following him down the path. "And 'tis more'n a year since you left us. Eh, I've yearned for you. And they say you're richer than the king now."

"What shall I give you, Tim?" asked Steven. "Say how much."

"But what do I want with money?" asked Tim. "Silly clinking stuff. 'Tisn't your money I want, Mas'r Steven."

All were indoors yet in the village, but the tide was on the flow now, and towards evening the fishing fleet would be setting out, drifting seawards on the ebb. Tim brought a small boat round to the steps by the pier, and soon they were at the beach onto which Steven and Betty had looked down that morning. More dreamlike than ever now to him was the memory of the day when last he had stepped ashore here with Jan Pentreath, while the company of big gulls wheeled overhead, and quite vanished was that nightmare of panic. Again and with rapture he felt the wholesome sting of the cool water and the glow of the strong winter sun, and he marvelled that he could have thought that he ran any danger in giving himself up to the spell that was woven in the sea and the woodlands. The curse was past, and within a few weeks now Betty would have proved it afresh. But till then no faintest echo of its history and of his own fear must reach her.

"Did you bring your pipe, Tim?" he said. "Play to me: play the new tunes you told me about."

Betty had slept for a little, but having woke up, no blankness of mind nor any soporific patents would enable her even to doze again, and soon she slipped off her sofa. She had left Steven sunning himself in a long chair on the lawn, but it was empty now, so perhaps he had gone off for a stroll or come indoors. Though she had promised to rest solidly, rest was impossible, but it was not restlessness so much as energy that possessed her, and she could not waste this golden afternoon in a bedroom void of sleep. She must inhale sun and sea air, drinking in the life of them like a child at the breast of the earth, and she went downstairs, prepared to plead and then insist, if Steven was in the hall and would have her go back to her seclusion again. But he was not there, and she slipped out hatless into the open.

Behind rose the hills, below dipped the wood, and now it was more to her mind to go upwards, for in this windlessness of the early afternoon she had a fancy for the air of the heights. Not yet had she seen anything of the country inland, and not far away was a hill that looked as if it commanded a wide view. She passed through a belt of trees above the house that hid the approach to it, and beyond was the down turf, delightful going for the feet, stretching smooth up to her summit. Great clumps of gorse studded it, sturdy ramparts higher than the head, and even now the flowers on them were plentiful, and in the warmed hollows by them the luscious thick scent hung heavy, cocoanut-flavoured to the nostril.

Up and always up she went, gaining vigour rather than spending it on her going, and now close in front of her was the ridge for which she had been making. She saw the grasses on the top waving and knew that there must be a wind there, blowing high above the combe from the north and passing over it. It would be good to fill her lungs with that, and in a couple of minutes more she would reach it.

She topped the ridge, which as she had guessed was the highest point about, and there, directly in front of her, was the circle of granite monoliths. She wondered at the greatness of the stones and felt a qualm of gooseflesh at the sight of these monuments so mutely eloquent of an antiquity which witnessed scenes of worship and sacrifice in some immeasurable remoteness. Those Druid priests—were they Druids?—must have looked on much the same scene then as she looked on now: the eternal youth of Nature recked little of centuries. She alone remained young when all else so quickly aged and was gathered in and forgotten. . . .

She sat down on the grass, with her back to a sun-warmed stone, stifled the reflection that it was odd of Steven not to have mentioned this antique sanctuary to her, and then for the first time she noticed the row of mounds which ran nearly from end to end of the diameter of the circle. She wondered what they were: they could scarcely be old ant hills with the turf grown over them, for they were too regular for that, and ant hills would have been round. These were oblong; and then with a little shiver the thought struck her that they were graves. Yet how was that possible? What manner of interment would this be, and for whom, that the dead should be unmarked by headstone or name? And what Christian would bury the dead in this place of antique worship?

A fanciful notion of hers, so she thought, but she knew that just below the controlled surface of her mind, now that her time was approaching, there swarmed a hundred fancies, buzzing about ready to settle, making shrill little pipings as they hovered. How she alternated, too, between fantasy and the stalest reflections about the swift-passing generations! She dismissed both, and told herself to what a home she had come: how warm it was, too, against this great stone where she sat propped, with the wind fallen, and the sun, now low and westering, shining on her. The slumber which she had vainly wooed in her bedroom now came courting her, her eyelids dropped, and she slipped into the gulfs of sleep. . . .

She woke with a start: the gold sunshine on which she

had closed her eyes was turned to gray, the warmth was chilled, and her heart was beating fast with some dream terror. Already the precise matter of it was gone from her, but Steven had been concerned in it, and Tim, and the scene had been set, not here, but in some woodland place haunted by mocking presences, careless and inhuman and gay, and older than time and younger than the dawn. All was vague, but it was frightful, and she scrambled to her feet, and set off with speed down the dusky hillside. She ought not to have allowed herself to go to sleep, for now it was late, and Steven, at home, would be in a fever of anxiety about her, for no one had seen her start, and no one knew where she had gone, while she was supposed, according to her own promise, to be resting upstairs. These self-reproaches winged her steps, but keeping pace with her was the wraith of her dream, flitting along by her side past the gorse clumps, and now diving with her into the shadow of the wood above the house. Then out she came onto the level, thankful that now in a moment she would put an end to Steven's anxiety, and passed into the hall where the lights were already lit.

A log fire crackled on the hearth, and he was sitting in front of it with his legs stretched out to the blaze, the picture of radiant tranquillity. He turned his head as she entered, smiling at her.

"Hullo, darling," he said, "there you are! May we have tea, do you think? It's ever so late. Nice walk?"

His complete unconcern was a shock to her. She had been prepared for his reproaches and his infinite relief at her return which would soon silence them, but not for his indifference.

"Oh, I'm so sorry, Steven," she said. "I went out for a walk, though you told me not to, and I fell asleep. I hurried back. I was afraid you would be awfully anxious."

"Not a bit," said Steven genially. "I've only just come in myself. Where did you go?"

She sat down on a corner of his big chair.

"Up the hill," she said, "and I found a great circle of granite stones. You never told me about it."

"Oh, the Druidical circle," he said. "Nobody knows much about it. A temple, perhaps: all the professors measure it and then quarrel about it. Ah, here's tea coming—hurrah."

"There's a row of mounds across it," she said. "What are they? I couldn't help thinking they looked like graves."

Did he stiffen? Did he get tense for a moment, or was that another fancy?

"Oh, those!" he said. "They are graves. Dog cemetery. My grandfathers for generations used to have their dogs buried there."

"But surely they are much too big for dogs' graves," she said.

Steven wriggled out of the chair which she had shared with him.

"Of course, you know best," he said in that rapped-out staccato voice. "Tell me what they are, then. I'm always ready to learn."

She was startled and amazed at this sudden fierceness.

"What's the matter?" she asked. "Why are you so cross with me?"

His ill-humour melted in a moment.

"Darling, I'm nothing of the kind," he said. "But what do those graves matter to you and me? Dogs, I tell you, perhaps a favourite pony or two, if you want something bigger. If you wish it, one was a giraffe that I used to play with when I was a boy. Anyhow, I swear to you that they are not the graves of human folk, if it's that which troubles you. . . . Come and have tea. And what do you think I've been doing? I bathed. I rowed myself out to that beach we looked down on this morning and had a heavenly dip and even basked in the sun afterwards. Not bad for mid-December: and then I came home and sat before the fire. I shall do it again to-morrow, and again and again and again. And you slept? I love sleeping out of doors; they say here that the dreams which come to you out of doors are true."

Some backwash of that nightmarish dream came combing through her again.

"Oh, Steven, don't say that," she exclaimed. "I had a horrid dream: something about you and that mad boy, and there was a wood full of presences, young and gay and antique, which were working on me——"

He whisked round on her in a flame.

"Betty, what utter nonsense you're talking," he said. "Really, between your graves and your dreams——"

He stopped: it would never do to agitate Betty or frighten her. Horribly startled for the moment at this sudden penetration of hers—she who had been so sunnily floating on the surface of Trenair—into the very heart of it, he had lost control of himself. But instantly he regained it, and with that marvellous quickness of his, bent his head over sideways, shaking it.

"I know I'm bawling at you," he said, "but I don't mean to. I got a dollop of sea water into my ear, and I can hardly hear myself speak. Ah, there, it's out! What was I saying? Oh, yes, you and your graves and your dreams! I bet you that you had been thinking about the graves just before you went to sleep, and that gave you the horrors in dream. Wasn't it so, Betty?"

It seemed a reasonable notion, and willingly enough she accepted it, just as she had accepted his story about the dogs' cemetery. But some inner arbiter told her that she did not really believe that dogs and ponies were buried there, or that the sea water in Steven's ear was responsible for that unmodulated snarl with which he had answered her when she spoke of her dream. Steven knew, said this calm referee, who it was that slept beneath the ancient turf, and Steven knew why that account of her dream had frightened him. There were things at Trenair about which she must not inquire: she must limit herself to the fair peaceful surface of it, its sun and its sea, and the air that made spring of midwinter. And she must not seek to know why Steven had refused to come here before.

CHAPTER XI

MAURICE duly arrived in the course of the next week. Steven's letter of invitation had been one it was impossible to refuse, and indeed he had no inclination to do so. That excellent advice which Maurice had given him had been taken: it was really only right that the counsellor should see for himself how wise he had been. Steven appreciated now how atrociously he had behaved towards him and others: so wouldn't Maurice come and by his presence signify his forgiveness? Maurice had written a very proper reply, correct in tone almost to loftiness. . . .

He had changed, Steven thought, during the last year, or perhaps he had only reverted to what he was before their friendship. There was a certain primness about him; his manner was slightly donnish; he began a good many sentences himself with the prefatory "of course," and constantly cleared his throat as if about to raise his voice to the audience of a lecture room. Steven made these observations of him without any malicious intent, but he wondered at himself for having ever supposed that Maurice was capable of perception. Yet he was very glad to see him, for these very limitations, this academic confidence, weatherproof and immune as regards anything crepuscular, was exactly what was wanted here in these days of waiting. There was no anxiety about Betty: Dr. Blaize, that admirably sensible doctor from Penzance, who twenty-one years ago had brought Steven into the world, pronounced her condition to be quite satisfactory; the little squalls of excitement, of misgivings and fitfulnesses that bore down on her now and then, were perfectly normal. Gentle exercise, plenty of rest, and, above all, plenty of unagitating occupation were indicated. Certainly it was a good thing that some old friend of Steven's was coming down, and indeed Maurice proved himself an excellent provider of occupation for Betty: she had a hostess's duties to discharge towards this prim, pleasant young man; she took him for drives to points of interest, the Land's End and the Logan Stone, and in the evening they played chess together, which seemed to occupy them in the most absorbing manner. From the first, in fact, Maurice fitted in beautifully: he was an academic sedative for all fantastic waywardness.

There was another reason why Steven found his advent altogether welcome. For the week before his arrival he had been very much tied to Betty, for she had shown a great distaste for being alone and yet was insistent that her mother, as Steven had proposed, should not come down here. She had become hysterical when he continued to urge it: she wanted nobody here but him and that friend of his who had promised to come. In consequence he had been obliged to be constantly with her, for there was no one else but he who could companion her, and though there was nothing he would not do to ensure her quietude and health of body and mind, he had found it very trying. He must always be on hand to sit with her or stroll with her, and this limited his freedom to the point of vanishment. Sometimes this incessant attendance was agitating as well as boring, for, in spite of medical reassurance, her moods gave him matter for secret apprehension. If they sat on the lawn she would suddenly look round towards the poplar wood, saying, "What is that stirring them, Steven? There is something moving in the wood." Then, laughing, he would say, "Now you've said that before, darling, and so I'm going to make a search." There would be nothing, of course, or at the most Tim crouching in a thicket, patiently and eagerly waiting. To him Steven made some negative gesture, and went back to Betty, with, perhaps, a newly blown wood anemone in his hand. "That's what you heard," he said. "The impertinent flower has come out a couple of months too soon and was crowing like a barn-door cock." And then her tense look faded, and she kissed it. "The sweet weak little thing," she said. "It wouldn't hurt me, would it? How fanciful I am, Steven: forgive me." And then she would look at him with some question in her eyes which remained unasked.

Maurice relieved Steven of the burden of this constant attendance, and acted, so he joyfully observed, as a powerful and beneficent sedative to Betty's restlessness and unfounded caprices. He had brought down with him the proofs of his book on the Age of Pericles, compiled from his lectures and now complete, and a box of fat volumes to check his references. Betty seemed to like sitting in the studious tranquillity of the room when he worked, having been assured that she did not interrupt the train of classical thought, and one morning (they had slipped into Christian names almost immediately) she said to him:

"Can't I be of any use in looking out some of your references for you, Maurice? You wanted the eighth volume of Grote's history just now, and you took up the seven other volumes of it first. Well, call out to me, 'Grote: volume eight, page so-and-so,' and while I'm finding it for you, you can be going on to the next reference that you'll want."

This was quite a useful idea: she hunted up a reference and laid the book open on his table, and while he was verifying there would be some further passage for her to search for. In the ways of academic humour she became Maurice's clerk, and he paid her one penny a morning for her services. "I shall be ready for my clerk at half-past ten this morning," Maurice would say, and so Betty got both emolument and steady occupation. Sometimes in her veering moods she now seemed to shun being left alone with Steven: if this happened she would ask where Maurice was. In the afternoon they would often go off on a motor drive together, and after dinner they played chess with absorbed attention and puckered brows. All this gave Steven liberty, and (which was more important even) Betty recovered her balance, and there were no more agitations and fitfulnesses. The day of her delivery was drawing near, and nothing could be more satisfactory than her regained tranquillity.

Steven had yawned and dozed in his chair one night while they were at their chess, and what a waste of time and energy it seemed to him that two people should enjoy cudgelling their brains over these artificial perplexities, and how delighted he was that they should do so! One of them said, "Check," and then after a while the other said, "Check," and then Betty said, "Humph," and Maurice lit a cigarette with the air of one who has delievered a serious ultimatum. It was the night of full moon, and straying to the door on the pretext of taking auguries about the weather, he had heard the sound of Tim's pipe in the wood. He did not want Betty to hear that, so he had come quickly in again, shutting the door, and had sat on, dumbly patient, itching to be out in the night and hating them both. Eventually, after much manœuvring, they settled that their game was a draw, and so all that time and thought since dinner had been spent over nothing at all.

"Good God, what children," thought Steven, "to be serious over that box of toys!" And Maurice said, "Of course, I ought to have taken your knight at once," and Betty said, "Oh, but then you would have unguarded your castle." But the hours were passing, and all was well with Betty. How admirably convenient it was to have Maurice here, and how good for Betty to be occupied in any pursuit that kept her mind from perilous trespasses.

The two young men never sat up together for long after Betty had gone upstairs, for the very fact that there had once been so intimate a bond of friendship between them made talk, as between acquaintances, impossible, and neither of them had the smallest inclination to go near the regions towards which friendship had once taken them: both of them, indeed, had presumably ceased to explore there.

Steven had once alluded to those early days of their friendship at Cambridge, when the squirrel had come to his summons, but Maurice's, "Ah, yes; very strange. I remember perfectly," was calculated to shut the door on any further reminiscences. Steven felt sure that in his accepting this invitation to Trenair there had been in Maurice's mind the idea of showing him how immune he was now to the lure of such wild and fantastic explorations as had originally brought them together, and how steadily he proceeded with the Age of Pericles in a milieu which had once been so full of thrilling possibilities of strange adventure.

But such an attitude did not conduce to tête-à-tête conversations, and after a few remarks to-night about Betty's chess and health, and an encouraging inspection of the sky, which promised well for their expedition to St. Ives to-morrow, they followed her upstairs, and Steven looked in for a moment on her, as was his usual practice. A nurse who was already installed in the house was with her, but she smiled brightly and professionally to Steven and said she would come back in ten minutes, for Betty must not sit up talking.

The topics, at this short bedroom talk, were always mild and of the dinner-table type.

"It's a glorious night, darling," he said, "for I understand that Maurice's clerk is having a morning's holiday, and is going off alone for a jaunt with her employer. I'm not sure that I ought to allow it."

This, as a humorous effort, was not very successful.

"Come with us, then," said Betty, without the ghost of a smile.

"Darling, I was only chaffing," said he.

There was something odd about her to-night. She began to talk excitedly, still with that grave, anxious face.

"Sometimes I don't know whether you're chaffing or telling me the truth," she said. "It has happened before. For instance, those graves in the Druidical circle. Are they really the graves of animals, some of dogs, some of ponies? And then what you told me about dreams dreamt in the open air coming true? Is that really so? Perhaps you were chaffing then: I hope you were. But, as I say, I can't always tell about you."

He came close to her, laying his hand on her shoulder. She seemed to shrink away from his touch, as he had often wanted to shrink from hers.

"Now, Betty, you must put all thought of those graves out of your head," he said. "I promise you that they are not the graves of human beings, if it's that which has been troubling you. I swear to you that they are not."

There was no need to force a tone of conviction into that. Though ghastly enough, and not to be inquired into with greater particularity, he was telling her the truth.

"And as to dreams out of doors coming true," he went on, "that's the merest bit of folklore, of superstition; there's nothing more in it than the notion that if you bow and curtsey to the new moon you will have good luck all that month."

That diverted her for the moment, but she was still grave and still excited.

"Ah, look out, Steven," she said, "and see if there's a new moon to-night. I should like to curtsey to it: that might please them. Them! I wonder who they are?"

He laughed.

"They're a pack of nonsense," he said. "But I promise you that you shall bow to the next new moon. It's no use my looking out to-night, for the moon's full, I know."

Her eyes, puzzled and troubled, dwelt on him, as if questioning him.

"So that's no use," she said. "But what's the right thing to do at full moon? There must be something. Ah! Didn't that awful mad boy ask if he might play his pipe to us at full moon? Don't let him come near me, Steven. I'm frightened of him. He's so terribly like you: he's more you than you are. . . . I can't express it, but I mean something."

Steven wished the nurse would come back, but it was wiser not to summon her, for that would make Betty think that there was something wrong. He could reassure her about Tim. . . .

"My dear, of course he shan't come near you," he said. "And as for his piping at full moon, why, he's probably been snoring in bed for the last two hours."

"I hope so; oh, I hope so," said she. "Steven, what is there about this place that enchants and terrifies me? How adorable I thought it at first, and it's adorable still, but there's something underneath it that's been dragging me in. Oh, I don't say that it's evil, but it's without a soul. And you know a lot about it; you always have known, it's in your blood. It's full of joy, too, so why should it terrify me? It dances and pipes."

Even as she spoke he thought for a moment that he heard Tim's pipe, or was it only a hallucination born of some intense desire? A huge exultation flooded him at the thought of the mellow night outside, and the full moon pouring down on the woods. That drew back, and in its place, following it like another wave, came fear, not for himself now, but for Betty. She was no longer floating on the surface tranquilly; something gay and terrible was dragging her in. And yet, how was that possible?

"Now you're talking absolute nonsense, darling," he said, "and I won't have it. Unless you promise me to throw all that rubbish out of your mind, I shall take you away from here to-morrow. We'll go straight back to London, to the fogs and the smoke. I mean it: I'm not chaffing now."

The nurse entered, and Steven instantly turned to her.

"Nurse, I've been talking very seriously to my wife," he said. "She's getting fancies into her head about this place, and I've been telling her that if we hear any more of them I shall take her straight back to London."

Betty got up.

"Ah, do, Steven!" she said. "Let's start to-morrow; or could we even start to-night? I want to go. Wouldn't it be lovely to get out of this valley altogether, to steal away from Trenair before they can stop us? Or is it too late already, do you think?"

The nurse looked at her sharply a moment, whispered a question to her, and nodded.

"That's all right, then," she said, "and all you want, Mrs. Gervase, is a good night's sleep, and you'll be as right as right in the morning. But now Mr. Gervase must leave you, and I'll get you to bed."

Steven's dressing room, where he slept, was next door, and as he kissed Betty and said good-night to her he saw the nurse make a little sign to him, which he took to mean that she wanted to speak to him, and he went into his room to wait for her. Presently she came tiptoeing in through the other door of his room, which led into the passage, so that Betty should not know she was conferring. Her news was quite cheerful.

"She's more than half asleep already," said the nurse, "and everything quiet. But she's got some queer idea into her head, no doubt about it, and it frightens her. Whatever can it be? Can you make any guess?"

"It must be something she's imagined for herself," said Steven. "I'm positive that no one has told her anything that—that could unsettle her."

"Well, I daresay we shall hear no more of it. But as to her going away now, that's impossible. I'll ring up Dr. Blaize at once if there's any fresh activity, but the chances are she'll sleep quiet till morning. And don't you be anxious about her, Mr. Gervase, for there's no cause. You go to sleep quietly, too: if it was morning, now, I should tell you to go out for a sail or a walk just as usual. I'll be sleeping in the room the other side of her, and if she so much as stirs I'll be with her in a jiffy."

She went back to her room, and presently Steven went to his window and opened it. . . . It was, then, Tim's pipe that he had heard just now: somewhere, not far off, in the woods below the house, he was playing. It would be risky, thought he, it would be provocative of that mysterious excitement in Betty, if she woke and heard him. Tim must be told at once that just now he must not play his pipe within sound of the house; and who, except himself, was to tell him? He could have laughed for glee at having found so laudable, so imperative a reason for going out now into the woods on this night of full moon to stop him. It was not, he told himself, for the assuagement of this thirst of his for the woods and the wildness and the rapture with which they brimmed that he went: it was because Betty must not wake and hear the sound of that music. He was sure her nurse would approve of that: she had said, too, that if it was morning she would have told him to go out as usual, but, since it was night, to sleep without anxiety.

But sleep was impossible, and where was the good of lying in bed when the magic of the woodland beckoned, and Tim had made a new fluting of springtime? The bushes and the thickets, where he must search for Tim to stop his music for Betty's sake, would be heavy with night dews, and the woodways miry, and in a moment he had slipped off his evening clothes and put on jersey and flannels. There was no need to turn up the clusters of electric lights with which Uncle Robert had endowed the house, for the drawn blinds dripped with moonshine, and where they were undrawn it lay in luminous pools on the stairs.

He closed the front door softly, and as he crossed the lawn that lay bathed in the intense white splendour, he seemed to strip the rags of humanity from him. He looked back for a moment at the house, before he dived into the wood, and saw that Maurice's room was still lit: with a choked-down laugh he felt sure that the Age of Pericles was occupying him.

Clear now and close sounded the notes of Tim's pipe: he was playing one of the tunes of springtime. It was formless in rhythm and melody, but it had the untutored rapture of bird song in it, and . . . where did it come from? Steven paused: the tune seemed to come from everywhere, as if it was an exhalation of the night itself and the wood. Could it be Tim who made that music? If it was, surely the spirit of the earth itself, of wet places and of night, breathed through him. High within Steven rose the bubbling ecstasy, and ebbed and flowed again, and now through the trees he caught sight of the boy in the clearing where the ruined walls stood. The moon, riding high, poured down into it, unshadowed by the encircling trees, and there was Tim bare-legged and stripped to the waist, whirling, as he played, in some wild dance of his own. Then he caught sight of Steven among the trees and ran to him, kneeling at his feet, with heaving ribs.

" 'Tis you!" he panted. "I was playing for you to come, I was calling you, and I knew you'd hear. And they're all abroad to-night, our folk: the woods are full of them playing and dancing. We'll roam through the woods, as we did of a night a year gone, when you came down to bide at the village with me. They're closer to us now, Mas'r Steven: maybe you'll see and hear them clear."

No thought of Betty lingered or called to him now: he was as oblivious of her as he was of any remembrance that on the night a year ago, of which Tim spoke, his mother had drowned herself. All human affections and relationships were as waves breaking inaudibly on remote shores.

"Yes, Tim," he said, "we'll go wide and far to-night—or maybe we'll just bide here. 'Tis long hours yet till the dawn, and we'll spend them in the woods."

Tim looked up towards the house.

"And she won't stop you or seek you?" he asked. "She keeps you from us, I know it. And she hates me, and, eh, I hate her blacker than night."

Steven brought his mind back to Betty with an effort.

"No, she's in bed and asleep," he said.

"And she's to have a baby, so the village tells," said Tim. "Rare rejoicings there'll be if 'tis a boy and comely. 'Twill be her fault if other, seeing as you begat it."

"She's safe and cared for," said Steven. "And it's the night of full moon."

Dappled and checkered lay the slopes, and silent but for the drowsy hiss of the ripples on the edges of the sea.

The moon had set, and in the east the dawn was beginning to smoulder when Steven crossed the lawn again, and, looking up, saw with a sudden gasp of his breath that there was a light shining behind the blinds in Betty's room. He guessed what that might mean, and now, as he hastened his step, he saw, too, that there was a motor car drawn up by the door. Suspense, with panic on its heels, crashed in upon him, for he knew the hour had come, and the sentence, for doom or acquittal, not on the child alone but on himself, was to be pronounced. A child human and without blemish would prove the untainted humanity of his fatherhood: if otherwise . . . The staircase was lit now and the passages above, and just as he approached Betty's room the nurse came out of it. She put a finger to her lips for silence till she had closed it, and beckoned him to his own room next door.

"What has been happening?" he asked. "All well?"

She shook her head.

"We can't tell yet," she said. "But she's had a shock of some sort. I don't know where you've been, but I wish you had gone to bed when I left you last night."

"Go on, go on," said Steven.

"She was sleeping quietly enough when I looked in on her," said the nurse, "and so I went to bed. I was awakened by a scream, and I ran in to see what ailed her: I thought the pains were on her. She had opened the door of your room, and she found you were not there, and she was screaming out, 'They've taken him: he's gone to them.' And then her labour began. I got Dr. Blaize over very quickly, and he's with her now. I must go back. I've been looking out every now and then to see if you'd returned. It was a bit of bad luck."

Steven sat on the edge of his bed, while the dawn, calm and lucid, brightened in the sky. He could hear footsteps now and then in the next room, and now and then a few words rapped out, and now and then a soft moaning sound. Then for a long while all was silent, and the silence was broken by the noise, not of a crying child, but of something bleating.

CHAPTER XII

AN HOUR afterwards Steven was sitting in the dining room with Dr. Blaize, who was having breakfast. . . . When he had heard that whimpering bleat there had shut down round him some horror of great darkness, for the fear which had driven him from Trenair a year ago was fulfilled. The curse was not finished yet, and he who had transmitted it to that little bleating creature, now hushed and still again, was tainted with it himself. In spite of the beauty and the perfection of his physical manhood he was not human, and at once he felt that he had known that for months. The great darkness was not new to him, he had long known that this ultimate night would close round him. Now it had come, and, like a man on whom sentence of death has been passed, he felt curiously indifferent. There he was in the dock, and the black-capped judge had just been addressing him. Yet all the time he was outside the jurisdiction of any, he was looking at this tragic spectacle, which did not concern him personally.

All that he had been actually told at present was that some little spark of new life had burned feebly for not many minutes and had expired again. He had not seen, nor did he wish to see, the vehicle which had contained it, for he had heard that bleating noise. . . . But now, when over his fragrant coffee Dr. Blaize was telling him just what he thought it would be good for him to know, some sensibility, some growing impatience at his words began to pervade that numbness. . . . The doctor was an elderly man, kind and grizzled and conventional. Never had he been called to Trenair to attend to any ailment of Steven's; his first service to him had been to bring him into the world twenty-one years ago, his second to tell him about the offspring of his wedlock.

"Very distressing indeed," he was saying; "you have my most sincere sympathy. Unformed, you know, unformed: it was as well, perhaps, indeed it was far better that the poor little thing should not live. But there is no reason, I guarantee you, why you should not become the father of a fine family. We must think, too, and that at once, of your poor wife: as yet she knows nothing at all. It would be very painful for you to tell her—indeed, I should not dream of allowing it. I have given her something which will keep her dozing or asleep, and after a visit or two elsewhere, which I must make, I will come back here and tell her myself."

Steven pushed back his chair: his impatience with this kind man broke all controlling bonds.

"What's the use of your talking like that to me?" he said. "You may tell my wife whatever you like: tell her that God sent a sweet little angel into the world for a few minutes and then took it back to heaven. She knows nothing about the curse that has been on my family for generations—at least, no one has told her—but you know about it and so do I. What came into the world this morning wasn't an unformed human child, as you said just now. It was something monstrous and not human. I haven't seen it, but I heard it. And if you persist in saying that it was an unformed human child I shall go to see it."

The doctor rose.

"I beg that you won't do that, Mr. Gervase," he said. "I would sooner tell you at once that it was monstrous. But such things do happen, and as for the curse, whatever the truth of it may once have been, it doesn't exist any more. Look at yourself: you've disproved its existence, thank God, in your own person."

"That's exactly what I have not done," said Steven. . . . "Ah, come in, Maurice: breakfast is ready. We're talking about my family history, most of which you know already. But another chapter has been added to it this morning, for Betty's child was born an hour ago. Let us call it 'child.' I haven't seen it, so I can't describe the exact species. . . . But there it is, and the doctor—oh, I beg your pardon, Dr. Blaize, Mr. Crofts—the doctor was telling me that the curse, which you know about, has nothing to do with it. Just a coincidence: he was saying that I am a proof that the curse is extinct. But that's not so, Doctor: I'm not human. I've got the body of a man, quite a good one, but not the soul. Tell Dr. Blaize what you know of me, Maurice: tell him what my own mother thought of me. You won't? Very well, it doesn't matter. Thank you for sparing my blushes."

His excitement ebbed from him, and now he stood looking from one to the other, dazed and appealing, like an animal in pain seeking aid from human friends. Then he spoke again, quite quietly.

"So go about your jobs, Dr. Blaize," he said, "now that we understand each other, and come back as soon as you can. You needn't be frightened for me, for I shan't do anything violent; I'm beaten. I'm as harmless as a man who has just been knocked out. When you come back you must tell my wife whatever you think judicious, and I'll back it up. I shan't go near her. . . . Oh, and one more thing: the little unformed child—that's our formula, Maurice—I shall have it buried in the Druid circle on the hill, the family menagerie, you know. The old carpenter, Tom Evans, who made the coffin for my uncle, is still alive, and he shall come and make another. They know all about the family history in the village: it's not unlocking the cupboard with the skeleton in it. I'll arrange that, so tell the nurse, please."

Steven went with the doctor to the door and breathed in the splendour of the morning: he had known at dawn that there would be another of these superb days. Then he sent for Tom Evans and told him to begin his carpentering: when that was finished he must see to one more grave being dug in the circle, next to the latest one, and in a line with the others. . . . His numbness of brain had come back, after that one ebullition, and again he had the sense of being merely a spectator of what was going on and in no way an actor. He strayed back to the dining room, where Maurice sat, feeling that he had just dropped in on his breakfasting at Cambridge.

"Maurice's clerk won't be at her desk to-day," he said. "Shall I look up references for you? Or perhaps you'd like to go away. You and I will be alone, you see, and you won't care about that."

"Steven, you know how gladly I'll stop here as long as I can do anything for you," he said.

Steven considered this as he might have considered the offer of some friend who was going shopping, to execute any little errand for him.

"I don't know that you can," he said. "I don't know anything I want. In fact, there's nothing whatever to be done for me. Just one thing I should like to know: what's to happen? What *can* happen?"

"You'll get over it, you'll live it down," said Maurice. "So will Betty: you'll have other children. . . . Good God, I'm so sorry for you."

Steven looked at him, as he would look at a child to whom he was trying to explain some very simple little situation.

"But don't you understand even yet?" he said. "Don't you realize that all that you and my mother feared about me is true? Literally, soberly true. You know quite well you believed it when it was a fantastic notion, but now you don't seem to get down to it. . . . You gave me excellent advice a year ago, and I took it. I fought against the doom, and now that it has come on me I know that you and she were right. Oddly enough, too, I feel as if I had known it all along. And there's no way out. As I was born, so shall I die."

"But you mustn't believe it," cried Maurice. "You've got to deny it, you've got to refuse it admittance till the thought of it leaves you, and it becomes untrue. Deny it."

Steven went patiently on.

"But how can I deny what is so obvious?" he said. "It's proved. And all the people who knew me best, you see, believed I hadn't got a human soul. The Child, you, my mother—and you're all right. Betty, too: she guessed. She used to say I puzzled her, and that's what she meant. And at heart you all looked on me, as you got glimpses of what I really was, with a sort of fascinated loathing. You can't deny that, at any rate. But I never cared; that was just my deformity, and I don't care now. I only wish I knew what was going to happen. Something must happen. When Betty gets well again: what then? Something pretty awful?"

"Nothing awful will happen," Maurice said, knowing that he was milling from his mouth the mere dry meal of words. "And before Betty gets better you've got to take hold again on normal life, you've got——"

Steven interrupted him with a laugh.

"What a baby you are!" he said. "Don't you see that I've got nothing left to take hold of? What happens, I want to know, to people in my condition? Perhaps I shall go mad: I daresay that's the simplest solution. I don't think I should mind being mad in the sense that you and the world understand madness. . . . My word, the woods last night! I was out all night, you know. That's where I belong, and now they've claimed me. They were seething with presences which were my kin, and which welcomed me."

He stopped suddenly: what was the use of talking to Maurice at all?

"You'd better get back to the Age of Pericles," he said. "Far safer. You're only interested in what's dead: you hate the perils of life, and its edges and the mists round them. Very wise. Order the motor to take you to the station, and leave the place where very unsettling things are on foot. I know it's much wiser for you not to meddle in them. Anyhow, do exactly what you like."

Dr. Blaize returned during the morning for his promised visit, and having seen Betty and told her that her child had been stillborn, came to Steven with disquieting news.

"I suggested that you should come and see her," he said, "but she got very painfully excited, and to quiet her I had to assure her that you should not do so unless she asked for you herself. I could do nothing more: my urging her to see you only agitated her. . . . Does she know, do you think, is it possible she knows anything about your family history?"

"She has never been told anything," said Steven. "Why?"

"Because she kept asking me whether her child was human. Very odd that she should ask that. Of course I assured her it was. And then, more strangely still, she asked me if it was to be buried in the Druidical circle at the top of the hill. Now what does that mean? She must know something."

Steven gave a sigh of utter indifference.

"No doubt she knows something," he said, "but I'm sure she's not been told. She went for a walk there one day, and was uneasy about the graves. I told her they were the graves of dogs and ponies. But it stuck in her mind, for she asked me again. Trenair's an odd place: you get to know things here without being told them. I suppose you'll go on denying the truth about her baby, though it won't be any use. Of course I won't see her till she wants to see me; I should hate seeing her. But what's going to happen?"

"I don't think you need be very anxious about the

future," said Dr. Blaize. "There's no symptom in your wife's condition that makes me really anxious. Her—her delusions will fade. You must be patient, Mr. Gervase. Time, its healing power: you as well as she."

Steven looked at him with a sort of pity.

"I wonder whether you understand nothing," he said, "or whether you only pretend not to. It doesn't matter, in any case. I'm sure you mean to be kind."

"But I want to be wise," said the doctor. "And I want you to be wise. Just take things as quietly as you can. Occupy yourself in ordinary ways."

"Certainly. I've only one engagement at all out of the common. That's the family funeral, as soon as the late lamented is ready. No flowers: no cards. Just earth to earth."

The day passed quietly; there was occasional news from Betty's room, brought by the nurse, but nothing alarming. Maurice had stopped on, for Dr. Blaize had told him that Steven, though he seemed indifferent to any presence or absence, had better have a companion, and when they went up to bed Maurice congratulated himself on having really been of some use. They had lunched and dined together, and after dinner had played chess, and though Steven's knowledge of the game was very elementary, he had agreed that it was most absorbing: it was impossible to think of anything else while it was in progress. They parted on the landing, and Steven went to his room and lay down without undressing on his bed, rather glad to get rid of Maurice, but not really caring, for he scarcely seemed to exist.

All day he had known that some intense activity was going on in his brain beneath the half-numbed surface perceptions which wanted to know what was to happen next. Plans were being made, though at present hidden from him: all was astir. It was as if he listened to some great ado from inside a hive of bees; who were getting ready for a tremendous adventure, some swarming, some nuptial flight. He would soon know, for something was imminent, and he need not puzzle himself about it nor wonder what it was, for it would declare itself when the time came. Lying thus, he dozed sometimes and went through vague scenes of horror with Betty, but such had nothing to do with the real thing. Sometimes—and this was nearer the mark—he was out in the woods with Tim under the moon, and the woods were tranquil and empty. Yet they were not asleep, the great activity was humming there also; it was still sheathed like the life in some ripened chrysalis, but ready to burst out into a new winged form into which had been transformed the crawling caterpillar that had encased itself there. Or again he would be standing where he had stood for just a few minutes this afternoon in the Druidical circle while the earth was shovelled in upon that square squat coffin which contained what his eyes had never looked on. All the village had attended: they had stood silently just outside the circle while he and Tom Evans had gone to the graveside. Now, in these dozings, he went through the whole scene again, but there were others with him by the graveside, vague figures and monstrous, who had come from their lodgings within the circle. Then he saw that they were not really monstrous at all: that hideous raiment of stricken form and feature was only some muddy vesture which now dripped off them and left them swift and radiant presences, like those which haunted the woodways. And in his dream he asked himself, "Have they come for me?"

He woke from this into a consciousness of huge happiness: all the horrors that had happened he now saw to be remote and unreal, bogeys invented by his mental sense. They had moved away from him, or rather it was he who had drifted away on some great sunny tide that bore him out to sea, while they remained crawling and shuffling about on the muddy shore. He lay there for a little, wide-awake and infinitely happy, and then, feeling that sleep was impossible, he got up, and without any purpose in his mind, let himself out of his room and went downstairs. It was not very dark, perhaps it was near dawn already, and just as he reached the hall he heard a hand on the latch of the door, which, as usual, was only closed and not locked. He knew who it was.

The door opened, and a white figure slipped in.

"Tim?" he said.

"Yes, Mas'r Steven. I thought you'd be in bed and asleep."

Steven switched on the light. Tim was dressed in shirt and shorts, with his wreath of ivy on his head. He carried in his hand a piece of thin rope and a wide-necked bottle.

"What are you doing here at this hour?" said Steven. "And what are you carrying?"

Tim looked at him smiling and eager.

"I came to kill her," he said. "A bit of rope noosed round her throat and a pillow over her face. You told me where she slept, and I can go like a ghost so that none hears. I know what manner of child she gave you, for Tom Evans told me, and she's not fit to live. Then you'd get another wife, Mas'r Steven, and breed proper sons. To kill her. 'Twas all I could do for you."

A great light began to dawn for Steven. He guessed what that joyful bustle in the hive meant.

"And the bottle, Tim?" he asked.

" 'Twas for me: 'tis a brew of the death herb I made, same as George Morgan gave his Sally. I asked Janet what they'd do wi' me if I killed a man, and she said they'd hang me, or more like shut me up in some dark house, so I should never sleep in the woods again and see the spring come. So the brew was for me when I'd done my service to you. If they'd hang me that would do fine, for then I should go free, but, eh, the high walls and the dark house! Not for me!"

"And you were going to do that for me, Tim?" asked Steven.

"Iss, sure, and welcome, and mine would be the gain, too for I should be one with the woodland, and not seeking and striving after it with my pipe and dancings. Eh, I shall surely be there, and I'll walk free along of you, and play my pipe so's you shall hear indeed. Let me get on with my job, Mas'r Steven. 'Twill be soon done, and you rid of her."

"Sit down, Tim," said Steven. "I want to think a minute. No, where's the need? I'm coming out with you now, and you must make me a brew of the death-herb. It grows on the slopes above our bathing beach."

"Sure it does, powerful and plenty. But whatever do you want to drink of it for?"

"Because I don't belong here any more than you," said Steven. "We're of the woodland, Tim, you and I, and we'll go back there together."

Tim's eyes sparkled.

"Eh, that would be grand, if you feel so," he said. "Gladly I'd go alone by myself, but I'll dance and sing to go with you. I'll not need my bit of rope then, if we're to quit them all."

"No, you won't need your rope. One moment, and I'm ready."

He sat down at the writing-table.

BETTY, I'm very sorry [he wrote] I hoped the curse would spare me, but it has got me. So I'm setting us both free.—STEVEN.

He left this where it would be easily seen.

"Off we go, Tim," he said.

Dawn was coming fast, though the sun was not yet risen on the earth, as they passed through the dew-drenched wood, and little wisps of memory, distant and rosy as the small light clouds in the sky, passed through Steven's mind: that dawn, for instance, on the river at Cambridge, when he and the Child had made sacrifice to the gods of wet places and of night; hours he had spent with Maurice; glimpses of childhood, all pleasant, all remote; but of the panic which had once driven him from this beloved Trenair, and of the horror that lay over yesterday, there was no trace at all. . . . The tide was just beginning to ebb from the full flood, and once more they floated out from behind the pier and came in sight of the beach for which they were bound. A flock of great gulls, shy and wary, were standing there, and they rose on their approach and circled high above them in the upper air where the sun gilded and enrosed their whiteness. Tim's brew was not enough for the two of them, but a dozen plants of henbane, on which the squibs of young leaves were bursting, grew a little way up the slope, and Tim gathered these and crushed them upon a stone, and put the green mash into his wide-necked bottle.

"That'll be plenty for us, Mas'r Steven," he said, "for 'tis more'n twice what I gathered for George Morgan to give his Sally, and she went off beau'ful, just slept herself away. And that was the old leaves, too, and the young shoots are rare and powerful."

The sun had risen now over the hills to the east, and flooded the beach where they sat with the warmth and brightness of the new day. The house from which they had come shone rosy-gray above the poplars, and now Steven emptied the bottle into Tim's cupped hands, dividing its contents.

"There, that's fair, Mas'r Steven," he said, "a palmful for each. Eh, 'tis bitter to the taste: a strange breakfast. Now 'twill soon be working."

Steven lay down on the sand, propped on his elbow.

"Come close, Tim," he said. "Lean against me and put

your head on my shoulder, so we shan't be lonely. We've always belonged to each other, you and I."

"Sure," said Tim, "and very soon we shall sleep, and, oh, 'twill be grand to awake together, and me serving you. . . ."

Tim turned his face to Steven's, smiling and radiant. There was the bond of blood between them, which had cast them, face and form alike, in that wondrous mould, but stronger and more intimate was the life spirit which united them and burned the brighter as they lay there.

Presently Tim's eyelids flickered.

" 'Tis the best we've known yet," he said. "I'm happy and sleepy-like."

Steven gave a long sigh, utterly content.

"We're two drowsy-heads, Tim," he said. "And we shall wake up at home."

"Sure," said Tim again, "and the springtime at hand. Eh, my pipe! I meant to play the spring tunes, but it's too late. I'm off now, Mas'r Steven."

Tim's head fell forward across Steven's breast, and he, through half-closed eyes, saw the bright edge of the sea shining near, and a long ripple hissed up over the sand. To his fading sight it seemed rose-coloured as with dawn, and the noise of it was like the ring of glass. Or was that Tim's pipe that sounded so clear?

THE END